THE TRANSFORMATION

Kate pulled me down on the bed. I didn't resist. Her lips found mine and her tongue slipped into my mouth. There was a trace of blood, left over from a bitten tongue or lip, and the taste was sweet, overpowering.

Her hands fumbled with the buttons of my shirt, pulling it open, over my shoulders. She began to kiss my chest and I twisted around so I could reach her as well, working my way downward, scraping the skin of her abdomen delicately with my teeth, scratching but not breaking it. Then her fingers were groping at my belt.

I felt light-headed and weak. She was becoming transparent to me, her skin dissolving, her bones no more than a ghostly image. All I saw was the delicate tracery of her circulatory system, branching and twining like some exotic flora, the oxygen-rich blood slamming through the fragile vessels of her body with every heartbeat. Her jugular was too far away, but it didn't matter. Her femoral artery would do . . .

—from "Confession" by Kurt Busiek

"*HOTTER BLOOD* is an outstanding collection . . . a daring combination of sex and terror . . . mixed with deadly intent by the best writers the horror field has to offer! A must-read for any horror fan!"

—*Cemetery Dance* magazine

Books Edited by Jeff Gelb

Hot Blood (with Lonn Friend)
Hotter Blood (with Michael Garrett)
Hottest Blood (with Michael Garrett)
Shock Rock
Shock Rock II

Published by POCKET BOOKS

Novels by Jeff Gelb

Specters

HOTTER BLOOD

More Tales of EROTIC HORROR

Edited by JEFF GELB and MICHAEL GARRETT

POCKET BOOKS

New York   London   Toronto   Sydney   Tokyo   Singapore

An *Original* Publication of POCKET BOOKS

POCKET BOOKS, a division of Simon & Schuster Inc.
1230 Avenue of the Americas, New York, NY 10020

ISBN: 0-671-70149-5

First Pocket Books printing January 1991

10 9 8 7 6 5 4

POCKET and colophon are registered trademarks of
Simon & Schuster Inc.

Printed in the U.S.A.

Copyright Notices

For our parents,
Marvin and Shirley Gelb
and
Herbert and Christine Garrett,
with grateful appreciation for their
encouragement of our early interest in reading
(even if it was monster comics and men's magazines!)

CONTENTS

CONTENTS

INTRODUCTION

Success is, in itself, a kind of horror.

When *Hot Blood* proved a winner, we decided the only way to make the next volume better was for it to be an anthology of all new stories. The idea was exciting, but we knew it would be quite a challenge. It had been simple to put together twenty-four tales of hardcore horror for the first edition because we had the entire history of short horror fiction to choose from, as well as a dozen fine new contributions. Could we find twenty-four equally stunning *new* tales of dread and debauchery? The thought was chilling.

The call went out to the cream of the crop of today's horror writers and our fears were quickly proven unfounded. We were deluged with new tales that met our primary requirement: that sex be the driving force in each story without being pornographic.

But our second horror lurked in piecing together *Hotter Blood:* Now we found we had to turn down excellent stories by name authors whose work, for a myriad of reasons, did not meet our needs for this volume. There is a lot of talent out there—enough to ensure equally great future collections.

You're sure to notice an intentional slant toward horror's new voices in *Hotter Blood.* These are the names we will be reading throughout the next decade and beyond, the authors whose works will top bestseller lists as King and Koontz have done for the past many years. These are the rising stars on the horror horizon, and their work deserves as wide an audience as we, as fans, have granted their horrific godfathers. In *Hotter Blood,* we are proud to give horror's new blood (so to speak) the exposure it is due (and, in some cases, overdue).

You never know where you'll find tomorrow's horror stars. Grant Morrison and John Byrne are already familiar names to hundreds of thousands of rabid fans as leading comic book writers. Morrison wrote the multimillion-dollar-success Batman graphic novel "Arkham Asylum," while Byrne revamped the Superman legend during his groundbreaking tenure on that title. We are extremely pleased to present the first published short prose fiction works of both gentlemen in *Hotter Blood*.

We were proud to see most of the original stories from the first *Hot Blood* collection nominated for various short fiction awards in the horror and science fiction communities. We're certain history will repeat itself with this collection.

Have we whetted your appetite for shivers and sex? Good! We meant to. After all, we already know how good this collection is. Now it's time for you to share our excitement, as you step into the world of *Hotter Blood*.

Just one warning: Get set for a new breed of horror!

Jeff Gelb
Michael Garrett
January 1991

HOTTER BLOOD

NOCTURNE

John L. Byrne

Monday brought the first miracle, as Edelman boarded the elevator, bound for the lobby. The doors opened and there she was, leaning against the rear wall. He almost fainted, seeing her in person for the first time. He thought for a moment she might be one of the terribly real flights of fantasy, his curse for so many years before therapy subdued them.

She wore cutoffs and a modest halter top, feet in ragged sneakers, chestnut hair spilling in wild disarray from a bright orange headband. No makeup, but Edelman recognized her immediately. He'd first seen that face on *Cosmopolitan* and *Vogue* covers nearly three years ago. One wall of his three-room apartment was a shrine to those dark eyes, pouting lips. His fantasies—especially his darker fantasies —were filled with her.

"'Morning," she said as Edelman stepped into the car. Her mouth was not so pouty without lipstick. Her teeth were bright, her smile genuine.

"Good morning," Edelman said, managing to keep his breakfast down. His heart thundered so hard he expected her to hear it in the confined space of the elevator.

They rode down to the lobby without further words. Edelman stepped back to let her out. She smiled again, said "See y'round," strode away with a purposeful, almost manly gait.

Edelman wandered after her, his knees weak, his heart still pounding. Rachel McNichol! In his building! At this hour, in those clothes, it seemed unlikely she was only visiting. It was barely eight o'clock, shadows still long on 75th Street, when Edelman stepped out into the August heat.

Rachel McNichol! He remembered the first time he'd learned her name. He'd seen her in catalogs piled up by the mailboxes in the lobby anteroom; fashion catalogs displaying beautiful, anonymous women. Long, firm bodies; proud, haughty faces. The kinds of faces Edelman always had that terrible love/hate thing about. Faces, bodies he craved, that were always beyond his reach, lofty and aloof. Mocking him, he sometimes thought, with their perfect beauty, their unattainability.

In their midst one dark-eyed, dark-haired goddess who stood out from the rest, seizing his heart and mind in a way he'd not experienced since the days of sneaking *Playboy* magazines into his mother's house, dreaming after airbrushed gatefold fantasies. Imagining the things he might do to them, given the opportunity. They had names, though; the catalogs' models were never identified.

Then, one day, passing the news vendor's kiosk in the 28th Street station—long gone with the renovations—he saw her face on the cover of *Vogue*. Heavily made up, after the fashion of the magazine that year, but he recognized the chin, the pout. He bought the magazine, found inside two dozen pages with her face. On the contents page he also found her name: Rachel McNichol.

Three issues later she was featured on the cover again, again four months after that. The next month, though she was not on the cover, Edelman bought the issue anyway, in the hope there might be interior pages—particularly lingerie ads—featuring her perfect face and lithe, athletic form. He was rewarded with a short article about her—a single-page feature on a fast rising star in the modeling firmament.

He learned she was from Texas—the accent in the few words he'd heard from her therefore came as no surprise—twenty years old, single. She lived alone, he read, even eschewing the usual bevy of cats with which the young women of Edelman's acquaintance seemed so obsessed. Edelman was allergic to cats and dogs. He was delighted to discover there was, in this, no barrier to his fantasies.

He spent the rest of the day in a daze, longing for five o'clock, aching to get back home. Thinking about her made his head ache, the way it did before the therapy.

That evening he invented excuses to ride the elevator in his building—three trips to the grocery store on Columbus Avenue, each time for a single item; garbage that *must* be taken out; over to Columbus again for a newspaper—in the hopes of seeing her. He checked the names on the mailboxes three times; the small cards over the door buzzers twice. She was not listed, might be subletting. He knew of at least three residents on the floors above him who took August off, abandoning the inhospitable city for the Islands or the Cape.

He did not see her that evening, and although he took the elevator at precisely the same hour for the next four mornings—even lingering in the lobby to the point of arriving late at the office on Thursday—she did not appear.

Friday afternoon found him coming home from work, tired, out of sorts, generally pissed off with the world. He worked for DeVere Pharmaceuticals, on Park Avenue South, near 28th. He was good at his work—better than almost anyone else there—knew the mixing of chemicals, had the touch, the art. But there were idiots above him who stood in his way, and his fellow employees were never much interested in the things he wanted to talk about. They'd even scoffed, some of them, when he'd let it slip he belonged to a fantasy and role-playing club.

"That makes sense, for somebody with your problems," Bill Whittaker said, making Edelman regret ever confiding in him.

Adding to Edelman's misery this particular day, he'd made the mistake of asking Carolyn Murray to have dinner with him that evening, an invitation she loudly and mockingly rejected in the middle of the lunchroom.

Life sucks, Edelman thought, riding the subway, imagining all the nasty things he could do to Carolyn Murray, hurtful things that had a lot to do with rage and frustration, little to do with the sexual forms they took.

On top of that, he had not seen Rachel since Monday morning. He was ready to believe he'd imagined the whole thing—not so unlikely as he would have wished, given his history, his problems. There was that time last Christmas . . . He shuddered at the clouded memory of his delusion. If the elevator encounter was . . .

There she is!

Coming down 75th from Central Park West. Casual business garb, skirt, blouse, sensible shoes. Hair shaped into a perfect frame for her exquisitely made-up face. Carrying a large stack of library books; seven or eight volumes, Edelman guessed. Piled against her right arm, pushing the breast on that side up into the deep V of her open-necked blouse.

She was distracted, Edelman could see. Her eyes were not on the street before her, on the hose snaking across the sidewalk. Young Sanchez, the summer doorman, was watering the potted plants along the front of the building, talking to a plain-faced girl in khaki cutoffs and a black halter top. The dark green garden hose looped and piled across the sidewalk. Two steps and Rachel would trip, Edelman was sure.

He bolted forward, crying "Look out!"—just as her right

4

toe hooked under the first loop of hose. She snapped back to the present, the place. Her eyes went wide. The library books arced out of her arms. She pitched forward.

Edelman was there. He caught her, smoothly, easily. He was bigger than her by half, a strong man. He caught her as he would a child, she weighed so little. He felt surprise, discovering this; the lingerie ads revealed no shortage of soft, supple flesh.

"Oh!" she said. Edelman felt her legs stiffen to regain weight and control. She lifted herself out of his arms, but he held on to the memory of her.

"Thanks." She smiled the covergirl smile. "That could have been . . . costly."

Edelman bent to gather her books—economics and real estate—his mind racing. "Costly?" he asked, as if he did not know how damaging to her daily job would be a skinned knee, a scraped cheek or nose.

"I'm a model," she said. She moderated the Texas drawl carefully. He might not even have noticed it, were he not listening for it. "I could have cost myself a few weeks' work. Oh, thanks." She took the pile of books back on her left arm, extended her free hand. "Rachel McNichol."

"Bob Edelman. We . . . met in the elevator the other morning, didn't we?" Now that he was into the flow of it, fabrication came easily. He could pretend not to know who she was, that it had been her Monday morning. Better than admitting to the wall shrine in his apartment.

"Oh, yeah." Her smile broadened. "You live here, Mr. Edelman?"

"Yes. Third floor." He pointed up, generally. His apartment faced out onto the park, not 75th.

"Then I guess we'll be seeing more of each other, won't we? I'm subletting the Richardson place." She dropped her voice at the last words. Subletting was not allowed in the building. Tenants developed distant cousins, come to house-sit in the summer months.

"Oh, yes," Edelman said. "I know Burt. We played handball a couple of times. I had dinner with him and Carrie last Thanksgiving. In their apartment." They'd seemed close friends, before he sensed a deliberate distancing, and Burt finally told him, flat out, that Carrie was weary of Edelman's moods and preoccupations. He'd seen nothing more of them after that, though he thought he might still have a key to their place, from an earlier time when they were called away unexpectedly and asked him to water their copious plants.

"Yeah. Well . . . thanks again." She was plainly interested in terminating the conversation. Edelman wondered if he'd somehow put a foot wrong, but he could find nothing wrong in the words he'd spoken. He made a show of stepping past her, as if it had always been his intent to continue toward Central Park.

"You're welcome. See you again." He watched her go up the steps into the shadow of the lobby, waited five minutes before going in himself.

Sanchez watched with raised eyebrows from his place at the end of the long green hose. He shrugged, dropped his voice to be sure no one but his companion heard. "That Mr. Edelman," he said. "An odd one."

The girl just nodded. Everyone knew that.

Saturday Edelman was up before the summer sun poked above the eastern skyline. He put on the jogging outfit he'd not worn in over a year. It struck him as the least conspicuous outfit for what he had in mind.

He went down to the lobby—no sign of Sanchez this early—and out onto 75th. He walked over to Columbus, bought a newspaper from the vendor just opening as he got there. He returned half the length of the block, remaining on the opposite side, leaned against one of the wrought-iron railings below a tall, old brownstone, opened the paper. He waited.

He had to move three times to avoid arousing suspicion. He was running out of places, on that short, residential street, where he could lounge inconspicuously and still be in line of sight to his doorway. After two and a half hours his mounting impatience was rewarded. She came out, dressed much as he was, turned right, began to jog along 75th toward Columbus.

He followed.

It was a glorious, glorious day. She went through an unstructured routine, jogging, stopping, looking in little shops along Columbus and the side streets, jogging some more. Edelman had no trouble keeping up with her. He even went in a couple of the shops, boldness overwhelming him. He tested how close he could get to her, how reckless without her seeing him.

He was getting one of those headaches, danger-sign headaches, playing this game of cat-and-mouse. He ignored it, concentrating on her, on ways he might get to know her, become . . . intimate with her.

In one of those little shops Edelman found the second miracle.

The moon was full, framed in the open window of Edelman's small living room. He sat in a chair positioned carefully in the long rectangle of pale white light spilling across his battered brown rug. Naked. Not even a wristwatch. Breezes from the park cool on bare skin. The city shedding the heat of the day.

He breathed slowly, evenly, despite the headache squatting just behind his eyes, the foolishness he felt. He could have picked up something for the headache at DeVere, during his visit that afternoon. But he'd had more consuming matters on his mind. Now, he hardly even remembered the stop, or its purpose.

He reread the old book open across his thighs. He'd recognized the title in the bookstore she'd gone into, on 68th just off Columbus. He was amazed to see it. David Sinclair —Edelman's favorite fantasy writer until he'd actually met him at the Dallas Fantasy Fair—never wrote a story without mentioning it in some context. Edelman never knew it was a real book.

Nocture, it was called, *The Book of Night Journeying.* He'd thought that a silly phrase. "Is it about going to the bathroom?" he'd asked once, trying to sound worldly at a club meeting.

It wasn't. It was about miracles. It was about *power.* Odd that the clerk in the store had not known what she had, what she was letting Edelman purchase.

Edelman read the fine, narrow print—surprisingly easy to read in the moonlight—listening to the clock on the mantelpiece, waiting for the last chime of midnight.

The clock chimed. One—Two—Three—

Edelman stood up. Four—Five—Six—

A long stride toward the window. Seven—Eight—Nine—

Step up onto the ledge. No one on the street looking up at the naked man. No one pointing. No police whistle blowing. Ten—Eleven—Twelve—

A long, deep breath. Whisper the words from the book. Heart pounding, he stepped off the ledge.

It was like stepping onto a firm mattress; some give, but he did not plummet to the pavement three stories below.

The book had not lied. Standing naked in midair over Central Park West, Edelman wondered how he could ever have believed the words in those fine, tiny lines, but . . .

The book had not lied! He was a phantom—yet something more than a phantom. Real in one sense, unreal in another.

He looked up, turning to face the side of the building, to see the windows of the topmost floor. Her windows. The motion caused him to rise. He drifted up. A little faster than the elevator, past windows dark and light, four, five, six floors. He stopped outside her bedroom window. He knew

8

the layout of the apartment on the top floor, knew in which room she'd be sleeping.

The window was open. He stepped onto the ledge, into the room, into a rectangle of moonlight very much like the one in his own room. It fell on a pale, uncarpeted floor. The room was large, spare. The decor was not as Edelman remembered, not at all the Richardsons' style. It was just the sort of room he'd imagined for Rachel. Low dressing table of modern design against the wall to the left. Rest of the room dominated by the huge double bed. Mosquito netting draped about the head of the bed, box spring resting on the floor, without legs. Sound of an air conditioner whirring— *Odd,* he thought, *with the window open.*

She was nude on the bed. Uncovered. Indirect moonlight bounced from the white walls, played elusive luminescence over the hills and hollows of her form. Dark hair spread over white pillow, perspiration a subtle sheen over her naked body. Edelman felt his phantom form responding as surely as flesh and blood. His manhood rose.

He crossed around the foot of the bed, knelt down to look at her sleeping face. Beautiful. More beautiful than he'd ever dreamed. Skin tanned, without the pale swatches a bathing suit would leave. Breasts full, lolling on her chest as she lay on her back, undulating slightly with each deep breath. Nipples small, dark coral.

Edelman looked down the length of her: smooth, hard muscle of her solar plexus; carefully trimmed and shaped V of pubic hair. She lay with one leg drawn slightly up and over the other. Moonlight threw deep shadow down the long muscle of her thigh.

He reached out a hand, touched her face. Smooth under his palm. Again the book had not lied, the sensation as perfect as if it were his true physical self occupying this space by her bedside.

He stroked her face, ran his hand along the curve of her jaw, the muscles of her neck. Drew a fingertip down the line of her sternum, tracing the valley between her pectoral muscles. Cupped her left breast, reaching across her chest to lift it in his hand. Ran his thumb over the nipple, saw it stiffen.

Just like the book says! She can feel me, respond to me, but she won't wake up. Because I'm nothing more than a dream to her. He bent to kiss her, certain he felt her lips respond to his, so slightly in sleep.

He dropped his face to the closer breast, caught the nipple between his ghostly teeth. It hardened. He bit down on the firm flesh. She moaned, stirred.

Edelman climbed onto the bed, draped himself down the length of her. He shifted his legs, forcing hers apart. He sank into the valley of her thighs, reached down between them to guide his member up into the parting of her pubic triangle.

Over the next few weeks she began to look tired, Edelman thought. As the book promised, he was able to use her in any way he wished, and in her deep sleep it seemed to him she sometimes reacted, moving with him, responding to his touch, his thrust. Sighing when he gave her pleasure, whimpering when he gave her pain.

He used her in every way his imagination could conceive, rolling her about on the big bed, taking her now from this angle, now that. One night he brought some lengths of cord and tied her, binding wrists to ankles. She moaned in discomfort when he mounted her thus restrained but did not awaken.

He used all parts of her, all openings. He rejoiced in it, growing bolder, crueler as he came to understand his mastery of her body. He could use the perfect, pouting mouth in any way that pleased him. He could squeeze and twist her breasts until tears flowed from her closed eyes. She did not awaken.

He turned her on her front one evening, took the same

lengths of rope he bound her with to beat her buttocks. She twitched and yelped with each stroke of the cord, but she did not wake.

But she was looking tired. When he saw her in the lobby—strange now to see her dressed, awake, conscious of him—she looked drawn. Dark circles under her eyes. He smirked to himself, and asked, "Are you all right, Miss McNichol?"

"Oh, er, sure . . ." She looked at him, as if trying to focus or—Edelman felt a passing chill in the pit of his stomach—to remember something. Something about him. But she only said, "I guess I've been sleeping badly. And every morning there's a . . . smell in my room. Like a hospital smell. I was thinking about having somebody come and look for a gas leak, but all the appliances are electric." She shrugged. The explanation of her condition clearly made no more sense to her than to Edelman.

Still, he was puzzled by her reference to hospital smells. He lived with such odors all day long at work, but according to the book there should be no such effect. He would have to double-check.

That night cold fury exploded under his heart as he stepped into her bedroom.

The slut was not alone!

There was a man in bed with her. Young. Dark. Long hair—longer than hers—falling in wavy ringlets over the pillow. Body—a sculpted thing, muscles in perfect array, shaped and hardened by careful exercise.

Edelman hated him on sight, would have hated him even had he not been in bed with Edelman's property. They lay close, her back spooned against his front. Edelman did not doubt they drifted off to sleep with the man inside her.

Edelman was furious, his first instinct to grab her, pull her from the bed, slap her bloody. He conceived the notion of binding her as he had before and lashing those perfect breasts until they bled.

But another idea came. A better idea.

Smiling, Edelman crossed the bedroom, turned left outside the door, walked down the hall to the kitchen. On the white walls Burt and Carrie Richardson looked down at him from fifty plastic-framed photographs.

The kitchen was as he remembered it: large, modern, with a central carving block of rich yellow wood on stainless steel legs. Suspended between two of the legs, a rack; in the rack, a large assortment of knives for all occasions.

Even the one Edelman had in mind.

He heard her scream through the six floors that separated their bedrooms. He lay on his back, on his own bed, looking up at the cracked and peeling ceiling, imagining the scene in the Richardsons' bedroom as the little whore awoke to find his handiwork.

She screamed six times, long, ululating wails that rose to piercing peaks before dropping down to begin again. A pause. Five more shrieks, each louder than the last.

Edelman could see her in his mind, writhing on the bed as she tried to free herself of the bonds that held her, wrists and ankles bound as one. Twisting and turning under the weight of the thing sprawled on top of her, dark blood staining white sheets, flesh peeled away in great, broad strips that looped around her arms and legs. If she turned her head enough . . .

Another scream, startled, horrified even beyond the horror of what lay on top of her. Edelman smiled. She'd seen her partner's penis and testicles, nicely arranged in a tidy—if bloody—little pile on the pillow next to her.

Half an hour later Edelman heard the thumping of feet, the crash of the Richardsons' door being broken down. The screaming stopped.

Pity about the door, he thought. *I'm almost sure I could have found the key for you.*

From his bedroom window he watched the ambulance pull out of 75th Street, turning right onto Central Park West. He smiled at the success of his evening's work. The little tramp—how could he ever have idolized her?—had been justly punished, as had the creature who usurped Edelman's place in her bed.

Edelman looked out across the lush greenery of the park—how resilient those venerable old trees, to grow so full and green in the foul air of New York—contemplating the marvels lying ahead.

Rachel was of no further interest, but this amazing power opened untold possibilities. He would begin to test them as soon as it was dark tonight. See how far he could float. How fast. A world of women and girls out there, all his, now. His to use as he liked.

Invigorated by the concept, Edelman left his apartment. He was going to wander through the park, study the lithe young bodies jogging, walking, tossing Frisbees. A smorgasbord laid out for the consumption of Robert J. Edelman. Almost as an afterthought he tucked the leather-bound *Nocturne* volume under his arm. He could read it in the park, sitting under a tree, watching all the pleasures that would be his in the nights to come.

There were other things he could do, too. No bank was sealed to him. Donald Trump's wallet might as well have been Edelman's.

He rode the elevator down to the lobby. Police were everywhere, as he'd expected. Edelman lingered awhile, listening to their words, their astonishment as they tried to understand what had happened.

A big man in plain clothes stood in the middle of the marble floor, everything flowing around him. Edelman heard one of the dozen or so uniformed officers call the man "Lieutenant," another plainclothesman called him "Shaw."

Lieutenant Shaw spent much of his time talking to a thin-faced man in drab civilian clothes who referred frequently to a small notebook. He carried a black bag, like a doctor's bag, Edelman thought. Edelman sidled close enough to hear the men's soft words.

"Not a professional job, for sure," the smaller man said. "Never seen such a mess. Clumsy."

"Not the girl, though, you think? She couldn't have tied those knots herself. And she sure wasn't faking the hysteria."

"No. And, anyway, the bloody hand prints everywhere . . ."

Edelman frowned. Hand prints? She couldn't have got up. He'd left her tied. They *said* she was tied.

"Yeah. Not her hands, for sure," Lieutenant Shaw said. "Or his. Too big. And, anyway, he wouldn't have been moving much."

"Plus there's the ether. You smelled it, didn't you?"

"Yeah. Like a goddamned hospital in that room."

Edelman remembered her mentioning a hospital smell. He'd not thought about it then. Now . . . A flicker across his mind's eye. The storeroom at DeVere. The little brown bottle. He tried to catch the image, but it was too fleeting.

"So you think somebody got in there," Shaw said, "probably brought along some knockout stuff to dope her . . ." He shook his head. "No sign of forcible entry, though. And the windows were closed and secured from the inside."

Edelman's frown deepened. He'd gone out by the window, as he always did. He left it open. Didn't he? Another flicker. The elevator. The Richardsons' door. The key . . .

"Inside job of some kind," the little man said. "She's subletting the place. Maybe there's a spare key floating around."

Shaw nodded. "Anyway, with all those prints, a room full of clues, it shouldn't be too hard to nail our man."

Edelman was trembling. His head pounded. Something was very wrong. The only hand prints they could possibly mean were his. But according to the book . . . The book . . .

The headache was very bad. The walls of the lobby wavered, dreamlike. The book . . .

He looked down at the copy of *The Fisherman's Bible* in his hand.

THE TUB

Richard Laymon

ello?"

"Guess who, Kenny." She spoke into the phone using her most sultry voice, which, she knew, was exceedingly sultry.

"All *right!*"

"Whacha doin'?"

"Nothing much. Hanging around. How about you?"

"I'm languishing in bed."

"Yeah?" Joyce heard his husky laugh. "You sick?"

"I'm sure running a fever," she said. "I'm hot. I'm just so hot I had to strip myself stark naked. I don't know *what* could be the matter with me."

"How high is your temperature?"

"I just don't know, Kenny. I don't have the strength to get up and fetch the thermometer. Why don't you come over and bring yours? That big one you've got between your legs."

Silence for a moment. Then Ken asked, "What about Harold?"

"Oh, don't you worry about him."

"That's what you said the last time, and he almost caught us at it."

"Well, it's absolutely safe tonight. I can guarantee it. He

17

went off to New York, New York, and he won't be back till Sunday evening."

"When did he leave?"

"You *are* a nervous nelly."

"I just don't want any trouble."

"Well, he left this morning. And you needn't worry that he missed his flight. He phoned me just a few minutes ago from his room at the Marriott. He's three thousand miles away, so I'm sure there's no danger whatsoever of him popping in on us."

"How do you know he didn't call from a pay phone a mile away and *say* he's at the New York Marriott? Maybe he's at the Brentwood Chevron."

"My, aren't we paranoid?"

"Why don't you phone the hotel? Just make sure he actually did check in, then call me back. If he's there, like he says, I'll come right over."

Joyce sighed. "Well, if I must, I must."

"I'll wait right here."

After hanging up, she rolled sideways, cradled the telephone, swung her legs off the bed and sat up.

What a nuisance.

Harold was in New York, just as he'd said. He had been nominated for a Bram Stoker award for that disgusting novel of his, and he certainly wouldn't miss his chance to bask in the glory. Tonight, he would be sopping up liquor in the hospitality suite with Joe and Gary and Chet and Rick and the others, yukking it up and having a ball. Joyce would be the farthest thing from his mind.

Even if he did have his suspicions about her—even if he didn't care a whit about chumming around with those other writers, even if he weren't nominated—he *still* wouldn't have the balls to pretend he'd gone to New York so that he could sneak back to the house and catch her with Ken.

Such a gutless wonder.

Such a wimp that even if he walked in on her by accident and caught her in full rut with Ken, he would probably do no more than blush, say nothing, and walk away.

Silly of Ken to worry about him at all.

What did he think, Harold might shoot him? Harold was terrified of guns. He probably wouldn't use one to save his own life, much less to blow away his wife's lover. And without a gun, Harold wouldn't stand a chance against Ken.

Ken, a 290-pound giant, all hard bulging muscles, could take care of little Harold without breaking a sweat.

She waited a while longer, then picked up the telephone and tapped Ken's number. He answered after the first ring.

"Hello?"

"Hello yourself, big man."

"Is he there?"

"According to the front desk, he checked in at six o'clock this evening."

"All *right*. I'm on my way."

"I'll leave the front door unlocked. Just come right in and see if you can find me."

"*Ciao*," he said.

"Yuck. Don't say that. That's what Harold always says. It's so pretentious."

"See you in ten minutes."

"Much better. See you then."

She hung up, stepped to the closet and reached for her satin robe. Then she decided not to bother with it. She *was* feeling hot. Though she would have to walk past windows to reach the front door, it was unlikely that anyone would see her. There were no other houses adjacent to their own, and hedges made it impossible for anyone to see her house from the road.

She left the bedroom, walking swiftly, enjoying the soft feel of the air stirring against her skin and the way her breasts jiggled just a little when she trotted down the stairs.

At the bottom, she saw her dark reflection in the window beside the front door.

She imagined a peeping Tom gazing in at her and felt a small tremor. Not a tremor of fear, she realized. For the benefit of the imaginary voyeur, she brushed her thumbs across the jutting tips of her nipples. The touch made her breath tremble.

She unlocked the door.

Her heart thumped and she trembled even more as she considered opening the door and stepping out onto the stoop. Waiting there for Ken. In the moonlight, in the open, the warm night breezes licking at her.

Some other time. Maybe later tonight, they could go outside together. But not now. She had already decided how to greet Ken, and she didn't have much time.

She hurried about, turning off all the downstairs lights before rushing upstairs again, where she shut off the hallway lights. Now the entire house was dark except for the master bedroom.

She entered, flicked a switch to kill the bedside lamps, then made her way carefully over the carpet to the bathroom. She put its lights on, but only for the moment she needed to find the matchbook and strike a match.

She shut the door and fingered the switch down. Then she touched the flame to the wick of the first candle. That was enough for now. She shook out the match. The single remaining flame was caught by the mirrors that covered every wall and the ceiling. The bathroom shimmered with fluttering, soft light.

Joyce smiled.

Harold has his damned tub, I have my lovely mirrors.

When they'd remodeled the bathroom, she had wanted a spacious sunken tub. Harold had insisted on his white elephant. It was a hideous ancient thing that stood on tiger feet in the middle of the floor. Like a showpiece. And he did enjoy showing it. He would bring his friends upstairs to the master bathroom so they could admire the monstrosity while he told them the whole long boring story of how he'd gotten it at an estate sale in Hollywood. Some bimbo actress from the silent-screen days had supposedly slit her wrists while she was in the thing. *Cashed in her chips,* Harold liked to say. *In this very tub.*

What a schmuck, Joyce thought as she bent over the tub and turned on its faucets. Water gushed from its spout. When it felt good and hot, she plugged the drain with the rubber stopper. She straightened up and wiped her wet hand on her thigh.

At least I got my mirrors out of the deal, she thought.

She had let him have the stupid haunted tub, and he'd let her have the mirrors.

She admired herself in them as she made her way around the bathroom, lighting more candles.

The wavering mellow glow made her eyes shine, her russet hair sparkle and gleam. Her skin looked dusky and golden. When the last candle was burning, she set down the matches and stretched, turning slowly, arms high.

She was surrounded by Joyces, all of them shimmering and mysterious. She gazed at their sleek, arched backs curving down to the perfect mounds of their buttocks. She gazed at the velvety backs of their thighs, legs tapering down to soft calves and delicate ankles. Still turning slowly, she lowered her arms and interlaced her fingers behind her head. All the Joyces did the same. They had such long, elegant necks. Shadows were pooled in the hollows of their throats and above the bows of their collar bones. Their breasts were high, the color of honey, tipped a deeper hue of gold. Below them, the rib cages were maybe a little too prominent. Harold certainly thought so. "Why don't you eat?"

The bastard.

I'm perfect the way I am.

She brought her hands down, savoring their touch, excited by the sight of all the Joyces caressing their breasts, gently squeezing their nipples, sliding their hands down their ribs (*which are just fine, thank you*), down the slim smoothness of their bellies, lower until their thumbs pushed into soft, gleaming coils of hair.

If Ken walks in and sees me like this, she thought, he'll never let me make it to the tub.

She hurried over to it. The water was high. She shut off the faucets and listened, wondering if he might already be in the house. She heard only her own quick heartbeat, her own ragged breathing, and quiet plops of water dripping from the spout.

Ken could be just outside the bathroom door.

Gripping the high rim of the tub, she swung a leg over. Hot water engulfed her foot. It was almost too hot. In the mirrors, she watched other Joyces climb into the tub, hold on to both sides, and slowly lower themselves. Then only their heads and the tops of their shoulders were visible.

Joyce slid herself forward. Her rump squeaked once against the porcelain as she leaned back. When she was submerged to the chin, she stopped her slide by raising her knees and pressing her feet flat against the bottom of the tub.

The damned thing was too long. She could never just stretch out in it, feet against the far end to keep her head out of the water. Which meant she could never truly relax. She had to keep her feet planted. Either that or prop herself up by spreading her legs wide enough to brace against the sides of the tub.

A real pain.

But this is one damned cloud with a silver lining, she told herself. The fucking tub's just the right size for fucking. Big Ken would be able to fit right in.

"Gonna do it right in your precious tub," she muttered. "How do you like *them* apples, Harold?"

She waited, savoring the water's heat, caressing herself. The ceiling mirrors reflected candlelight down into the tub. She watched her hands move, her body writhe as she squirmed with pleasure.

She flinched at the sound of a floorboard creaking.

He's here!

In the bedroom?

She scooted backward, sliding herself up until she was sitting. She rested her arms on the sides of the tub. She wanted to look just right when he entered, and the mirrors showed that she did. Water covered her like an iridescent mist from the belly down. Her arms, shoulders, and chest were wet and shiny.

She turned her eyes to the bathroom door.

What's taking him so long? she wondered. And then she heard a faint, muffled footstep.

Definitely a footstep.

What if it isn't Ken?

A shiver crawled up Joyce's body. She felt her skin tighten and tingle with goosebumps.

Anybody might've walked into the house.

But it has to be Ken.

It doesn't have to be.

But if it's a stranger out there, maybe he thinks the house is deserted. Maybe he won't find me. Maybe . . .

The door flew open.

Joyce gasped and flinched.

Ken strode into the bathroom as if parading onto the stage at a body-building contest.

He had removed his clothes. He had oiled his skin.

"It's you," she whispered.

He began to pose. He turned this way and that, moving and pausing and flexing with slow, graceful elegance. His muscles bulged and rippled. Joyce watched, breathless. She had seen him do all this before, but never in the fluttering gold of candlelight.

He looked magnificent and strange. A gorgeous, hairless monster of dancing mounds and slabs.

When he strutted to the rear of the tub, Joyce didn't have to turn her head. She watched him in a mirror, watched him bend and reach down and slip his hands around her breasts. They touched her only for a moment. Then he pranced backward, curling his arms and twisting his torso.

He twirled around. With coy glances over his shoulder, he came to the side of the tub. He raised his arms and flexed, displaying the bands of muscle crisscrossing his back, the hard mounds of his rump. Joyce smiled when he made his buttocks bounce. One side at a time. She reached up and stroked one slick cheek.

He gently swatted her hand away as if offended, strutted away from the tub, then whirled around and sashayed back to her. Hands on hips, he bent his knees. His rigid penis, inches from her face, jerked up and down. He hopped closer. Joyce twisted toward him, rolling onto one hip, clutching the rim of the tub with both hands. Her breasts pushed against the cool porcelain wall. She opened her mouth. He brushed against her lips, teasing her, not entering. Then he pranced backward.

"Quit it," she gasped. "Get in here. I want you *in* me."

He returned to the tub. Peering down at her, he whispered, "You look delicious."

"You look pretty good yourself."

"You seriously want me in the tub?"

"There's plenty of room."

"The bed would be more comfortable."

"But not as exciting."

He shrugged his massive shoulders. Bending over, he clutched the side of the tub and climbed in. He stood at her feet, glanced down at her, then turned his head slowly, surveying his images in the mirrors.

"Quit admiring yourself and fuck me."

He sank slowly to his knees, flinching a bit when the hot water met his scrotum. Joyce slipped down into the warmth. As it engulfed her to the neck, her feet met the slippery skin of Ken's thighs.

"You don't want me on top, do you?"

"Of course I do."

"You want to drown?"

"I want to be crushed." She lifted a foot out of the water and stroked him. "I want to feel you on me, that whole gorgeous body pounding me senseless."

He moaned. He nodded. He muttered, "Let's lose the water."

"Hurry. Just hurry."

He reached down behind his rump. Joyce heard a quick sucking gurgle, then the soft rush of water flowing down the drainpipe.

She spread her legs. Ken crawled forward slowly. His hands glided up her thighs, caressed her hips and belly, moved up the slope to her rib cage. They cupped her breasts. As they squeezed, she lifted a hand out of the water and curled her fingers around his penis.

"In," she whispered.

His hands slid away and down her sides. Bracing himself above her, he lowered his face into the water. His tongue flicked her right nipple, swirled and pressed. His mouth opened, and she felt his lips around her breast. He sucked. He sucked it deep into his mouth.

"God!" she cried out. She let go of his penis and clutched his back.

He let go. He came up gasping. His dripping face smiled at her, then plunged down again. She felt lips on her other breast. They were like a soft, pliant ring encircling her

25

nipple, making a tight seal. This time, they didn't suck. They blew. Blew like a kid making fart sounds on his arm. Lips and air and water vibrated against her nipple. Bubbles erupted on the surface.

Gasping, she pushed his head away.

"Did it hurt?" he asked.

"No. Just . . . quit it and fuck me . . . *now!*"

He struggled, trying to reposition himself. Joyce realized that their differences in size were causing him problems. That and the water. He was still worried about drowning her.

Suddenly, he reared back onto his haunches, dragging her up out of the water by the armpits, lifting her, planting her down on him, impaling her.

A club shoving high up into her.

She cried out and shuddered and clamped herself tight to his chest as spasms quaked through her body.

Spasms also quaked Ken.

He dropped forward, driving her down. Her back splashed, then slammed the bottom of the tub. Her head snapped down and thunked. Lights exploded in her vision as water rained down on her face.

When the exploding lights went away, she realized she was sprawled beneath Ken, her chin resting against the top of his shoulder.

"Christ," she gasped. "You hurt me."

He didn't apologize.

He didn't say a thing.

She realized that he couldn't. His head, next to her own, was facedown in the water. The level was lowering, but slowly. The heat enclosed Joyce's head like a warm hood. Only the front of her face was in the air.

So Ken's face had to be submerged.

He's going to drown!

"Ken!"

He didn't stir.

He wasn't making bubbles. He wasn't breathing.

His chest was mashed tight against Joyce's chest. She felt her raging heartbeat. Whether *his* was beating, she couldn't tell.

Though she was pinned down by his weight, her arms were free. They'd been around him at the moment of the fall. So she made fists and pounded on his back.

"Ken! Ken, wake up!"

He's not sleeping, you idiot.

"Ken! Get your head up! Ken!"

She kept hammering her fists down against his back. They made meaty thuds. She had no idea whether pounding on him would do any good, but she'd seen it done on doctor shows. Also, in a way, it felt good. Each blow sent quick little tremors through his body. Like rapping a watermelon at the grocery store. The tremors made him vibrate on top of her. They gave Joyce a tingle.

The blows even jostled his penis a little.

It was still buried in her. Still erect.

"I *know* you're faking," she said. "Now, come on. Dead guys don't have boners."

He didn't move.

"Come on, Ken. This isn't funny. I bumped my damned head. Besides, you scared me. I thought you were dead or something."

He still didn't move.

"All right. You're asking for it." She jabbed the long nail of her forefinger into his back. She felt it pop into his skin. He didn't flinch.

A sick, icy chill snaked through her bowels.

"Oh, my God," she muttered.

She nudged his head with the side of her face. It moved easily. She bumped her cheekbone against his ear. His head swung away, then flopped back and hit her as if trading blows.

"Shit!"

27

He's dead! The bastard's *dead!*

Joyce squirmed under his terrible weight.

This won't be easy, she thought.

She took a deep breath, then attacked. She bucked, she twisted, she shoved and tugged at Ken, she kicked and thrust at the bottom of the tub with her feet, she clawed at the sides with her hands. But she couldn't roll him off. She couldn't lift him. She couldn't writhe her way out from under him.

All her efforts hardly moved him at all.

Finally, she was too exhausted to continue the struggle. She lay beneath him, limp and sweaty, arms at her sides, fighting to breathe.

Calm down, she told herself.

Right. Calm down. I've got a fucking stiff on top of me. Not to mention . . .

Don't even think about that.

There has got to be a way out of this.

A way out of it fast!

Use your head, use your head.

The problem—the major problem—is the damn tub. The way it's holding us in. Of course.

If only we'd done it on the bed! I could've just rolled him off me . . .

If only. A lot of good that'll do you.

If only he hadn't fallen on me, that's what.

What happened to him? A heart attack? An aneurysm? Who knows? Who cares? The jerk was pumped up with steroids, probably fucked up his system.

And now I'm the one who's fucked.

For the first time since she'd landed on her back under Ken, Joyce noticed the overhead mirror. She stared up at it.

No wonder she was trapped. She could hardly see herself. Only her face and legs were visible. The rest of her was hidden beneath Ken's massive body. She raised her arms.

They came up into view below Ken's armpits. They looked so small.

Her legs looked useless. Beautiful, useless legs, with their knees in the air—legs spread wide and painfully apart and jammed against the walls of the tub by Ken's thick thighs.

She tested them. She was able to unbend her knees. She could straighten her legs, lower them, and raise them high.

When she moved her legs at all, Ken seemed to shift position deep inside her, probing and exploring.

She didn't let that stop her. She watched her legs in the mirror and kept on testing their maneuverability. She found that she could kick around pretty well, but mostly just from the knees down. What she couldn't do was bring her legs together. Though she tried, they remained tight against the walls of the tub.

Maybe . . .

She lifted her right leg high, hooked its calf over the edge of the tub, shoved her right elbow against the bottom, and struggled to raise and turn herself, hoping to roll Ken off. She couldn't budge him.

Okay. This doesn't work. Something *has to work.*

She lowered her leg. She tried to relax.

I can't actually be stuck *here.*

But I'm certainly being *stuck.*

At least I should be able to do something about that, she thought.

She slid her open right hand into the tight crevice between her belly and Ken's. His skin was slippery against the back of her hand. She shoved downward. Their pelvises, locked together, stopped her fingertips. She tried getting to him from the side of her groin. No way.

"Great," she muttered.

Then she screamed and kicked and pushed and twisted and squirmed, determined to get him off her, out of her, knowing she could do it—she had to do it and she could—

29

mothers picked up cars, didn't they, when they had a kid trapped under a wheel? She could lift Ken. She would. She would hurl him aside and scamper out of the tub.

When she found that she couldn't, she wept.

Sometime later, the candles began to die. One by one, they fluttered, flared brightly and went out. She was left in darkness.

Just as well, she thought at first. Nothing to look at, anyway, but a dead guy pinning me down.

She didn't feel that way for long.

Terror began creeping through her.

A dead guy. A corpse. I'm trapped by a corpse.

What if it starts to move?

It's only Ken, she told herself. It's not any fucking ghoul or zombie or spook, it's just Ken. And he's dead, kaput. He isn't about to start *moving*.

But suppose he does? Suppose he wants revenge? I'm the one who killed him.

He had a heart attack or something. Wasn't my fault.

Maybe he doesn't see it that way.

Shit! He doesn't see anything. He's dead! Besides, he died happy. What a way to go, right? He came and went.

She heard a laugh. It sounded a trifle mad.

He didn't come, she reminded herself.

Coitus interruptus croakus.

She laughed again.

She went silent, the sound of her laughter frozen in her throat as she imagined Ken lifting his head, kissing her mouth with his dead lips, whispering, "I've got some unfinished business," and starting to thrust.

It took the light of morning to ease her terror. She slept.

She woke up aching and sweaty, her rump numb, her legs lifeless. She flexed her muscles, kicked and squirmed as much as she could. Soon, circulation came back. Her buttocks and legs burned. They felt as if they were being pricked by thousands of needles.

When she felt better, she noticed the odor.

The overhead mirror revealed its cause. Down between Ken's feet, a turd was hanging over the edge of the drain.

"Shit," she muttered.

She closed her eyes.

Don't sweat the small stuff, she told herself.

Think, think.

Okay, it's Saturday. If he doesn't miss his flight or something, Harold will be getting back tomorrow evening. Around seven. That gives me better than a full day to get out of here. Or hubby'll get the surprise of his life.

How's this for a horror story, Harold? Write this one up, why don't you? Maybe you'll win a fucking award!

Won't happen. I'll be out of this mess long before he gets home.

Right.

How?

I can float Ken off me!

She thought about that for a while. If she filled the tub, wouldn't the rising water lift him? Sure it would.

I might drown in the process.

But if I can hold my breath long enough . . .

She raised her legs, stretched them out, tried to squeeze them closer together . . . and came nowhere near the bathtub's faucets.

So much for great ideas.

There has to be a way. There . . .

"Get off me!" she shrieked, and fought the body. It was rigid with rigor mortis. It felt even heavier than before. Finally, exhaustion made her quit.

There *is* no way, she realized.

I'm gonna be trapped under this goddamned stiff until Harold gets home.

After that, she spent a long time crying. Later, she dozed.

When she woke up, her butt and legs were numb again, but she no longer felt the horrible desperation. She felt resigned.

"When rape is inevitable," she muttered, "relax and enjoy it." What asshole thought up that one? she wondered.

This isn't the end of the world, she told herself. It may be the end of my marriage, but that's no great loss. Harold will come home tomorrow and get me out of this.

It's awful and disgusting, but I'm not going to die from it.

Later in the day, the stench got worse as her own excretions joined Ken's.

When darkness returned, so did her terror.

She lay motionless, hardly daring to breathe, waiting for Ken to stir. Or to speak.

Joyce.

What?

I'm hunnnngry.

She imagined his head turning, nuzzling down against the side of her neck, biting.

When she finally did feel him move, she shrieked. She screamed until her throat felt raw and burning.

Later, she convinced herself that Ken hadn't come back to life. The motion had probably been caused by something natural. Like decomposition. Shifting gases. Tendons or muscles turning soft. Gross. Disgusting. But he wasn't coming back to life. He wasn't going to start talking to her. He wasn't going to bite her. He wasn't going to start humping her.

Just make it through the night.

Later, as she was starting to drift off, Ken moaned.

Joyce gasped. She went rigid, goosebumps squirming over her skin.

It's just escaping gases, she told herself.

He did it again, and she whimpered.

"Stop it," she whined. "Stop it. Get off me. Please."

32

She exploded into another frenzy of struggles, then lay sobbing under his bulk and prayed for daylight.

When the first gray light of dawn came into the bathroom, Joyce's panic subsided and she closed her eyes.

It's Sunday.

Harold will come. He'll be here around seven. Before dark.

There won't be another night under Ken.

Exhausted, she drifted into sleep.

The jangle of the telephone startled her awake.

Who is it? Maybe someone had heard her screams in the night and was calling to check on her. *When I don't answer . . .*

Fat chance.

Nobody had heard the screams. Probably just a friend calling to chat. Or a salesman.

The ringing stopped.

Or Harold. Harold calling to say he'd missed his flight, or he'd been bumped, or he'd decided to stay on another day or two in New York to meet with his agent, his editor.

"No," she murmured. "No, please. Harold, get back here. You've got to."

I can't go through another night.

It's all right, she told herself. He'll come. He'll come.

A few more hours, and he'll be here.

She wondered if Harold would be able to get her out from under Ken. Probably not. Such a weakling. He might have to call the fire department. *I hate to bother you folks, but I'm afraid my wife is stuck in the bathtub. It seems she was screwing this muscle-man and the fellow pitched a coronary or something.*

The idea of it made her laugh. The laughing made her chest hurt. Worse, it jostled her insides and jiggled Ken's penis.

She groaned.

There's nothing funny about this, she thought.

But if Harold can't get me out, the fire department will. It'll be a little embarrassing, but so what? I'll be free.

She imagined herself running down the corridor, buck naked, the firemen gaping in shock and maybe just a bit turned on. Running to the other bathroom, the one with a shower.

First, she would drink cold water. Fill her parched mouth with it. Drink till her belly bloated. Then she would take the longest shower in history. Sudsing and scrubbing until there was not a trace left of Ken's foul dead touch. Douching, too. Getting rid of his death.

Afterward, cocktails. Vodka and tonic. Ice clinking in her glass. A twist of lemon. Drinking until her head was full of soft, cozy cotton.

Then, a steak dinner. A thick slab of rare filet mignon, charcoal broiled.

I'll have to broil it myself, she thought. *Harold isn't likely to be in any mood to cook for me. If he sticks around at all.*

Thinking about the steak, her mouth watered. Her stomach growled.

I'll be eating soon, she told herself. *In just a few more hours . . . if that wasn't Harold on the phone, calling to say he wouldn't be home.*

It wasn't.

Please, it wasn't.

He'll be here. He'll come.

He came.

Joyce, lost in daydreams about his arrival, heard nothing until the bathroom door swung open.

"Harold!"

"Joyce?"

She heard his quick footsteps. Then he was gazing down at her, at Ken. His face turned a shade of gray almost the same color as Ken's back. His mouth drooped open.

"Get me out of here!"

He frowned.

"My God, quick! I've been pinned under him since Friday night!"

"You can't get up?"

"Would I be here if I could?"

"Jeez, Joyce."

"Get your thumb out of your ass and get me out of here!"

He kept staring down into the tub, shaking his head slowly from side to side.

"Harold! Get me out of here!"

"Uh-huh. Right."

He turned and walked away.

"Ciao," he said. The bathroom door bumped shut.

Harold flew to Maui and spent a week relaxing on the beach, reading horror novels written by his friends, dining at fine restaurants. He ogled some beautiful women, but he stayed away from them. He didn't need any more traitorous bitches in his life.

Upon his return, he stepped into the house and called out, "Joyce, I'm home."

She didn't answer.

Grinning, Harold trotted upstairs.

The smell was not good. It made him gag. It made his eyes water. With a handkerchief over his nose and mouth, he hurried across the bedroom and entered the bathroom.

He went numb.

He dropped the handkerchief.

He stared.

The tile floor near the bathtub was strewn with body parts.

A bloody orb that he recognized as a head. Part of a head, anyway. It was missing its jaw. The ragged stump of its neck looked *chewed.*

He saw an arm. Another arm. Big, muscular things. So

much missing from around their tops. The knobby ends of the humerus bones looked as if they'd been licked clean.

The floor was littered with other pieces. Curving slats of rib bones. Chunks of flesh. Slabs of stringy muscle. Slimy gobs that might have been interior organs—parts of lungs, maybe, or kidneys—who knows?

Harold *did* recognize a heart among the assortment of litter.

Over the rim of the tub hung coils of intestines.

Harold threw up.

When he was done, he approached the tub, careful not to step on any mess.

Joyce wasn't in it.

Her boyfriend was. Some of him. From the ass down, he appeared to be in fine shape. Excellent shape.

Most of his torso, however, had been hollowed out. He was an armless, headless husk sprawled in a swamp of blood and puke and floating bits of God-knows-what.

"Welcome home, honey."

Harold whirled around.

Standing in the bathroom doorway was Joyce. Clean and fresh and smiling. Wearing her red satin robe.

"My God," was all he could say.

She grinned and clacked her teeth together. Then she brought her right hand around from behind her back. It was holding a jawbone. "Ken has good, sharp teeth. He was of enormous benefit."

"My God," Harold muttered.

She tossed the jawbone, caught it with her forefinger behind the front teeth, and twirled it. "Let's talk settlement," she said. "I get the house. The tub is yours."

THE PICTURE OF HEALTH

Ray Garton

Caryl Dunphy was no longer a virgin. At the age of twenty, she had finally done the deed, as the girls used to say in school; she'd lost her innocence, popped her cherry, become a woman. But she had not done it with just *anybody*. Caryl had done it with *somebody*.

Hawk.

He stirred next to her beneath the covers, smacking his lips in his sleep and sighing as he rolled away from her, taking his hand from her breast, pulling his moist cock away from her thigh.

Caryl propped herself up on one elbow and just stared at him in the dingy light of the dressing room.

His face was so finely sculpted, its complexion so perfect, that it did not look real; it more closely resembled a beautiful mask. His shoulder-length hair spilled over the pillow in wavy reddish-brown strands. Long lashes rested on his high cheekbones and full lips parted slightly with each exhalation. His broad shoulders spread above a smooth muscular chest which rose and fell rhythmically with his flat rippled belly.

Caryl touched his hair gently with two fingertips and her stomach fluttered with excitement.

I'm actually here! she thought. *With him! With Hawk! My first time . . . and it's with the biggest rock star in the world . . .*

He'd first appeared about twenty years ago as the lead guitarist and songwriter for a band called Birds of Prey. Back then, he was Darren Hawke. When the band broke up in 1980—after only two top-forty hits—Hawke continued to perform on his own, mostly in nightclubs and small auditoriums, but only for a while. He disappeared for three years—the equivalent of a death certificate in the music business—and rumors blew around like the wind: Darren Hawke, the sexiest and most admired member of the Birds of Prey, had died; he was in hiding because he had AIDS; he was in a drug-induced downward spiral; he'd had a sex change operation and would soon reappear as a *female* rock musician.

But no one really knew what had happened to Darren Hawke during those three years of invisibility. Then, suddenly, as if he'd never been gone, he reappeared as, simply, Hawk. He had a band, but its members were incidental. Hawk was the only star of *this* show. There was an album from which four songs became number-one hits. A series of steamy videos on MTV just fed the flames of his popularity. The music was at once dark and uplifting, romantic and shamelessly sexual. Suddenly, Hawk was the favorite target of gossip columnists and tabloids. A week did not pass when he was not paired with a new woman: a movie star, a recording star, a model, writer or television actress. Sometimes the tabloids even paired him, both subtly and blatantly, with other men. But his career flourished and his popularity only grew. His reputation as a man who never spent more than one night with the same woman only helped his career.

And Caryl had followed it all. She'd savored every picture of Hawk in every paper and magazine that featured one. And then he'd come to San Francisco. In spite of the limitations of her budget and the complaints of her mother, she'd bought a ticket. She'd gotten a seat in the third row and was shocked when Hawk had pointed at her several times during the concert, smiling and winking. Afterward, as she was making her way out of the auditorium, she was approached by a man in a black leather jacket who gave her a backstage pass and told her that Hawk wanted to see her. At first she thought it was a joke. But when the pass got her past the guards and into his dressing room, she knew it was for real.

Caryl was led down a long poorly lighted corridor with doors on either side. *Dressing rooms,* she thought. Some of the doors were open and Caryl couldn't keep herself from peeking into a few as she passed. Three half-naked bodies writhed on the floor in one room; in another, a man with long platinum hair injected something into his bony arm as a girl's head bobbed up and down on his lap. Caryl didn't look into any more rooms, but she could hear sounds: muffled laughter . . . crying . . . sucking . . . "Now lick my ass, bitch!" was snarled through clenched teeth. Caryl became frightened and, for a moment, considered running back the way she'd come.

"Right here," the leather-jacketed man said, opening a door.

Hawk was shirtless, barefoot and sweaty as he sat on the edge of a narrow bed drinking from a flask. Smiling, he offered her a drink, but she declined. What was her name? Did she like the show? Did she come alone? Did she need a ride home? Or maybe she'd like to go out? Go to his hotel for a late dinner?

Dinner with Hawk, she thought, her jaw slack. "Yuh-yeah. Sure. That would be nice." Her mother would never have to know; Caryl could say she went out with friends. And that wouldn't exactly be a lie, would it?

"Lemme get dressed." He put the flask aside and stood, removing his tight black pants in one graceful sweep of movement, and Caryl spun around with a gasp, her heart pounding like a jackhammer in her chest.

Hawk chuckled. "What? You never seen a naked man before?"

She closed her eyes but the image would not go away: his perfect body, smooth skin, firm muscular thighs and . . . and *that* . . . smooth and cylindrical . . . not too big, not too small . . . at least, as far as *she* knew. And what did *she* know?

"A-a-as a muh-matter of fact," she said, her mouth dry, "no. I haven't." She kept her back to him, head bowed, afraid to turn around, and stiffened when she heard him coming toward her.

Hawk stepped in front of her, completely naked and smiling, and said quietly, "Really? Never?"

She just stared at his bare legs and feet, but when he hooked a finger under her chin and slowly raised her head, her eyes traveled the length of his body and her breath caught in her throat. She stopped at his eyes—sparkling and slightly narrowed—and there her gaze held.

"Really?" he asked again, stroking her cheek with a finger, and she nodded; her mouth was too dry to speak now. "Well, you got one right here. Look all you want." He held her hands lightly and, grinning, took one step back so she could look him over.

Her face burned, but, as if with their own will, her eyes moved down his body slowly, lingering on his muscular torso, passing over his hairless, unblemished skin to the patch of hair surrounding his penis. It moved. Twitched. Began to grow. Caryl thought her heart would jump out of her mouth.

His hands were on her shoulders and she found herself moving backward and sitting when her legs bumped the edge of the bed, where her purse dropped from trembling fingers. He knelt before her, closed his eyes and pressed her hands to his face, his hair, moved them down his neck, over his shoulders, down his chest, holding her fingertips to his nipples, and—

—Caryl felt weak, felt a warmth in her middle that she'd never felt before, growing warmer, *hotter,* and—

—Hawk moved his hands up her arms and began removing her clothes smoothly, gracefully, until she was in nothing but her underwear, and—

—she knew there was something she had to say, something she had to do, to make *sure* of, but she couldn't remember *what,* until—

—he pushed her down on the bed gently and laid down beside her, pressing his erection to her bare thigh, and then—

—she remembered. Caryl's mother, Margaret Dunphy, was a devout Christian and disapproved of premarital sex. But, unlike many others who shared her belief, she condemned no one who felt otherwise and always knew Caryl might choose to live her life differently than Margaret had. For that reason, she'd told her daughter to make sure she was prepared and never to engage in sex without protecting herself, not only to prevent pregnancy but also to prevent the transmission of diseases. "The Bible doesn't condemn promiscuity just because God didn't want us to have fun," she'd told Caryl once. "It just took a few thousand years for the reasons to become painfully obvious." It was not Margaret Dunphy's belief that AIDS was God's punishment to the sinful; it was, quite simply, she thought, the result of man's lack of common sense. "Whether you're married or not," she'd said, "screwing around is just *not* common sense. Right?" So, because of her mother's concern, and with her approval, Caryl kept a few condoms in her purse at all times. And if this was *it,* if this was going to be her first time, she was going to use them.

"Wait," she whispered hoarsely, the frantic pounding of

her heart making her voice hitch rhythmically. "Just a second."

"What?" He raised his head, frowning.

As she reached for her purse, the only thing she managed to say was "Pruh-protection."

He chuckled and wrapped his fingers around her wrist, pulling it away from the purse. "We don't need that."

His words broke through her hypnotic stupor and she pushed herself into a sitting position. "Oh, I think we do. *I* do, anyway."

He leaned close and gave her a little kiss. "Have you ever heard the phrase, 'It's like taking a shower with a raincoat on'? That's what it's like for a guy. And besides, you don't have anything to worry about."

"Buh-but I know about your repu-reputation," she breathed. "I've heard the stories. All those women . . . some say men, too . . ."

He laughed loudly this time. "And you *believed* them? They're just *stories.* Anybody in my position has to put up with that. I don't even pay attention to them anymore. It comes with the territory. I just wanna make music. Jeez, you think I'm screwin' around as much as they say? I'd be in an AIDS ward by now if I was!" He stroked her breasts, slipped his fingers under her bra while tugging at the strap with the other hand and kissing her shoulder gently. Electric tingles shot down through Caryl's body from the spot touched by Hawk's lips. "We don't need one of those things," he whispered, kissing her again. "We want skin, right?" Another kiss. "Flesh against flesh." Another. "Our juices mixing with nothing in between." He had the bra off and was working on her panties now as he sucked on her breasts and rubbed himself against her.

But she didn't feel right about it, couldn't enjoy what he was doing to her because her stomach suddenly welled up with fear at the idea of having sex without any protection and her mother's calm, rational voice echoed in her mind:

Whether you're married or not, screwing around is just not *common sense. Right?*

Right? Right? Right?

His tongue was on her nipple and his hand was between her legs, fingers making their way between her lips, which had grown so wet and—

—she reached down and grabbed her purse with one hand, trying to push him away again with the other, gasping, "No! Wait! A second! No!" but—

—he straddled her, held her head between his hands and massaged her temples with his fingers as he looked into her eyes and whispered, "We're going to make love . . . and it's going to be beautiful."

Caryl's muscles relaxed. Her legs loosened and she allowed him to remove her panties completely and lower his head between her thighs. His lips made her arch her back; his tongue made her whimper like a child; his fingers made her cry out. He moved up her body, licking all the way, and hiked her legs over his shoulders. Slowly, carefully, he slid his erection into her, staring into her eyes during every moment of it. Caryl bit her lower lip so hard she tasted blood and her hands clutched at the bedsheets as if for life. Her breasts rose and fell with pistonlike speed as Hawk began to move inside her, and after a few moments of stinging pain . . . it was wonderful . . .

And now she lay beside him, stroking his satiny skin and watching him sleep. His eyes opened suddenly and he turned to her, smiling, as if he'd never been asleep.

"I'll get a car for you," he whispered. "You can go home and get anything you need. I want you to come to L.A. and live with me. Our plane leaves in three hours."

Caryl let herself into the apartment quietly. Something by Mozart was playing softly on the stereo in the living room, and the lamp by the recliner cast a shaft of light into the hallway. Caryl braced herself, hoping that her mother had

Ray Garton

fallen asleep while reading in her chair so Caryl could just leave her a note, but she suspected otherwise. She suspected correctly.

The recliner creaked as Margaret Dunphy stood up, and her footsteps sounded on the hardwood floor; Caryl's back stiffened as her mother appeared in the hallway.

Margaret Dunphy was tall and slender with graying brown hair and a soft face. She wore a long bathrobe of maroon velour and smiled at her daughter warmly.

"So, how was the concert?" she asked, folding her hands.

Caryl felt herself blushing and turned away, whispering, "It was . . . guh-good."

"Did you go out afterward?"

"Uh-huh." She nodded.

"What did you do?"

Caryl's gut tensed into a knot. "No," she breathed, "I didn't. I-I'm sorry. I can't lie to you. I didn't actually . . . go *out* afterward."

"Oh. What did you do?"

Tears burned the back of her throat as she spoke, trying to control her voice. "I, um . . . Hawk? The singer I went to see? He . . . invited me backstage."

"Really?" She smiled as she said it, with no sign of anger, as if she were happy about the honor given her daughter.

Caryl had expected that; although her mother was a Christian, she was neither a Bible-beater nor a tyrant. But that only made it worse, because Caryl knew she was going against her mother's wishes, and that hurt.

"So you got to meet him," her mother said.

"Uh-huh."

"Well, that must have been nice. I know how much you admire him. What was he like?"

Staring at her feet, Caryl said, "Nice." There was a long silence, so long that Caryl could not bear it any longer and suddenly, unexpectedly—

—she told her mother everything. *Everything.*

44

The next long silence was even worse. Her mother's smile disappeared, but slowly. And it was not replaced with an angry glare—only a raised eyebrow.

Finally, Margaret said, "I hope you were . . . careful. You know what I mean, don't you?"

"Yes. I know what you mean." Caryl couldn't bring herself to tell the whole truth about *that*.

"So, you've decided to go? And live with this man?"

Caryl nodded.

"Do you think it's serious? I mean, do you think there's, you know . . . marriage in the future? Or is this just . . . oh, I don't know . . . an affair?"

Still not looking at her, Caryl said, "I don't know. I only met him tonight. I mean, really *met* him."

"Well." Margaret put her hands on each side of her daughter's face and smiled. "You know what you want. I just hope what you *want* is what's *best* for you. You might think I'm a fuddy-dud, but I'm aware of this Hawk's reputation, you know. I read magazines and papers. I watch television."

"Yeah, we talked about that and . . . he said they were just rumors and he's not like that at all. He said . . . well, he told me that . . . oh, Momma, I don't want you to hate me. I know you think this is wrong and . . . well, I just don't want you to hate me."

Embracing her daughter, Margaret sighed. "Oh, I could never hate you, Caryl. I just want you to be happy. That's all."

Hawk's three-story house in Bel Air was spectacular. The yard was like a green shaded field with a pond and ducks and so *many* singing birds, and inside, the rooms and hallways were endless. Secretaries, assistants, butlers and maids attended to Hawk's slightest whim and they all treated Caryl as if they worked for *her* as well as for Hawk.

She was given free reign of the house and Hawk encouraged her to look around as much as she liked; he would be busy with meetings for the next few days, then he had three weeks free and they could do whatever they wanted, spend all of their time together, stay in bed for days at a time if they felt like it.

So Caryl looked around.

She went from room to room and floor to floor, staring in awe at framed pictures of Hawk with the Who, the Rolling Stones, Elton John, Led Zeppelin, Joe Walsh, Roxy Music, Peter Frampton and more, all of them signed. She admired his Grammys and American Music Awards and People's Choice Awards, all on dustless shelves behind spotless glass. She went from room to room, finding giant blowups of his *Rolling Stone* magazine covers and his album jackets, paintings of Patti Smith and Stevie Nicks and Joan Jett, framed gold and platinum records. The halls were lit by wall sconces—white ceramic hands that held glowing globes—but on the top floor of the house at the end of the hall, the last few globes were dark and the shadows were long. Caryl reached for the knob of the very last door and a hand touched her shoulder. Starting, she spinned around.

Barnes, one of the butlers, a tall, balding, black-haired man, pulled his bony-fingered hand away and smiled, inclining his head slightly as he said, in a low, quiet voice, "Mr. Hawk prefers that this room remain closed. It's locked anyway."

"Oh. Oh, sure. Okay, sure, I'm sorry." Embarrassed, Caryl nodded as if her head were about to bob off. As Barnes walked away, she asked, curiously but timidly, "Um, what's in there?"

Barnes turned slowly, his thin face still smiling. "Just some dusty old personal items. We aren't even allowed to clean in there," he added with a soft chuckle.

Caryl nodded and smiled and said, "Ah, I see," and Barnes headed back down the hall. But before following him, Caryl turned back to the door and stared at it a moment. Above the knob was a second lock, a deadbolt. She tossed a glance back to make sure Barnes was gone, then tried the doorknob. It was, indeed, locked.

But something was wrong.

There in the shadowy end of the hall, Caryl could see the faintest orange glow seeping from beneath the locked door.

The next few days were like a wonderful hazy dream to Caryl. She only saw Hawk for a few minutes in the morning and then in bed after he got home, when they would make love so furiously that a couple of times they actually ripped the sheets. Hawk still refused to wear a condom and it terrified Caryl just as much as it had during their first time in his dressing room. She was scared of picking up any diseases, of course, and she most definitely did *not* want to get pregnant. Not yet anyway.

"You don't have to worry about that, babe," Hawk told her one night as he moved inside of her. "I can't make babies. I've been fixed."

Caryl thought that was kind of sad, but they were too busy to talk about it then. In fact, they were always too busy to talk about much of anything. When they were together, they were either making love or sleeping, or Hawk was just on his way out. And he went out every day, long after his promise that he'd be busy for just a few days. Caryl was still so overwhelmed by the fact that she was actually living with Hawk that she was able to ignore the inadequacies easily. At first. One morning after breakfast, as Hawk lit up a joint before leaving, she asked him why he was gone so much . . . every *day*, in fact.

He kissed her, pulled a wad of cash from his jeans pocket and pressed it into her hand. She shuffled through it and, shocked, discovered twenties, fifties and hundreds. "Whuh-what's th-*this* for?"

"I'll have Kelsey drive you into town. Go shopping. Beverly Hills is great for shopping. Get some clothes. Some jewelry. Go over to Gucci and get yourself a nice leather outfit. Have lunch. Baby yourself a little. And don't come back till you've spent all of that." He kissed her again, slipped his tongue into her mouth and squeezed her ass as he held her close for a moment. "I've got a few meetings to go to. Some asshole video director wants to tell me his ideas for the new song. Then I'm going to the studio for a while. I'll see you tonight."

And then he was gone.

Caryl was afraid she would stick out like the proverbial sore thumb in Beverly Hills, but riding through the immaculate streets in a black limousine with tinted windows made her blend in like a chameleon.

She did buy a leather outfit at Gucci, just as Hawk had suggested, along with a gorgeous pair of shoes. At Tori Steele she bought two dresses (one of which she wore out of the store) and a coat, and at Tiffany's she got a beautiful diamond necklace and a pair of ruby earrings. She'd felt guilty at first and was hesitant to spend so much of Hawk's money, but he *had* told her to spend it all, so she decided to find someplace quiet and elegant for lunch. Maybe Kelsey the driver would have a suggestion.

On her way out of Tiffany's she stumbled to a halt with a startled gasp when a woman stepped in front of her suddenly, stopping just inches away. She was tall but stooped, leaning on a cane in her left hand; her right hand held the collars of her heavy ragged coat tightly together, although it was a warm, sunny day. Both of her trembling hands were skeletal and blotched with scabrous sores, as was her long, flour-white face. Her scalp was visible beneath her dark greasy hair which fell in thin strings around her skinny, frail neck, where more sores disappeared beneath her collar. The worst of it was that in spite of the pasty skin and the horrible wounds all over her and the stick-thin wrists and the pasty eyes, she looked young . . . and she looked as if she might have once been beautiful.

"Excuse me," Caryl said, going around her, but the woman stepped in front of her again.

The woman's mouth opened, and a few slow seconds passed before she finally spoke. "Have you been with him yet?"

Caryl flinched and stepped back, but the woman just stepped forward, her cracked lips curling up in a rictus grin around darkening teeth as she nodded knowingly. "You have."

"I'm sorry, but I don't think I—"

The woman leaned even closer, so close that Caryl smelled her putrid breath when she hissed, *"Have you been tested yet?"* Then she turned and, as quickly as she could on unsteady legs, hurried away, disappearing in the crowd of pedestrians.

Caryl had lunch at a small sidewalk café. She ordered a glass of white wine before her cobb salad; the woman had shaken her up. She was obviously some hopeless street person who appeared to have reached the end of her drug-addicted rope and probably had no idea what she was saying. But that didn't make it any less upsetting. What she'd said had been so . . . so frighteningly appropriate.

Don't be stupid, she thought, sipping her wine. It was warm in her stomach; she wasn't used to alcohol.

She nibbled on a bread stick as she waited for her order, wondering how her mother was, reminding herself that she *had* to call her soon before she started to worry.

A metallic squeaking behind her made her look over her shoulder. A well-dressed but frail-looking man was walking into the café, slowly pulling a green oxygen tank on a dolly at his side. A thin transparent hose stretched from the tank's nozzle to the man's face where it wrapped around his head just beneath his razor-thin nose. Although he walked slowly, he took short labored breaths. He glanced at her, and she saw the dark gray circles under his shadowy eyes, the blue veins in his skull-thin temples and the gray patches of skin on his sunken cheeks. His blond hair was cropped short and his hairline receded halfway back on the top of his head. He looked at her and smiled, and the taut skin of his face looked ready to split and peel back over his skull; there were dark gaps between all of his upper teeth, which were small white beads.

Caryl jerked her head away so quickly she almost spilled her wine.

The man wound his way around the tables to the far corner of the short wrought-iron fence that surrounded the café; he seated himself so that he was facing her. Caryl diverted her gaze by reading the small dessert menu. As she sipped her wine, she tossed a casual glance toward the man's table. He was just sitting there without a menu or a glass of water or any food in front of him. But he was still watching her with a hint of a smile on his cadaverous face. Caryl returned her eyes to the dessert menu and studied it as if it were fascinating until her cobb salad and croissant arrived. As she ate, she tried to cheer herself with the thought of all the wonderful things she'd bought that day—the beautiful clothes and jewelry—and with thoughts of what she might buy for Hawk to surprise him when he came home, but she could not shake the feeling of being watched by that gaunt balding man at the corner table with the oxygen hose under his nose.

Finally, she heard the squeaking again. *He's leaving,* she thought with relief.

She took a bite of salad.

The squeaking stopped beside her. She could hear his ravaged lungs fighting for air. His voice was soft and tremulous.

"He wouldn't wear a condom, would he?"

Caryl gasped, and a few chunks of lettuce caught in her throat, making her choke. She grabbed her ice water and took a few swallows.

"Have you been tested yet?"

She coughed again and water shot from her nostrils. She dropped the glass, and it shattered her salad plate and knocked the wine over. She coughed and fought for air. A waiter approached her in an instant with another glass of water. She drank, caught her breath and looked up but—

The man with the oxygen tank was gone.

"Where did he go?" she gasped.

"Who?" the waiter asked.

"The man. With the tank. The oxygen tank."

The waiter looked confused. "Oxygen tank?"

"Yes. He was just *standing* here a few *seconds* ago *talking* to me!"

He shook his head and looked at her somewhat suspiciously. "Sorry, lady. I didn't see nobody."

After the waiter had calmed her, Caryl left and went straight home instead of buying Hawk a gift. She decided to fix him dinner instead, but once in the kitchen, she realized her hands were too shaky to cook, so she had another glass of wine and sat in front of the television for a while and watched Oprah and Phil.

When Hawk got home that night, she was still upset; she'd spent the day trying to keep those two thin voices out of her head . . .

Have you—
He wouldn't use—
—been tested—
—a condom—
—yet?
—would he?

When Hawk came into the bedroom to find her trying to read a magazine, she smiled with relief and sat up to embrace him, but he wandered around the room distracted-

51

ly, undressing, mumbling to himself. Then he said, "Gonna take a shower," and went to a dresser, opened his bottom drawer, removed something that jingled metallically and left the room.

Caryl thought that was odd. They had their own bathroom adjoining the bedroom; why would he leave the room to take a shower? And what had he taken from the bottom drawer of his dresser?

The wine had made her sleepy and she felt even worse than she'd felt before. She put the magazine aside, turned off the light, rolled over and went to sleep. She dreamed of walking corpses that whispered of tests and condoms . . .

When she woke the next morning, suddenly, drenched in sweat brought about by the visions in her sleep, Hawk was already gone. He'd left a note on his pillow that read, *"See you tonight, babe. Think dirty thoughts and have your legs spread when I get home. We'll fuck till our gums recede."*

The note depressed her so much she skipped breakfast. She wanted only to get out of the house. Instead of a limousine with a driver, she took one of Hawk's cars, a Corvette, and drove herself into town with no idea of where she was going. As she drove out the front gate, she saw a woman standing across the street near a patch of bushes. She was very thin, wore a sweater and had her arms folded tightly over her breasts as if she were cold. She stood as still as a mannequin, just staring at Hawk's house with deep-set shadowed eyes.

Caryl tried to fight back the shudder that passed through her and just drove. She found herself in the village of Westwood near UCLA and looked for a restaurant where she could have brunch. When she spotted one that looked good, she parked the car and walked back toward the building, strolling past a police officer who was writing a ticket for an illegally parked car. A woman walked toward her on the sidewalk. She was black and, although Caryl didn't think it was really possible, she looked rather pale. Her hair didn't look real; she was obviously wearing a wig. Just as they were about to pass, the woman stepped in front of Caryl and asked, "He's using you, isn't he?"

Caryl stopped and, suddenly angry, fed up with questions from strangers, she snapped, "Who *are* you? What do you—" She swallowed her words when she saw the woman's throat. It was bulging with hideous lumps, as if a number of small rocks had been slid beneath the skin. "—want from me?" Caryl finished in a breath.

The woman looked deeply into Caryl's eyes, frowning, and asked quietly, "What does he keep in the room upstairs?"

"What do you want?" Caryl shrieked. *"Why are you asking me these things?"*

"What do you suppose he keeps up there?" the woman whispered. Then she stepped around Caryl and walked on.

"No!" Caryl shouted. "You *wait!* You wait *just* a second, lady! Who *are* you? Why did you *ask* me that? What do you *want?*" She broke into a run and almost fell when—

—a police officer stepped in front of her, a ticket book in one hand, a pen in the other. "Excuse me, lady. Can I help you? Do you have a problem?" His voice was firm.

Caryl fought back tears, closed her eyes and whispered, "Thuh-that woman. That woman I was just talking to."

"What woman?" the officer asked, frowning.

Caryl pointed down the walk. "That wo—"

She was gone.

The officer shook his head, trying not to smirk, and said, "I'm sorry, ma'am. You *look* sane enough. But I'm afraid you were just, um, talking to yourself."

Caryl felt dizzy for a moment, scrubbed her face with a trembling hand, turned and walked away.

Two hours later, she was still wandering the sidewalks of Westwood, staring blindly into store windows, trembling in the warm sunlight as she rounded the same corner she'd rounded just a little while ago.

What does he keep in that room upstairs? . . . What do you suppose he keeps up there?

Staring at her reflection in the window of a small dress shop, Caryl began to think she'd made a horrible mistake in coming to Los Angeles with Hawk, although she wasn't quite sure why she felt that way. Surely the people who had been accosting her on the street knew nothing of her personal life. It was *impossible!* She'd never seen them before. They never mentioned any names. They never said anything specific.

What does he keep in that room upstairs?

Well . . . nothing *too* specific. And just because other people hadn't *seen* them didn't mean they hadn't *been* there. It had to be some incredible coincidence.

But she couldn't shake the feeling that she'd made a dreadful mistake. Maybe her mother had something after all.

The reflection of a woman standing behind her and to her left appeared in the window beside her own, slightly blurry and undefined. Another appeared on her right. And behind that one, a man with a gauze patch over one eye stopped, also facing the window.

A hand touched Caryl's left shoulder and she gasped, started to spin around, but a woman's quiet, weak voice said, "Don't turn around."

"Just listen," the man rasped.

"We want to help you," the other woman said.

"He's doing to you what he did to us."

"Making you feel so important," the man said. "At first, anyway."

"But he's just using you. Someone to come home to."

"Someone to come home and *fuck*," the man added.

Caryl took in an unsteady breath to speak, but the woman said, "Just listen."

The man said, in his gravelly voice, "What he *really* did to us was far worse than that."

"It's what he does to everyone," the second woman whispered.

"He doesn't go to the studio," the first woman said. "He doesn't go to meetings. He goes to see his lovers. All day long. Sometimes prostitutes."

"Sometimes bathhouses and gay bars," the man said. "He's insatiable."

The second woman: "And they're always nobodies. Never celebrities."

The first woman: "He saves the celebrities for parties and concerts and premieres, when he knows the press will show up. And the *celebrities* he never *touches.*"

"Otherwise his secret would be out." The man chuckled.

"Secret?" Caryl muttered, staring at the glass.

The man: "People would find out what he's doing."

The second woman: "He would be destroyed."

The first woman: "Now we come to all of his lovers—"

"His *conquests,*" the man interrupted.

"And try to warn them, stop them before it's too late," the first woman continued.

The second woman whispered sadly, "But it's always too late."

"What're you—" Caryl breathed, her gut swelling with a sick fear.

"Sshhh," the first woman hissed reassuringly, patting her shoulder. "You can stop him."

"Get into that room," the man said.

"The room upstairs. Get into that room and stop him."

"And whatever you do," the first woman whispered ominously, "don't let him touch you again."

"At least," the man added, "not without a condom."

Her fear began to melt away and was replaced with the same anger she'd felt toward the black woman earlier. With teeth clenched, she spun around to shout at them, tell them to go away, *threaten* them if necessary, but—

They were gone.

That night, Caryl pretended to be asleep when Hawk got home, hoping he wouldn't try to wake her so they could fool around. He didn't. Instead, he paced the room and mumbled, as he'd done before. She could hear liquid sloshing in a bottle and, after a moment, caught the stinging odor of whiskey. He chuckled, mumbled some more, then opened the dresser drawer again. She heard the same jingle she'd heard before and he left the room.

Caryl threw the covers back, slipped into her robe and peered out the door cautiously. At the end of the hall, Hawk was just rounding the corner, still mumbling; she heard his feet clump up the stairs as she hurried down to the corner. As soon as she heard him walking down the third-floor hallway, she glanced around to make sure no one was nearby and started up the stairs silently. As she reached the top step, she heard the door at the end of the hall close with a muted click, followed by the sounds of two locks being turned in succession.

Walking on the balls of her bare feet, Caryl went to the end of the hall, where the light was dim, and approached the door carefully. The soft orange glow still flickered through the narrow crack beneath the door, then disappeared . . . flickered some more, then disappeared . . .

Hawk was pacing inside. She heard his voice, soft and indecipherable but frantic, breaking occasionally into a soft, breathy laugh, then falling back into sibilant mutterings. Caryl flinched when she heard a loud thump, as if Hawk had fallen heavily to his knees, and his voice rose, but only slightly. She leaned closer to the door, until her ear was almost touching the wood, but could only pick out snatches of what he was saying.

". . . am thankful once again . . . fair and just and . . . be transferred to my image on this . . . for you in return . . ."

Caryl's brow wrinkled so hard that it hurt, and she realized her white-knuckled fists were pressed together between her breasts. She wasn't sure of what she'd just heard and thought she might have misunderstood his words altogether, but for some reason it sent an icy blade of fear into her gut and twisted it.

Keys jingled.

Footsteps approached the door.

Caryl thought her heart would stop as she turned and ran down the hallway as quickly and quietly as she could, and her feet tangled together for an instant as she turned to rush down the stairs, and when she reached the bedroom, she couldn't get the doorknob to turn at first because of the cold, clammy sweat that coated her palms, and when the door finally opened, she fought the urge to slam it behind her and tore a seam in her robe as she ripped it off her body and tossed it aside and threw herself onto the bed, pulled up the covers and turned on her side as—

—the bedroom door opened again and Hawk came inside.

Caryl closed her eyes and tried to breathe normally, tried not to let her chest heave, tried to calm herself so he wouldn't be able to hear the drumming of her heart.

Please don't let him try to wake me, God, she prayed silently. *I'll leave tomorrow and never do anything like this again, I swear, I swear, I will, just DON'T LET HIM TRY TO WAKE ME!*

The drawer was pulled open again, the keys dropped inside, and she could tell he was moving unsteadily, drunkenly, as he undressed. A match was lit, Hawk inhaled deeply and the cloying smell of marijuana filled the room. The bottle sloshed again: another drink. And then a throaty chuckle, as he walked to her side of the bed.

He touched her shoulder, shook her gently, then a little harder. He pulled back the covers and got on the bed, straddling her and rubbing his erection on her thigh as he took another drag on the joint.

She didn't stir, tried not to move a muscle, kept her eyes closed.

—Hawk slurred, "C'mon, babe, dincha get my note?" He shook her some more, a little too hard this time, and she knew he'd never believe it if she didn't wake up.

She rolled her head slowly toward him, mumbling.

He cupped one breast and squeezed it too hard, then reached down and tried to wriggle his fingers between her closed legs.

"Time t'plaaay," he gurgled through a broad grin. He leaned toward the nightstand, put the joint in an ashtray, picked up his bottle of whiskey and finished it off, then tossed it to the floor, getting off her. He pulled her toward him and said, "Sixty-nine."

Trying hard to feign waking up, she muttered, "Huh? What?"

"C'mon, babe, sit on my face while you suck my cock. S'all nice'n hard for ya."

Her mind raced and her stomach turned. "Oh . . . oh, honey, I can't."

"What?" He squinted at her, annoyed. "H'come?"

"Oh, honey, I've been sick all evening. Didn't Barnes tell you?"

"Sick? No, he didn't. Wha's matter?"

"Flu, I think. My . . . stomach." She wasn't lying. Her guts were moving and she felt like vomiting. But it wasn't the flu, it was fear. "In fact . . ." She sat up slowly. "Well, I don't think I should . . . oh, no." Caryl slid off the bed, hurried into the bathroom and leaned over the toilet, emptying herself loudly.

"Sheee-yit," Hawk groaned from the bed.

When she was finished heaving, she remained on her

knees, trembling and weak, and whimpered, "I'm suh-sorry. Muh-maybe I shuh-should sleep in, you know, another room, so . . . so you won't cuh-catch this. Huh? You think?" She stood on wobbly knees, leaning on the edge of the sink, and flushed the toilet. After rinsing her mouth she said, "You think so, Hawk? Hawk?"

When she came back into the bedroom, she found him sprawled over the bed, mouth yawning open, snoring.

"Hawk?" she said loudly, then, even louder, "You awake, Hawk?"

He didn't move.

That room upstairs. Get into that room and stop him . . . stop him . . . stop him . . .

Caryl stared at the bottom drawer of the enormous dresser, then again at Hawk. She didn't know if she could take the stress, the pressure—

Get into that room and stop him.

But she had to try. With her robe back on, she crept to the dresser and pulled the bottom drawer out slowly, cautiously. It was full of underwear and socks, a couple of dirty old marijuana pipes, a dildo that looked like a real penis only *much* too big (and *that* one surprised her) . . . Hawk was such a slob.

And there they were, two keys on one little ring nestled in a pair of undershorts in the back corner of the drawer. To keep them from jingling, she wrapped the undershorts around them, put them in the pocket of her robe and closed the drawer silently. Then she left the room.

Afraid of being caught, Caryl instinctively wanted to hurry; terrified of being heard, she was afraid to move too quickly. As a compromise, she went upstairs **and** started down the hall. It seemed much longer this time and the far end seemed much darker. And the hands . . . they chilled her . . . so patient and motionless as they held up the globe lights. All but the ones at the end that held cold dead spheres of darkness.

At the door, holding the keys level with the knob, she froze up.

Just go, she told herself. *Just go back downstairs, get dressed, grab some money and go home to Mom.*

But other voices spoke to her, too: *Stop him . . . get into that room . . . stop him . . . stop him . . .*

She tried one key, it didn't work, so she tried the next and the knob turned. She unlocked the deadbolt. Taking a deep breath, she opened the door.

Candlelight. That was all she noticed at first as she closed and locked the door behind her. They were everywhere in the room: fat black candles, at least six inches in diameter, dozens of them arranged in no particular order, flames dancing and flickering in the darkness. There were shelves of them on the walls, shelves on top of shelves, and as she looked up, she saw a three-foot-tall crucifix complete with a bleeding figure of Christ painted black and hanging upside down on the far wall.

Caryl staggered backward and slapped a hand over her mouth as if she were about to be sick again.

"Oh, dear Jesus, I'm sorry," she breathed, "I'm so sorry for being here, for, for, for being with *him,* please forgive me, please forgi—"

Her breath stopped when she saw what was beneath the desecrated cross.

It was an enormous painting on an equally large easel, a painting of the most hideous creature Caryl had ever seen, something out of a madman's worst nightmare. Gulping at saliva that wasn't in her dry mouth, she stepped forward, wincing as she got a closer look at the painting.

The creature resembled a human being, but in form only. Its arms—which dangled helplessly at its sides—and legs—bent at the knees as if they were about to buckle—were reduced to white, brittle sticks. The ribs pressed dangerously hard against the paper-thin skin, as if they were about to slice through and open the entire abdomen to reveal whatever foul things were being held inside. Shadows were dark just above the collarbone where the skin had sunk into virtual canals below the bony shoulders. The neck was painfully thin except for the dreadful bulges like—

Like small rocks beneath the skin, she thought, remembering the black woman she'd seen in Westwood.

And all over the flour-white body there were sores, dark scabrous sores that glistened and ran, some of them small, some of them huge, as if they'd grown and were still growing, intent upon covering the entire body, devouring it as if it were food. They even covered the face. And the *face . . .*

It was nothing more than a skull coated with a thin layer of paste. The nose was a razor and the cheeks disappeared into black holes beneath the knifelike cheekbones. The lips were so cracked they looked ready to crumble. The mouth gaped as if in a desperate effort to draw in a breath that would not come, and the teeth inside were dark and rotting away; some of them were already gone. The head was bald except for a few patches of colorless, thin, dry-looking hair. The ridges of the forehead stuck out over two pits, from the bottom of which the eyes stared in pure, hellish agony. The eyes . . . what was it about the eyes? Or was it something else that disturbed her even more deeply than the decayed thing hunched on the canvas?

Caryl wasn't sure what repulsed her more: the image or that indefinable thing about it that moved her, that . . . haunted her.

She moved closer to the painting and bumped into a wooden dais on which she found a large leather-bound book that resembled a photo album or scrapbook. There was nothing written on the front, and a strip of leather was snapped onto the cover holding it closed. Hesitantly, she unsnapped the strip, and the cover crackled as she opened the book slowly.

At first she turned the heavy black pages looking only

closely enough to see that the book was filled with small newspaper clippings, some of which were accompanied by grainy black-and-white photographs. It took a few moments for her to realize they were all obituaries. Frowning, she stopped and read one. A twenty-seven-year-old woman named Phyllis Browning, who died of complications due to AIDS. The next was accompanied by a photo of a handsome man named Walter McClaren; he also died of complications due to AIDS. She began scanning the obituaries of men and women more rapidly, squinting in the candlelight . . .

". . . died of pneumonia due to AIDS . . ."

". . . of complications brought on by the AIDS virus . . ."

". . . of bone cancer due to AIDS . . ."

". . . due to AIDS . . ."

". . . AIDS . . . AIDS . . . AIDS . . ."

Caryl was finding it more and more difficult to breathe as she read and finally stopped breathing for a long, long moment when she saw one particular picture.

A beautiful, smiling black woman. Twenty-nine years old. It was the woman she'd seen in Westwood. But this was her obituary.

She swept through the book until she found another familiar face.

The man with the oxygen tank in the sidewalk café.

And the sore-covered woman outside Tori Steele.

Caryl tried to breathe but couldn't at first as she raised her head slowly, her eyes moving up the dilapidated body on the canvas. The same hideous sores . . . the same sickening lumps under the jaw . . . and the eyes . . . those eyes . . .

Something else caught her attention. It was a shallow wooden box with a glass top on a three-foot-tall platform between the painting and the dais. A single candle burned brightly in front of the box.

Breathing shallowly now, Caryl walked around the dais and hunkered down to look in the box. It held a single sheet of paper—heavy paper, it seemed—on which was written a lot of indecipherable gibberish in black, beautifully formed letters. Even some of the *letters* were unfamiliar to her. But one word stood out, one word that made her upper lip curl in disgust and made her want, more than she'd ever wanted before, to be with her mother, to see her face and her smile, to hear her warm, comforting voice:

SATANIS

Caryl made a low, miserable whimpering sound in her throat as she began to stand again and then she froze. There was something else at the bottom of the page. Something that was written differently and not in ink but in what appeared to be a brownish-red paint that had dried to a crust. Something familiar. Something that made the confusing writing above much less confusing . . . and much more frightening.

It was Darren Hawke's signature.

He goes to see his lovers . . . all day long . . .

Have you been tested?

She looked up at the painting, at those eyes that looked so familiar.

. . . sometimes prostitutes . . .

Have you been tested?

They were Hawk's eyes.

. . . sometimes bathhouses and gay bars . . .

Have you been tested?

She looked at the crusty brownish-red signature again.

"Oh, dear God," Caryl whispered, burying her fingers in her hair and pulling . . . pulling . . . grinding her teeth together. "Oh, dear God, dear God."

That room upstairs . . . get into that room and stop him . . . stop him . . . stop him . . . STOP HIM!

Something stirred inside Caryl, something hot and writhing and angry. She no longer felt like herself. She was a different person now . . . a person defiled and filthy and—

Oh God no please no don't let it be God please—

63

Infected.

She wrapped both hands around the fat black candle before her. "Oh . . ." She stood slowly. "Dear . . ." She lifted the candle, paused a moment, then brought it down hard on the box's glass top as she screamed, *"GAAAWWWD!"*

The glass shattered into half a dozen deadly sharp shards as her scream went on and on, and when that scream was done, she sucked in a deep breath and let out another as she looked up at the painting, swung the candle back and threw it with all her strength. It tore through the canvas, ripping a hole in the dying Hawk's chest and knocking the painting over before thumping the wall behind it.

There was another scream, then, from downstairs. A man's scream. It was just a sound at first, but in a moment it formed words: *"What? What? What are you doing? WHAT ARE YOU DOOOIIING?"* A door slammed open and feet pounded the floor, then the stairs, as the scream continued. *"WHAT THE HELL ARE YOU DOOOIIING?"*

Caryl continued screaming, too, as she reached into the box and took out one of the glass shards, holding it so tightly in her hand that it cut into her palm. She threw herself on the painting, attacking it, lifting her arm and bringing it down again and again, ripping through the canvas with the shard, slicing through the emaciated diseased body in the painting as she screamed senselessly, spittle spraying from her mouth.

Footsteps in the hall outside. Screaming. Pounding on the door. *"STOP IT! STOP IT! NO PLEASE NO STOP PLEASE STOP IT YOU'RE KILLING ME YOU'RE KILLING MEEEE!"*

But she didn't stop and the house rang with their screams.

The canvas was little more than shreds, but Caryl didn't stop in spite of the pain in her arm and the heat on her sweaty face. Then her voice became dry and hoarse, and the movements of her arm slowed and she became weaker and weaker because of the heat . . . the burning heat . . . and the crackling . . .

She stopped, heaving for breath, and raised her head.

Flames from the fallen candle were slithering up the wall, licking at the inverted crucifix.

"No, oh-no, no," she croaked, dropping the glass. She ignored her bloody hand as she stood and staggered away from the fire, stumbling toward the door.

There was pandemonium outside, running feet, screams, pounding on the door. Caryl recognized Barnes's voice as he screamed, "Oh my God! Oh my God!" One of the maids shrieked, "What's happening to him?" But Hawk's voice was gone.

Caryl unlocked the door, opened it and looked into the hall. If she had had any voice left, she would have screamed.

Hawk lay on the floor, his back against the opposite wall. He was naked and he was changing rapidly.

As Caryl watched, black-red sores blossomed and spread over his body, which had turned a sickly pale. He convulsed as his skin seemed to shrink around his body. His ribs became more and more visible until there seemed to be almost no skin over them at all. As his neck grew thinner, bulbous lumps swelled on his throat, and he hacked as if he were about to spit up parts of his lungs. His long wavy hair fell away from his head and fluttered around him to the floor. A few teeth fell into his lap. He vomited uncontrollably and his bowels let loose with a sickening sound. The coughing grew worse quickly, as did the convulsions.

In moments, as the fire grew worse in the room behind Caryl, Hawk was a shriveled husk on the floor, motionless, reeking and dead.

Two weeks later, Caryl knocked on her mother's front door at a little after four in the morning, trying hard to hold in her sobs. She had a key and could have let herself in, but it didn't seem right. Not anymore.

In a few minutes, Margaret Dunphy called sleepily, "Who is it?"

"I-it's me, Muh-Momma."

The door swung open and Margaret cried out as she threw her arms open. "Caryl, oh, Caryl!" she cried. Caryl's purse dropped to the porch as she returned her mother's embrace and began to sob uncontrollably.

"Oh, baby, I was so worried, so scared. I heard about the fire but nobody knew anything about you and I thought maybe . . . I was afraid you'd . . . oh, thank God, thank *God,* I'm so glad you're okay, so glad you're home."

But, as she held her mother tightly, all Caryl could say again and again through her tears was "Positive . . . *positive,* Momma . . . positive . . ."

CHANGE OF LIFE

Chet Williamson

When Leonard Drew checked into the Ramada Inn, he was polite and dignified with the girl at the registration desk, bluff and hearty with the middle-aged man who carried his luggage, and debonair and witty with the woman at the bar, who, for a certain sum, was willing to meet him in his room later that evening. It wasn't just the money, Leonard told himself. She liked him, he was sure of it.

And why shouldn't she? Leonard was well liked everywhere because, as he told the junior sales trainees, he was *adaptable*. People liked him because he became one of them, because he used their language, because he said "So the bitch don't work so good, huh?" to the guys in the machine shops that used his company's products, and because he told marketing managers that he would make his report "just as soon as I access the data and interface with my associates." Leonard was adaptable, and that, he well knew, was why he was going places in Bentson Industries.

Now, as he kicked off his Florsheims, undid his yellow power tie, and flopped down on a bed as solid as his portfolio, he became aware of a sound issuing from the throat of the only sort of human with whom he did not feel comfortable—children.

"Daddy? Izzis the one?" Leonard Drew's doorknob rattled as the, no doubt, filthy urchin out in the hall shook it.

"Just a minute, Tommy!" came a woman's voice weakly.

"Izzisit?" The doorknob rattled again, and the door clunked against its frame.

Leonard nearly shouted, *No, iz izn't it, you little asshole,* but restrained himself, and instead, in a more devilish mood, leapt from the bed, tiptoed to the door, and growled as deeply as he could.

"Grrrr-*aaaahhh!*" said Leonard.

"*Waaaaaaah!*" the urchin remarked, and his cry grew fainter as he ran down the hall. "A *bear!* A *bear,* Mommy!"

"Aw, f'crissake," came a man's voice, followed by the woman's clucking. Leonard giggled and listened, his cheek and ear against the cold metal frame, to the boy's insistent cries of *A bear, a bear!* and then a key seeking its hole, a door opening and closing, and silence. Leonard giggled again, climbed onto the bed, and closed his eyes for a little nap.

When he woke up fifteen minutes later, he did not get upset about the growth of new, black, wiry hair on his hands. He was too busy being upset about the way his fingernails had grown into hooked claws. But that was before he noticed that his body, which was *also* covered with wiry, dark hair, was about three times its normal size and had burst out of its clothing. The thing that upset him the *most,* however, was that he could see his nose. Not see it as he'd always seen it before, a little pink lump when he went cross-eyed, but really *see* it, far enough out there to be in focus. It too was black. And moist.

When Leonard finally roused the courage to look into the mirror, he saw that the sum of the parts did indeed make a whole. He had become a bear. A good-looking bear, well-built and with a handsome, shiny coat, but a bear who certainly had no future with Bentson Industries.

Leonard was not only adaptable, he was logical, and after only ten minutes of ursine blubbering, he realized that the boy in the hall had had something to do with his metamorphosis. It was absurd, but the little brat had called him a bear, and now he *was* one, so what Leonard had to do now was—

FIND BOY

It was a fat and lumpy thought, not at all like Leonard's usually quick and incisive ones, and he realized with a shock that it must have come from the fat and lumpy bear brain that was in the process of replacing his own.

FIND BOY said his brain again, and he wondered when he *did* find him, if he'd reason with the kid or eat him.

His bear body, primitively reacting to his human thoughts, lumbered to the door. Leonard had enough presence of mind to snatch his yellow tie from the bed with a hairy paw and toss it around his thick neck, hoping that no one would shoot a bear in a power tie.

FIND BOY

It wasn't easy to get the door open, but Leonard did it, sticking a Florsheim between the door and frame since he knew damn well he'd never be able to work a key. At that moment a door opened halfway down the hall and a man stepped out of a room.

"Can I come, Daddy?"

"I'm just going for ice. You stay with Mommy."

"All alone?"

"She's in the bathroom . . ." The door closed and the man went down the hall in the opposite direction.

BOY

Leonard trundled down the hall on all fours, feeling rationality slipping away from him, knowing only that he had to find the boy, and not knowing what he would do when he did. He sat up on his hind legs in front of the room from which the man had come, and scratched on the door with the long nails of his forepaws.

"Tommy, see who that is!" came a voice from inside. Leonard scratched some more, heard a thumping, and realized that the boy was jumping up and down, trying to see through the peephole.

"Tommy?"

"Huh?"

"Who *is* it?"

"I dunno . . ." Tommy answered, obviously afraid to open the door. "Just some man . . ."

Leonard felt something wiggle inside him, felt the clumsy bear thoughts begin to fade and be replaced by his own clear impressions.

Just some man . . .

God bless you, you little fucker, Leonard thought, shambling back to the door of his room, feeling himself get thinner and thinner, welcoming the chill, poorly heated hall air on his rapidly balding skin, and best of all, seeing his nose disappear.

And as he dashed through the door, a bear no longer, but a stark-naked man, he thought once more, God bless you, you weird little bastard, and I'm never gonna get near you again . . .

"Oh yeah, baby," moaned Lisa, the woman he had met in the bar, "you are *somethin'* . . ."

It was the usual patter, but tonight it sounded good, and he smiled as he thought how close he had come to doing it in front of a zoo audience. That kid, that weird little kid. Christ, if he hadn't said that to his mom about it being some *man* . . .

"Oh *baby,* oh *God* . . ."

He felt Lisa begin to convulse and speeded up. After they both shuddered for the last time, she collapsed on top of him. "You are *incredible*. You are an absolute *stud bull,*" she said huskily, and in another moment he knew that it hadn't been the boy's fault after all.

As he struggled to extricate the tip of his right horn from Lisa's left earring, and heard the bed frame crunch beneath his weight, he thought that perhaps there was such a thing as being *too* adaptable.

DEMONLOVER

Nancy A. Collins

Sina was restless. She couldn't squat in front of the television set and act as if nothing was wrong between the two of them. She finally decided to go out and catch some live music, shrugging off Mike's silent reproach. She knew she'd have to deal with his pouting when she came home, but she didn't care. She had to get out of the house or go mad.

As she pulled into the club's parking lot, she saw a man loitering in front of the building. He stood with his hands in his pockets, one leg drawn up, the boot heel resting against the doorframe. He was cool and he knew it. The wall behind him bristled with rusty staples like a buzz-cut porcupine. The bar's door was propped open, allowing the music to thump and crash its way onto the street.

As she drew closer, Sina saw he was tall and lean, with a handsomely muscled waist. His hair was blond and cut so it fell across his brow with practiced nonchalance. His eyes were electric blue, cold as witchfire. They were the eyes of a white tiger on the prowl.

Something detonated inside her. She grabbed the car's fender in order to steady herself. Excitement turned the oxygen in her lungs into ice crystals and helium.

A blond. Funny, she'd never been attracted to blonds before. She normally preferred dark men, the closer to the Mephistophelean ideal the better.

Her throat constricted into a dry tube and her ears filled with the sound of blood. She felt clumsy and ridiculous, but there would be no running away. The longing would not permit it. A horrible giddiness surged through her, just like the time she'd taken nitrous oxide at the dentist's prior to losing cavities.

Sina hesitated, digging into her pocketbook for the cover charge. She could feel his eyes flicker over her like lasers. She looked up, forcing herself to keep from trembling. He was studying her, his lips compressed into a flat, unreadable smile. His eyes were those of a debased angel, blue as Depression glass.

She averted her gaze and moved into the thundering dark of the club. She didn't have to turn to see if he was following her. She could feel his presence, as if she were joined to him by an invisible cord.

The club was close and smoky, the walls painted flat black in an attempt to create the illusion of space. The band was thrashing away on the stage, surrounded by a knot of wildly pogoing dancers. She wound her way to the bar and was startled to see him already lounging there. The only open space was at his elbow. Setting her jaw, she moved next to him and ordered a beer.

She had to fight to keep from gasping aloud when he shifted his stance. His hip rubbed against her like a tomcat. The beer bottle shook as she lifted it to her lips.

She had found him. It *had* to be him! The sexual arousal she experienced was so powerful it was almost unpleasant. Her crotch ached just looking at him. But what could she do about it? She wasn't drunk enough to simply swagger up and tell him to take her home and make her like it. She'd been out of circulation too long. She'd forgotten the anxiety and paranoia inherent in the mating ritual. What if he didn't want her? What if he was gay? The stainless-steel death's head leering at her from his earlobe didn't help matters either. As much as she loathed frustration, she feared rejection even more.

"I noticed you looking. See anything you like?"

For a moment she didn't realize he'd actually spoken to her. She blinked rapidly, as if startled from a daze. His face was inches from hers and she inhaled his musk, pleasantly redolent of masculine sweat. Her brain froze like a rabbit pinned by the headlights of an oncoming car.

He's bad news. You can tell by looking at him. No. On second thought, don't look at him. Don't do it. Don't say anything. Finish your beer and go home. That was the last she heard from her common sense.

All attempts at witty remarks and sly come-ons fled. Her prepared speech died in her throat. All she could do was answer with the truth.

"Everything."

His name was Feral. He smiled when he said it. He pulled her onto the dance floor, his personality sinking its fingers into her will. Had he asked her to cut off her right hand, she would have gladly done it.

Every time he touched her she felt her skin tighten, as if a mild electric current had passed between them. She'd forgotten the exhilaration that comes with a sensual high. When Feral wearied of dancing, he suggested they go outside. The night breeze rapidly cooled the sweat on her body, making her shiver.

As she leaned her back against the wall, Feral tucked his left leg between her thighs and ground himself against her hips. It was an incredibly juvenile, but deeply gratifying, public display.

He kissed her, his tongue probing with expert thrusts. His arms encircled her, locking around the small of her back.

She felt like she was in a vise and, for a few brief moments, he lifted her on tiptoe. She could not control her breathing or pulse. Her fingertips vibrated against his skin.

He disengaged himself from their embrace and motioned for her to follow. Feral ducked into the alley that flanked the club, negotiating the garbage-strewn passageway with the grace of a panther. Sina wasn't quite as certain.

"Feral?"

He turned, his eyes glowing in the darkness. He reached out, quick as a snake, and drew her to him, capturing her left wrist and pinning her arm behind her. There was no violence, no struggle; just the sound of their mouths meshing. Feral's free hand explored her body under her blouse, his fingers tracing the curve of her rib cage, squeezing her nipples and rubbing them with the ball of his thumb. She gasped aloud, writhing against him like a cat in heat. His mouth covered hers and she had to remind herself to breathe.

Feral backed her against the wall, plucking at the snaps on her jeans. His erection, lumped in his pants, was nestled against her hip. Feral reached down to pull on his belt buckle, and for the first time since she'd entered the alley, she was afraid.

"No!" She freed her left arm and placed her hand atop his own.

Feral stopped, his blue eyes questioning her. What could she say? That she was scared of fucking? He'd think she was some kind of neurotic cocktease.

"No, Feral. Not here. Not like this." She nodded to the heaps of reeking garbage that decorated the alley.

He stood there for a second, then nodded. His hand dipped into his pants pocket and handed her a motel key.

"When you're ready, just come on over. I'll be there."

Sina sat on the edge of the bed and stared at the man she'd once imagined she would spend the rest of her life with. She knew she should feel guilty there was so little remorse to be scavenged from the death of a five-year-old relationship.

She studied Mike's familiar features, now rendered alien by the hollowness inside her. She tried to remember what it had been like, before the tedium and resentment leeched the passion from their lives. Her head began to throb.

She closed her eyes, trying to summon pleasant memories of their life together, but all she could feel was the longing, roiling like a storm cloud inside her.

The years they'd spent together had not been *perfect,* but they had been good. At first she didn't mind the long evenings at home; after the numerous chaotic affairs she'd suffered through, it was somewhat novel *not* to party every weekend.

Yet, although her previous lovers proved to be highly unstable, sex with them had been like walking on live coals and swimming the Arctic Ocean at the same time. She was dismayed to find sex with Mike lacked the delightful friction she'd grown accustomed to. She hoped that as they grew together, their sex drives would adapt accordingly—his increasing while hers decelerated, until they reached a suitable, mutually satisfying compromise.

At the end of two years Sina marveled over how they'd succeeded in reaching a level of stagnation it had taken her parents two decades to attain.

After their fourth anniversary passed without comment or celebration, Sina knew she'd been deluding herself.

It was then that the longing began. At first it was shadowy, ill-formed post-coital dissatisfaction. She no longer made advances toward Mike, preferring to accommodate him whenever he felt the urge, which, thankfully, proved to be infrequently. Sex, once her drug of choice, had become housework.

She knew she was being silly. So what if sex with Mike didn't sparkle? He loved and respected her. He offered her shelter and stability. She forced herself to recall her earlier relationships; the ones that had left her—emotionally bruised and physically battered—on his doorstep in the first place. The memories were sordid, tinged with self-disgust and more than a little sexual excitement. The hunger grew.

It was sheer accident she'd come across the poem.

When she read of the nameless woman, wailing for her demon lover, her face burned with the heat of recognition.

She realized she was mourning the lover she'd gone so long without. The lover she'd pursued in all his varied, imperfect guises for close to a decade.

She knew that the only love her demon was capable of was self-destructive, cruel, vampiric, parasitic, and all the other words her best friends had used to describe Jerry, Alec, Christian, Matt, and the others whose names, faces and genitalia had now blurred together in her memories. They were men incapable of love yet able to inspire suicide threats.

There was something about the love they offered her that friends could never understand, and it was beyond her ability to explain. Despite the unhealthiness of the attraction, Sina had experienced ecstasy with her would-be demon lovers. In order to taste the kind of love the poets rhapsodized about, Sina knew she had to suffer. To love as the immortals do is to know damnation.

At first she'd felt guilty for being unable to transcend the demands of the flesh, but that was soon replaced by resentment of Mike's inability to provide her with what she needed. He could not save her from herself and she hated him for that.

The longing continued to grow. She couldn't close her eyes without seeing disembodied sex organs pumping away like Victorian steam engines.

She was hesitant about taking action. She still remembered Lee and how he'd dislocated her shoulder and blackened both her eyes. She had loved him with a passion that was close to maniacal. She had lost control that time—and it nearly cost her life. It had certainly robbed her of her self-respect.

One evening when Mike was not home, she went out to a bar, intent on screwing the first man who looked at her sideways. Once she got there, she discovered she couldn't settle for just *any* man.

The older men in their synthetic-fiber suits were ridiculous, if not actively repellent. Sina visualized them naked: paunches overshadowing their erections, their bandy legs white and absurdly hairy compared to their heads.

The younger boys with their acid-washed jeans and silk tour jackets were incapable of appreciating the lyricism of sexuality; all they were interested in was hopping on, getting off, and pulling out.

There'd been no demon lover there to satisfy her. She knew that when she finally found him, the recognition would be immediate. Her heart, soul, and womb would know him the minute she saw him.

She knew Feral was the one she hungered for. She glanced at Mike's slumbering form, his back to her. She promised herself to sleep on it before acting on Feral's offer. She climbed in bed next to Mike, pulling her limbs tight against her body in order to keep from accidentally touching him in her sleep.

She needed to get her head straight and think about what had happened. She had security, a home, and someone who cared for her. She couldn't throw that away.

When she closed her eyes Feral was there, shimmering like an ice sculpture in the Mojave, and she knew what her decision would be.

The motel was every bit as seedy as she'd expected it to be. Men like Feral didn't shack up at the Hilton. The motor court centered around a swimming pool with fungus-dappled tiles and a basin spider-webbed by slippage. An overweight woman in maid's whites pushed a housekeeper's trolley along the second story's promenade. It was hard to tell if the towels on the cart were clean or dirty.

Sina stood outside the door to Feral's room, working the key between her fingers like a rosary. She was walking the razor's edge. She'd almost forgotten what an exquisitely scary experience it was, like hanging over an ice chasm with nothing but a piton for support.

I should leave now. While I can. I could still go back. Mike would never know the difference. We could start all over again. I could do it.

She unlocked the door and stepped into Feral's room.

With the curtains pulled and the lights off, the room was as dark as a movie theater. There was a stale, closed odor permeating the air. Something heavy struck the carpet, as if someone had fallen from the bed onto the floor.

Feral's voice came from the darkness, his tone urgent: "Close the door. Now."

She did as she was told. Her eyes had grown accustomed to the gloom, although she found the smell stifling. She could see Feral on the opposite side of the double bed, his elbows propped against the mattress. She wondered if he was a pusher. If so, she was lucky she didn't have a bullet in her skull from walking in unannounced.

"Feral . . . remember me? You gave me your key . . . ?" She took a hesitant step forward.

"Sssina." It sounded strangely sibilant. "Yes. I remember. I've been waiting for you." He pulled himself upright, exposing bare white flesh down to his waist. He appeared to be supporting his entire body on his forearms, the muscles rigid as marble. Sina was relieved to find the insides of his arms free of needle tracks.

His chest was hairless. In fact, except for the champagne-colored hair on his head and his slightly darker eyebrows, Feral's entire body was as smooth as glass. At least, those parts of his body she could see. She took another step toward him. Funny, he didn't seem to have either nipples or navel.

Feral smiled and moved to meet her, gliding from behind the bed. His naked flesh glowed in the near-dark, as translucent as opal. His genitals were overlarge, and as she watched, his penis grew to full erection. It was almost enough to take her mind off the fact that from the crotch down Feral was a snake.

He was at least fifteen feet long, from his pointed ears to the tip of his tail, legs merging into a seamless column as thick as his torso. Like his human upper body, Feral's serpent half was as pale as milk. Sina was reminded of the albino snakes found in deep caverns.

Feral moved like a cobra, holding his human self upright as he slithered forward. He towered over her, swaying slightly with every ripple of his abdomen. The revelation of Feral's inhumanity was nowhere near as terrible as Sina's realization that she still wanted him.

Feral's erection was now parallel with her sternum, his amber hair brushing the mottled plaster ceiling. His eyes were still blue, only now the pupils had become reptilian. She could not look away and she recalled how, as a child, her grandmother once told her about snakes charming birds out of the trees and into their jaws.

"I've been searching for you for so long." Feral's voice managed to sound earnest, despite the forked tongue. "It took me so long to find you . . . to pinpoint the source of the Call that drew me from my place in Hell. I'm sorry I kept you waiting for all this time. I can only move amongst your kind at night. I was afraid I would never find you. But your Call was strong and it would not let me rest until I found you."

He wrapped her in a moon-pale coil, his scales whispering against her flesh. He didn't feel slimy at all. He felt so good she wanted his touch all over her body. She shed her clothes and gasped as his scales brushed against her naked flesh. Her hands caressed him and Feral hissed his pleasure. What was left of her sanity fled as she felt herself respond to his sinuous constrictions and undulations.

Feral's coil tightened, lifting her within reach of his human self. She clasped his forearms, reaching up to kiss him, and wrapped her legs around his waist, lowering herself onto his erect penis. Feral's split tongue flickered out, tasting her moans.

She pressed herself against his cool, dry skin and shivered as his tongue played across her breasts. For the first time in her life she was truly happy, cradled in the coils of the demon who'd braved the dangers of the mortal world in search of his human lover.

"So this is it, huh?" The john grinned. He smelled of Southern Comfort and his words came out slurred. He wore an ill-fitting polyester suit that did little to conceal the beer belly hanging over his belt. He stuck his hand up her skirt as Sina unlocked the motel-room door. "You bring all the guys you pick up here, you whore?"

"All of them."

She opened the door, motioning for him to follow. As the john crossed the threshold, he sniffed and made a face.

"Phew! It sure does smell in here! You need to air this place out!"

"Don't worry. In a little while you won't notice it at all," she assured him.

He giggled and licked his lips. "Ain't that the truth."

As Sina locked the door, Feral moved from his hiding place in the bedroom. The john had time and breath for one muffled shout before the coils silenced him.

After making sure he was suffocated, Feral and Sina quickly stripped the corpse of its clothes and wallet. The naked dead man's belly overshadowed his pubis and his legs were hairier than his head.

Sina tossed the wrinkled polyester suit onto the mound of similar garments in the corner of the motel room. She'd have to make another trip to the Salvation Army pretty soon. She retired to the bed to sort through the wallet, leaving Feral to finish what he'd begun. She'd gotten used to the sound of cracking bones, but she still had a hard time watching when it came time for him to unhinge his jaw. Besides, he wasn't the only boyfriend she'd had whose table manners left a lot to be desired.

She stuffed the bills and travelers checks into the shoebox she kept under the bed and dumped the credit cards and ID into a paper bag, to be disposed of in the nearest Dumpster.

It wouldn't be much longer before someone noticed what was going on. But by then they would be well on their way. Feral made it sound really nice, not at all what she'd been led to expect. She was looking forward to meeting his folks. She had to be sure to stay on her best behavior. After all, every girl wants to make a good impression on her future in-laws.

CONFESSION

Kurt Busiek

My name is Roger," I lied. "And I'm an alcoholic."

They say confession is good for the soul, but it's never done much for me. I was in a basement room a few blocks off Union Square. There were about thirty other people in the room, sitting around card tables on folding chairs, smoking, sipping coffee and listening to me. One or two of them were newcomers, checking out a meeting for the first time. The rest were familiar to me, faces I'd seen at other meetings. Smoke hung thick in the room, like nobody had ever heard of the Surgeon General's report. Pretty typical for an AA meeting.

I went through the rest of it, how both my parents were alcoholics, how coming home and finding one or both of them passed out in the living room revolted me so much I knew it'd never happen to me. But it did. I was establishing a career as a securities broker when I started winding down from the day with a beer or two. Then it was screwdrivers, then scotch, and by the time I got fired I could knock off a bottle of tequila while alone, watching TV. After that, of course, I *needed* the booze to cope with how those assholes had treated me. It wasn't until I woke up in Hoboken, bleeding on somebody's BMW, and couldn't remember how

I'd gotten there that I faced up to the fact I was in trouble. It was a stirring story. I'd told it so many times I almost believed it myself.

There was a girl at a nearby table. I'd seen her before, even spoken to her once or twice. Wendy something. Maybe Cindy. She watched me closely, and when I looked over, she smiled. There was warmth in her eyes and her pulse went up slightly, her steady strong heartbeat pumping the blood through her veins a little faster. I smiled back. I shouldn't have—she'd take it as an invitation—but she looked like Kate, with that silky red hair, an expressive mouth and a sharp little chin.

I swear, I deserve all the shit I get.

After I finished my qualification, there was a round of applause and some guy started a collection to help pay for the room and the coffee and all. I drew myself a black coffee from one of the urns in the corner and drifted over to join the only all-male conversation in the room.

Mike was talking about a murder, listing detail after detail of knife wounds, finger marks, torn clothing. It was the same conversation as always, just a new installment. Some nights it was baseball, some nights politics, once in a while the deplorable state of Broadway. But it always boiled down to the same thing—how bad New York had gotten. They'd chew over the latest news, trade the latest stories, compare failures, atrocities, outrage. Then Lou would shake his head slowly and the others would join in. Not like that when they came to the city, no sir. Tonight's tidbit was a dead woman found on a tenement roof. Lou took it as a sign nobody cared about people anymore. Fred disagreed. Contract killings, he said. They made it look like a crazy, killed ten or twelve to hide the real motive and got off scot free. Mike didn't think that was how hired killers worked, but he wasn't making much headway against Lou. I just listened. The ritual of it was oddly comforting.

Sure enough, she came over. "Some of us are going over to LB's for coffee and sandwiches afterward. You want to come along?" Her pulse was really going now, and blood filled her face, coloring her cheeks and filling out her lips, making them deeper, heavier, inviting. What was I supposed to do? Women at AA meetings aren't generally overflowing with self-esteem to start with, and it obviously took a lot for Wendy (or Cindy) to do this.

"Look, I'd love to," I said, "but I've got to meet this guy." I smiled in a you-know-how-it-is way.

It didn't work. She opened her mouth to say something and I knew what was coming. A "Half an hour won't kill anyone" or a "We'll be there late; you can stop by after," something along those lines. I locked on her eyes and thought, *Go away. Just go away.* "Maybe next time," I said aloud.

She closed her mouth. Looked around in transient confusion and absently turned, not seeing me anymore. I watched the way her hips rolled, making her wool skirt twitch as she headed back to her friends. She even dressed like Kate. I wanted to call after her, to change my mind, but I knew better.

Oh well. There were other meetings I could go to for a while. I put my Styrofoam cup down and headed for the door before she remembered me.

Outside, the air was cold and crisp, and the night sky was bright, the city glare that generally shrouds Manhattan thin enough to let a couple of stars through. Nights like that make New York seem small and cruddy, no more than a crusty infection on the side of a diseased planet, and all its inhabitants inconsequential and irrelevant. I didn't need that; I needed to feel human, plugged-in, like life was crucial and death was a horror, like moral choices had weight and power. I went up to 16th Street, walked into Shay's and ordered bourbon, straight up.

I knocked it back, ordered another.

The anonymous hubbub calmed me down a little. I realized I was breathing heavily and slowed it down, settling back on the barstool and looking around. There was the usual crush of evening revelers: couples, knots of workplace buddies and solo cruisers looking for action, mixing and mingling in their urgent quest for camaraderie, comfort, sex or oblivion. One of them, about ten feet down the bar, was staring at me.

She was a cowgirl type, lanky and lean with streaked blond hair, a wide-brimmed leather hat, a fetching overbite and long, long muscular legs that promised action, energy and staying power. The legs were sheathed in skin-tight denim, and when she saw she'd caught my eye she flexed them, arched a little and pursed her lips at me in an insolent smile. Her heart beat like a racehorse's, sluicing the blood around her body with more gusto than your average beer commercial. My teeth hurt and I wanted to test my strength against hers and see who collapsed first.

I shot her a c'mon-aren't-you-too-old-for-this-shit look and turned back to my drink.

The bartender, Rachel, was right in front of me, offering to top up my glass. *Shit,* I thought, *I must really be on tonight.* I knew Rachel from a few other nights at Shay's, and she struck me as the tough, no-nonsense type. I thought she was immune. But her pulse was up, her breathing shallow, and she looked at me without quite focusing. She leaned forward, crossing her arms under her breasts, lifting them and pushing them together, emphasizing her cleavage. Her chin was up, exposing the long line of her neck and the vulnerability of her throat. She was talking about how dangerous the streets were—especially late at night. It made her nervous, or so she claimed, walking home alone.

I said something I forgot as soon as the words left my mouth and looked past her at the mirror behind the bar. When people in a bar don't know what to do, they look at their reflection in the mirror. Out of long habit, I do the same, despite the fact there's no reflection to see.

I took Rachel up on that refill. I needed it. But don't get me wrong, I'm not an alcoholic. Alcohol has no effect on me—it just gives me something to do while I'm out, something to concentrate on other than blood and the thirst. Sometimes it's harder than others, like now. Shay's had been the wrong place to go to forget about Wendy.

There was another vampire in the place, at least one. I didn't know where exactly, but he was there. I could feel it. It's like sharks—one vampire alone is usually okay, but if others are nearby, each one's thirst will affect them all, increasing the buzz of the blood around them and their need for it, like an addiction that makes it hard to think about anything but your next drink, your next fix. Vampires tend to avoid each other—alone, they can be clever and canny, but together they get blood-crazed and stupid and sloppy.

I was starting to get it bad—there was a crimson haze over everything, and the murmur I heard wasn't the crowd but their pulses, throbbing loudly enough to overwhelm ordinary sound, the sweet call of the blood tugging at me, making my throat dry and hot and my hands and feet cold.

"Look," Rachel said, low and husky. She brushed my hand—hers was warm, very warm. "There's something I've been wanting to tell you."

"Not tonight, huh, Rache," I said, running my knuckles across her arm. "I'm just not in the mood for confessions right now."

She jerked back as if struck, and the blood rushed to her face—this time in embarrassment rather than arousal. Tight-lipped, she fled for the other end of the bar. I put a twenty by my glass and left. If I was starting to think about confessions again, it was going to be one of the bad nights.

I left the blood-haze behind in Shay's, but couldn't just shuck off the state it had left me in. I was aroused and jangly, a hot ache in my throat and a dull throbbing pain at the back of my teeth. I needed blood, but that wasn't the problem—I had six jars of plasma in the fridge. What I felt went beyond thirst.

The blood of the living is a constant temptation, but I've never surrendered. When I (What? Emerged? Arose? Awakened?) in a Dumpster off Bleecker five years ago and felt my humanity sloughing off like a childhood memory, I swore I'd never forget, never succumb to this perverse state, as if by force of will I could keep at least a shred of what it felt like to be alive. A modern vampire, that's me. Sensitive. No mess, no fuss. Well-behaved. The AA meetings help a lot, the feeling that I'm not alone, that others have a constant craving and can control it. One day at a time, like the Big Book says—that's how I do it. There are troublesome nights, sure, but I just stay home with my plasma and read some Austen, some Eliot, something that affirms the innate dignity of man, and I get through. No, the thirst isn't the real curse. Not by a long shot.

A couple of girls passed me in Village uniform—black skintights, black leather and crucifix earrings. The crucifixes hit hard. The pain didn't bother me—I deserve it when I'm like this. It was the thought of the needle spearing through their lobes, the momentary pain, the small welling of blood that followed. They were too absorbed in their conversation to see me, and for that I was grateful. After they passed, however, I could still sense them, a twin nimbus of heat and life pulsing with energy and release. I wanted to turn back, to go after them. I forced myself to walk onward.

I was seven blocks away from my apartment building and the streets were busy, a small knot of people at every intersection, waiting to cross. Most nights I can handle it—a breast nudging my arm as a woman squeezes by here, a thigh brushing mine there, the momentary flash of eyes and lips and throat and flesh—but tonight I couldn't shut it out, the pulses hammering at me in syncopation, buffeting me from heartbeat to heartbeat. The blood-haze returned, and the sense of the passersby lingered after them, mingling in an undertow of desire that threatened to sweep me off my feet and pull me along. I hunched deeper into my jacket, warding it off, concentrating on my feet, on each individual step.

Up ahead a couple of women in wool overcoats stood behind a rickety card table, hawking animal-rights literature and begging signatures. They frowned at me as I approached, and I welcomed the distraction of their scorn. My jacket always attracts their attention. It's an ostrich-hide flight jacket, imported from South Africa, and it reeks of political incorrectness. I'm not insensitive to their message —but it eases something in me to be near something dead, particularly something that died in pain. Whenever I hear about a company being boycotted, I write for catalogs. I have a fabulous collection of objectionable shoes, belts, cuff links and tie tacks, and I often wish raccoon coats hadn't gone out of style for men. I'm not proud of it, but if it keeps me from feasting on the living, it's worthwhile.

As I approached, the frowns disappeared and the younger, more vulnerable of the women smiled tentatively at me. I suppressed the urge to backhand her into the wall (though the image of the rough concrete tearing a gash in her scalp and the blood mixing with her lustrous auburn hair flashed into my mind and took a long time to fade). Even if I can't see my reflection any longer, I know what I look like. I'm nothing special, never was. I never made women melt, never was particularly desirable. My love life was unenviable at best—oh, I had relationships, but they were never easy, never solid—and I'm no different now than I was then. Except, of course, that I'm a vampire—and vampires draw women like dog shit draws flies. And what a piece of self-knowledge that is—I'm sexually irresistible to women because I've been damned to hell. It's not even like they want me because I'm rich or famous. That I could deal with—at least that might be something I earned. But this—these deeply felt, seductive smiles on the faces of women who would have had nothing to do with me in life—it isn't me they're smiling at at all, it's the curse. It's insulting to me, degrading to them and it never, never ends.

I reached my building, but it no longer seemed to be a construction of stone, wood and masonry, glass and mortar. Instead, it was a living thing, pulsing with pockets of life, each individual blood-signature intimately familiar to me, the smell and rhythm of them, nightly visitors, old temptations. The crimson glow behind that window was Mrs. Wintour, behind that one Anna Berkowitz and her niece Brenda. My inflamed senses faultlessly registered who was home and who was out, longtime tenant or relative newcomer. They also told me I had a visitor.

She waited by my door, clutching her coat around her in the chilly hallway. Her pulse was sluggish, but she saw me and it jolted to life, her eyes lighting up and her skin taking on a rosier tone.

The ache in my teeth was like a knife. "Kate, you should be at home. You shouldn't be here. You should be with Tim, asleep."

"I couldn't stay away." She looked away, then back, defiance in her eyes. She set her lips in a determined line and I knew what was coming. She'd done it before.

"Kate, no—" But she opened the coat. She was naked underneath, as I knew she would be. Her body gleamed in the dim light, but it wasn't just her body I saw. I could see the blood racing up and down under her skin and my hands ached to trace it. It collected, taunting me, in the hollows of her pelvis, in her nipples, her lips. Heat poured from her and I knew I couldn't resist. My good intentions vanished, my need exploding in a crimson fog behind my eyes.

She must have seen it, because as I took a half-step forward, she gave a little cry and leapt, her arms wrapping around my neck, her body flattening against mine. I buried my face in her throat, the powerful flow of her jugular enfolding me, begging for the release of my teeth. I held back, instead tasting her with lips and tongue, the salt tang of her sweat and the musk of her perfume filling my senses, masking momentarily the siren call of her blood.

She bit my ear and pulled back. "Well," she said throatily, looking into my eyes, "aren't you going to invite me in?"

Once inside, she shucked the coat and headed for the bedroom. I thought of the cold, bitter taste of the plasma in the refrigerator, of my sturdy, lockable closet, lined with furs and leathers (I didn't have a coffin, was never interred; it'd be no more than a box to me), of *Mansfield Park* or yoga breathing or self-hypnosis or just plain teeth-gritting waiting, waiting for dawn, and made one last attempt to extricate myself.

"How can you, Kate? How can you demean yourself? You're educated, an adult—a lawyer! You have a life, a husband who loves you, kids, for God's sake!" The holy name ripped through my larynx like broken glass, but I needed the pain, needed anything to help me break free. "If self-respect won't stop you, then what about them?"

"Oh, fuck 'em," she answered, a savage glint in her eye. "I don't care about anything but you. And you want me too—you know it!"

It was true. I'd met her in college, when she was already going with Tim. I was attracted to her, and she was flattered but didn't feel anything for me—not when I was alive. We'd become friends, the three of us, and I'd settled for that. My mistake was thinking I could still hang around after my death—that my vampirism wouldn't matter. By the time I realized what I was doing to her, to them, it was too late. Horrified, I cut off all contact, but it didn't do any good. We'd been too close for too long, and now, when my need got too strong, she felt it as much as I did. I moved three times before I realized she wasn't finding me through an address book. She was following my need.

One of the things I do to control the need, to beat it down

and shut it away, is to tell myself as brutally as possible that these women don't want me, wouldn't be interested for a second if I was alive—and that, if not for the curse, I wouldn't want them either. I avoided old lovers, long-ago crushes, anyone I felt anything for before, and for the most part it worked. But not with her. She was a real person to me, someone I not only wanted but also maybe even loved.

She pulled me down on the bed. I didn't resist. Her lips found mine and her tongue slipped into my mouth. There was a trace of blood, left over from a bitten tongue or lip, and the taste was sweet, overpowering. I caressed her back, her hips, her breasts. Her skin tingled beneath my hands as I traced veins, arteries, the delicate fuzz of capillaries tiny fractions of an inch away from my fingertips. I could feel a power building up within me and shuddered.

Her hands fumbled with the buttons of my shirt, pulling it open, over my shoulders. She began to kiss my chest and I twisted around on the bed so I could reach her as well, kissing the underside of her breast and working my way downward, scraping the skin of her abdomen delicately with my teeth, scratching but not breaking it, still holding back. I felt her hands and lips work lower as well, pausing at my nipples and then my navel. Then her fingers were groping at my belt as my lips nibbled at her inner thigh.

I felt light-headed and weak. She was becoming transparent to me, her skin dissolving, her bones no more than a ghostly image. All I saw was the delicate tracery of her circulatory system, branching and twining like some exotic flora, the oxygen-rich blood slamming through the fragile vessels of her body with every heartbeat. Her jugular was too far away, but it didn't matter. Her femoral artery would do—less than an inch away from my teeth, swollen with pleasure and life and release. My lips parted.

She slid my zipper down and reached for me, finding me, as always, limp, flaccid, unresponsive. She stiffened, her heat suddenly tainted with confusion.

She pulled away to look at me, and the uncertainty in her face triggered a surge of rage in me, the power I'd felt earlier turned dark and ugly.

"What's wrong?" she asked. "Don't I—"

I lashed out, grabbed her by the throat, and stood, lifting her. Her body dangled weightless from my hand, and her pulse throbbed under my thumb, throbbed like my teeth, my throat. "Oh yes—yes you do." She twitched, trying to free herself, her legs kicking out gracefully. Her hands came up to pull at mine. It felt like the flutter of a bird's wing.

I put her against the wall. I thought I was gentle, but the wall shuddered when she hit, and she winced in pain. "Be still. Do you know? Do you know what it is I want?" She looked back at me, her head cocked to the side, her eyes meeting mine aslant. There was worry in her eyes, but it was clouded with desire. I had to find a way to get through it—I had to make her see my ugliness, my depravity. "I want to rip your throat out! To tear your flesh with my teeth and nails and drink your blood! To have it smeared on me like paint, to sink my hands into it, to bathe in it until it grows cold!" She licked her lips. "I want to kill you! That's what does it for me. That's the *only* thing that does it for me. Do you understand?"

She nodded, slowly. But there was no resistance in her. The worry slipped away. Deliberately, carefully, she lifted her chin, exposing her throat to me as best she could.

I would do it. This time, finally, I would.

"No!" I shouted the word, flinging her to the bed. I am not an animal. I would not give in.

I dropped to my knees, leaning on the edge of the bed and running my fingers along the edge of her jaw. So warm. There would be a bruise on her neck soon. I could see crushed capillaries oozing below the surface of her skin. "I don't like this, Kate. The fear, the pain. I'll do something bad, I know it. I've been strong, but I can't be strong forever. Somebody has to do something—don't you see?"

I cupped her face in my hands, stretching out toward her, begging for understanding. "I'm vulnerable during the day. I can be stopped. I can be killed. It would be easy. No risk, no danger.

"All you'd have to do would be to open the drapes. I took the apartment because it gets a lot of sun. Or would—I've never checked it out." I laughed, a sharp, bitter bark. "The forecast's good for tomorrow. It's good all weekend."

The heat still smoldered in her eyes, and I could see she was still caught up in it, still welcoming death. She could hear me, but my words didn't penetrate. "Please, Kate. You're my friend. I need your help."

I slumped to the floor by the bed, looking away from her, at the wall. There was only one way. "I hurt somebody, Kate. I don't remember much about it. Her skin was so soft—her heart beat so fast. I wanted to bite her, to tear at her throat, but I didn't—I didn't. I promised myself I'd never do that." I took a breath. "But I remember hurting her, hurting her badly. She needed help, I think, but there was no one else around. All I could do was leave—stop hurting her—and hope that was enough.

"I'm scared, Kate," I whispered. "Scared of what I might do."

Finally. The heat left her face and she shivered, naked in a cold apartment. Fear flickered through her eyes. Death in passion was one thing. Pain, disfigurement—that was something else.

I reached out to comfort her, but she pulled away. "Oh, Kate. Don't think that way—I'd never hurt *you*. I could never do that." I was smiling. It was going to work.

"Why—why are you telling me this?" When her eyes darted toward the doorway, I reached out without thinking and clutched her arm. It was right then my mood collapsed. Right then I realized it wasn't going to work after all.

"I've told you four times before," I said dully. One of these times, one of these nights, I'd have the strength to let her remember, and there'd be an end to it. And it'll be over. When I let her remember.

One of these times. I looked at her, and she forgot.

While she dressed, I threw on a clean shirt and headed to the kitchen. I opened the refrigerator door and looked at the plasma. It looked like homemade soup in its jars. Warm, thick soup, a reminder of homey days and good times. I wouldn't be needing it tonight. I heard her close the door after her, and I opened the utensil drawer, pulling out a carving knife. Oneida steel. Long, sharp, with a guaranteed stainless blade.

They say confession is good for the soul, but it doesn't do a thing for me. Maybe it soothes my soul somehow, prematurely damned to hell and writhing in flame and agony for eternity, but up here it doesn't do shit.

I slipped the knife into my jacket, absently grabbed an empty jar from the shelf, and headed out. It was still a long time until dawn. There were still people out. Hell, maybe Wendy was still at LB's. Couldn't hurt to drop by.

WOLF IN THE MEMORY

Stephen Gresham

Into the classroom walks our new music appreciation teacher and she winks at me. Of course, winks come in about as many shapes and sizes and models and horsepowers as new cars, so you have to know a little more about this particular wink: first of all, it was slow and deliberate, not a fast, flashy meaningless one that a mature woman can toss out at just anybody. No, this one had style and substance and yet was somehow delivered at full throttle. From that very first day of class, I knew that this woman had something special in mind for me; never did I see that distinct wink offered to anyone else, not even to Starkey Conway, our resident stud.

Her name was Miss Lavenia Wolf—"one 'f' instead of two," she purred—and that one "f" was something Starkey later translated to mean "one fuck daily," but who of us listened to Starkey? Well, we did, but only because he was seventeen and still in the eighth grade and tall (I was the only guy as tall) and muscular in a street-fighting sort of way and, most important of all, experienced with women. Older women. Those sixteen and older, though how much older than that we were never able to determine. But I digress.

Back to Wolf. She had black hair, the kind romance novels describe as the color of a raven's wings (I, for one, have never seen a raven in Alabama, but I can assume they're as black as a crow), and, of course, it was long and softly framed a pale, pouty face that reminded me of . . . well, a pudgy Natalie Wood, and in 1961, sweet Natalie was driving adolescent boys bonzo with every film—heck, I think I fell in love with Natalie back in that weird movie about Santa Claus, and she must have been about ten years old in that one, just a pup.

Wolf was certainly no pup. She had dark, hungry eyes. Smiling eyes. And the smile in those eyes was always connected to the right side of her mouth, her lips moving always in concert with the twinkle or glimmer in her eyes. Never one without the other. She had a cute nose, and her lips were almost too thin to be seductive, but you see, that's the point of this recollection. The woman wasn't simply sexy; no, hardly the right word. She was . . . okay, I'll get to what she was and how what she was led me to the most excruciating decision of my adolescent phase.

I wouldn't say she had a super figure. She wasn't a classic, not *Playboy* centerfold material, but she was nice. Very nice. Rather small breasts complemented by ample hips and the beginning of a potbelly—definitely not regulation *Playboy* centerfold stuff, and yet . . . maybe it was her legs that saved the day, I don't know. They were a touch muscular, especially in the calf, and the swell of her skirt that first afternoon testified to fulsome thighs, their promise delivered more than adequately when she perched upon a piano stool and talked about the coming nine weeks. I swear I can't recall much she said. Neither can my two best friends, Chick and Mance. They were there, too, on that warm September afternoon nearly thirty years ago. They, however, were not aware of how on that day Miss Wolf had proffered me a "gift" (henceforth in this narrative to be capitalized—

"Gift"—affording it the proper respect), one for which I shall always be eternally grateful.

We had all dreaded the class until Miss Wolf positioned herself atop that stool, crossed her legs, smiled, and said, "I plan to have some fun with you fellas. So how about not forcing me to have to get after you and spoil the good times."

She propped a heavily powdered chin on her knuckles and cocked one eyebrow saucily—no, not quite Natalie, but dang close. You could tell right then that she could use her sexuality to discipline us anytime she needed to. We were flies in her web—yeah.

The next thing about that first meeting I recall is the way she strode before each of us derelicts (as if we were soldiers lined up for inspection) and asked us to sing the opening lines of "Sand in My Shoes." When she halted before me, she winked again. A hot shout of embarrassment burned in my throat, and she said, "What's your name?"

Three heartbeats later, I remembered. "Dyson, ma'am. Dyson Bonner."

She bit softly at her lower lip and said, "Let me hear the range of your voice."

Sounds innocent, huh? Well, when she said it the way she did (coupled with that wink and that bite), she might as well have said, "Drop your jeans and let me see what you have." My voice cracked on every syllable. Thank goodness everybody else had pretty much the same experience so that the laughter was passed around in equal portions.

Music appreciation was the last class of the day, and after that first day, Mance, Chick and I gathered in Chick's bedroom and took inventory. Obviously they had not been affected as powerfully by the demeanor of Miss Wolf as I had. Chick, whose father was a Baptist minister, sat as usual on his bed thumbing through the lingerie section of the Montgomery Ward catalog, ogling at women clad only in bras or girdles or slips or some combination thereof. Though Chick was normally reserved and soft-spoken, when he had that catalog in his lap his eyes glazed and he would stare at those women the way a dog on a chain stares at freedom. He would whistle and snort and howl and suck disgustingly on his tongue and thrust it rapidly between his lips—then he would turn the page.

Mance, who possessed more philological curiosity than Chick, would often sit at Chick's desk attacking the dictionary, asking me how to spell such words as "cunnilingus" and "fellatio." In 1961, such words were (to Mance at least) frustratingly suppressed from inclusion in most dictionaries, but when he did succeed in finding a dirty word, Mance would read the definition loudly and with much passion, followed by a throaty, infectious, boyish laugh.

On that particular day, he was reading a sex manual he had spirited away from his older sister.

"Listen to this," he exclaimed, rocking in the chair as if on the verge of an orgasm. Thereupon he read aloud the directions to the female sex partner, who, during intercourse, was coached to whisper, "Oh, honey, you're really giving it to me tonight."

We all laughed. What else can you do when you're so horny you don't know the time of day? At that point I tried to elevate the proceedings ever so slightly, remarking upon our music appreciation class and sharing my assessment of the new teacher.

"Miss Wolf is very . . . *erotic,*" I said. The word just slipped out.

Chick frowned. Mance's mouth fell open, and he reached for the dictionary.

"Howja spell that?" he queried.

"E-R-O . . ." I stopped. Tiny bubbles of spittle had formed in one corner of the questioner's lips, and the underwear voyeur looked no less dumbfounded. How could they possibly understand? Miss Wolf had ceremoniously presented me the Gift of the erotic. Or was it that she herself was the very eidolon of eroticism? Was the Gift mine for the taking—no strings attached—or would I somehow have to *earn* it? Was the Gift actually a "Grail," thus requiring me to advance upon some perilous quest or arduous pilgrimage? The mystery of it all gave me a headache, but my heart and hormonal areas were not the least bit confused.

To Mance I said the only sensible words to cover the moment: "Never mind."

The mock splendor of an Alabama September made passage into the gloriously real splendor of an Alabama October, and Wolf—she of the Gift and/or Grail—appeared each day of the week to coax song from our pubescent vocal cords. And in a splendor all her own she would sit upon her throne (a.k.a. piano stool) and casually allow one of her black, wickedly spiked high heels to lose contact with the floor. At such times my crude brethren would often be mindlessly engaged in guessing what color panties she was wearing that day. Not me. I saw what she was up to, though, admittedly, I had to fight hard not to become thoroughly transfixed by the subtle movement of that high heel as she inched her nyloned foot free from its leather housing, letting the spike heel dangle.

Oh, my.

Perhaps nowhere in the pages of the history of eroticism has such a gesture been properly described. Nor can I describe it. But the tightness in my jeans wordlessly voiced my appreciation of the moment. Wondrous to me was the fact that *she* knew that *I* knew that no one else in the class fully appreciated the erotic ritual of that dangled high heel. More than that: There was no need to ask for whom that heel dangled—it dangled for *me*.

Alas, though, a Grail legend would not be a Grail legend if a venerable truth were not evident: For every Fair Damsel living only to offer the Gift of the erotic to some adolescent knight sans armor, there is a counterbalancing creature known as the Hideous Damsel—and Soldier Junior High School, Soldier, Alabama, was no exception. Opposite Lavenia Wolf in my dreams skulked Mrs. Eudora Hoagland, my English teacher. I sensed that were it possible for her to lay her sausage-link fingers on my Gift—as if it were a delicate, crystalline globe—she would have most gleefully dashed it to the floor, where Mr. Rydel, the janitor, would have swept its splinters and shards in with the other school-day dust and detritus.

Hoagland's favorite ploy was to delay me after class, drape her meathooks on my shoulders, and say, "Don't keep company with Starkey or Mance or Chick. Your job is to keep the right company."

My job? My job? What in the hell did she mean?

Then she would tighten those menacing fingers onto the thin rods of my clavicles, and I would imagine them breaking under her brute force like the bones of a small bird. I never failed to shudder when she touched me like that. A Hideous Damsel, yes. But worse. A genuine psychopath. This woman, I constantly reminded myself, could kill. The death-washed gray of her eyes told me that she wanted to. Needed to.

Halloween soon approached. Good thing, too, because aside from the daily dose of the erotic administered by Miss Wolf, the body of the school year was showing signs of jaundice. Our junior high football team (of which I was a member—wide receiver, though we lacked a quarterback capable of throwing me a pass) accepted its winless state so willingly that our head coach stormed home at the half of our third game and did not return until game six. After games there were dances which became moribund within thirty minutes. I did try to kindle a romantic fire with Tressie Sue Gimbel, one of the cheerleaders, but it was no use. How could Tressie's teasing flirtations compete with Wolf's archetypal eroticism? I mean, can a lady finger make as much noise as a cherry bomb? Is a BB gun as powerful as a cannon?

So there was Halloween and a school party put on by the PTA and starring the teachers and even our skeleton of a principal, Mr. Johnston. Naturally, Mance, Chick and I shunned such an unpromising *mise en scène,* opting to chase about our small town raising as much hell as possible. By mid-evening we grew bored enough to hurriedly don some makeshift costumes—Chick dressed as Satan, Mance as a pirate, and I as a vampire—and hustled to the junior high gym where the first person I saw was Tressie garbed as Snow White. What a tease!

But then I feasted my eyes on Miss Wolf.

Never have I seen such a comely witch. Never has black taken upon itself a neon jangle as it did flowing from the tip of her tall, peaked hat to the hem of her ankle-length gown—with her bare feet gracing the gym floor, each toenail screaming a red that I have yet to find on the color spectrum. Her lips were painted the same color. And I was enthralled.

Wolf was manning (why isn't there a word "womanning"?) the apple-bobbing caldron and the touchy/feely display supposedly of dead body parts. You've seen the stuff I'm sure: peeled grapes for dead man's eyes, cold cooked spaghetti for brains, etc., etc. Nothing *sui generis.* Or so I thought. The apple-bobbing caldron was a huge crock pot that was blackwashed appropriately; the apples were buoyed in a gray, sudsy concoction that reminded me of dishwater.

As I observed from an oblique angle, Mance breathlessly exclaimed in my ear, "Nipples. Nipples." And he danced a little jig which I recognized as endemic to Mance. His southern drawl is so pronounced that I thought he said, "Naples, Naples," and I wondered why he was talking about Italy. Then I chanced a look at the front of Wolf's gown and I experienced a flash of intense white light, something of the nature of what folks encounter near death—a glance at Heaven I guess you'd call it. At that point I must have made my way to the caldron, probably lurching more like a zombie than gliding sinuously like a rakish vampire.

Wolf smiled at me. She hooked a brilliant red fingernail toward me and then reeled me closer. Closer to those hardened nipples and red lips and the Gift. She leaned forward—I smelled her perfume and my right leg went numb—and she whispered, "I like vampires."

"Oh, yes, ma'am," I said quickly. "So do I."

If memory serves me correctly, I hung around, occasionally bobbing for apples (temporarily losing my paraffin fangs) and smiling vacuously at Miss Wolf. The night wore on; ten o'clock—PTA quitting time—drew near. I had lost track of Mance and Chick and had nervously chewed through my waxy fangs when Miss Wolf, having dismissed some dorky seventh graders, cocked an eyebrow and said, "Would you like to put your hand in my special box?"

In times of extreme stress, the rushing of blood in the body of a thirteen-year-old boy has a geometry all its own; the heart pumps thunderously, in defiance of all laws of physics and physiology.

Hot blood.

She took my hand. From a shelf apparently below the Tupperware container of cooked spaghetti she lifted a shoe box with a fist-size hole in one end. There was a lid on the box so I couldn't see what was inside—more peeled grapes or spaghetti, I guessed.

I was wrong.

She pushed my hand within the opening and my fingers brushed a silken maze of materials—nylon, cotton, and powder puffy things. I started to jerk free, but she held my arm until my knuckles pressed against the nipple end of a balloon filled with warm water.

I believe I gasped. Somehow through the roar in my ears I heard Wolf's soft, apologetic laughter. I tried to act cool, but over Wolf's shoulder I noticed that Mrs. Hoagland had been watching from her sentry beneath the basketball goal.

She was frowning.

In that moment she became a vampire hunter stalking me with the sharpened point of an ash stake, hungry to plunge it into my heart. Hey, I'm serious. I'll never forget the look of hatred in her eyes. She hated Wolf (Jealousy? Envy?). She hated me. She hated my Gift. Even across the gym floor, her eyes whispered threateningly. I caught their vicious sentiment: "So you like to put your hand into strange boxes, eh?" they seemed to say. "How would you like it if I put yours into a paper shredder? Or a bear trap? Or a tank of piranhas?"

You get the idea.

Her eyes also had a few choice words for Wolf: "I'll have your job, bitch. I'll find a way to put your tit in a ringer."

The gym reeked of Hoagland's perfect hatred.

Her actions struck me as motiveless malignity. But whatever it was, it worked. She had me scared. My Gift was in danger.

And yet the Halloween episode—the "shoe-box gambit" as I came to call it—had taught me an important lesson about the erotic. It went something like this: At the pulsing heart of the erotic is mystery. Throw in surprise, too. Mystery and surprise. And fear. They guaranteed that a certain energy would always be available to anyone who had been given the Gift of the erotic. What did it all mean? Hey, I was just a kid, but I think I came to realize that the erotic—Wolf-style, at least—meant that I might live life more "livingly." That is, if Hoagland didn't castrate me first.

But through it all the Gift was growing. It had a secret life, and only Wolf and I knew about it, and that, of course, made me feel terrific, and I continued to feel terrific until a few weeks of November slouched by. November. Some poet has called it the month of the drowned dog. He's right.

November was a month of tension crowned by a mixture of disappointment and hope. Here's what happened. At the suggestion of Mrs. Hoagland, the eighth-grade boys were paraded, once a day, into the auditorium where our emaciated principal would stand before us, tottering as if buffeted by some inner wind, and lecture us. And show us films— films supposedly on the facts of life. Not only that, but on two occasions, the Reverend Finebaum of the First Methodist Church was asked to address us on morality. Chick, of course, just about turned into a pillar of salt at the thought of his father possibly being asked to speak to us. And what was this charade designed to do? Answer: rid us at once of our alleged foul language, purge us summarily of our dirty thoughts, and exorcise forthwith our demons of sexual obsession.

Naturally it didn't work.

About all it accomplished was to give Mrs. Hoagland a month's worth of jollies, make the girls snootier than ever, make Chick's face break out, and provide a new list of words for Mance to look up. I survived by dwelling constantly upon Wolf and the Gift. However, one day even those saving graces appeared to have forsaken me.

Seems like it was the day before Thanksgiving break, Wolf had us practicing for the Christmas program scheduled for three weeks hence. We had been singing our little throats raw in the days preceding, straining to make "Silent Night" sound like . . . well, like "Silent Night." Starkey was up to something. Before class he passed around this mimeographed poem, a sort of parody, which began, "On the night before Christmas ole Santa was humpin' everything in the house." Starkey had written the entire poem himself and threatened to pound anyone who laughed at it. Starkey the poetaster. Oh, well. I didn't think much about it—just a stupid poem, the kind adolescent boys usually adore—but then Wolf perched herself on her throne and it appeared that Starkey was going to show her a copy of his poem.

He approached her sheepishly. Our motley group collectively held its breath. My heart slowed—maybe even stopped, I'm not sure. What I *was* sure of was that Wolf would scorn such drivel and such affrontery. A true woman of the erotic would not acknowledge such prurient nonsense.

Wrong.

"My father would love this," she mused.

Starkey's face lit up like the lights on the football field. Then Wolf glanced up at our group and realized we knew the text of the poem. She raised a cautionary finger and smiled.

"Now fellas, no one else must hear of this. I could lose my job. This (she held up the poem) is just between me and all of you. The girls and the other teachers mustn't know a thing about it. Will you promise me that?"

Some of us dully nodded, and then Starkey stepped in front and shook his fist.

"If any of you nerds squeal about this I'll punch a lung out of you. Get me?"

We did.

I couldn't look at Wolf. God, was I disappointed.

Class seemed to last about three days. I was so depressed that I sang "Joy to the World" as if it were a dirge. I never once all the hour let my eyes meet Wolf's. When the bell rang, Mance, who was in such a tizzy I thought he might wet his pants, whispered to Chick and me, "Can you believe this? Geez, can you believe this?"

Chick was of the opinion that Miss Wolf's tenure at Soldier was inexorably doomed—well, he may not have used those exact words.

My friends waited breathlessly for my response to the shocking developments.

"I don't give a damn," I said, the lie scalding my tongue.

We started to split. Basketball practice was scheduled to begin at four o'clock, but Miss Wolf held me back, requesting that I try on one of the new choir robes for the Xmas songfest. As frostily as possible, I agreed to stay. The robes were hanging in the mammoth closet near the door of the room, a multipurpose closet where Mr. Rydel stored janitorial supplies and where Starkey boasted he had made out with numerous girls *and* Randy Tyburn's mother, a recent divorcée; he had further hinted of having cornered Wolf there for a passionate exchange or two. You can believe what you like.

In the closet, Wolf switched on the single naked bulb. Then she smiled at me.

"Boys and their dirty poems—so silly, aren't they?"

"Yes, ma'am" stuck in my throat.

I slipped into one of the robes. She stood close to me as she zipped up the front of it. God, she smelled so good.

"It fits okay," I said, straining to be businesslike.

She stepped back, cocked her head to one side, and winked. As she helped me out of the robe she said, "You're not like the others, are you?"

"No, ma'am. I mean . . . yes, ma'am."

I didn't know what I meant. I hurried from the scene, but I felt better. Yeah, much better. The Gift had not been shattered. Only threatened. I would live to face another December—just had to stay clear of the Hideous Damsel.

Of course, every good story of the erotic should reach a climax. The big moment—make that the Big Moment—occurred the evening of the Christmas program. In passing, I'd like to mention that while Mrs. Hoagland suspected something was up in Wolf's class, she, much to her chagrin, could not ferret it out, a fact which gave me immense pleasure. I believe Wolf secretly delighted in the situation, too.

Anyway, before the program began, Wolf asked me to help her move the piano to the gym, and I obliged, foolishly insisting that I wheel it all by myself. Well, I wrestled that beast to the gym, but it almost turned me into a soprano. With a wink and a playful touch of a long red fingernail to the tip of my nose, Wolf said "thank you," adding a request for me to assist her again afterward. No problem.

As you might expect, our part of the program left something to be desired. Have you ever heard of an entire singing group completely forgetting the lines to the second half of "The First Noel"? Performance amnesia or something. Suffice to say, the Vienna Boys' Choir would receive no serious competition from us. I felt sorry for Miss Wolf. But you know what? Our screw-ups didn't seem to bother her. She appeared to enjoy the evening, going so far as to joke about it as I rolled the piano back to the music room once the program had drawn mercifully to a close.

"I'm real sorry we sang so poorly," I told her as I opened the closet door and began to take off my robe.

"Please don't think a thing about it. I enjoyed working with you fellas."

She had slipped in behind me; I was standing beneath that single naked bulb when I heard the closet door softly close. To be honest, I didn't give a second thought to it because the damned zipper on my robe had stuck halfway down.

"Would you mind unzipping me, Dyson?" Wolf purred. No problem.

Her robe had a zipper in back, so she turned and lifted her long black hair and, fingers trembling just a bit, I zipped away . . . and saw a mile of silken bare flesh and felt its warmth radiating outward. I'm afraid I didn't stop unzipping until I nearly reached the bottom of her spine—I guess I kept thinking I would see some article of clothing before then.

But I didn't.

She spun around and stepped out of that robe like a butterfly emerging from its cocoon in a speeded-up nature film. Clad only in a black garter belt and hose and those marvelous spiked heels, she smiled, bit her lip softly, and winked at me.

Oh, Lord.

And I thought: what if Mance and Chick could see me now? Now. Here. My Gift surrounding me like a huge, glass bubble.

"I would like very much for you to touch me," she said. What could I say?

I distinctly remember that she took my hand and guided it toward her. With her other hand she switched off the light. And the darkness roared in my ears. I touched something— it *might* have been her breast, but then again I was so deeply in shock it could have been Mr. Rydel's plumber's friend. Her lips brushed the corner of my mouth and produced a tingle I can still feel during the middle of a sleepless night.

Then we heard it: the voice of the Hideous Damsel.

"Lavenia, are you here?"

We tensed. Waited. I prayed I wouldn't faint. I promised God I would never spell another dirty word for Mance if He got me out of this. Like most of my deals with God, this one didn't work out.

Light rushed in with a thunderous whoosh—the way it does in horror movies these days. But this was no movie. No fantasy. No hallucination. It was the real thing. And I was in real trouble. And real scared.

Hoagland had a nest of snakes in her eyes. When she focused on us, her face transformed into that of a dragon. I could feel the heat from her breath as she stood there, motionless, staring. I actually prayed that she would say something; that look was scaring the holy shit out of me.

Then she wiggled her fingers.

The sight of Hoagland's fingers was more terrifying than anything ever conjured up by H. P. Lovecraft or Stephen King. And she was coming toward us, those fingers raised.

This gorgon had killing on her mind.

I stepped protectively in front of Wolf. She cowered against my back like a frightened animal. The scent of her fear wafted over my shoulder; her skin goose-pimpled. Her breathing was low and raspy.

I decided to challenge the would-be murderess.

"We were helping each other with our robes," I stammered. But her eyes burned holes in my words, and her hands continued drifting at my throat. Was she going to strangle me?

Behind me, Wolf whimpered, "Please, Mrs. Hoagland."

"Shut up!" the Hideous Damsel screeched.

Then she lowered her hands and picked up one of Mr. Rydel's wooden-handled mops, raised it to eye level, and snapped it in two. The snap sounded like the report of a rifle. I sucked in so much air that my lungs stitched fire.

What followed knocked the top off my scale of terror.

Hoagland took one half of the handle, its splintered, razor-sharp point gleaming whitely in the shadows, and elevated it so that the deadly fang was directed at my face.

Oh, Jesus.

I could imagine that hideous frog-sticker being thrust into my eye socket or into my stomach. Or my groin.

She leaned close. The tip of the mop blade rested against that soft flesh just under my chin. I couldn't swallow. Hell, I could barely breathe. Sweat ran in rivulets down my cheeks, mingled with stinging tears.

And Hoagland whispered menacingly, "This is not your job."

She pressed the mop tip and it ever so slightly broke the skin. To an innocent observer the wound would have appeared to be a shaving nick. Nothing more.

Wolf whimpered "Please" again, and I started to pray.

Then one of those medievallike miracles occurred.

Somebody came shuffling down the hallway outside the music room. I never knew who it was, but they quite likely saved my life and Miss Wolf's.

Sometimes I wonder how so many people in the days following came up with so many different accounts of what happened. Truth is, I became a celebrity of sorts in the time leading up to the school board hearing. On my locker someone taped two small signs; one read, "Closet King"; the other, "Bonner Bags Wolf."

Mance and Chick hounded me unmercifully for details and—get this—Starkey Conway suddenly wanted to be pals. In addition, Tressie Sue Gimbel began to look at me with one eye of disgust and one eye of embryonic lust.

But, mostly, the closet scene had a downside: Mr. Johnston called my parents. Mom cried. Dad frowned. Two or three times he started to say something, yet found that he couldn't. I like to think maybe he understood.

I had a series of bad dreams in which Hoagland killed me and stuffed me in a Hefty bag. I couldn't report her because it would mean tarnishing my Gift. Besides, she had as many goods on us as we on her.

A week later, the Inquisition was held.

God, I was scared. Rumor had it I might be expelled from school or kicked out of the state or sent directly to Hell—or maybe all three. As I entered the principal's office, I saw that Miss Wolf was seated by a window staring off vacantly. I ducked quickly into the conference room, and adult heads —like something out of one of those horrid Greek myths— swung toward me. There was Mr. Johnston, Mrs. Hoagland, and four other sort of faceless adults. They directed me to sit down.

Mr. Johnston got right to the point. He said no one was blaming me. Whew—I breathed more easily. There would be no firing squad or guillotine or, apparently, expulsion. But then something weird began to occur.

They began to catalog, in some detail, various complaints against Miss Wolf, and I got the strangest sensation that I had been transported back to Salem in the days of the witchcraft trials. They were defaming Wolf; worse yet, they were besmearing my Gift. I could barely hold my tongue.

Then questions were fired at me from all sides like machine-gun rounds: "What went on in that closet? What else has Miss Wolf done? Don't you think it's your responsibility to bring this immoral woman to justice?"

My head swam. My neck ached from glancing from one adult to another as if I were watching a tennis match.

"What do you have to say for yourself?" they demanded.

"I won't give it back," I announced frantically.

There was silence. Almost funereal silence. Mr. Johnston's skeletal face seemed to leer at me.

"Give what back? Did Miss Wolf give you something?"

"No. Yes. I won't tell you."

Mrs. Hoagland—the Hideous Damsel was in her element —leaned forward to deliver what she must have felt would be the deathblow to my defense of Wolf. I pressed my fingertips nervously into the soft skin beneath my chin.

"Dyson, it's your job to tell us. Be a young man. Do your job. It's your job to tell us what that woman did."

My job? My job?

The words, outlined in blood, pulsed in my thoughts, intensified by some inner strobe light.

Shaking, nerves roller-coastering, I stood up and pushed away from the table. And I shouted, "I quit!"

I heard my voice echo behind me as I scrambled out the door. I slowed by where Wolf was seated; she glanced up at me. Know what she did? Yeah, you guessed it: She winked at me.

After I crashed through the school doors, I leaped onto my bike, and as I pedaled away the anger and frustration began to dissolve, and I reached deep into my thoughts and held the image of my Gift and felt the residue of the mystery and anguish and horror of growing up. But I pedaled faster and faster and faster. And it felt good. Yeah, real good.

Y'all might be interested to hear that the Hideous Damsel —dear ole Mrs. Hoagland—murdered her husband. One day she just snapped, and that snap led to another, because she snapped his neck one morning when he disregarded her request to take out the garbage.

Guess he wasn't doing his job.

Well, I never saw Miss Lavenia Wolf again. Never heard where she went or what became of her. Now, years and years later, I've learned that Nature's central fire can grow cold on a man. At such times you need a glimpse of the erotic, a darkness that roars, and a touch of Wolf in the memory.

TO HAVE AND
TO HOLD

Gary Brandner

In the sixteen years of their marriage, sex with Lilian had never been this good.

Harry Crofft held her close, savoring the satiny feel of her flesh against his. It was hard not to cry out, but Harry knew he must not. He clamped his lower lip between his teeth and moaned deep in his chest.

Sweat ran in rivulets from his body, soaking through the sheet beneath them and the mattress under that. Harry used all his willpower to sustain the moment, to hold off the thumping climax.

Think of something else. That was how you did it, delayed the orgasm. Think of something depressing.

Harry Crofft did not have to dig too deep for a melancholy thought. He had only to go back to that terrible night a month ago. The night of the horror downstairs, right under the room in which he now lay with his wife. What a cruel irony, he thought. Only after that unspeakable tragedy did he and Lilian find fulfillment in their bed. Sometimes Harry allowed himself to wonder if it was so good now not in spite of what happened but *because* of it. At least the children would never again walk in to interrupt them in the act.

Shuddering, he pushed that unworthy thought away,

ashamed of himself. Even in his mounting passion tears blurred his eyes. Lilian, supine beneath his pounding need, was so innocent, so unaware of what had happened to her. To all of them. Seeing her bland, guiltless face, how could he possibly blame her for what happened? It was not her fault. She could not possibly have understood what she was doing. And now . . . now she was like an innocent child. And yet, very much a woman. A much different woman than she had been before. So receptive to his needs. So compliant, so eager to please him. The catharsis of tragedy had left them freely animalistic in their coupling.

The doorbell.

"Damn!" he growled through clenched teeth.

Lilian stared up at him, her mouth slightly open, as he pulled away. Harry put a finger to his lips and shook his head. Poor Lilian did not understand the danger.

He waited. Maybe it was just a salesman or one of those fresh-faced young idiots peddling their religion. Maybe they would go away. Harry squeezed his eyes shut, trying to will them to go away. But no, they would not give up. When the doorbell got no response they knocked. Persistent devils. How could they know he was home? With a little snort of disgust he remembered his car was parked out in plain sight in the driveway.

Carefully he withdrew from Lilian. "Stay here," he said, "and be quiet."

An unnecessary precaution. Lilian had not spoken an intelligible word in a month, only strange little sounds. Not since that frightful night when the children . . .

In a perverse way, Harry could almost enjoy her new-found silence. Since the day they were married it seemed that Lilian had almost never shut up. She had babbled on incessantly about the most trivial matters. Privately, Harry had to admit that it was a relief now not having to pretend to listen. There were distinct advantages in being married to a mute.

Still, there were times when he would not have minded a little friendly conversation. The physical communication they had now was great, but a guy had to stop screwing once in a while. It wouldn't matter what they talked about. Naturally, he would stay off the bad business of a month ago, even though it had to be uppermost in their minds.

Quickly he pulled on pants and shirt and stepped into his slippers. He smoothed back his hair and left the bedroom.

Descending the stairs he pulled in deep, controlled breaths, composing himself to face whoever was at the door. The persistence of the knock gave him a pretty good indication of who it would be.

He pulled open the door and nodded to the two men who stood outside.

"Sorry to bother you again, Mr. Crofft, but we were wondering if you'd heard anything at all from your wife." Sergeant Verick's eyes were the color of pewter—cold and steady.

"I haven't heard a thing from Lilian," Harry said. "I would have called you if I did."

"I hope that's true," Verick said. "You do realize that you could be in danger."

"Me? From Lilian? I hardly think so."

"Mr. Crofft, are you forgetting what she—?"

"You understand that we're just doing our job," Detective Ash put in. He was ten years younger than Verick and had a kinder, more sensitive face.

"I thought your job was to find my wife. Keep her from hurting herself. Or anyone else."

"It's also our job to protect you. There is no way of knowing what your wife's mental state might be today."

"I'm sorry," Harry said, relaxing his stiff posture. "I'm sure you're doing your best. This is just . . . difficult for me."

"Of course it is," said Ash. "Please understand that we don't like to intrude on your grief. But it's frustrating for us to run into dead ends everywhere. We've checked all your wife's friends and what family she has left. No one has seen or heard anything of her since . . . since the night it happened."

Harry shook his head. "After this long . . . maybe we should all just give it up."

"The police will never give up on this one," Verick said. He shuddered. "Those children . . . we're not going to rest until we find her. I'm sorry if we have to invade on your privacy, but this isn't just a personal matter for you, it's a crime of the ugliest kind."

Detective Ash touched the sergeant's arm and gave him the tiniest head shake.

Verick coughed into his fist. "Don't think we're unsympathetic, Mr. Crofft. I have children of my own, and I can imagine how this must tear you apart. I just want to assure you that we won't rest until we locate Mrs. Crofft and . . . see that she gets whatever treatment is necessary."

"Yes, thank you," Harry said.

What was that? A noise from the bedroom? Did the policemen hear?

"We'll be in touch, Mr. Crofft," Ash said. He looked as though he wanted to take Harry's hand, but he did not. The two detectives walked back to the street where their car was parked.

Harry closed the door and stood for a moment with his back against the cold wooden panel. His eyes ranged over the neat, comfortable living room. For a heart-stopping moment he saw the room as it had been on that dreadful night. The beige carpet soaked scarlet with blood. Twelve-year-old Justin, partly on the floor and partly across the big chair facing the television set. And little Kimberly at the foot of the stairs, her tiny hand across her face in a pitiful attempt to ward off the fatal attack. And Lilian. Oh, God, Lilian staring at him with that innocent, uncomprehending look. The bloodied ax lying at her feet.

Harry squeezed his eyes closed and let the pain subside. When he looked again the blood and the ax were gone, the walls repainted, the carpets new, the big chair replaced. The living room was empty. No one was standing on the stairs. He hurried up to his wife.

Lilian welcomed him back into their bed. The cool, moist touch of her flesh instantly revived the passion that had been damped by the visit of the policemen. *Treatment,* Sergeant Verick had said. Harry knew what that meant. It meant they would take Lilian away and lock her up where he would see her maybe once a month. And he would never, never be allowed to hold her like this again. He could not allow that to happen. Not now when they had found the perfect physical expression of their love.

The past month had been difficult, there was no denying that. The police were all over the place, of course, right after it happened. They were efficient, businesslike, and sympathetic, while trying hard to hide their real emotions. And there were the reporters. The media loves a story of nauseating violence. People were horrified at the thought that a mother could do such a thing to her own children. But they loved hearing about it and reading the details and watching Harry's stricken face on their television screens. It was a rough time, but after a couple of weeks there was a new horrifying crime to take the public's attention.

Some well-meaning people, seeing Harry's distress, tried to make excuses for Lilian. She was a "sick woman," they told him. She "needed help." Well, she had help now. She had Harry's help. Even that first night, as the police and the reporters prowled through the house, Lilian was right upstairs, hidden in their bedroom, not making a sound. Harry was proud of her for being so quiet. That was before he discovered she no longer spoke.

On that first night he had yet to appreciate the good part of all this. Then, much later, after everyone had finally left him alone and he had declined all offers to stay somewhere else, the sex with Lilian had been sensational. So often in the past she had pleaded the traditional headache or had performed in a perfunctory manner, the better to get it over with as soon as possible. Now, suddenly, she was insatiable. As often as Harry wanted to do it, she was receptive and ready.

No, there was no way he would let anyone take Lilian from him now. Not after the month he had enjoyed with her.

There had been the one close call with his mother a week ago. Right from the start she and Lilian had never gotten along. *There's something wrong with that woman,* his mother had said prophetically. *She just isn't right for you.* On her last visit, Harry's mother had sniffed the air and looked around the empty living room as though it were filled with garbage.

"You really should come and stay at home," she said. "I've got plenty of room. This can't be healthy for you, living here alone like this."

"I'm fine, Mother. Really." He had glanced up the stairs and caught his breath when he saw the bedroom door was open. The full-length mirror on the inside of the door reflected Lilian's naked body as she lay on the bed. On her lips was the slight, taunting smile.

He had quickly moved in front of his mother to cut off her view, and he hustled her out of the house as soon as possible. He sent her away with false promises to visit her. When he returned to Lilian he intended to scold her for taking the chance that his mother might see her. But as always, the proximity of her soft white body and the ineffable look of innocence in her eyes fired him with desire, and all else was forgotten.

Now, so urgent was his ache that Harry did not take the time to undress. He fumbled to unzip his pants and push them down on his thighs. With a little moan he dropped on top of his wife.

While Lilian's naked body flopped around beneath him, he thrashed and pumped and rolled from side to side on the king-size bed. With his eyes tightly closed he felt as though he could lose himself entirely in the mysterious inner darkness of the woman. The scent of her was sharp in his nostrils. The little sounds she made teased his ears.

The climax crashed around him like a towering wave over a solitary beachcomber. In his right hand he squeezed her breast as though holding on for his life. His emotions boiled over and out in a screaming, jabbering orgasm.

It was a full minute before he became aware of the sound. Door chimes, followed by an urgent pounding downstairs.

"Mr. Crofft!" Sergeant Verick's voice.

What were they doing back here? Harry pushed himself up and off Lilian and saw the open bedroom window. Damn, that was careless. He disengaged himself from Lilian, took a moment to calm himself, and walked downstairs.

The two policemen stood outside, their eyes watchful, muscles tense under their rumpled suits.

"Are you all right?" Verick said, his cold eyes probing Harry's.

"We heard someone shouting from the bedroom," Ash said, glancing toward the stairway.

"I'm fine," Harry said, pleased with the steadiness of his voice. "You must have heard the television. When I turned it on the volume was way up. Everything's all right. Really."

But the two policemen were not listening to him. They were staring down at his hand. His clenched right hand.

Harry followed their eyes and saw the shriveled tissue in his fist. A crusted brown nipple peeked out between his knuckles. His fingers loosened. The withered breast of a woman, thirty days dead, dropped softly to the floor.

CRUISING

Lisa W. Cantrell

Danny Norvill opened the door to the sleek gray Jaguar and slid behind the wheel.

Darkness coiled around him. Silence. The allure of the night.

A cool October wind cut sharply through the light clothes he wore and chilled his blood. But that was all right. He'd soon be warm. He'd be with Karen.

He reached over and closed the door.

Smiling, he placed his hands on the steering wheel—lightly, lovingly, rubbing his open palms against the black leather wheelcover.

Sitting in the car always affected him this way: an initial rush of pleasure, a tightening at his crotch. It was almost a sexual joining, and it fed the hunger in Danny the way a storybook woman sparks fire and passion in her man.

The long hood stretched endlessly before him; night-damp and shimmery, slick and sweet, it caressed his eyes like a silver dream:

It was the first time he'd seen the car, sitting in Fat Jack "Have WE Gotta DEAL For YOU" Carson's Used Car Lot over on Fourth and Main. He hadn't even known it was a Jag then, but he'd known he wanted it. Wanted it like he wanted

Karen. Wanted it until the pain of that wanting was a constant ache in his groin.

He still marveled at how Fate had dealt him a winner's hand: the not-unreasonable asking price; the sudden big sale that had netted his old man a sizable commission; the final payment on his Mom's Chevette. He hadn't quite believed it the day Fat Jack placed the keys in his hand and slapped him on the back, making some nowhere remark with a wink to his old man. They'd laughed, but it hadn't mattered. Nothing mattered but the keys in his hand and the car that had been in his blood from first sight. A special car. It made Danny Norvill special, too.

A turn of the ignition key, the car sprang to life, first with the growl Danny knew so well, then smoothing into the purr of the beast at rest that lures the reckless and cautions the wary.

He checked the gas gauge, smiled to see it near "Full." The old man had taken to giving him hell when he asked for extra cash, crappin' about lousy gas mileage and cost of upkeep and repairs, *"not to mention insurance; shoulda never bought you that damn Brit car!"* The old man's sales were down.

Danny didn't care. The Jag was worth it. Worth the extra work and expense. Worth the old man's flap. Worth it all when he sat behind the wheel and threaded the car like a silver needle through the staring eyes of the other kids.

Danny backed off the gas and let the XJ6 idle on its own, savoring the thrum of power, the headiness of being on the edge. The car consumed him like it always did, making him feel a part of it: the mind in the body, the hand in the fist.

He switched on the stereo.

Music spilled around him, the deep, primordial hammer of heavy metal bass—just the way he liked it. It pounded at his eardrums, drove into his body until he felt its rhythm like the beating of his heart.

The turn of a knob: running lights blinked on, wicked amber eyes gleaming in the darkness. A second revolution brought the headlights to full.

He cupped his right hand over the rounded gear shift lever mounted in the center console. Cool and slick, it fit his hand like a lover.

Slipped the lever into reverse.

Easing his foot off the brake, Danny backed the car out onto the main road and shifted into drive. The XJ6 began to roll forward. He didn't even have to give it any gas. On a flat, hard-surfaced road the car would do thirty by itself.

Another flick: Powerful halogen beams flashed to bright, shoving night back at least another fifty yards.

"*'Let there be light.'*" Danny chuckled and gunned the Jag down the empty street.

Another Saturday night.

Time to go cruising.

He played the car gently around a corner and headed up Liberty Drive. It felt good driving the Jag again, real good. It was where he belonged on a Saturday night—him and the Jag, cruising the strip. So what if he wasn't a jock? So what if his family didn't belong to the Country Club set. So the fuck what?

Across the intersection of Liberty and Main.

Lights from the shopping center appeared up ahead on his right. Danny cut his speed. He could visualize the scene: some kids sitting in their cars, others lounging against front fenders or perched on hoods, a few inside the Pizza Den grouped around Cokes and pepperoni pizzas.

Karen would be here.

Karen . . .

For a moment he imagined she was already sitting here beside him, her hand on his leg, fingers creeping ever closer toward the bulge at his crotch. He could see them driving up to Sparrows Point, visualize her soft and yielding in the back seat . . . tight jeans rolling past her hips . . . blouse open, his hand on her breast . . .

Danny jerked himself back to reality, wiped sweat from his face with his sleeve and slowed even more, switching to running lights as he pulled in the side entrance to the shopping center's parking lot. He wanted to make a pass around behind the line of parked cars first, see if he could spot Karen in one of them.

Turning down the tape player, he crawled the Jaguar silently forward. A string of vehicles formed a close-knit semicircle beneath phosphorescents and neon. Familiar. Closed. Just like always.

But that was okay. He didn't need to be included. The Jag set him apart. In it, Danny was better than them all.

Keeping to the outer edge of the light, he scanned the parked cars—she wasn't inside any of them—then pulled back around behind some big green garbage Dumpsters and switched off his lights. Through a space between two Dumpsters, Danny watched . . . waited . . .

She came strolling out of the Pizza Den, flipping her long blond hair back in that way she had. God, she was beautiful. Jeans hugging her ass, jammed into her crack. He wiped away sweat, reached down to massage his swollen cock—

She wasn't alone.

Danny tensed as he saw Brad Simpson's tall, beefy form swing in beside her. One hand stuffed into the pocket of his jeans, the other draped possessively across her shoulders. His Varsity letter jacket billowed in the breeze.

Dammit. God damned son-of-a-bitch. Bastard.

He watched them saunter by a couple of cars, stop to talk at another, then head toward Brad's red Camaro. Opening the driver's door, Brad allowed her to slide in first, then followed. The Camaro's lights came on. It headed out of the lot. Danny watched it turn left onto Independence Boulevard and go speeding away.

He switched his lights back on and eased the Jag out to

follow, taking his time. He didn't need to keep their taillights in sight to know where they were headed.

Sparrows Point.

Where else would they go?

Anger churned hot and sour in the pit of Danny's stomach. Desire coiled tight as a snake. It hissed its venom as he cruised the silver Jag down Independence Boulevard, turned left at Sakers Mill Road, climbed Mabry's hill to the Point.

There they were, the red Camaro parked all by itself at the edge of the cliff. He kept the powerful car on its leash, though it strained to break free, go leaping out of the final turn.

Cutting his headlights, he pulled onto the grassy embankment and rolled silently toward the Camaro. A smile stretched his face. Wind sang through his brain.

They were creatures of the wind this night, he and the Jag, and nothing—*nothing* could take that away.

Turning the tape player up again, he slipped the Jag's nose up close to the rear of the Camaro and stopped, letting the engine idle quietly. Then he popped the headlights on full.

Blond hair dripped over the back of the seat, cascading like ripples on a pond. Brad loomed over her, hands bracing the seat on either side of her head. He looked like he was eating her face.

Bastard! Bastard! Bastard!

They sprang apart, Brad jerking his head up with a startled look on his face, Karen swinging around. Danny watched her bring her hand up to shade her eyes from the glare of his lights.

Exhilaration took hold. He popped the Jaguar into reverse, lurching backward about twenty feet, then started inching forward again in little jumps and spurts. One foot on the gas, one on the brake, he revved the engine between each burst.

Brad whirled around, wrenched open his door and

jumped out, striding toward the Jag. Fury radiated from him, hands clenched at his sides. Mr. Macho Man, ready for a confrontation.

Danny smiled and slammed into reverse again, spinning in an arc away from the Camaro. Wheels churned up the ground, throwing clumps of grass and gravel in their wake.

Brad stopped, was standing uncertainly at the rear of the Camaro. He'd recognized the Jag. Karen had her window rolled down, leaning out to see.

For a moment, Danny ignored the pair of them, listening to the feral purr of the Jaguar's engine, hearing it thrum through his veins, flame like a geyser of hard-rock sound. A wave of dizziness took him, lust—for the Jag, for the night—blurring all other emotions.

Then he looked at Karen. She was sitting there, face freeze-framed in the window, hair ruffling in the breeze.

He wanted her—*God!* How he wanted her.

Gradually, he began easing the car forward again, nosing it toward Brad, keeping him square in his sights.

Brad began backing away. He didn't look so macho now, he looked scared.

Danny liked that look. Liked it a lot.

He pulled to within a yard or so of the Camaro's rear bumper, blocking it in, angling the car to bring his window in line with Brad's gaping stare.

Danny mashed the brake hard, feeling the car tug against the leash, pressed the button to the power window. The glass slid downward with a soft hum.

Brad's eyes widened. His face blanched, ghost-white against the night.

Danny grinned, peeling his lips back off his clenched teeth, exploding the smile outward in a burst of pure hatred and anger and pain. Then Brad was scrambling backward, bolting off into the night.

"Brad? Brad, what's happening?"

Karen's frightened voice floated to him on the wind.

Danny ignored her—for the moment—gunning the Jag forward, releasing the leash. It leapt toward Brad's retreating back, headlights stabbing him, zeroing in.

It struck and kept going, on top of him when the body hit the ground, rolling over it again and again, circling around to pounce, maul, until the ground was as torn and gutted as the kill.

Then it was over. Bloodlust momentarily spent.

Danny let the car idle for a moment, then began easing it forward, taking up the slack between him and his new prey.

She'd started getting out of the car, thought better of it, was slamming doors and locking them, rolling up windows on both sides. He heard the engine grind and flood out.

He pulled in behind the Camaro.

She whirled around, looking back at him through the rear glass:

Like she'd stared at him that day at school, that day he'd finally gotten up the courage to ask her for a date, stared at him sitting at the wheel of this car and he'd known she was his for the taking, always known she could be his for the price of a Coke and a great set of wheels—

Except it hadn't worked out that way, instead she'd turned and begun walking off, laughing with her friends, and when he'd called her back, he asked her if she'd like to go for a spin in the Jag, not believing she'd say no, not believing it! She'd laughed in his face—LAUGHED IN HIS FACE!—and made some comment about a great car with a geek at the wheel.

The heat of that memory pumped new energy through him, surging from his gut like bile. He put the car in park, pulled up the emergency brake, got out. The Jag thrummed softly behind him, cheering him on.

He approached from Brad's side, never taking his eyes off her, watching her trace his progress around the side of the car, up to the door. He wrenched it open.

She screamed, "No. No, Danny, you can't be here. You can't be here, Danny."

He grinned again, remembering how he'd felt as he peeled rubber out of the school yard that day, remembering how he'd felt as he raced away from the laughter, the hurt:

Remembering the bridge.

The crash . . .

Wind sang through the moment, telling him *go on, go on, now, she's yours, yours for the asking price, yours for the car and the pain and the night . . .*

He reached for her—and the skin on his arms was patchy dark and oozing; the flesh was beginning to rot, shrink back from his nails. They looked like claws.

She shrank against the far door, hands scrabbling behind her, searching for the handle, the lock, *anything* to get away!

Little animal sounds whimpered from her, and he savored them. He'd always known she'd sound like that.

He grabbed her arm, pulled her shrieking, struggling body from the Camaro, dragged her over to the Jag. This time he wasn't going to take no for an answer. This time they were going to go for that ride.

Smiling, Danny opened the door to the back seat.

DREAM ON ME

Mick Garris

*I*t's not my fault!" he said through the chill that dried his sweat.

"Of course it isn't your fault. It happens sometimes. I understand."

He was startled to look up into Martika's eyes as she cradled his head in her lap. He expected to see Linda, though he should have known better.

Martika, of course, didn't understand. This wasn't about detumescence defeating penetration. The blood that had pounded through his veins had stalled out, defusing any active organs. The passion had been sapped by Linda, who had invaded their lovemaking even from the grave.

He looked up, crushed by guilt and nausea, past Martika's breasts and into Linda's face. It was Martika who continued to speak, but Linda who stared. And Linda who understood . . . and tried to blame him.

But he was the Blameless Man. He couldn't bear the guilt, never had. Not only over Linda. Ever. He couldn't bear fault and was expert at rationalization that relinquished him from responsibility. He was unable to shoulder hurt feelings or pride, and unwilling to accept fault for pain.

Martika leaned over him, the brown nipple of one newly drooping breast brushing his cheek. "You're shivering. You cold?" She stroked his face, which broke out again in a chilly sweat. He wanted to open his mouth and nurse away the pain, let it draw out a lust that would overpower his memories with carnal bullets, to pull her legs open and part the red sea with his Moses.

But Linda sat on his shoulder.

He was back in the Mazda; Linda had insisted on driving the new car. Bob's Big Boy and a drive-in movie: Let's play teenager. He honestly didn't care. "Whatever you want" was the refrain. It had become a joke to him. He meant it; when it didn't matter, he said it: "whatever you want," even though he knew it made her defensive, as if she were a spoiled little princess being indulged, getting her way. He could tell that this night it pissed her off. They sped down Ventura as he hid in the movie section.

"What do *you* want to see?"

"Whatever you want . . ."

"Don't you have an opinion? Doesn't anything *matter* to you?"

But he didn't have time to answer. He saw the pipe truck before she did; his scream made her crush the brake pedal to the floor, and the car made a screaming doughnut before righting itself just in time to slam head-on into the flag-tipped pipes jutting out of the back of the truck.

Miraculously, they missed him; predictably, she had been impaled. The half-inch aluminum javelins made webs of the windshield and a pincushion of the bucket seats. She was spiked to her velour seat like a butterfly pinned to its velvet showcase, the anger still gripping her face. Her blood watered the asphalt through the feeding tube that pierced her heart, first in beating gushes, soon in a weakening, dribbling flow.

She was still looking at him, her eyes sightless but filled

with blame and fury, her hand a claw, digging into his thigh so hard that blood was drawn: his only injury from the accident.

And then . . .

"It's not my fault."

"I can't do this anymore. I'm not going to share you with a ghost."

He could see Martika with sudden clarity, as if the camera operator had suddenly racked focus. And what he saw shook him. She could see through him, see the deceit, the wicked core he'd gone to such lengths to keep secret under a hide of humanity. His heart of guilt was laid bare to her.

"I'm sorry," he said, feeling doubly naked as she watched with the lidless brown eyes that suddenly saw all. It was all he could say.

"So am I. If I'm going to be with you, I want to be *with* you. I mean, I know you don't want to hear this, but I love you, Andy. I really do care about you. But Linda is dead! Get her out of my bedroom!"

Or he'd lose her. As he'd lost them all since Linda.

Martika was the first who really mattered. Her sweetness was genuine, deeply rooted, not a ruse to be dropped when he'd been captured, only to be replaced by ball-snipping PMS madness. Her temperament was steady, intelligent, nurturing; she forgave easily, and without battle, and seldom considered the imagined hidden agenda. And she never sought out the hidden dark side; she seemed blissfully oblivious to shadows.

But now, allowing herself to look beyond the shell, she saw that he was agonized by Linda's spirit. He couldn't bear it if Linda pulled them apart. He had never told her, but he probably loved Martika even more than he had loved the dead one. And now she'd found him out. He couldn't let her leave him.

* * *

Martika watched him; he seemed so weak and vulnerable, hardly the man most people saw. He needed her so much, and—she had to admit—she needed him. But even as she held him, she felt his skin go clammy, and prickle into goosebumps. The conjoining of their flesh had been more than physically rewarding; she loved the feeling of being entered by his warmth as she wrapped him in a blanket of her arms and legs. They were a flesh sculpture, a Japanese puzzle box that only became two separate pieces when taken apart.

But it was not only fluids and a mutual heartbeat symphony that they shared. There was a level of sanity above and beyond the world outside. Their eyes locked during sex, the shared gaze broken only by the occasional blink. It was a silent communication that allowed them to see directly into one another's brains, to see the electrical impulses at work. It surprised them when one day they noticed they were both making the same sound when they made love: a Zen sort of hum that seemed to place them on clouds, looking down at the earth before they fell back to the planet.

Martika never wanted to notice the gradual change that crept into their love life. They still looked into one another's eyes, but she could see a vacuum forming behind his pupils. The connection was not being made. There was a distance she could sense . . . an obstruction. He was looking beyond and through her now. At someone else? At Linda?

It was his charm and strength and confidence that had first attracted her, and that dreaming thing, but now that she could sense something hidden, his weaknesses were becoming increasingly obvious. She knew about Linda, indeed had nursed him through recovery. But there were darker secrets within him, guilt and melancholy that were becoming increasingly difficult for him to hide and for her to ignore. She would do almost anything for him, but he had to do something for himself, too.

She couldn't carry his burden any longer. She didn't care

about a former lover; what in the world did she have to do with his life before they ever met? But she would not let their life together be spoiled by a third party. Even if it meant losing him.

More than anything, she wanted to feel him touch her, not only with his hands. She wanted their bodies to pretzel together, she needed the Vulcan mind-meld that happened on their best linkages. But, knowing it wasn't going to happen that way tonight, Martika knew she had to sleep alone. Without him. And, goddamn it, without *her*. Even if she is dead.

He lay on the couch, staring at the door, dreading the breach in his Good Guy Suit that Martika had at last detected. He couldn't sleep, not after Linda's visit and certainly not after he'd driven a wedge between himself and Martika. Well, *he* hadn't done it himself. It was Linda, really. Why wouldn't she just leave him the fuck alone? He couldn't let her push Martika away.

He just looked at the door, saw the little slice of light underneath go out, and remembered the feel of Martika against him.

It hurt Martika to sleep apart from him. Just knowing that he was on the other side of her closed door felt wrong, as if she were punishing a child for hurting himself. The bed felt too big, too empty, but she lay in it, knowing that she was right this time. She could only see clearly from a distance.

She looked at the door, could hear his even breathing. She knew what his breath felt like against her ear, his scent still lingering on her pillow. She was tired, worn out but wired. Her eyes flickered and the bed did a high-seas dance as she watched the closed door.

She pressed her thighs together, flexing the muscles, wishing her legs were wrapped around him. The area between remembered him and was wet. She wished they had finished, and she drew her legs up against her chest. She wasn't about to touch herself.

As the bed swam, the door opened, revealing his silhouette in a wedge of moonlight. She couldn't speak, though she felt she ought to turn him away. He stood strong and tall and naked. And he spoke.

"I really do love you, you know. And I don't want to fuck that up."

He came closer to the bed, kneeled on it. She wanted to say "not now," but her voice wouldn't work. She wanted to stop him because she knew she should, but she wanted him the way he was and the way they were.

"I need you, Martika."

He'd never said *that* before, though she'd craved hearing it.

And he lay behind her fetal ball, spooning from behind. He kissed her back, his hands strong, working their way in a walking massage that began at her neck and led to her ass. He followed his hands with his mouth and reached around to feel the front of her.

She was gratified that he didn't reach first for her breasts, as every man before him had. He caressed her face, her shoulders, her stomach, and by the time he discovered her goose-pimpling breasts, he found them wanting and pointed. He turned her onto her back and tasted her. She sat up in front of him, and he nursed.

She wished she had milk to feed him, but all she could give were body and soul. And they were his. He rolled her onto her back, grabbing her wrists and holding them tight against the bed, and she opened up to him, wrapped around him, and clenched him, rocking, in her vise as he took her. She rolled him over, taking control for the moment, thrusting him into her as deep as she could take it. They gave and took and gave and took, the overpowering becoming the overpowered, and met in the fabled Land of Climax with a heaving sigh.

And she dared open her eyes, knowing even before she saw that she was alone.

The bastard had dreamt all over her again.

He stared at the door, the puppet master of dreamland, hoping he'd made things right. He felt like Barbara Cartland or one of those gothic pulp novelists, creating breathy women's romances of seduction and submission, and the guilt bore on him. Martika deserved more than that. So he had let her get on top for a moment before being overcome. He knew what she liked by now, he hoped.

He waited on the couch for her invitation to return to the bed. The dreams always woke her up. He didn't wait long. The door opened, and she stood there in her chenille robe. That wasn't a good sign. He'd hoped to see her naked.

"You don't play fair."

He knew that. He would if he could . . . but he didn't know any other way. She stayed in the doorway, keeping her distance.

"It used to be that way for real, you know." Her tone was wistful, yet broken. Caved in. "A long time ago . . ."

"I want it to be that way again," he said. "It can be."

"I don't know. I'd like to think so. But when things start to slide, I don't know if they ever get better." And then, hopefully, because she wanted it, too: "Do they?"

"They can with us."

She took a deep breath, gathering the strength to say it, to take her position and stand her ground.

"Not as long as you keep Linda alive."

She expected a defensive reaction, but got silence instead. He was actually considering what she'd said. He looked so hurt that she wanted to hold his hand and apologize . . . but she realized she'd done nothing wrong.

"I know how hard it was; I know what you saw. But you're with me now. You say you love me; you used to show me."

He looked up and their eyes locked. "I'm sorry. I *do* love you. And I need you. More than anyone before. Linda is gone."

She wanted to believe him, saw new strength in his eyes. No, the old strength, the confidence. Now, if only he would come to her and show her he meant what he said.

He stood up and went to her, taking her in his arms. "I don't want to lose you."

He wouldn't.

They embraced, they went to bed, they made love, and the clouds behind his pupils parted. He was home.

In the afterglow, he refused to roll off and surrender to the sleep that dogged him. He could see she was watching him, almost dared to call her expression inscrutable, but she would have slapped him for it. Even though she'd have laughed afterward, she'd have meant it.

He tried to read her face. "What?"

"See? You didn't have to dream on me."

"I think maybe I did. This time."

He watched her consider that for a moment. "Please don't dream on me unless I ask for it. Okay?"

"Okay. I love you."

"Parrot fashion . . ."

She watched him fall asleep.

The defenses tumbled, and his youthful, unlined face cried innocence. He lost a good ten years as he slept, and every experience that lined his visage fled. He was newly minted in repose.

But now Martika was wide awake. Wasn't that always the way? He conked, she buzzed. It was hard not to resent it, but, of course, it wasn't *his* fault. She lay on her side and watched him sleep; his breathing was deep and even, with a light whistle through the hairs in his nostrils. He fell deep and quick. His eyes did a REM dance under their lids. His hand spasmed; he was dreaming.

She could only wonder what he dreamt. He swallowed, his hand clutched, jerked, scratched her, so she pulled away. His breathing came harder, and the breath deepened, soon dropping down into a trancelike hum, just like during the best times they made love . . . just like only half an hour ago.

She saw another spasm; a wet spot was growing on the sheet.

He was dreaming that they were making love. It made her smile. Maybe things would get back to where they were . . . where they should be. Maybe they would be okay.

Suddenly his eyes snapped open.

"Linda?"

The fantasy crashed to earth, plummeted to hell.

"No! Not Linda! Martika! Say it! Martika! Remember me?"

Even as she screamed at him she knew she was being irrational, knew that he couldn't control his dreams . . . only hers.

But she just . . .

Couldn't.

Take.

Any.

More.

Linda!

He saw her clearly, and his eyes shone with regret. "I'm sorry. It wasn't—"

"I know it wasn't your fault! It's my fault!"

"It's nobody's fucking fault!"

She knew that. But she wanted him gone. She needed to be alone. She sent him home . . . to a hollow shoe-box apartment he visited only occasionally to pick up his mail.

* * *

He walked through cobalt moonlight. He wasn't sorry he'd run the dream thing. It was the only way to restring the broken web of their faltering relationship. But he didn't dare tell her he'd learned it from Linda. Martika wasn't jealous of Linda, not really, but she'd certainly feel like a third-generation lover knowing he'd used Linda's stuff on her.

He'd tried it professionally for a while, actually made some money manipulating people's dreams. But he could see little future in sitting in the homes of the lonely, the depressed, and the depressing, watching them sleep and giving them their own James Bond and Marilyn Chambers fantasies. He grew to resent them and didn't want to get as close to these strangers as he needed to be to dream on them. And even though it was only fantasy, he didn't want to share in their sex. He'd certainly had his fill of watching soft-bellied mommy's boys sleepwalking as they Errol Flynned around cheap apartments and squirted in their slumber.

He wanted to teach Martika to power dream, but she didn't possess the guile and cynical bitterness it seemed to require to reach the plateau. Not that it was ever a problem for Linda; she specialized in cat-claw resentment. He was glad that was beyond Martika.

Linda's beauty was in her imagination. The dreams they shared traveled the universe, and their waking hours seemed mundane by contrast. They were far happier in the controlled world of sleep than they were when the fantasies ended. How could real life ever compete?

But she sure knew how to dream on him.

Martika felt guilty. She'd turned him away, even after he'd told her he'd loved her, needed her, cared most of all for her. But, goddamn it, if he loved her, why did he dream about *her?*

She'd never get to sleep that night. Not without help. She gulped down two dry Xanax and turned on the TV. She stared at the screen for several minutes before realizing she was illuminated by ceramic dogs marked down to three payments of $14.65 on the Home Shopping Channel.

An electric current pulled her attention to the curtains; she rose, reeling as she stood, the Xanax marching to her brain, and pulled the gingham open. Andy was on the street below, and their eyes connected for the briefest of moments before he turned away in shame and she let the curtain fall closed.

Her face heated as the sedative stirred her mind of molasses with anger and confusion. She had to sit down . . . lie down . . . let him go . . . just let him walk away . . . just stop the bed from spinning, stop the laughter from the closets . . . and just hitchhike to dreamland. Martika wound down like a grandfather clock. Nobody pulled the chain, and she sunk deeply into sleep.

Andy finally stopped walking, surprised to find himself standing—once again—before Linda's grave. Why the surprise? A little metal plaque in the sod with her name on it: That was Linda. The sight of her resting place, her name coldly inscribed, made him shiver. Now, as he stood before Linda his mind—a fickle gray muscle—turned to Martika. Martika loved him as he loved her; Linda only wanted somebody to take responsibility and blame. The dreams were almost worth it; her temper and her death were not.

He suddenly felt depleted, exhausted. He needed to lie down on the grass and let his whirling brain slow down. The earth rocked and reeled under him as he stared up at the sliver of moon peeking through the clouds. The moon was shaped like Martika's face . . . but it had Linda's expression.

Martika's hands clutched in her sleep, her face darkened, troubled. Her closed eyes danced in drugged REMerobics.

* * *

143

He'd closed his eyes in the cemetery, and he opened them in bed. With Martika. The Woman in the Moon. He saw her clearly, unfiltered, and found her irresistibly beautiful. Her skin was an even bronze, her black hair cut blunt and glossy, her crescent eyes an even and piercing brown as they opened up to him. Her face gave its apology, and he climbed on top of her, needing to press the full length of his body against her skin.

They met with cool fire: night skin burning hot a couple layers lower. He tried to enter her without hands, but was unable. To his surprise, his groin ended in a thatch of soft hair. There was no divining rod to join them.

But another body pressed against him from behind. He didn't need to look over his shoulder: The pressure of the tiny breasts that were all erect nipple gave Linda away at the first zap of their electric contact. He looked over his back anyway, when he felt her enter him with his penis.

He tried to fight her off, but she was intent on impaling him as she'd been impaled, hoping to draw blood as she'd spilled it to the highway pavement. He felt his flesh tear and tried to throw her off. He screamed like a girl until Linda used him up and rolled him off the bed and onto the floor.

Not finished, Linda dropped onto Martika and entered her, too. The dark-haired one gasped as she took the full length of his penis from Linda, bucking it deeper, not wanting to like it as much as she had to. And the room spun into darkness, with laughing voices coming from under the bed fading into her ears.

The alarm made Martika's heart club her awake the next morning. She was hung over from the drug, and her eyes felt swollen and sandy. At first she was surprised to be alone in bed, but it didn't take long to reach a high enough state of consciousness to remember the events of the preceding night.

Another dance with Dr. Guilt. How could she have

treated him that way? He'd been through some heavy times;
the guy had watched the woman he loved die, hadn't he?
Would she deny him his feelings? She felt selfish and
shrewish, and she wanted him in her bed with her more than
anything, to hold and rock and caress and nurture and help.
She was so, so sorry.

She grabbed the phone and called. And got the machine.
And didn't leave a message. And called again, and did leave
a message.

When she stood up, she almost toppled over again. She
needed some coffee, at least. The night before the morning
after had ripped her up and spit her out. She had to sort it
out; she'd make it up to both of them.

He was waiting for her in the living room, and her heart
leapt at the sight of him. Until he didn't move.

"Andy?"

His naked body was huddled in front of the fireplace . . .
motionless . . . cold . . . dead. She ran to kneel in front of
him, and her knee skidded across the gelatinous curdling
puddle of his midnight blood. He was impaled on one of the
andirons . . . a cold satay, skewered from behind, basted in
his own blood. Horrified, she slid back against the wall,
urging down her bile as she remembered the night's events
. . . the fight, the Xanax, the hurt and anger . . .

And the Dream.

Her Dream.

Her taste of the Power.

"I don't want it!" she screamed. "No more fucking
dreams!"

DeVICE

Stephen Gallagher

I wouldn't blame you if you didn't want to hear this. I mean, it *is* pretty disgusting.

But I was sitting there in the corner of Flanagan's bar on Christmas Eve, on my own and starting to realize that I wasn't going to be meeting up with anyone that I knew after all, when this expensive coat with a bony old guy rattling around in it—he must have been at least seventy, and he was as white and frail as a scrap of rice paper—sat down across from me and, without even a hello or an introduction, said, "How would you like to make a thousand dollars for one night's work?"

I sighed and looked around the place. Christmas Eve seemed to be losers' night at Flanagan's; I mean, let's face it, nobody was going to be here if they had somewhere real to go.

And I said, "Thanks, but I don't do that kind of thing."

My friend Colin, *he* used to do that kind of thing. Colin was the one who told me the story about how he'd gone from this very bar to the hotel room of a visiting Japanese businessman, where for once all that he'd had to do had been to lie there without the guy even laying a finger on him. Apparently the man had used chopsticks. *A wank,* Colin would say, *is just too coarse a word for it.* I used to like Colin but we don't see much of him around, anymore. These days he spends a lot of his time checking for skin blemishes in a magnifying mirror and wondering if he'll ever be able to get up the nerve to go for a blood test.

But this big-money Methuselah said, "You don't understand," and, with the air of a man satisfied that he'd at last found the one he'd been looking for, he started to unbutton his coat. My heart sank, the way that it does when you open the door and realize that it's somebody who wants to talk about your salvation and you just lost the option of hiding behind the furniture until he goes away.

"I'm sorry," I said, "but I'm really not interested."

"A thousand before and a thousand on completion," he said. "And I'll guarantee that it'll involve nothing that affects you in any direct or personal way."

"And it doesn't involve chopsticks?" I said suspiciously, but he didn't understand.

Listen, I've got my pride.

But Christmas Eve is no time to be broke.

We went out to his car. It was a big Mercedes, and it had a driver in a uniform. The driver didn't even look at me as I got in. I sat there uneasily. The old man sat alongside, dropping back gratefully into the upholstery as if the evening so far had been something of a physical ordeal for him. Our arrangement was that I was going to hear him out, look the job over and then, if I didn't like the setup, I could walk and I'd still have five hundred for my trouble. It was all so painless, I hardly realized I was being carried along with it until I looked back and saw the Flanagan's neon disappearing into the night.

There was rain on the car's window. I was spending my Christmas Eve sitting in a strange car on my way to hear about a job which I just *knew* was going to be something dubious, at best. It made me feel pretty low.

But the thought of the money made me feel a little better.

He had a big house on the hill above town, with a big wall around it and gates on the driveway that opened at a signal. I looked back and saw them closing again behind us and the man said, "I can see you're nervous. But please don't be." And I tried to look as if I wasn't.

I mean, you hear things. I reckon I can take care of myself, but that driver—he looked as if he wouldn't have seemed out of place in a bloodstained apron with a beef carcass under each arm. And who could say what else was going to be waiting on the other side of that big door under a vast stone portico where only a single light burned?

We went up the steps. The car headed off around behind the house somewhere. The door was open before we reached it. The old guy held back and gestured me in, smiling, like I was some honored guest instead of a hireling that he'd picked up in a dive. There was a maid waiting in the hallway, and she offered to take my jacket, but I kept it on. She wore a uniform, too. One of those with a little hat and an apron. It might have been quite sexy if she hadn't been almost the same age as her employer. She didn't seem at all surprised to see me.

"Please," the old man said. "Follow Elspeth up to the library. Make yourself comfortable. I'll join you in just a few moments."

The library? I was moving up in the world. Most of the time I tended to reckon that I was in a cultured household if there was a book in it somewhere, even if it was only holding up a table leg. But this place didn't just have books, it had a *library*.

And it looked like one, too. It was all polished wood and red velvet and deep leather chairs with buttons on them. The books lined every wall and even went across the top of the door, and there wasn't a paperback among them. The maid asked me if I wanted anything to drink, and I said I'd like a beer, and she brought it to me a few minutes later on a silver tray with what I guessed had to be a crystal glass. After that she withdrew and left me alone. The old boy seemed loaded, all right.

But given that I'd told him how I was nobody's idea of rough trade, I still couldn't guess what he might need from little old me.

Nothing happened for a while and so I went over to look at the shelves. Most of the titles were foreign; I recognized some German, but most of the others I didn't recognize at all. I took one down and flicked through the pages. It was a picture book.

But, the *pictures* . . .

I mean, I thought I'd been around. But as soon as I saw the one with the donkey I realized that I hadn't—at least, not as much as some of *these* people, and it was no great matter for regret. Just to give you an example, there was this woman and this man and they were . . . well, I've got my own idea of what constitutes a hot lunch, and that isn't it.

I never heard him coming in. When he cleared his throat, I slammed the book shut and I could feel my face burning redder than a desert sunset. As I fumbled it back into its place on the shelf, he was smiling. His eyes were a very pale blue, the palest blue I've ever seen. His weariness seemed to have vanished, and I wondered if he'd been off to take a shot of something. I think he might have been wearing makeup, just a hint. I didn't want to get close enough to be sure.

"My collection," he said. "I can see you've been getting acquainted with it."

"Strictly as an outsider," I said. "I'm not into that kind of stuff."

"Don't worry," he said. "Don't worry. All I'm proposing for you is a half-hour's wait around followed by a cab ride. For that, and for that alone, you get the two thousand."

"You've got a houseful of servants here. You've got a big car and a driver of your own. So what makes *my* time worth so much to you?"

"Come along," he said, "and I'll show you."

We went out of the library and up to the attic, with him leading the way. It seemed like a little-used part of the house; the carpeting on the stairs wasn't cheap, but it was old and dusty, and the walls were spotted with mildew. The attic door was double-padlocked, and it took him a few moments to undo the locks and get the door open.

The first room was nothing special—just a bare floor and boxes and a naked bulb and another door. There was a padlock on this one, too, even bigger than the previous two.

I swallowed hard, wondering what was I about to see.

We went in. Again there was a single unshaded bulb, again nothing to cover the unvarnished boards, but the mess and the bric-a-brac were missing. Instead, standing in the middle of the floor, where the ceiling was highest, was the most peculiar-looking device that I've ever seen.

How to describe it? Well, think of the Time Machine in the old Rod Taylor movie. Then cross it with one of those pieces of apparatus that they use to train astronauts, kind of like a big gyroscope, where they strap them into the middle and then spin them in two or three different directions all at once to simulate weightlessness, and then add lots of leather straps and strange pieces of knotted rope and a toilet seat and an elephant's tusk and a folding music stand, and you'll probably have a mental picture of what it was like. It had springs, it had levers. From the state of the brasswork and the well-preserved leather, I'd have guessed that it was some kind of an antique.

"You're looking at a true collector's piece," the old guy said to me. "Made in Italy by Vicenzo di Amalfi in 1875. Restored in Edinburgh by Robert Cotton sometime around 1932. Three previous owners ruined themselves just to have their hands on it for a little while. I picked it up more than twenty years ago from an estate that didn't know its actual value. There have never been more than half a dozen like it in the world, and this is the finest. You might call it a Stradivarius of pleasure devices."

A pleasure device? I looked again.

That knotted rope hung at head-height, and the knots were roughly where the user's eyes would be. The elephant's tusk was engraved with minute calibrations, and it appeared to be on a spring-driven arm. Its pointed tip was just below the opening of the toilet seat, which was equipped with a lap strap.

My idea of pleasure was a can of cold beer and a Clint Eastwood movie on the VCR, preferably in the company of Cheryl the Nurse from the apartment downstairs. She wasn't really a nurse, but if you could catch her in the right mood she'd sometimes dress up as one for you. This machine appeared to have been designed for torture rather than turn-on.

"You ever actually use this thing?" I said.

"Not yet," he said.

"Thanks for the drink, I'm out of here."

But he smiled to show that he wasn't taking me too seriously.

He carefully locked all of the doors behind us and, as we made our way down, he explained something of the background.

He was eighty-three years old (I'd thought he was a wasted-looking seventy; I suppose that for eighty-three, he didn't look so bad). He had inherited a ton of wealth originally made on the railways, had never done a stroke of work in his life, had never married and had no heir. He had one sister, whose family despised and disowned him and had a good chance of getting their hands on everything when he died.

"Leave it to a cats' home," I suggested.

"I wish it were that simple," he said. "And, besides, I can't abide cats."

We went back into the library.

The family rift, he told me, all dated back to the embarrassment of a court case and a brief period of imprisonment back in the early fifties. "But I've lived a blameless life for the past twenty-five years," he insisted. "I was something of a libertine, I admit . . ."

"A what?"

"A libertine. I existed for pleasure, all kinds of pleasure. As each was sated, the next became more extreme. Some people live out their lifetimes on their yearnings; I could afford to satisfy mine like *that*"—he snapped his fingers— "and then immediately look beyond. I was a libido with a bottomless bank account, and I was unstoppable."

He sat down in one of the big leather chairs.

"But look at me now," he said. I looked at him. He was old, but he was no Father Christmas. "You can only recharge a battery so many times. Mine died somewhere around 1965."

"What you're basically telling me," I said, "is that you can't get it up anymore."

And it was his turn to color up a little and look away.

I said, "But it hasn't bothered you in twenty-five years."

He shook his head.

"So why the sudden need?"

And it was then that he told me about the arrangements he'd been making.

And *I* sat down, because this was getting interesting.

The terms of his inheritance had been complicated. The essence was that it was family money and would ever remain so; he could spend all the interest, but the capital was out of his reach. On his death, the river of loot simply diverted to the next family member in succession.

And of course, he had no heir.

This, I suppose, should hardly have been a surprise in the case of someone who'd probably squandered his entire sex life on a succession of circus animals, French loaves, little boys, and various items of gardening equipment. But having seen how reproductive technology had come along in the past few years, he'd made plans. He'd fixed it all up with his lawyers, he'd hired a surrogate mother, and he had one of the most expensive and discreet clinics in town lined up and waiting; they'd handle all the test-tube stuff, and the member of his sister's family would probably chew one another's legs off with the frustration of it all when this infant appeared out of nowhere with the ability to sail through any legal or genetic test that could be put in its way.

There was only this one small obstacle. The clinic, he'd been assuming, would be geared up to handle every small technical detail; but there was one aspect on which his entire plan depended and around which it threatened to fall apart. It was a small matter of a private cubicle and an empty bottle and the clinic's well-thumbed copy of *Penthouse*.

And from the old battery, not a flicker.

So he'd dug out the device, the ultimate pleasure contraption of another age, and he'd dusted it down and made it ready to perform. If this didn't do it, he reckoned, nothing ever could. He'd been psyching himself up, and he believed that he was nearly ready; all that he needed now was someone who could stick around in case there were any problems and who would then be a dependable courier.

"And you can't send one of the servants?" I said.

"Oh, no," he said, and he seemed shocked at the very idea. "Oh, *no*."

I told him I wanted to think about it and asked if I could have the five hundred now. He said he'd have his man drive me home and I'd be handed the cash when I got there.

Which is exactly what happened.

There seemed to be nobody else around but me. I knocked on Cheryl the Nurse's door, but she wasn't home. Then I went upstairs and sat in my own place and fiddled around with the wire coat hanger that I've had to use to get a TV signal ever since the antenna broke, but it wouldn't come right. I looked at the mess on the screen and thought, Well, at least you're seeing *some* kind of snow this Christmas.

And then I went out to the pay phone in the hallway and called the number that the old guy had given me.

"I'll do it," I said.

I had to meet him out at the clinic on the next working day, mainly so that I'd know where it was and to give the staff a chance to get a look at me, since they were the ones who'd be releasing the second half of my money across the counter on receipt of what everybody was coyly calling "the material." It was an expensive-looking place that stood in its own grounds, and there wasn't a single sign anywhere to tell you what it was or what they did there. The reception-area nurses all looked like catwalk models, with outfits to match. They were polite to me and called me "sir."

I didn't kid myself.

The big night came two days later, the one before New Years' Eve. The pay phone rang, and when I got out there and picked it up, I heard him say, "I'd like you to come over as soon as you can, please," and under the politeness I could hear a kind of controlled tension in his voice that told me, Yep, tonight was going to be the night we launched the Shuttle.

The entrance gates were open. I stood under the portico and rang the bell. The old man's driver opened it—only now he was out of uniform and wearing an overcoat, and I supposed that he'd only been waiting for my arrival before he could leave. As I went in through the door, he went out and closed it behind him. We exchanged a nod and I was about to speak, but by then he'd already gone.

I stood alone in the entrance hall. I seemed to sense a great emptiness in the house. "Hello?" I said uncertainly, and I could hear the echo.

"Thank you for coming," the old man said, and, reacting

to the sound of his voice, I looked up. He was upstairs and looking down over the rail. He was wearing a long white bathrobe and carpet slippers. His legs were skinny and were veined like marble.

"Please," he said, "please, come on up."

I went up the stairs. My heart was hammering. I can't explain it, but I was unaccountably nervous. I mean, I wasn't going to be doing anything much, and certainly nothing extraordinary; this was going to be the easiest money I'd ever made.

We went on up to the attic. All the padlocks were off, and the door between the two rooms stood open. Someone had cleared a space in the junk and placed an armchair in the outer room, with a small table and a few magazines alongside. Through the doorway, I could see the device.

It waited.

"First I want to run one final test, and then I'll have to ask for your help in getting aboard," the old man said apologetically. "I'd thought that I could manage on my own, but I find that I can't. After that, you can go outside and close the door and amuse yourself until it's over. I'll call you then."

I stood back and watched while he fiddled around. The device looked like the world's kinkiest piece of gym equipment. Or the world's most sadistic birdcage. After a moment it started to move, and the old man stepped back.

Clockwork. It all ran by clockwork. I could hear the whirring and the clicking and the spinning of escapements as the entire structure-within-the-structure began slowly to rotate. It was awesome, in its way: strangely cruel, strangely beautiful. When the central part was fully inverted, everything locked into place and a new phase of the mechanism began to operate. The elephant's tusk was now raised above the saddle like death's scythe on a cathedral clock tower, and as I watched, it began to bear down on its levered arm.

Jesus, I thought. *No.*

But it stopped. It stopped with its silvered tip protruding

no more than an inch through the gap in the saddle, and there it began to oscillate gently.

I wanted to snort. And without thinking about it, I looked at the old man to share the joke.

But then our eyes met, and I stopped myself. Because I don't think I've ever seen anyone looking so utterly vulnerable; not before, and never since. His eyes seemed to be pleading with me.

So I said nothing.

The machine reset itself smoothly. The old man dropped his bathrobe self-consciously and stepped forward. I have to say that I've seen more meat on an X-ray. I held his elbows and helped him up, and that was the only contact we had. I noticed that there had been a couple of changes since I'd last seen the device. There was a magazine on the music stand, its pages pinned so that it couldn't fall off. It was an old movie fan magazine and it was open at a picture of Joan Crawford in a bathing suit. The other addition consisted of a small clear plastic bottle that hung empty on some buckle-on webbing. This, I had to assume, was the collection point. There was a drop of something swilling around in there already, maybe some preservative or anti-congealant. I had some gloves and a supermarket carrier bag folded up in my pocket; no way did I want to have any closer contact with that stuff than I had to, and I didn't even want to have to look at it.

"Thank you," he said. "I can handle it from here."

"Are you sure?" I said, not knowing how I'd respond if he were to ask me for anything more.

"I'm sure," he said. "I'll call you when it's done."

So I left him there, hooking himself up and strapping himself in, and went through to the other room and closed the door behind me.

I don't know how much time went by. Half an hour, maybe. No more than that. I sat in the chair and I tried to look through some of the magazines, but I couldn't concentrate. I felt disturbed. You come across something like this and, whether you want to or not, you find yourself taking a hard look at what makes you tick. I could sit there and honestly swear that there was nothing about this whole business that connected with me; not the pleasure device, not the books in the library, none of it. And yet . . .

And yet I still found myself fascinated, unable to look away. That has to mean something.

Doesn't it?

I heard him calling, weakly.

I hesitated for a moment, and then I stood, dropping the magazine, and went over to the door. I could hear him coughing on the other side. I went through.

The central part of the device was still in its inverted position. He was hanging upside down in the straps like a stranded hang glider. The knotted rope was across his eyes like a blindfold, which meant that he could no longer see the magazine or anything else. It was a comical sight. But I could feel only pity.

And then he coughed again and sprayed blood everywhere.

I ran to the machine and tried to find some kind of a release lever on the panel; I don't know what I did, but after a few seconds it all came back to life, and the entire inner cage began to swing back around. He coughed again, and the blood came out in a bright red foam.

The whole thing locked back into its original position; he whimpered at the slight jarring but otherwise made no sound. Something was different here, but I couldn't work out what it was.

And then I realized that the elephant's tusk was missing. The lever mechanism was there, back in its original position, but the calibrated ivory wasn't.

Stupidly, I looked around on the floor to see where it had fallen; as if it was something that you wouldn't notice if you didn't look twice. There was nothing on the floor but dust and footprints, and the old man's slippers lined up exactly where he'd left them.

And blood on the floorboards. The kind of blood splashes that you get under hanged meat.

And I thought with dismay, as I realized that this was no accident but the way that he'd actually planned it, What, the *entire tusk?*

"Did everything work?" he gasped, and I knew without a doubt that I had a dying man on my hands, here.

"Seems there were one or two things you didn't warn me about," I said.

"I know," he said, "I'm sorry, I'm sorry. I've left letters, you'll be in the clear. But you've got to tell me. Is the material safe?"

I gave it a long pause before I spoke. He turned his head from side to side, like a blind man searching an empty room for reassurance.

And then I said, "I'm sorry. But you completely missed the bottle."

His face crumpled in despair.

"No," he said. "No."

And then he coughed up a couple more pints of his own lifeblood, spraying it all about like a lawn sprinkler first thing on a spring morning so that I had to dodge back or get spattered, and died.

I've no conscience about it. Not even though it had meant that I'd sent him on into the Great Beyond in the most acute state of misery imaginable; in the knowledge that all of the pain and the self-sacrifice were for nothing, and that his last act had been rendered essentially meaningless by what he'd think was a stupid miscalculation.

He hadn't missed the bottle, of course. I left him there for the servants to find and delivered the material to the clinic as we'd agreed. I completed the deal and I picked up the money. As far as I know, everything should have worked out and his relatives ought to be screaming and banging their heads on the walls about now.

But I see no reason to feel guilty at all.

I mean, come on, the man was a masochist.

So far as I could imagine, it had seemed like the kindest thing I could do.

THE BEST

Paul Dale Anderson

Both of us?" He gasped. "Both . . . at the same time?"

She was already unbuttoning her blouse. "I need to be *filled*," she said, and there was a longing in her voice that seemed irresistible.

She slid out of the blouse and let it drop to the floor. She reached around and unhooked her brassiere. "I feel so *empty*," she moaned. "I need to be *filled*. Fill me, please!"

Gordon glanced nervously at the other man. Was it more than homophobia that edged into his consciousness and made him afraid? Was there something else, too?

Something he didn't want to think about?

"My fantasy," she explained, as she stepped out of an ankle-length wool skirt, "is to have two men inside me. One man is never enough."

She slid panty hose down both legs and stood naked, fully exposed.

She spread her legs and opened her sex.

Two slim fingers disappeared inside.

While two fingers of her left hand toyed with a pointy nipple.

"Indulge my fantasies, and I'll indulge yours," she promised, her voice husky, practically dripping with dew.

"Hell, why not?" the other man said, unzipping his fly. "I'm game."

"What about you?" the girl asked Gordon. "Or aren't you man enough?"

That was the trigger. Gordon shot out of his seat and grabbed the girl's hips, throwing her roughly to the floor, falling atop her, mauling her flesh, slapping her face. He hurriedly fumbled with the front of his pants, got them open somehow, and thrust his rage at her center.

The other man pulled him off.

"I don't like sloppy seconds," he spat at Gordon. "Go play with yourself in the corner while I check her oil, pump the tank full of no-lead premium, and recharge her batteries. You can have what's left as soon as I'm finished."

"Both of you," moaned the girl. "One isn't enough."

The man shoved his dipstick at her wide-open mouth. "Suck it," he demanded. "Prime the pump and see how big it gets. You don't need anyone else."

"No!" Gordon protested as the man's engorged muscle disappeared—one inch at a time—into the damp darkness between her luscious lips.

"Why don't you get lost?" the other man suggested. "Can't you see we're busy?"

Something snapped inside Gordon's head, then, and suddenly he had to prove himself. He had to prove he was bigger and better, not just better than the man she had in her mouth at the moment—but better than any of the other men she had ever had.

Better than them all.

He had to prove that Gordon Sommers was the best.

Nothing else mattered.

Homicide Lieutenant Ralph Bergstrom shook his head sadly. He'd seen it happen before, hadn't he? And he knew he'd see it a thousand times again between now and the day he retired.

"Why'd you do it?" he asked Sommers. "Jealousy?"

"Not jealousy." Gordon sobbed. "It was something else."

"What?"

"You wouldn't understand."

"Try me."

Gordon Sommers said nothing.

"Okay. Start at the beginning. Where'd you meet this broad?"

"Not a broad, Lieutenant. A *lady*."

"All right. She was a lady. Where'd you meet her?"

"At the track."

"The race track?"

"Yeah. I'd just placed a big bet at the two-dollar window. I turned around and there she was—the most beautiful woman I've ever seen."

"Describe her."

"Every man's fantasy come true—big breasts, nice ass, long blond hair, everything you could want in a woman. And she had this look about her that said she was all primed and raring to go."

"Primed?"

"You know. Ready to fuck. Right there in front of God and everybody."

"She looked like a prostitute?"

"No, no. Far from it. Dressed conservatively in an expensive-looking white blouse and ankle-length skirt. She didn't want money. She'd won odds on the last race and she had a roll of two-dollar bills in her hand big enough to choke a horse. Money was the farthest thing from her mind. What she wanted was *sex*. Pure, unadulterated *S-E-X*. You could tell just by looking at her. She radiated this sense of desperate urgency—a kind of combined look and smell—that said she needed a man in the worst way."

"And you were that man?"

"I thought so. She caught me staring at her and licked her lips—you know, slowly and seductively: sliding the tip of

163

her tongue around those luscious lips until I thought I'd cream in my pants."

"So you propositioned her?"

"No, no. She propositioned *me!* She swiveled her hips over next to me and whispered in my ear. 'I bet you want to fuck me, don't you?' she said. 'I want to fuck you, too.'"

"And that's when you gave her the key to your hotel room?"

"Yeah. I knew I could get another key at the front desk."

"What about the victim?"

"Another guy she met at the track. I don't even know his name. She didn't know his name, either."

"Go on."

"She brought him with her. Said she wanted to fuck both of us at the same time. I thought she was kidding, at first. But she wasn't."

"She wanted to get it on with both of you?"

"Yeah. She said one man wasn't enough."

The cop grimaced. How many times had he heard this same story repeated by perps? A hundred times? A thousand?

When would the nightmare end?

Lieutenant Bergstrom stopped by the bar around the corner from the station. He needed a drink—desperately. Hell, he didn't need just a drink. He needed a whole damned bottle.

"Heard you had another one tonight," Earl Danzig said, sidling up to the stool next to Ralph's and signaling the bartender for a Scotch. "Same MO?"

"The same," Bergstrom confirmed.

"Still no leads?"

"None."

"Christ," Danzig said, taking a sip of his fresh Scotch. "What kind of woman is she? Some sort of siren out of Greek mythology? I still can't believe she's real."

"She's real, all right," Ralph said.

"I don't know. Those guys might have made her up."

"All of them?"

"Maybe some kind of mass psychosis. Isn't that what lawyers say when they cop insanity pleas for perps?"

"Look, Earl, I don't want to talk about it. I came here to have a drink and forget."

"Well, if she's real, I'd sure like to meet her. Sounds like every man's wet dream, doesn't she?"

"Shut up, Earl. Shut your fat face."

"Hey. Don't get sore, Ralph. I know you just got married. But that doesn't mean you can't have wet dreams like the rest of us poor slobs. Does it?"

Bergstrom picked up his drink and moved to the other end of the bar—as far away from Danzig as he could get.

Danzig ordered another Scotch. And followed.

"Just think about it, Ralph," Danzig continued, almost drooling. "Here's this gorgeous blonde, built like a brick outhouse, and everyone says she fucks like a mink—never gets enough, always wants more. Don't tell me you wouldn't take a piece of that if you had a chance."

"Get out of my face, Earl. I'm too tired to think about it."

"You getting old, Ralph? That new wife of yours wearing you out? If you can't handle it, old man, just say the word. I'd be willing to help you out in the sack . . ."

Ralph's fist flew straight for Earl's face. Earl blocked the blow and countered with a quick kick to Ralph's groin.

"Break it up!" the bartender yelled, rushing from behind the bar with a baseball bat in his hands. "Take it outside if you have a score to settle."

"'S awright," Ralph gasped. "Fight's . . . over."

"What the fuck got into you?" Earl demanded. "Can't even take a joke anymore, can you? Jesus Christ, Bergstrom. Maybe you are getting old. You okay?"

"Wind . . . knocked . . . out."

"Didn't bust your nuts, did I?"

"Hurts . . ."

"C'mon. I'll take you to the hospital."

"No . . . hospital."

"Look, Ralph, I'm sorry. I saw your fist coming at me and I overreacted. Let me give you a ride home, at least. You don't look in any condition to drive, and it's all my fault."

"Forget . . . it."

"No. If I can't take you to a hospital, then I'm driving you home."

"Won't . . . let . . . you . . ."

Earl laughed. "Think you can stop me?"

Before Ralph could protest again, Earl bent his back and snatched the injured man up in a fireman's carry.

And headed out the door.

"We used to be best friends," Earl said as he drove. "We were partners for four whole years, back when you worked the burglary division. Then you got promoted, transferred to homicide, and now we're like strangers, trying to kill each other in a barroom brawl. What the hell happened, Ralph? What changed you?"

Ralph didn't answer.

"You used to be a real card, you know that? Life of the party. Real skirt chaser, too. Suddenly you turned serious. And now you can't even take a good-natured ribbing."

"Getting old," Ralph mumbled. "Slowing down."

"No, you're not. I just called you old to get your goat, make you react. I shouldn't have done that, Ralph. I'm sorry."

"Forget it."

"I guess I was sore that you got married and didn't ask me to be best man. Hell, you didn't even invite me to the goddamned wedding. Come to think of it, you've never introduced me to that new wife of yours, have you?"

"No."

"Least you could do is tell me her name."

"Helen," Ralph said.

"I hear she's a lot younger than you. That true?"

"No. Actually, she's older."

"Real looker, though. Right?"

"Right."

"So. You gonna introduce us?" Earl pulled into the driveway and parked next to Ralph's back door. "Gonna invite me in for a beer and satisfy my curiosity?"

"Some other time," Ralph said. He opened the passenger door and got out.

And fell flat on his face.

"Jesus Christ! You okay?"

Ralph retched and copious vomit spewed through his clenched teeth.

Earl left the car and walked to where Ralph lay on the lawn.

"Delayed reaction to a kick in the gut," Earl said knowingly. "You won't be able to walk right for a week."

Suddenly the porch light came on and the back door opened. "Ralph?" a woman's voice called from the house. "That you?"

Ralph tried to answer, but bile still clogged his throat and made his body convulse with dry heaves.

"It's all right, Mrs. Bergstrom," Earl said. "I'm Sergeant Danzig. Ralph isn't feeling well. If you hold the door open for us, I'll help get him inside."

Ralph tried to resist, but Earl—two inches taller, fifty pounds heavier, and five years younger—managed to lift him and move his struggling body toward the door. In the eerie glow from a mercury vapor porchlight, Ralph's face looked pale, drained of blood. Spittle clung to the stub of five o'clock shadow that dotted his chin.

Then they were inside the house and moving into the bedroom. Earl heard Mrs. Bergstrom's footsteps two steps behind his own.

"What happened?" she asked.

Earl laid the resisting Ralph down on a king-size water bed. "Nothing serious," he said. "We were practicing hand-to-hand combat and Ralph got hit in the gut by accident. He'll recover in a day or two."

She said something he didn't catch. So he turned around to face her.

And then Earl saw her for the first time.

Oh.

God.

She was *gorgeous*.

Wearing a black-silk kimono that barely hid her voluptuous body from his prying eyes, she was the sexiest thing he'd ever seen in his entire life. Twin mounds pushed seductively against their silk sheath, and the thin material curved delicately around shapely hips and buttocks like a second skin. Ending—rather abruptly, he noticed—midway down milky-white, smooth-as-silk thighs. Since she was standing directly in front of the room's only lit lamp, the bright light was filtered through her thin kimono from behind, clearly outlining the precise juncture of legs and . . .

Obviously, she wasn't wearing underwear. Earl thought he could count pubic hairs, if he felt like trying.

He felt like trying, all right. But he didn't dare.

"I'm Helen," she said, subtly shifting her weight so Earl could get a better look. "Like what you see?"

Earl attempted to swallow, but his throat was far too dry. His tongue wouldn't work either, and his voice got lost as his heavy breathing accelerated to a fevered pitch.

He could hear his heart pounding in his head.

"Want to see more?" she asked, fingering the belt at her waist.

He licked his lips.

Is the Pope Polish? he wanted to say.

She slid the kimono from her shoulders and let it drop silently to the floor by her feet. Her nipples stuck straight out like twin spikes aimed at Earl's eyes.

"Helen," Ralph's voice croaked from the bed. "Don't . . ."

"I want you," she whispered. "I want you to fu—"

"Helen!" Ralph said again, louder. "You promised."

"I can't help it," she sighed. "I need . . ."

"I know what you did today," Ralph said, his voice strained. "You went out again, didn't you?"

"Yes. I went to the track."

"I *know*, goddammit. I know where you went. I saw what happened."

"It just . . . happened," she said. "I got carried away."

"And now," Ralph said, "you want more, don't you? When will it stop?"

"I'm never satisfied," she said. "Can I help it if I'm never satisfied?"

"Fight it, Helen. Fight the urge. You can do it. I know you can."

"I can't."

"Earl, listen to me. You must leave here. Now. Get away. Go home. Go to a bar. I don't care where you go, just get the hell outta here. . . ."

"Earl doesn't want to leave," Helen said, licking her lips. "Do you, Earl?"

Earl shook his head.

"Helen's on fire," she whispered in Earl's ear. "Touch my pussy. Feel how hot I am."

Earl did.

Ralph closed his eyes. He didn't want to watch.

He couldn't help hearing, however.

He'd seen and heard it a thousand times before, but he was still powerless to put a stop to it.

Marrying Helen had been his one and only way of controlling her, of protecting her. Hopefully, of changing her.

But it hadn't helped.

Helen's appetite was voracious. He realized now that nothing he could say or do would ever change her.

Nor change the way he felt about her.

Eyes closed, he groped with his fingers for the handle of his service revolver.

They were doing it on the floor at the foot of the bed. Earl was on top. His breath came in tiny gasps as his buttocks rose and fell, rose and fell.

Ralph could tell that it was time.

"Now, Ralph!" Helen screamed as Earl pumped his seed inside her. "Do it now!"

Ralph didn't want to open his eyes, but he had to. His eyelids snapped open as he leveled the gun.

At this range, he couldn't miss.

Blood and brains splattered the walls.

Half a second later the sound of a shot assaulted Ralph's ears. He closed his eyes and tried—unsuccessfully—to block all further sight and sound from his tortured mind.

But he'd seen it too often before, and his mind—like a video recorder—insisted on replaying the entire scene, complete with all its gory details, in living color.

Helen, her naked body covered by what was left of the corpse, experienced pure ecstasy as multiple orgasms, triggered by Earl's death throes, vibrated her beautiful body like some kind of uncontrollable palsy. Rich red blood flowed from the hole where Earl's head used to be, and Helen's face and hair were thoroughly soaked and matted with slime; bits of bone, and spongy gray stuff that had to be parts of Earl's brains, obscured half her forehead.

Her eyes sparkled. She seemed to be smiling.

This, after all, was what she lived for, wasn't it? Her entire raison d'être.

Nothing else mattered.

Ralph felt suddenly sick to his stomach, but there was precious little inside him he could still vomit out.

"I love you," she said after a time. "No one else can

satisfy me the way you do. You know that, don't you? You're the best, Ralph. The absolute best."

"Are you sure?"

"I'm sure," she said.

"You won't go out again tomorrow, will you?" he asked.

"No," she answered. "Not tomorrow."

He wanted to believe her.

"Maybe the next day, though," she said, her voice already sounding emptier.

SOMETHING EXTRA

J. N. Williamson and
James Kisner

My wife said she didn't really mind if I thought about someone else when we made love," I told her on impulse. "So I thought of you."

Monica's response was instant. She slapped me across the face, stingingly, and then walked off in a huff. Her hips were fighting her natural impulse to wiggle and I was glad I'd said it on the premises of Rollins Advertising Agency. If it had been a less public place, she might have torn my head off. If Monica's husband had been around, he *would* have. Larry still has a tattoo of an eagle on the back of his right hand, and I've heard that bird takes wing when he gets good and pissed.

Sighing, I poured myself a cup of coffee and took it back to my desk.

I hadn't meant to blurt that out to Monica Patterson, but what I'd said was true. When I'd seen her standing next to me in the kitchenette, where the agency always has two pots of coffee brewing, the words had just tumbled out of my mouth. Maybe it was her perfume or merely the fact that Monica looks like such a naturally sexual woman—not sexy, sexual. She has long black hair that tucks in at the ends and a figure that's more like seventeen than early thirties, so I had to say something.

No, it was none of that. It was her dark brown eyes that seem to be far away and fixed on something far more interesting than writing ad copy, and how she said "Hi" as she accidentally brushed against me. She'd reached for a Styrofoam cup and her left breast had touched my shoulder as it rose, she had let it stay there for a second, and . . .

No, I admitted as I returned to my little cubicle, it wasn't those things either. I'd wanted her to *know*. Out of perversity, maybe—just to see what she would do, perhaps.

I worried that one of our co-workers might notice how my face was red from Monica's slap, but nobody paid much attention to me. Everyone was busy at their word processors, banging out copy. Which was my job, too. Banging out copy. I sat down and stared at the word processor screen. I was banging away about sleeve bearings for one of Rollins's biggest clients. It wasn't exactly like writing the Great American Novel, which I didn't especially want to do anyway, but it paid the bills. The majority of them, anyway.

I sipped some coffee, set it down, rested my fingertips on the keyboard. My mind searched for some brilliant phrase to describe the client's new sleeve bearings, but it proved elusive. Instead, my thoughts drifted to the night before. When I was making love to Sheila and Monica Patterson popped into my mind, saying "Hi" in the breathy way she did it at the office.

I felt guilty at first. There I was, dutifully pounding away on my wife Sheila (who isn't bad-looking, has always been faithful, has kept slim after bearing two children, and who can even cook without looking anxiously to the microwave), and I was imagining another woman. One who is definitely good-looking, slim only where it counts, has macho Larry-with-the-tattooed-eagle and no kids, and might or might not be faithful.

To my surprise, Sheila told me what I'd done was okay.

She didn't specifically say it was okay to picture Monica beneath me, but Sheila is a liberated woman and reads a lot about sex. Dr. Ruth, Graham Masterton, Masters and Johnson. Once she read that it was healthy to fantasize about someone else while making love to the spouse. The newer sex books even encouraged mental cheating, Sheila explained. She startled the hell out of me by admitting she sometimes thought of Tom Selleck when we were going at it; so she didn't really mind if I imagined Elvira or Kathleen Turner or Kim Basinger.

Trouble is that I'd *tried* those women, mentally, and they didn't do the trick. They were beautiful, desirable, and inaccessible. Remote. Unavailable. Additionally, I hadn't been able to persuade my libido to believe that any of those women would look twice at a junior copywriter named Ron Bowers.

So I'd begun thinking of someone real (so to speak). Someone I knew.

Monica.

I guessed I'd sort of spoiled it by letting her know and getting slapped. I'd been stupid, ignorant. Monica had probably believed I was hitting on her, and I really, truly was not.

Of course, I'd *thought* about it a lot.

I bumped into Monica later at the front door when we were coming individually back from lunch. I blushed; she gave me a dirty look. I followed her to her cubicle anyway, needing to explain. She was secretary to the media guy, who buys the ads for the firm that makes the bearings I try to describe. Monica never exposes an inch of the flesh I'd imagined infinitely better than sleeve bearings, and her clothes aren't tight-fitting but they're far-out, unmatching blouses or sweaters with long skirts that sort of swing between her legs or jeans that are always worn at key spots and look as if just a tiny *bit* of earnest rubbing might make the skin show through.

She sat behind her desk, pretending I wasn't there. Trying to come up with something clever as an opening, I hovered around until I noticed a big jar of peppermint pinwheels rising from a stack of printed-out pages. "Can I have a mint?"

She stared at me. *Through* me.

I took a mint, unwrapped and popped it into my mouth. I figured it might sweeten my pizza breath. "I'm sorry," I said. The pinwheel was rolling around on my tongue and making me mumble. Another stupid mistake, I realized. "I wasn't coming on to you but I shouldn't have said that." I turned to leave. "I didn't mean to be insulting." Abased, I grinned a little and took a step away.

"Wait," Monica said.

I stood stock-still. She was glancing around as if she intended to say or do something and needed privacy. No one else was back from lunch yet, and we were alone. "Do you want to slap my other cheek?" I asked her.

"No, I—I just wanted to say that *I'm* sorry." She got her cigarette case out of her purse, evading my gaze for another moment. "I shouldn't have hit you, Ron."

"Sure you should," I disagreed. "You've met Sheil, I've met your husband Larry at the Christmas party. We might've all been friends and I messed it up."

Monica lit a Vantage Ultra Light, puffed it with an enigmatic expression. The puffs of smoke came my way like hot breath. "Did you really mean it?" she asked.

"Did I mean what?" Hell, I could be mysterious, too.

She frowned. It made her prettier than ever. "You only *said* one thing." Monica leaned across the desk. "Were you really thinking about me while—while you were with Sheila?"

"Sure," I confessed. "It was okay with Sheil. She's very liberal."

"But," Monica continued, "why me? I'm married, too. It seemed kind of *weird* when I heard it." She sucked in smoke. Lucky Ultra Light, I thought, it had the *ad*vantage. "Don't you think that's—well, sick? A little?"

"Nope. And why not you?" I asked. "Sheila read a book about sexual fantasies and said that it's normal for a man or woman to think of somebody else during lovemaking. Because it enhances the relationship, not just the sex. Adds something extra."

"Really?" A lot of smoke came my way then and from her flared nostrils, too.

"Really, according to my wife's book. Because it doesn't hurt anyone, and—"

Her eyebrows arched, her head lowered a fraction of an inch. Her twerp boss—which is what my boss calls him, too—was on a straight line toward Monica.

Under my voice, I muttered, "We can rap later," and then I stole another mint.

"Fine," she replied. She got her body arranged in a businesslike posture. "And, thanks. I think!"

At five-thirty I'd banged out three pages of decent copy concerning sleeve bearings. Also roller bearings and plain, old ball bearings. It should've been more like twenty pages but my thoughts kept meandering back to what Monica had said before we parted: "Thanks." Why "thanks"?

I didn't know why, but it bothered the crap out of me.

It was very busy at the agency the next couple of days, and I didn't see or chat with Monica. We passed in the hall en route to the coffee makers or the copy machine, but that was it—a glance and a nod. Yet I detected something brewing in Ms. Patterson's mind and believed it was every bit as hot as coffee. An expert with women isn't required when they are onto something truly serious, important to them. And that's good, since I am definitely not an expert.

The phone on my desk buzzed on Friday morning. "Ron Bowers."

"Hi." Monica, maybe smoking a Vantage again. "Tell me, are you free for lunch?"

"Yeah. I guess so." Mystery for mystery. My blood warmed up, churned a bit.

"Meet me at the front door," Monica proposed. "Eleven-thirty?"

"Okay. If you want."

"I want," she answered and rung off.

I got the goal of twenty pages within range at seventeen sheets of tribute to bearings of all kinds, but that was because I'd banged out twelve of them over the past two days. Maybe Monica had rethought our discussion and Larry would be there with the eagle on his fist spreading its wings, but I doubted it. *I want,* Monica had told me. What?

She was wearing a sweater and skirt that matched perfectly, clung to her body like wallpaper that had just been hung again at Monticello and advertised the exciting news that she'd abandoned brassieres—for lunch, at least. We walked together to a tavern around the corner from Rollins where they served decent sandwiches and a wide range of imported beers. Management didn't mind our mild imbibing if there were no afternoon meetings with clients. I listened to the brunette's unexpected high heels going *tap, tap, tap* while we took a table in a back corner, hoping to dodge any fellow employees and starting to wonder what I'd do if Monica Patterson was considerably more available and accessible than Elvira and Company. I'd always been a loyal husband except once that didn't count.

Point is, we gulped down two beers apiece along with most of our sandwiches while Monica discussed every subject under the sun except the one that had made her ask me to lunch. Then the cigarette case came out, I was taking her lighter to ignite it, and she was jumping on the topic at hand with both feet.

"Ron, you were *great* last night," she said in a breath.

I sputtered, "What?" and drooled imported beer down my chin to the collar.

She touched my hand. "I did what you and Sheila recommended!" She freed my hand so I could mop off my face with a napkin. "I imagined it was *you* when Larry was on top of me! And it made for an entirely new, wonderful experience!"

"I should be flattered," I answered when I could speak. "I suppose."

Monica's brown eyes smoldered with a memory that included me—but one I could not share. "And the more I thought of it being you and not Larry, the better it became. We did it *twice!* Why, it's like having an affair but not worrying about being caught!"

I studied her eyes without knowing what to say. Monica was really excited. What had I started? It seemed very strange to me, just then, not the way it had seemed . . . before.

"Ron, it's truly wonderful." She wanted me to understand. Her hand reached for mine once more and I pulled it back. "We've come up with a terrific new kind of safe sex!"

I looked away, out the window. "Well, maybe not quite that, not ex*act*ly that."

"It's fun and satisfying, anyway." Now she was pouting. She put her hands in her lap, crimsoning slightly. She was gorgeous. "Just like you said, it doesn't hurt anyone."

I managed a grin. "I was okay, then?" I asked. "I was really good?"

"God." She gasped, rolling her melting chocolate eyes. "Were you ever!"

I felt my frown come back. "But it was Larry—Macho Man with the goddamned bird on his hand—not me!"

Monica shrugged. "Maybe. Maybe not. You know what I mean."

"No, I don't," I snapped. I suppose I wanted details, wanted to know how I'd made it so great for her. Share *some* of the high. "Not really."

Monica put her head forward across the table to speak with as much confidentiality as humanly possible, there in the tavern. Her dark hair framed her very sexual face (I'd been right about that part); she'd lost most of her lipstick having her sandwich and the beers, and her mouth was moist. "Thinking it was you, *believing* it was you instead of Larry—the fact that it was another man, a *different* man— was very much like it *was* you. I feel as if I know"—she blinked in embarrassment, nibbled her lower lip—"every inch of your body. Do you see?"

"I guess." It sounded peculiar as the devil to me, even dangerous in a way I hadn't imagined. But I couldn't have stood away from our table then without embarrassing myself badly.

Her voice was husky. Her gaze wasn't on my face. It had dropped considerably lower. "Isn't that how you do it, don't you absolutely *see me* under you?"

My God, I thought. "Well, hell," I said, "if it was good for both of us!"

She laughed loudly, irrepressibly. It was the sort of teasing laugh, when a woman's mouth widens in a very distinct, certain way, that makes a man think of things he could do with her lips.

I went on picturing her mouth the rest of the day, even when I was reaching my twenty-page goal. It was that or put my job right on the line. I didn't have any idea whether my boss would approve my copy or not, but I'd done a solid piece of work in passionately putting on paper the way our client's parts rested on other parts and made them turn, slowly, with mechanical and well-oiled precision . . .

When I made a similarly persuasive approach to red-haired, slender Sheila that night—my thoughts already on where I'd put my latest issue of the adult comic book *Cherry*—Sheil responded as if I had suggested that she might possibly like to have a new house or automobile. Or Tom Selleck, perhaps. Since I have never been one to look gift horses in the mouth, I began helping my wife remove her clothes while she returned that favor and, subsequently, several others. We hadn't done that in years. Or the "several other" things I cited.

She didn't even appear surprised when I was the one who reached up from bed to switch off the light.

She didn't appear to wonder if the children were sound asleep, and neither did I.

For an incredibly long period of time, in fact, neither one of us wondered about anything except the products of human nature and human need.

Sleeve bearings and ball bearings, I rediscovered, weren't the only things that performed as though they were well-oiled and perfect at a level far exceeding anything of which the mechanical was capable.

I stole one of my wife's cigarettes from the headboard—her cigarette lighter, too—and lit up.

She was lying on her side, faced away from me. Her long black hair was asprawl on the pillow and, even that way, the ends of the beautiful hair were tucked in. When I glanced down at the cigarette in my hand, I saw that I was smoking a Vantage Ultra Light.

The hand that held it carelessly and manfully between index and middle fingers had an eagle on the back.

JUICE

Kiel Stuart

I want juice tonight."

Rory Thomas Blaise MacLaren heard the promoter's order. He set his jaw, staring down at the locker-room floor. Ah, yes, the smelly little tiled room, the wrestler's home away from home, whether high school or hired hall.

At his side, his partner Sam grew quiet. Rory cocked his head, feigning respect and attentiveness.

The promoter took the cigar out of his face for a moment. "Juice," repeated Banks, in his flatlands voice.

Rory hated juicing. He kept his mouth shut about it most of the time, because if you protested (even to peers instead of promoters), you didn't work much.

The marks came to wrestling matches to be taken in by its faked violence. To Rory the real violence was more subtle, more revolting. The real violence was this person who owned you, commanding you to take a sliver of razor blade and slice open your forehead.

Rory took his gaze off the floor, fixed it on Banks's rug. A yellowish stain marred the promoter's greasy old wig, where it was supposed to pass for scalp. "Anything else we can do for you?"

Banks squinted up into Rory's face. "Get a haircut."

As smoke from the cigar assaulted him, Rory shifted his two hundred fifty-odd pounds casually. "Which is it? Haircut or juice? Gotta know."

Banks narrowed oysterish eyes. "Why?"

Rory tossed his Irish Setter mop. "'Cause I don't have enough blade for both."

It brought some stifled laughs.

On a bench next to them, Sam coughed. Rory exchanged a quick glance with his partner, as Banks bit down on his cigar.

"Juice," came through it, loud and clear. "I don't care from who." He turned his back on them and left.

Rory sighed, lacing up his boots. What the hell. Blading was the easy way; just raise your hand to your head and *voilà*, Christ at Calvary.

Everyone knew it was better than hardway blood—having a ring partner bust open some fragile scar tissue or getting hit over the head with a metal chair. Anyone with an IQ over twenty could tell the difference between a neat razor slash and the mess that resulted from fists or a chair.

For all Rory knew, some wrestlers liked the slice and dice. Enough of them had foreheads resembling the canals of Mars.

Rory wanted to keep his looks intact, not to mention keep away from whatever diseases he could get, wading in blood.

Sammy poked him one in the ribs and smiled. The smile spread out his mustache, the one he'd grown to look older than his twenty years. Rory never had the heart to mention it made Sammy look even younger. "Ten points, Rory."

"Yeah," he said, breathing out. "What a reach."

"*I* thought so."

He shook his head. Stirring up psychological turmoil in others, even a rudimentary life form like a wrestling promoter, rapidly reached the point of diminishing returns.

Rory flopped on the bench and stared at the wall. Sam said something, twice. Finally, he looked up. "Huh?"

"Your mind is in another dimension." Sam waved a hand in front of his face. "But then it always is."

Rory laughed. From anyone else, that remark would have rated a black eye, at least. But Sam meant it as a compliment. He said Rory was a deep thinker. Sam was just a kid.

The kid checked out his own blade. "No sweat," he said. "I'll do it again."

Rory watched Sam wrap the blade in his wristband and silently contemplated the mysteries of his trade. He believed that the letting of blood was somehow symbolic, connected with washing one's sins clean. What would Sister Loyola have said about this, back at St. Luke's? Would she say wrestlers were closer to God because they willingly shed their blood? Probably not. Slicing open your head with a razor hardly qualified as stigmata.

He felt a brief flash of guilt for permitting Sam to take on the burden of his sins. He should have opened himself up now and again.

Rory looked around the locker room and sincerely doubted that any of his colleagues ever had similar thoughts.

There was Badass, dark and morose, rumored to have killed several men, only no one could remember exactly where or how. And Red Man, the practicing alcoholic (nobody on this particular circuit made enough money to be a practicing cokehead). Rory thought a lot of what he'd seen of wrestling would make for a good movie some day. A horror film.

Chuck "The Lumberjack" Little brushed past them on his way back from the previous match. The big moose beamed at them. "Playtime. Maybe I'll have a touch of that *blonde.*"

Rory rolled his eyes. Chuck couldn't seem to get enough of her. Neither could most of the others. Rory supposed that she was attractive. Him, he'd rather read a book.

But Chuck's playtime meant their showtime. "Let's go." Time to head for the ring.

Sam checked his wristband again.

"Look." Rory lowered his voice. "Don't knock yourself out tonight. Take it easy." Sam, young and elastic, was a vigorous if overeager worker. It made up for his lack of size, it got him jobs, and Rory knew from experience it would eventually get him a bad back, hips, shoulders, and, Rory's own personal favorite, bad knees.

He heard the distant whine of the ring announcer: "From the fabulous Hamptons, New York, at two hundred and fifty-three pounds, Rory the Ripper!"

He saw the girl as he went down the aisle, ducking insults and beer baths. Long ice-colored hair, the oval face that just melted away from angularity, the greenish eyes . . . she was very striking, he'd admit. Their "stage door" was usually knee-deep in groupies fighting for attention by now. This one could probably cut right in line.

He and Sam had time for some conversation in the ring, during rest holds. "Who knows? I may get lucky tonight instead of Chuck." Sam had Rory in the dreaded abdominal stretch which looked painful as hell but was merely awkward.

The referee hovered near as Rory helped Sam sail over in a hip toss, ending in an armbar to the mat, where they could both be comfortable.

Sam grimaced as if Rory was about to tear his arm from the socket. "She probably wants to go through the whole roster. Your turn may be next." He tapped Rory, signaling their switch to standing wristlock.

"I can hardly wait," Rory snorted.

Sam covered his laugh in a scream of faked pain.

They went to ten minutes, twenty seconds, then Rory put Sam's face into the ring post for the blading, after which he helped him over the top rope and got DQ'd. Rory felt the crowd's hate, aimed right between his eyes. Sam, wearing his own blood, got the cheers. Rory saw the blonde get up and head for the exit.

"Listen," said the ref, just as they were about to leave the ring, "you think she goes for short guys?"

"I'll give her your number," Sam said.

The next night, the wrestler's home away from home happened to be an American Legion hall. But as Rory drove there, it seemed to him the Texas highways had been his real home, his and Sam's, for the past three years.

Before that, Rory remembered working the Mid-Atlantic area, and before that, Oregon, and before that, the Deep South, and before that was a pretty fuzzy memory. He'd worked with part-timers who came and went, star wannabes, and a few genuine celebrities, like four-hundred-and-fifty-pound Blubber Boy McKay. Many were cast in Sam's mold, young eagers who would eventually settle into a comfortable living in the wonderful world of pro wrestling, not household names but not paupers either.

Changing lanes, Rory caught a glimpse of himself in the rearview mirror. He looked quickly away, laughed. *There you are. Typecast. The good-looking, sullen heel.* That was the "Ripper" persona. It played beautifully off Sam's fresh baby face. The innocent victim, Sam always had the crowd on his side. Maybe they all identified with the "victim" part.

Sam was, in many ways, a lot like him. No family, no roots. And no secret of his flaming hero-worship, openly envying Rory's size and skills in whipping crowds to a frenzy. A budding Rory MacLaren. As he got out of the car he wondered if that was exactly something to aspire to.

Inside, Rory tossed his bag down where his partner usually was. The chaos of preparation was all around him: taping of joints, physical warm-ups, last-minute instructions. He waited a few minutes. No Sam. He turned to Chuck. "Where's Sam?"

Chuck shrugged. "Maybe he got *real* lucky last night."

He set his gear down inside the locker and went out into the hallway. No sign of Sam there. Rory frowned. Down the hall was Banks's setup.

Though it was against his religion to enter the realm of the promoter unless absolutely necessary, Rory took aim and fired himself into Banks's little room.

Banks was on the phone. Rory ducked away, but the promoter put his hand over the mouthpiece and motioned him in with a wave of cigar smoke. "Wha?"

Might as well discover if Banks knew anything. "Sam isn't here yet."

Banks shrugged. "So? Work it with, ah, Whatsisface in the first."

"Red Man?" Rory inched away, heading for the safety of the hall.

"Naw, the other one. Tell him to put on a mask and— yeah, hold on, I'm still here!" Banks began shouting into the receiver; Rory took the opportunity to flee before the word "juice" could leave his lips. Without Sam's obliging presence, he couldn't be sure of avoiding the blade himself.

Whatsisface—Badass—in the first was wheezing a bit from having to do the extra match with Rory, but he lived through its seven minutes.

Not having Sam to work with made him vaguely uneasy. He took the feeling and stuffed it away.

That night he buzzed Sam's room. No answer. He gnawed on a cuticle for a minute, then silently toasted the kid's luck and turned over to sleep.

"Get used to working with Whatsisface." Banks took the cigar from his teeth just long enough to get the words out. "Your little buddy won't be back here." He was already moving out the door.

Rory let his teeth show. It was not a smile.

Shit! Sam was going to be pissed! Rory felt his skin

tighten. Swell—no one worked as well with him. Who would he play off now? Ah, the kindliness of wrestling promoters. "You can him, for *one* lousy no-show?"

"I didn't have to. He's dead."

Dead. The word echoed down the length of the hall. Dead.

Rory's face went stony. He moved instinctively in front of Banks, putting an arm against the open door. The promoter took a step back and the cigar from his teeth. Rory struggled to formulate a sentence. "You mind telling me what happened? If it's not too much trouble."

"Who the hell knows? What's it matter? Probably drugs." A particularly unpleasant smile curled the promoter's lips.

Rory let his arm drop and said tightly, "Sam is clean." He corrected himself. "Was clean. Didn't even take steroids."

"It ain't my problem. Just trying to make a living." Banks shrugged.

Rory watched his retreat from cold, lidded eyes. Had Banks known him well enough to realize what that look meant, he would have turned pale and fled.

Rory remained staring at the pattern in the floor tiles for some time. Then he walked back to the locker room on legs that felt numb.

He passed the heavily bleeding Chuck on his way out, and the next thing he saw was the ring. Rory knew he had somehow gotten from the locker room to the mat.

It hardly registered. His mind was somewhere else. He thought of blood, of sins, of Sam, and of how Sam always commented on Rory's faraway gaze. *"You're a deep thinker, man."* His teeth clenched tighter and tighter.

He went through his match, an efficient machine that knew the task at hand. He barely felt Badass's hands as they moved from hold to hold, barely heard the bell at match's end. Barely noticed when he vaulted out of the ring and landed wrong. His knee blew.

Damn you, Sam! he thought. How could you let this

happen? Limping back to the lockers, his faraway gaze swept the crowd, blank with growing rage. Then he stopped in midsweep.

Long spill of cold hair. Riveting eyes. That blonde, at ringside again.

She looked at him for a second or two. Then she rose and made for the exit, as she always did.

Rory hit the showers, chewing at the inside of his lip. The blond groupie might have been with that damned fool Sam. She might have something to tell him. Maybe she talked him into snorting the white stuff for the first time. Maybe he pulled a Len Bias.

In the meantime he needed to let the steaming water run over him until he felt like moving. And he didn't care how long that took.

He finally toweled off, dressed, and went looking for Chuck. Yes. That was a good idea. Start with Chuck, who might know where to find the girl.

A quick check of the halls showed no one. Oh, hell; by now Chuck might be back at his hotel. His knee hot and swelling, Rory realized dimly he should ice it. He shuffled back into the locker room to grab his bag.

Heard running water and went to the showers to look.

The blonde. There she was, in the shower with Chuck. They both appeared to be enjoying the experience, she with her long wet hair and Chuck with an idiot's grin on his bearded, bloody face as he groped her.

Rory shut his eyes.

Blood. Sins. Washing them clean.

He opened his eyes. Rory forced himself to watch them in silence for a minute, then slipped away without being seen.

He sat in his car but didn't start it. Aside from Blubber Boy McKay's bare butt, this was the most vividly repulsive thing Rory had ever seen. He closed his eyes and their embrace remained etched against his lids.

He coughed violently, as if clearing his lungs of poison.

Rory twisted the key in the ignition and gunned for home. The long Texas span of road sang blackly at him.

The ice pack didn't work. He didn't care. Rory's limp worsened. Banks booked them into one high school after another. Sam haunted his dreams almost every night. Banks still bugged him for juice, almost every night.

He never got around to meeting with the blonde.

Maybe tonight, in the fourth or fifth nameless high school with the same clamorous audience.

Rory waded through the groupies already piled at the exit. His colleagues were already there, joking about the lineup.

"A battle royale," cracked Red Man. "That's what we got."

"Yeah," said Badass, pumping his hips in a juvenile obscene gesture. "And I got your blonde right here."

Rory said nothing, taping his knee to ready it for the match. He'd stopped making jokes. He'd begun thinking about blood and sacrifice. *God's bleeding clowns. It's our job. And I let Sam do it. Mea culpa, Sam . . .*

As he headed for the ring, the blonde's green-eyed gaze followed him. What did she offer that was different from the hordes of other women at the door? Intensity?

Whatever it was, he would have to talk with her. She might have something to tell him about Sam. Yes, he promised himself, soon.

He went to work. Halfway through the match with Badass, Rory's brow opened up: hardway blood, which wasn't exactly pleasant but not unexpected when a mis-timed knuckle hits just the right spot over a prominent brow bone.

Hardly a gusher. A mere trickle. One towel held in place by pressure, five minutes, a tiny Band-Aid, and he'd be good as new.

When the match ended Rory limped deep into the locker room in search of a clean towel. He hadn't been paying much attention to what went in his gym bag the past couple of days.

Pretty deserted back in the supply room, he thought, reaching down for a towel. The shadowy atmosphere enveloped him; for some odd reason his scalp prickled. Without knowing why, his hearing was instantly acute. He was alert for footsteps he could have sworn were there.

His breathing quickened, echoing in the small room. Then stopped.

Nothing. His laugh was a short bark, the product of air held inside too long.

He straightened, folded the towel and pressed it to his eyebrow, turning back for the showers.

It was then that the blonde stepped from the shadows, blocking his way.

He noticed for the first time that only her face was the same—that riveting face. The body was swollen.

Rory backed up. There was a glow to her skin, the way skin gets when you clamp your hand over a flashlight and can see the blood lit from within. She had that quality all over, like a fat red light bulb.

He took another faltering backwards step; she followed, glaring at his face.

With effort, he drew a breath. "Were you with Sam when he died?" His own voice sounded hoarse and weak.

She didn't speak. She grabbed his shoulders to pull him even closer, shocking him with her strength.

He tried to shove her. She didn't shove. Her grip on his shoulders was talonlike.

Run! Every nerve flashed the message. His muscles jerked involuntarily, struggling to tear loose. Useless.

Suddenly she whirled, letting go.

He heard the sound of approaching people, of booming male voices and scuffling feet. She sprang away from him and was gone.

Rory sagged against the wall, looked at the towel in his hand, and dropped it.

He slid down the wall until he touched the cold tiled floor. Silent, weak, he watched Chuck and the others pass by. And he began to make some fairly athletic leaps in the chain of logic.

Big Chuck. Big bulky 280-pound Chuck.

Lithe, 185-pound Sam.

Blood.

Always the blood. On this circuit, blood made up for the heat that other, more creative bookers could get through dramatic angles.

Run. He struggled to his feet and got out.

Rory went back to the hotel and looked down at his hands. They trembled slightly.

Quit, then. Tomorrow—that one last paycheck would come in useful. Head back East.

He sat still, wondering if the things Sister Loyola had said long ago were true. Was there a heaven? And could Sam look down and see him? *"You're a deep thinker, Rory . . ."* Yeah, right. Couldn't think his way loose from a paper bag—

He reached out to zip his case shut.

Underneath an old photo—their first publicity shot together—he saw it, and he held it up by its thick gold chain.

His old crucifix. He put it on. It made him feel safer, somehow.

He looked at the picture again. Sam looked back at him, through those brown curls he used to wear, before he cut them to look older. Quickly, he put the picture facedown.

Rory's eyes stung. Tears? Hell, he hadn't cried since he was six. Why break a track record like that?

When Rory arrived at the high school, Badass told him that he'd be working the last match with him, instead of Chuck, who'd called in sick.

He shuddered.

"Hey, whatsa matter with you, man?" demanded Badass. "Doncha like me no more?"

Taping his knee, Rory scrambled for an answer. "I'm crazy about you. It's Banks that I—"

The locker room noises cut off suddenly. Rory looked up from lacing his boots. Banks was framed in the doorway.

"Double juice tonight, boys. We got a big crowd and I'm aiming at a bigger one next time."

"No way," murmured Rory, and if the room was quiet before, it was tomblike now.

Banks strode toward him, taking a blade from his own pocket. He waved the blade in front of Rory's face. "I've *had* this crap from you, MacLaren. Now put this fucking blade in your mouth or up your ass, I don't care. Double juice tonight, and this time you ain't walking away spotless, pretty boy."

Rory was aware of everyone watching him, waiting for the smart remark.

Cold-eyed and silent, he took the blade from Banks and wrapped it tightly in his wristband.

"Good boy. I want this last match short and sweet, a five-minute bloodbath. You got me? Nice." Banks smiled and walked out, his back to Rory.

Rory set his face and counted out the minutes to the last match.

From a distance: "Ladies and gentlemen, making his residence in the fabulous Hamptons . . ."

He followed Badass out, cross thumping against his chest. Yes, she was at ringside, fat and malevolent, green eyes glowing like evil gems.

Rory climbed into the ring and began trading chops with his partner. Badass took the opportunity to hit a gusher early on. He wiggled his eyebrows at Rory, mouthed, "What are you waiting for?" as they switched from a standing armbar to a wristlock. Badass was right, he knew it, knew Banks could fire him. Still Rory resisted.

Four minutes into the match he had a vision of Sister Loyola talking about the blood of the Lamb. He saw Sister Loyola's white face stark against her black habit.

Confiteor Deo omnipotenti. . . .

Badass was hissing into his ear by now, as they practiced bear hugs on one another: "Are you nuts? Did you hear Banks or what? Jesus. Tell you something. Your little pal wouldn't give me this shit. He was for real."

Rory lidded his eyes again, sudden ice racing through his hot muscles. *Mea culpa, mea culpa, mea maxima culpa . . .* He did a half-twist out of the bear hug, raised his wrist, as if saluting, and hit himself just above the left eye, so angry he didn't even feel the pain of the blading or the thump of the ring as Badass put him in an inside cradle for the count.

He pushed away from the referee, from Badass, and stumbled out of the ring for the lockers.

His vision smeary with blood and sweat, Rory found the showers full.

He went painfully around to Banks's "office" of the evening—a little hole in the corridor, away from the lockers.

It was time to tell the bastard off. He opened the door. The office was black, deserted.

Banks wasn't there. Probably in the showers or the outer hall, berating everyone's performance. Rory looked around the tiny room.

Now what? He sank against the cramped desk. Wait here until Banks came back from yelling at the boys? He'd already run out of steam, sitting here bleeding like an idiot, all set to give Banks what for, and Banks wasn't there.

Now he was beginning to feel the blood loss. It seemed to pound in his ears. Or was it only the throb of an old heater system, echoing around this little dark room?

The hell with Banks.

Wearily, Rory got up and pushed back the door.

And she sprang at him from the hall.

He drew back, saw her take in the cross. One unaffected

glance, not even a hitch in her movement. She'd been out there, waiting for him. Waiting to do what she'd done to Sam . . . *Your turn may be next . . .*

Run! His nerves screamed. He could see light from the hall; there was just enough room to get by now. Her leer shone at him like a thin ray of moonlight. And in that leer gleamed teeth jagged as a shark's.

Go! Now! Run!

Sam's face in the photo. While he could still remember. He closed his eyes and met her charge.

She surged forward, foul-breathed, clawing at him, her tongue a greedy slug lapping his face. He tried to flip her, but his knee betrayed him. She knocked him backwards with all the force of her soggy weight, pressing him into the floor.

Rory gasped, struggling to push her off, but thick spongy thighs clamped his body. Her teeth lashed across his split skin. He saw the spark of saliva dripping between them. Her breath reached his ears in eager, short grunts, hit his nostrils with the stench of rotting meat.

Rory strained. She didn't yield an inch, bearing down on him, heavy with the blood of the others, of Sam.

Teeth raked the side of his neck. His skin flashed a warning as the needle points opened a nick just inches from the main artery. Her snarling was the song of death. Weakening, desperate, Rory wrenched his arm free, frantic to ward off the relentless teeth.

The forgotten blade in his wristband ripped across her bloated chest.

And the blonde popped, exploding in blood like an engorged leech.

It washed over him, a crimson ocean, sucking at him with riptide force as it lashed against the walls. Then it subsided, a warm and stagnant pool.

When he struggled to his feet, all that remained was blood and a gelatinous sac that might have once been the blonde's outer covering.

Rory lurched to the desk, collapsed against it, his breath rasping. Banks's office was now wallpapered in a sticky scarlet film. Rory used Banks's overcoat to clean himself.

Slowly, enough strength returned for him to lever open a window, climb through, and head for the parking lot.

Rory turned, taking one last look through the open window.

"You want juice, Banks?" he said softly. "You got it."

SURPRISE

Rex Miller

Warren Childress had everything. It came to him magnified, amplified, multiplied times a thousand—the awareness that he was the king of the hill—as he reached the 8th hole of the front nine at Brook Hollow. His kind of hole, he thought with a smile.

You reached it by traversing a quaint wooden bridge that spanned a picturesque winding stream dividing the 7th green and the 8th tee. Some viewed it as a water hazard. Not Warren. To him it was just one more chance to grandstand. He never overshot the 7th and never flubbed one into the drink off the 8th. Invariably there were one or two foursomes stacked up waiting to go off the 9th and into the clubhouse. It gave people on the 8th hole a little captive gallery, so that a perfectly hit ball could be watched and admired by the golfers waiting to tee off up by the 8th green.

"You're up, Warren," one of the guys said to him.

"Right," he said, getting a tee and sliding a gleaming Ultra-flite Gold out of his expensive leather bag.

He had a pro swing. Fluid. Grooved. Beautifully smooth. The contact was solid and full, that great feeling when you know it's dead bang on. He didn't even lift his head for a second, just stayed down over the tee, arms in the top of his backswing arc, wrists cocked, not having to look, knowing he was there even before he heard the oohs and aahs of the other envious players.

Unconsciously, as he took a tee out of his left trouser pocket, he'd let his fingers slide across his groin, feeling for the small growth he'd noticed that morning. When you're pushing the big five-oh and you have everything to live for, the way he did, you become very aware of your mortality.

That's not quite true. He'd noticed it the night before. Late for a dinner party neither of them really wanted to go to, Warren Childress had said to his wife, who was carefully applying makeup in the next room, "Do you know what really hurts?"

When there was no answer, he pulled his long silk socks on, and then she said, after a few beats, "What hurts, darling?" She held her mouth in that funny way women do when they talk while applying lipstick.

"I'll tell you later," he said, knowing that he wouldn't. His wife was even less interested in him than he was in her. He didn't give two hoots in hell about Lois and hadn't for years. His mistress never wore lipstick. She never smeared herself with that coating of orange-looking crap that seemed to end right at the neck on so many women of Lois's age. God, how he loathed that look. The hair so meticulously coiffed, every strand sprayed in place just so by the idiot at the beautician's, and then that orange mask of thick makeup and the bright lipstick and the green eyes. Jeezus.

"Tell Mother," she said patronizingly as she waltzed into the room, "what hurts Daddy?" Her voice carried through the master bedroom with a theatrical echo.

"Nothing." He smiled with fake whimsy. "I was grumbling and bitching. The Levitt account."

"What else is new?" She smiled back. "Now what?"

He'd have to make up something. "It's the same old song and dance. They want the impossible—" And he began improvising.

Warren didn't feel like sharing his irritations with her any more than he felt like sharing anything else with her, so he ad-libbed something about one of his proverbial nightmare accounts, his brain on autopilot and hers disengaged entirely.

He missed Jacqueline desperately. She was twenty-two. Beyond fabulous-looking. So gorgeous his heart hurt to think about her. She loved him and she could suck the brass off a table lamp and her greatest joy in life came from playing slave for him.

A twenty-two-year-old *pony*. Six hundred thousand dollars' worth of split-level in Blue Springs. Olympic pool. His and hers saunas. A Corniche. The neo-Impressionist hedges. The CDs. The little special fund that neither the IRS nor Lois knew a damned thing about. The biggest agency in North Kansas City. He had the world by the tail.

Warren Childress had been pulling on the silk briefs when he'd spotted a dime-size mole on his groin. Something he'd never seen before. Sort of an ugly little purple-brown cauliflowerlike growth. Nothing to concern himself about, but it paid to watch these things.

A few years ago he would have said something about it to Lois.

"Hon, are you too busy to come in here and help me with this tie?"

"Ek-shually I yam." He could hear her coming in. She made a grand entrance in a swirl of French perfume. They were both forty-nine. "But I'll take time."

"You look very nice," he told her.

"Thank you," she replied indifferently, working on his tie. True romance for the nineties, all right, each partner loathing the other. No, that wasn't true.

Just cold ashes, gray hairs, too many resentments and harsh recriminations. A man and woman weren't made to stay together for a quarter century. It was too long even for a good relationship, and theirs had withered long ago.

Jackie, on the other hand, was something else. Tall. Legs up to her neck. Showgirl busty. God, he never tired of touching those beautiful breasts. Kissing them. And she was so much more than just a great-looking young woman with nice boobs—she was exciting. She was inventive. Wild. And the lady was crazy about him.

His mind returning to the present, he decided he would finish the front nine and then he would drive on to the subdivision where his mistress kept an apartment. The idea of lovemaking was already beginning to turn him on.

He putted out and picked up his ball, moving to the 9th tee. He was still up.

He wiggled his two-hundred-dollar brogues into a comfortable stance, compensating with the grip just so, pulling it over so he wouldn't slice, and smacked his tee shot toward the clubhouse.

It arched into the blue sky, the perfect, cloudless Brook Hollow landscape a classic background as the small white ball fell into the green fairway some two hundred and fifty yards away.

"Not too shabby," one of the guys in his foursome said, as he stepped up to tee his ball.

"It'll play," Warren Childress said, thinking of Jackie and what they would do together, as he walked toward the clubhouse. The stirrings of an erection felt delicious, and he fantasized about the way the afternoon would go and he was hard, thinking about their last session together.

She had coaxed him out of his controlled facade, turned him, made him so hot he forgot to stifle his inhibitions, reached down into his darkest corner and pulled the wild and nasty and twisted Warren out of there. Made him sit up and beg for it and roll over and be her puppy—Jeezus, who's kidding here, she was *his* slave? He was *hers*. He'd do anything for this beautiful, kinky bitch lover.

"I'm Daddy's girl," she said, putting on, playing little nympho Lolita, doing what some beautiful women do so well, so achingly well, so organically, naturally, enticingly, heartbreakingly well, and she smiled coquettishly; she pouted, preened, posed, played like she was a fast, fuckable fourteenybopper, and she touched him like a man touches a woman, controlling, manipulating him, her incredible cover-girl face, movie-queen bananorama face, seductive stiffener of a tanned, young, Ipanema-beach-bossa-nova face that said let me eat your lips and suck on your delicious ice cream cone of a mouth—a mouth opening and a tongue coming out and touching him just so.

"Mmmmmmmm," he moaned.

"Daddy?"

"What. Jeezus! *What?*"

"Daddy, will you do anything your little girl wants?" she asked, pouting with her mouth still there.

"Yes."

"Tell Daddy's girl."

"Anything."

"Make-believe things for his little girl?" He wasn't sure what she said, but he answered again—his breath coming in ragged gasps.

"Yeah. Anything, baby."

"Here's what I want Daddy to do," she whispered, and she told him awful, weirded-out, mondo bizarro things, and he did them for her, letting her enslave him, and when it was all enough for her—finally—she kissed him softly, and he held her and cherished her face and tried to tell her so, but a long and hot and delicious tongue was inside his mouth and spearing his soul, the pink and wet tongue of this movie star piercing into him and inflaming his desire, and within the next couple of minutes of Fucking Standard Savings Time, which is when time compresses in on itself and ceases to tick within those unaccountable sweeps of the second hand, there was an eruption, and he felt her hand on him and the volcanic surging lava from his loins was spurting uncontrollably all over them, splashing on the pretty flowered sheets and getting them all gooey and sticky, and the heat of her hand on him was causing his exploding fluid to shoot out prematurely, and she moved the hand up and down quickly and each move threatened to tear his guts out of his body, and each move killed him a little, and each movement of her small, fragile-boned hand pumped out another couple of c.c.s of the hot, cloudy, milky jism, and each movement got him off again and he'd never come like this and, ohmygod, he was afraid she'd opened some physiological door with her beautiful body and face and tongue, and now this and what if he could never stop coming and he'd die like this, the first man to break through the come barrier, the test pilot for the Mach 4 Jack Off, the pioneer of a brave new world of spermshooting where, like a worker drone in the hands of the queen bee, you bop till you drop and, yes, he could go this way any moment, in fact he was on death's door and, yes, don't stop, it's to die for, you're killing me, and *seismic* was the word that came to mind, and he felt the earth move, and his heart shuddered as the tremor split the world in half and the last drops of his life force shot into the room and covered them in yech nasty hot sticky stuff and, spent, he gave up the ghost.

"You're sweet, you know that?" she said after a minute or so of snuggling. She had the wisdom of silences. He made no noise or movement. She smiled and he could feel his dead body starting to warm again, just at the shape of that luscious, edible mouth of hers. What a face.

She got up and went back into the bathroom. He could hear her running water. She came back out wearing his silk bathrobe, even managing to look sexy and cute in that, and the sleeves were rolled back, and she was carrying a damp cloth, and she began cleaning up the mess he'd made in the bed, and he made his first noise as the wet cloth touched him:

"Nnnnn." Just a soft whimper escaped from his lifeless, inert body. Dead on the bed.

"Don't worry, honey," she purred to him as she leaned over, "Jackie's gonna kiss it and make it well."

"NNNNNNN," he moaned in agony/ecstasy, and she laughed.

"But next time we're going to take our time, aren't we?" she chided, as she laughed into his mouth.

"Mmm."

"Three, four minutes, anyway. No more of the old thirty-second Vesuvius," she teased him. "Deal?"

"Three or four minutes?"

"Yeah," she said.

And somewhere in all of that he decided that she'd given him the secret of life. This was what it was all about.

He thought about her, hard and hot now, and had to fight to yank his mind back to the present and calm down enough so that he could hit his approach shot to the green.

In a few minutes they'd reached the clubhouse, he'd bid a hasty goodbye to the guys, changed into some mocs, and was on his way to the burbs.

Warren Childress parked and tipped the parking attendant, Pedro, who always gave him special attention.

"I might be a while," Childress said.

"Hokay," the small man said in a downbeat, meek voice. He was usually a bubbling little bantam kind of guy and Childress looked at him as he moved toward the elevator.

"You doing all right, Pedro?" Conversational. Just asking.

"I don't think Missy up there now."

"You don't think Missy—? Oh. Did Miss Jordan go out?"

"Missy gone," he said.

"How long has she been gone—do you know?" Misunderstanding him.

"Leave yesterday. Missy gone."

"What the hell are you talking about, Pedro, my man? Talk to me."

"I don't know nothing," Pedro said, shrugging and moving to the expensive car. "Luis say Missy go. She move out."

His eyes were downcast as if he was ashamed for the way Childress had treated this lovely lady to make her leave. What the hell was this shit?

"You're mistaken, I'm sure," Childress said, but his thumb was on the elevator button.

He rode to three and got off, striding briskly down the hall, the thick carpet muffling his footsteps.

Room 305. Right side of the hall. He slipped his key into the lock, felt the familiar turn of the mechanism, the give of the metal, the door opening. The furniture he'd picked out for the apartment looked just the same as always.

"Jackie? You here, doll?" His voice loud and metallic in the apartment, the silence of no response even louder. He walked through the room and opened the bedroom door. The bed was stripped of linens, a bare mattress, his first stab of shock. He flung open the clothes closet. Empty. Drawers. Nothing. Into the bathroom. Bare. Only a few used containers scattered about and in the medicine cabinet. The apartment screamed at him and he was suddenly very afraid.

He went over to the phone to call the apartment house management whom he paid directly, but the telephone was dead. She'd had it disconnected. He looked in the kitchen. Some food in the fridge, a few things in the cabinets. She'd left in a hurry. He was getting frantic. He went through the whole place looking for a note—something. Not a word. What in the *hell* was going on? Jackie would never leave like this.

Warren got the car and drove over to the management complex. Yes, Miss Jordan left yesterday. She had turned in her apartment key. Said we could go ahead and rent it out for the first of the month—she was leaving. She didn't leave a forwarding address—said she'd be in touch when she was relocated. No—there was no message of any kind for you.

He phoned the doorman and the garage attendant who'd been on duty when she left. Had she left in a taxi? No—took her car. Some luggage. That was it. She had been vague about her destination. She hadn't responded when they'd told her how sorry they were to see her go—she just smiled, Luis the garage man told him. *Smiled?* He had to get out of there. He couldn't breathe.

He sat in the car debating whether or not to go to the police. There would be questions. Problems. He couldn't chance it. Maybe it would be better to call them anonymously later. Where had she gone?

No, there hadn't been any messages for him at the office. He started the car and drove home, blindly, mind buzzing with the possibilities. Another man? Illness in the family? She'd been so happy when they'd been together last time. Jackie loved him. She couldn't just pick up and leave. Something had happened to her. Should he call the hospitals? The word *abortion* nudged him for a second.

He knew that his worst fears were right—that something had happened—when he pulled into his driveway and saw two official-looking guys standing there waiting. They walked over and were standing beside the door when he got out of the car. They had the smell of cops, or private heat.

"Mr. Childress?" the first one said, a rough-looking man who seemed out of character in a three-piece business suit. Warren's heart started hammering; he feared something awful had happened to Jackie.

"Yeah?"

"We represent Mrs. Childress. May we see your keys, please." The hand outstretched—no question mark in the statement.

"My keys?" he started.

"Hand your keys over," the other man said. In a thickening fog, he handed his key ring to the first guy.

"Do you have duplicate house keys and car keys, Mr. Childress?"

"No."

"The house keys have been changed," the first man told

him. "Step this way, sir." They escorted him to an un-marked Pontiac, and Childress sat in the back seat. The second man sat in the front.

"You guys going to tell me what this is all about?"

"We're employed by Mrs. Childress's attorneys, sir. They'll be in touch with you as to the details of the divorce." The words stabbed into him like sharp knives.

Lois got the house. The Corniche. The neo-Impressionists. The CDs, of course. He was getting to keep whatever he could pull out of the agency, but he was to immediately "relinquish" the monies that Jackie had told them about. Jacqueline Jordan, whose fucking *deposition* was one of the sharp knife wounds that left him bleeding as the man spoke. When he was through, the man tapped a small envelope that lay in the seat between them. Something rectangular, about an inch thick. "You can keep this. Mrs. Childress said it was a little souvenir for you." He said it without any irony.

Warren picked it up and looked down into the envelope, knew what it was the moment he saw the TDK T-120HS on the top of the box. A copy of a videocassette. Shot from the clothes closet, he supposed.

They let him out at a cab stand, opened the trunk of the Pontiac and unceremoniously plunked his luggage beside the first cab. They didn't ask him if he had cab fare, even—they just pulled out. Hell, he'd never tumbled a hooker he didn't slip fifty bucks to for a taxi.

He got into the cab and the driver loaded his luggage, getting in with a grunt of effort, turning and saying, "Where to, bud?"

"Just drive," he said.

"It's your money," the driver sneered, dropping the meter. It's your money, chump.

Warren Childress, head of the biggest agency in North Kansas City, sighed and leaned back into the seat of the cab as it pulled out into traffic. All he could do was see his wife say to him, "Tell Mother," over and over, "what hurts Daddy—"and know now that she was cutting his nuts off even then. She'd probably already watched the videotape. Seen and heard him getting off. Heard "Daddy" and "Daddy's girl." God—she must have been enjoying herself.

The car. The CDs. The house. The paintings. And that bitch cunt even told her about the money he had squirreled away. It couldn't get much worse than this, he thought. But he was wrong.

Because Warren Childress had everything. And that night, in a lonely hotel room, watching the cancerous mole begin to bleed, he would start to comprehend just how much worse it could get.

ROCOCO

Graham Masterton

It was such a warm spring day that Margot had decided to brown-bag it in the plaza outside the office, next to the ultramodern Spechocchi-designed waterfall. The plaza was always bustling with pedestrians, but after the high-tension hyper-air-conditioned chill of her single-window office in the Jurgens Building, eating lunch here was almost as good as a Mediterranean vacation.

She was as classy at brown-bagging it as she was at her job; and she laid out a crisp pink Tiffany napkin with *sfinciuni*, the thin Palermo-style pizza sandwich, with a filling of unsmoked ham, ricotta and fontina; a fruit salad of mangoes and strawberries macerated in white wine; and a bottle of still Malvern water.

It was while she was laying out her lunch that she first noticed the man in the dove-gray suit, sitting on the opposite side of the plaza, close to the edge of the waterfall. Most of the time he was half-hidden by passing pedestrians, but there was no doubt at all that he was staring at her. In fact he didn't take his eyes away from her once; and after a few minutes she began to find his unswerving gaze distinctly unsettling.

Margot was used to being stared at by men. She was tall, just over five feet nine inches, and she had striking dark brown hair that was upswept into curls. Her ex-fiancé Paul had told her that she had the face of an angel about to cry: wide blue eyes, a straight delicately defined nose, and subtly pouting lips. She was large-bosomed and quite large-hipped, like her mother, but unlike her mother she could afford to flatter her curves in tailored business suits.

She was the only female account executive at Rutter Blane Rutter. She was the highest-paid woman she knew; and she was determined to reach the very top. No compromises. The top.

She began to eat, but she couldn't help raising her eyes to see if the man was still staring at her. He was—no doubt about it. He was sitting back on one of the benches in a very relaxed pose, one leg crossed over the other. He must have been about thirty-eight or thirty-nine years old, with shining blond hair that was far too long and wavy to be fashionable, at least in the circles in which Margot moved. He wore a pale cream shirt and a dove-gray bow tie to match his suit. There was something about his posture which suggested that he was very wealthy and very self-indulgent, too.

Margot had almost finished her *sfinciuni* when Ray Trimmer appeared. Ray was one of the hottest copywriters at Rutter Blane Rutter, although his lack of personal organization sometimes drove Margot crazy. He slapped a huge untidy package of sandwiches onto the concrete tabletop and sat down too close to her.

"Mind if I join you?" he asked, opening up his sandwiches one by one to investigate their fillings. "My daughter made my lunch today. She's eight. I told her to use her imagination."

Margot frowned at the sandwich on the top of the pile. "Tuna and marmalade. You can't say that's not imaginative."

Ray began to eat. "I wanted to talk to you about that

Spring Flower spot. I'm working toward something less suburban, if you know what I mean. I know a bed-freshener is an entirely suburban product, but I think we have to make it look more elegant, more up-market."

"I liked your first idea."

"I don't know. I ran it past Dale and he wasn't too happy. The woman looks like she's fumigating the bed to get rid of her husband's farts."

"Isn't that just what Spring Flower's for?"

Ray bent forward to pick up another sandwich. As he did so, Margot became conscious again that the man in the dove-gray suit was still staring at her. Blond shining hair, a face that was curiously *medieval*, with eyes of washed-out blue.

"Ray, do you see that guy over there? The one sitting by the waterfall?"

Ray looked up, his mouth full of sandwich, then turned and looked around. At that moment a crowd of Japanese tourists were shuffling across the plaza, and the man was temporarily obscured from view. When the tourists had gone, so had the man; although Margot was at a loss to understand how he could have left without her seeing him go.

"I don't see any man," Ray told her. He pulled a face, and opened up the sandwich he was eating. "What the hell's this? Cheez Whiz and Cap'n Crunchberries. Jesus!"

Margot folded her napkin and tucked it into her Jasper Conran totebag. "I'll catch you later, Ray, okay?"

"Don't you want to see what I've got for dessert?"

Quickly, Margot crossed the plaza toward the waterfall. The water slid so smoothly over the lip at the top that it didn't appear to be moving at all—a sheet of glass. To her surprise, the man was standing a little way behind it, in a brick niche where a bronze statue of a naked woman was displayed—a naked woman with a blindfold.

The man saw Margot coming and made no attempt to

walk away. Instead he looked as if he had been expecting her.

"Pardon me," said Margot, as commandingly as she could, although her heart-rate was jumping around like Roger Rabbit, "do you have some kind of eye problem?"

The man smiled. Close up, he was very tall, six foot three, and he smelled of cinnamon and musk and some very perfumed tobacco.

"Eye problem?" he asked her, in a soft, deep voice.

"Your eyes seem to be incapable of looking at anything except me. Do you want me to call a cop?"

"I apologize," the man replied, bowing his head. "It was not my intention to intimidate you."

"You didn't. But there are plenty of women who might have been."

"Then I apologize again. My only excuse is that I was admiring you. Do you think I might give you something, a very small token of my regret?"

Margot frowned at him in disbelief. "You don't have to give me anything, sir. All I'm asking is that you don't stare at women like Sammy the Psychotic."

He laughed and held out his hand. In his palm was a tiny sparkling brooch—a minuscule pink-and-white flower embedded in glass.

Margot stared at it. "It's beautiful. What is it?"

"It's a jinn-flower, from Mount Rakapushi, in the High Pamirs. It's extinct now, so this is probably the last one there is. It was picked high up on the snow line, and taken to Hunza, where it was encased in molten glass by a method that has been completely lost."

Margot wasn't at all sure that she believed any of this. It sounded like an extremely devious and complicated line but a line all the same. She slowly shook her head. "I couldn't possibly accept anything like that, even if I wanted to accept anything at all."

The man said gently, "I shall be extremely hurt if you don't. You see, I bought it especially for you."

"That's ridiculous. You don't even know me."

"You're Margot Hunter. You're an account executive for Rutter Blane Rutter. I've seen you many times before, Margot. I made a point of finding out."

"Oh, yes?" Margot snapped. "And who the hell are *you?*"

"James Blascoe."

"Is that it? James Blascoe? And what do you do, James Blascoe? And what right do you think you have to check up on me, and then to stare at me?"

James Blascoe raised both hands in apologetic surrender. "I don't really do anything. Some people, like you, are the doers. Other people, like me, are the watchers. You do, I watch. That's all, it's as simple as that."

"Well, do you mind going someplace else to do your watching, Mr. Blascoe?" Margot demanded. "Someplace where you won't scare people?"

"Your point is well taken," James Blascoe told her, and he bowed his head once again and walked off across the plaza. Margot watched him go and was both relieved and disturbed. He had been remarkably attractive, and he was obviously rich. As he reached Bowling Green on the far side of the plaza a long midnight-blue Lincoln stretch-limo appeared and drew up to the curb. He climbed into it and closed the door and didn't look back once.

Margot returned to her office. Ray was waiting for her, with a whole sheaf of messy notes and layouts spread all over her normally pristine desk.

"You look like you saw a ghost," said Ray.

Margot gave him a quick, distracted smile. "Do I? I'm okay."

"You want to look at these new ideas? Kenny did the drawings. They're not exactly right yet, but I think you'll understand where we're coming from."

"All right." Margot nodded. She shuffled through the layouts, still thinking about James Blascoe. *Other people, like me, are the watchers.*

"Neat pin," Ray remarked, as she lifted up another layout.

"I beg your pardon?"

"Your pin, your brooch, whatever it is. Where'd you get it? Bloomingdale's?"

Margot looked down at her fawn linen business suit, and there it was, sparkling brightly in the exact center of her lapel. The tiny jinn-flower embedded in glass.

"Now how the hell did he do that?" she demanded. Then, indignantly, to Ray, she said, "This isn't Bloomingdale's. This is just about the rarest brooch in the whole darn universe! A real flower, handmade glass."

Ray took off his spectacles and peered at it more closely. "Really?" he said, giving Margot the most peculiar look that she had ever seen.

He was waiting for her the next morning when she arrived at the office. He was standing by the revolving doors in the bright eight o'clock sunshine—immaculately dressed, as yesterday, in gray. He stepped toward her with both hands held out, as if to say, I'm sorry, I didn't mean to impose on your life yesterday, I don't mean to impose on your life today.

"You're angry with me," he told her, before she could say anything. She had to step out of the way to avoid the hurrying crowds of office workers.

"I'm not *angry* with you," she retorted. "It's just that I can't accept your gift."

"I don't understand," he replied. For the first time, in the morning light, she saw the small crescent-shaped scar on his left cheekbone.

"It's too much. It's too valuable. Mr. Blascoe, I don't even *know* you."

"What difference does that make? I wanted you to have it."

"In return for what?"

He shook his head as if she had amazed him. "In return for your pleasure, that's all! Do you think I'm some kind of Romeo?"

"But why me? Look at all these pretty girls! Why choose me?"

James Blascoe looked serious for a moment. "Do you always have to know the reason for everything? There's a pattern in the world, that's all. A symmetry. Blessed are those who have, and cursed are those who don't. You're one of the haves."

"Well, I'm flattered, Mr. Blascoe, but I really can't—"

"Keep the brooch, please. Don't break my heart. And, please . . . accept this, too."

He held out a small purse of pale blue moire silk, tied with a gold cord.

Margot laughed in disbelief. "You can't keep on giving me gifts like this!"

"Please," he begged her. There was a look in his eyes which made it oddly difficult for her to resist him. The look in his eyes didn't match his voice at all: It wasn't a begging look. It was level and imperative. A look that said, *You will, whether you like it or not.* Before Margot had time to analyze what she was doing, and the implications of what she was doing, she had taken the silk purse, and she held it up, and said, "All right, then. Thank you."

James Blascoe said, "It's an ounce of perfume created by Isabey, of the Faubourg St. Honoré, in Paris, in 1925. It was specially blended for the Polish baroness Krystyna Waclacz, and there is no more left but this one bottle."

"Why give it to me?" Margot asked him. For some reason, she felt frightened rather than pleased.

James Blascoe shrugged. "What will happen to it, if you don't wear it? Wear it tonight. Wear it every night."

"Hi, Margot!" called her secretary, Denise, as she passed close by. "Don't forget the Perry meeting, eight-thirty on the button!"

Margot looked up at James Blascoe, but he was standing against the sun and his face was masked in shadow. She hesitated for a moment, and then she said, "I'd better go," and pushed her way through the revolving door, leaving James Blascoe standing outside, watching her intently, his features distorted by the curved glass.

In the elevator, she felt as if she were being compressed. Breathless, squashed, tightly surrounded by people who were determined to press the life out of her. By the time the chime rang for the thirty-sixth floor, she was shivering, as if she had contracted the flu, and when she reached her office she stood with her back pressed to the door, taking deep breaths, wondering if she were terrified or aroused, or both.

That night she was taken to see *Les Misérables* by Dominic Bross, the record producer, whom she had met while working on the Bross Records account. Dominic was fifty-five, gray-haired, handsome, talkative, opinionated, and Margot wouldn't have dreamed of going to bed with him in a million years. However, she always enjoyed his company, and he always behaved like a perfect gentleman.

Halfway through the second act, Dominic leaned over to Margot and whispered, "Do you *smell* something?"

Margot sniffed. All she could smell was the musky Isabey perfume which James Blascoe had given her. Once it had warmed on her skin, it had started to give off the deepest, most sensuous fragrance that she had ever experienced. Maybe it had been wrong of her to accept it, but it was something erotic and very special, something that made her head spin.

"I don't know," Dominic complained. "It smells like something died."

* * *

James Blascoe was waiting by her apartment door when she returned from her dinner with Dominic. She was tired and quite angry. For some reason Dominic had been unusually hurried and offhand, and he hadn't even accepted her invitation to come up for coffee. Finding James Blascoe at her door didn't make her feel very much better.

"Well, well," she said, taking out her key. "I'm surprised Leland let you in to the building."

"Oh, you know me." James Blascoe smiled. "Bribery and corruption are second nature to me."

"I'm not going to invite you in," Margot told him. "I've had a totally terrible evening, and all I'm going to do is take a bath and get some sleep."

"I'm sorry," James Blascoe told her. "I quite understand, and I won't intrude. But I wanted to give you this."

He reached into his inside pocket and took out a long black jewelry case. Before Margot could protest, he had opened it up and shown her what lay inside. It was a shimmering diamond necklace, so bright that it was almost magical, seven diamond festoons attached to ten diamond-encrusted bows.

"This is absurd," Margot protested, although it was hard for her to keep her eyes off the necklace. It was absolutely the most beautiful thing she had ever seen in her life.

James Blascoe slowly smiled. It was like somebody slowly drawing a spoon through an open jar of molasses. "Traditionally, this necklace was supposed to have been part of the ransom offered by Catherine the Great to the Sultan of Turkey."

"Well, who does it belong to now?" asked Margot. The diamonds shone in tiny pinpricks of light across her cheeks.

"Now," James Blascoe said, with utter simplicity, "now, it belongs to you."

Margot lifted her eyes away from the necklace. "Mr. Blascoe, this is ridiculous. I'm not a whore."

"Did I ever suggest that you were? Take it. It's a gift. I want nothing in return."

"You really want nothing?" Margot challenged him.

"Take it," he said. "I want you to have the finest of everything. That's all. I have no other ambition."

There was an unblinking look of command in his eyes. Margot knew that the jinn-flower brooch and the Isabey perfume had been one thing. But if she accepted this necklace, no matter how much James Blascoe protested that he wanted nothing at all, she would be beholden to him. It was probably worth over a hundred thousand dollars. It was certainly exquisite: the kind of jewelry which most women can never even dream of owning.

"Why me?" she whispered.

"Why not?" he replied, with the faintest shrug.

"No, tell me," she insisted. "Why me?"

He was silent for a disturbingly long time. Then he touched the crescent-shaped scar on his cheek with his fingertip, stroking it and stroking it, and said, "There are some people in this world who have been overfavored. The brightest and the best. God has given them everything. Looks, brilliance, wealth. And then—as if in a kind of madness of overgenerosity—He has given them even more."

He hesitated for a while, with the side of his mouth lifted by an enigmatic, self-satisfied smile. "You are one of those people, that's all. Now, please . . . accept the necklace."

"No," said her mouth. *What am I doing?* said her mind. But her hand reached out and took it.

Two days later, at a cocktail thrash at the Plaza Hotel for Overmeyer & Cranston, one of their biggest clients, Margot decided to take a risk and wear the necklace for the first time. She matched it with a simple electric-blue cocktail dress and wore the simplest of diamond-stud earrings.

The party was already noisy with laughter and conversation when Margot arrived. She smiled and waved to O & C's president George Demaris and then to Dick Manzi of NBC. However, she was surprised when both of them frowned at her and gave her only a half-hearted wave in return; she was even more surprised when the cocktail waiter stared at her in what could only be described as dumbstruck astonishment.

She took a glass of champagne and challenged him. "Something wrong?"

"Oh, no, no. Nothing's wrong, ma'am."

A few moments later, however, Walter Rutter angled his way across the room toward her and took her arm and tugged her almost immediately to the side of the buffet table.

"Margot? What's with the necklace? You can't wear something like that here!"

"What do you mean, Walter? This necklace is worth a fortune! It was part of the ransom that Catherine the Great gave to the Sultan of Turkey!"

Walter narrowed his crow's-footed eyes and stared at Margot for a long time. Margot defiantly stared back at him.

"Catherine the Great gave that necklace to the Sultan of Turkey?" Walter said. He sounded short of breath.

Margot nodded. "A very dear friend gave it to me."

"I'm sorry," Walter told her. He was obviously choosing his words carefully. "But—if it's worth a fortune—maybe this is not quite the place to wear it. You know, for the sake of security. Maybe we should ask the management to lock it in the safe for a while."

Margot fingered the necklace in disappointment. "You really think so?"

Walter laid a fatherly arm around her bare shoulders. "Yes, Margot. I really think so." Then he sniffed, and looked around, and said, "Those fish canapés sure smell strong. I hope nobody goes down with food poisoning."

* * *

221

The next morning, James Blascoe was waiting for Margot in the foyer of Rutter Blane Rutter, with a large gift-wrapped box in his hands. Black shiny paper, a black shiny bow.

"Mr. Blascoe," she said, emphatically, before he could open his mouth, "this really has to stop. You can't go on giving me all of these ridiculously expensive gifts."

He thought for a moment, lowered his eyes. "Supposing I were to tell you that I loved you, beyond all reason?"

"Mr. Blascoe—"

"Please, call me James. And, please, take this gift. It's an original Fortuny evening dress, made for the Comtesse de la Ronce, one of the wealthiest women in France, in 1927. The only person in the world who could possibly wear it is you."

"Mr. Blascoe—" she protested. But his eyes told her that she must accept the gown, no matter what.

"James," she whispered, and took the box.

That evening, he was waiting outside her apartment, with a black silk shoe bag. Inside were the softest pair of pointed suede ankle boots, handmade by Rayne. They were meticulously hand-stitched and dyed to the color of crushed loganberries to match exactly the color of the Fortuny gown.

"Take them, wear them," he insisted. "Wear them always. Remember how much I love you."

She was awoken the next morning by the phone ringing. Tugging her fingers through her tangled curls, she found the receiver and picked it up.

"Margot? Sorry to call you so early. This is Walter Rutter."

"Walter! Hi, good morning! What can I do for you?"

"Margot, I wanted to catch you before you left for the office. You see, the point is I'm in some difficulty here. I have to make some savings in the agency's overall budget, and that regrettably means shedding some staff."

"I see. Do you know how many?"

"Not exactly, Margot. But the problem is that it has to be last in, first out. This is nothing to do with the fact that you're a woman—and nothing to do with your abilities, which have been tremendous in the past, and have earned us a great deal of acclaim. But . . . as things stand, I'm afraid that I'm going to have to disemploy you, as of now."

Margot sat up straight. "You mean I'm fired?"

"Nothing like that, Margot. Not fired. But not continued with, staffwise."

Margot couldn't think of anything to say. She let the phone drop onto the comforter. She felt as if someone had suddenly lashed her with a birch, stinging her face, cutting her hands, slicing her self-assurance into ribbons.

She was still sitting upright in bed twenty minutes later, when the doorbell rang.

Mechanically, she wrapped herself in her short silk robe and went to answer the door. It was James Blascoe, with a long gift-wrapped box and the smile of a man whose will can never be denied.

"I've brought you something," he announced.

Without waiting to be asked, he walked into the living room and laid the box on the table. He tugged free the gift ribbon himself and eased off the lid. Inside, wrapped in dark brown tissue paper, was a huge greenish scepter, almost four feet long, embossed with thick gold bands and complicated knobs and bumps. James lifted it up, and Margot saw that the scepter's head had been cast in the helmeted shape of a man's erect glans, except that it was nearly twice human size.

She stared at it, her cheeks flushed, strangely excited by its decorative blatancy.

"Do you know what this is?" asked James. "The phallus used by Queen Nefertiti of Egypt to give herself erotic pleasure. It's over three thousand years old. It has been passed down from one century to another, from one royal court to the next. It has slid its way up between the thighs of more celebrated women than anybody could count."

He grasped the glans in his hand, rubbing his thumb against it as if it were his own. "It is said to give more pleasure than anything you could imagine, man or beast. Now it's yours, to keep, and to use."

He brought it across the room and laid it in the palms of her hands. "Tonight, at midnight, dress in the jewelry and clothes that I have given you, perfume yourself with my perfume, and then think of me, and give yourself the pleasure that only you deserve."

Margot still couldn't speak. James kissed her forehead with a cool, dry, almost abstracted kiss, and then he left the apartment and closed the door behind him.

At eleven o'clock that night, like a woman in a dream, Margot ran herself a deep perfumed bath. She washed herself slowly and sensually, rubbing the soap over her full white breasts over and over again, until the nipples rose between her fingers.

At last she rose naked from the bath and dried herself in a deep warm Descamps towel. Her apartment was filled with mirrors: She could watch herself walk from room to room.

She brushed out her curls and made up her face, starkly, very white. Then she dropped the velvety Fortuny dress over her shoulders, and it touched her bare body like a series of soft, hurried kisses. She pinned the jinn-flower brooch to her shoulder, fastened the diamond-festoon necklace around her neck, and slipped on the handmade ankle boots. Last of all she sprayed herself with Isabey perfume.

It was almost midnight. She went to the table and lifted the huge copper-and-gold phallus out of the tissue paper. It was very heavy, and it gleamed dully in the lamplight. *It is said to give more pleasure than anything you could imagine, man or beast.*

She knelt in the middle of the floor and lifted up her gown. Holding the phallus with both hands, she parted her thighs and presented its massive green glans to the dark, silky fur of her vulva.

At first she didn't believe that she would be able to insert it, and she clenched her teeth. But then, little by little, the huge cold head buried itself inside her, and she managed to force it farther and farther up, until she was able to kneel upright, with the base of the phallus flat against the floor.

The sensation of having such a huge rod of chilled, uncompromising metal up inside her made her wince and quake with erotic anticipation. Her hands smoothed and massaged the swollen lips of her vulva and then caressed the slippery meeting place between metal and flesh.

Think of me, James had asked her, and as she pressed her whole weight down onto the phallus, she tried to visualize his face. As flesh parted, as membranes tore, she tried to remember what he looked like. But she couldn't. She couldn't even think of his eyes.

He had been right, though. The pleasure was beyond all belief. She gasped and shook in the most devastating of climaxes, and then the blood suddenly welled in her throat and poured out over her lips.

Ray had been trying to call her all day, and when she didn't answer, he went around to her apartment and persuaded the concierge Leland to let him in.

The living room was dark, with the blinds still closed. In the center of the room, surrounded by mirrors, Margot lay with her eyes still open and her mouth caked with dried blood.

Around her neck she wore a piece of twisted wire, decorated with Pepsi caps and unrolled condoms. She was wrapped in a frayed pink candlewick bathrobe and worn-down Keds. The bathrobe was stained dark with blood, and out from between her thighs protruded a long section of scaffolding pole.

Shaking with shock, Ray knelt down next to her and closed her eyelids with a gentle touch of finger and thumb. He had realized for some days now that she was going off the rails. Pressure of success, that's what Walter Rutter had called it. But he had never imagined for one moment that she would kill herself, not like this. How could any woman kill herself like this?

The room stank of sardine oil—the same smell that had been following Margot around for the past few days.

Ray stood up at last and looked around. The concierge was standing in the doorway, pale, paralyzed with uncertainty, and Ray said, "You'd better call an ambulance—and the cops."

Outside in the spring-sunny street, a man stood watching as the ambulance arrived. He was unshaven and wore a soiled gray suit. His eyes were red from lack of sleep and alcohol. He waited to see the blanket-covered body taken away, and then, as the sirens whooped, he started walking southward, sniffing from time to time and ceaselessly searching through his pockets as if he expected to find a cigarette butt that he had previously overlooked or even a couple of quarters.

It was always the same after he had snuffed out another of the world's brighter lights. A dull headache, trembling legs. But that was the nature of his work. Balancing the world, exercising social justice. For every bag lady who died in a trash-filled doorway, one of life's brighter flowers had to be plucked. Justice—that was all it was. Somebody had to do it. Somebody had to keep the balance.

When he reached Herald Square he stood on the curb outside Macy's for five or ten minutes. Then he saw a pretty, well-dressed young woman crossing the street toward him, pushing a golden-haired child in a baby buggy. He gave a last sniff and straightened himself up and smiled at her.

Inside Margot's apartment, Ray reached down and picked up the small plastic flower-brooch which had fallen from her bathrobe. He looked down at it for a moment, then dropped it into his pocket. It would be something to remember her by.

DEAR DIARY

Elsa Rutherford

August 3

This afternoon when I went for my visit with Dr. Fillmore, we prayed for the dauphin and the future of France. Dr. Fillmore understands that I must follow the visions God has given me. I said ten Hail Mary's, and Dr. Fillmore just listened. He isn't Catholic, but I can tell he's a very spiritual person.

I go on my own now. They trust me. I'm sure it's because Dr. Fillmore has told them how trustworthy I am.

After Nurse Samuels unlocks the door behind her cubicle and walks with me to the elevator, I go down to the main floor by myself. The elevator creaks and chugs; this place is old, but I don't mind. Dr. Fillmore's office is at the end of the hallway to the right of the elevator.

When I came into Dr. Fillmore's office this afternoon he smiled and said, "Good afternoon. I'm Dr. Fillmore, and who are you?" We've been having these little visits for some time now, but Dr. Fillmore seems to think it appropriate to reintroduce ourselves each time we meet. He's very courtly and proper, except when he brings up the subject of my parents. I'd rather not talk about my parents. May they rest in eternal peace.

When I go to visit Dr. Fillmore, I never stop or dawdle along the way. I don't understand people who waste time; it's as though they have no sense of who they are, no purpose in life. Unfortunately, so many of the guests here seem to have nothing better to do than stand around staring off into space. When I have places to go and things to do, which I always have, I get on with it. On my way to see Dr. Fillmore I never even pause to talk with the doorman who stands guard at his post beside the front door. I give him a courteous nod and continue on about my business.

Of course, I sometimes stop by the water fountain in the hall. People do have to quench their thirst. And I have been known to take a moment or two to admire the giant potted ferns that sit beneath the window just past the water fountain. They're always green and pretty. Someone here must know exactly what to do and what not to do to keep them healthy. They do try hard to take good care of things here.

Occasionally I allow myself a glance at the fire extinguisher outside Dr. Fillmore's office. Well, perhaps fire extinguisher isn't the right term. It's the old-fashioned kind, very interesting—the kind inside a glass case with a hose on a rack. The nozzle on the end of the hose is brass and very shiny. There's an ax inside the case, too. A rather small ax with a short handle. I like to look at my reflection in the glass. It's almost as good as having a mirror.

I'm not sure I like my hair the way it is today. Plain brown and all chopped off. I think I look like a boy. I wonder if Dr. Fillmore thinks I look like a boy. No, I'm certain Dr. Fillmore doesn't see people as male or female but as God's creatures who must strive diligently to do His blessed will. I like Dr. Fillmore. My name is Joan.

August 9

My hair looks terrific today. It's long and fluffs out around my shoulders. And I'm crazy about the color, sort of platinum blond. Real sexy. I gave myself the once-over in the glass on my way to see Fillmore. I know I look good. God, I just love having big boobs, having them poke out the way they do. Fillmore couldn't keep his eyes off them. I looked him straight in the face, gave him that look that said, *I know what you're thinking, buster!* He glanced down real quick and fidgeted with some papers on his desk, pretending nothing was going on. Silly man. I guess I'm too much for him. I guess he doesn't know what to do with me, but I wouldn't mind giving him a lesson or two. He's a good-looking hunk.

But I'm getting sick and tired of hearing: *"Let's talk about your mother. Let's talk about your father. Let's talk about your childhood."* Same old thing. Boring. Boring.

About halfway through the visit, I got up and sidled over to where Fillmore was sitting behind the desk, as if I was kind of restless and needed to stretch my legs. I leaned over, pretending to look at something on his desk, and brushed against him so that my boob rubbed against his shoulder. Then I sat down on the corner of his desk and squirmed around so my skirt was hiked up to my thighs, and I didn't bother to cross my legs or keep them together. Fillmore got a good crotch shot. I know he did. His face turned red, and he said, "I think you'd be more comfortable back over there in the chair, Mae." So *he'd* be more comfortable. That's what he meant.

But he loved it. I know how men are. They've all got just one thing on the brain. They'll do anything to get what they want. And they'll talk others into helping them get it, too.

Fillmore never got up from his desk, so I couldn't see below his waist, but I bet he was hard as a rock. I bet he would have loved pushing me down on that desk and having somebody hold me there while he crawled on top. He wanted to put it to me. I know he did. That's what they all want. To heave and shove and grunt like nasty old pigs. I can't help it if I'm sexy. I guess I was born that way. But when you're a grown woman you can choose who gets into your pants.

When I left, I told Fillmore he ought to get out of that stuffy old office once in a while and come up and see me sometime.

August 16

I'm wearing a very beautiful headpiece. Much like a tiara. But, instead of gaudy jewels, it's ornamented with an exquisite golden serpent. It is a symbol of my high station. I wear it on certain occasions—such as my visit to Dr. Fillmore today. To be perfectly frank, I was rather dismayed that he failed to bow when I entered the room. Not the slightest sign of obeisance. The man is impudent. Perhaps I should have rebuked him immediately. Instead, displaying great forbearance, I chose not to do so. We of noble birth often find ourselves obliged to tolerate the ill-bred and the low-born. There are so many of them and so few of us.

The doctor wanted to talk about my relationship with my parents. He pressed me to speak of certain incidents from my childhood. I declined. Why dwell on unpleasant matters? I am growing weary of this inquisition. I offered to discuss life along the Nile . . . or Julius or Antony . . . but the learned doctor did not seem interested.

I am sure he is jealous. It's obvious that he dreams of how it would be to lie with me. I can see it in his eyes though certainly he dares not speak of it. Well, let him dream. Even dogs are permitted their dreams. Let him imagine bringing his swollen loins to my silken couch. Let him picture in lusty detail the glory of such a coupling. Let him imagine the perfection of my alabaster breasts and the ecstasy of my embrace. I allow him his fantasy, for that is all he will ever have. Though I have a generous nature, there are limits to my indulgence and he would pay dearly should he forget his place and so much as lay a finger on a lock of my ebony hair.

August 23

Today, before my visit, I looked in the glass again. The nozzle is still so shiny. It looks as if they open the glass and polish it every day. I know they don't, of course. There's no way to open the glass except to break it. And it's not easy to break. You have to hit it really hard. I never noticed before, but the ax blade is as shiny as the nozzle. And sharp, too. A sharp ax can be a very handy thing to have around.

I cut my hand today. It bled. I hate the sight of blood. It's sickening. When I went in to see Dr. Fillmore, I kept my hands behind my back. Fillmore's got eyes like an eagle. I tried to forget about the blood, to forget about what was behind my back. I can block anything out of my mind if I try hard enough.

Dr. Fillmore wanted to talk about my parents again. I knew he would. He always does. If he doesn't shut up . . .

If he wants to talk about somebody's parents, let him talk about his own. I bet his old ma and pa were as ugly and hateful as he is. I bet they made him do nasty things when he was little. I bet he remembers every filthy detail to this very day. Every terrible, terrible detail . . .

When I let Fillmore see my hands, when I raised them high, his eyes went wide, and, after that, he made an odd, gurgling sound.

I don't know why Dr. Fillmore has become such a slob. After I'd been there for a while today, I noticed that his hair was damp and matted and that his clothes were all blotched with stains. It was sickening. I stood right over him and he just stared up at me, never blinking, his mouth gaping open, as if he didn't have a clue to why I was looking at him. When I glanced up, I saw that the office was in pretty foul shape, too. Right away I began to feel dirty, as if the place was rubbing off on me. I had to get out of there. So I just turned my back on the sickening mess and walked out. I went straight back the way I'd come. I didn't stop or dawdle or slow down for anything. In fact, I barely spoke to the nice doorman who took my arm when he saw me coming down the hall and insisted on escorting me back up in the elevator. I didn't say a word when he took the ax from me.

My name is Lizzie.

THE SPLICER

Don D'Ammassa

*I*n retrospect, Scott suspected that the first tampering with the film program had occurred during the Godzilla Festival.

Saturday was always science-fiction night at the Managansett Cinema, just as Fridays were reserved for horror films, Mondays for swashbucklers, and so on. Old Man Bradford couldn't afford to show first-run movies in the town's only theater, but he made up for it by sheer volume. Every show was a double feature on weeknights, triples on weekends.

The same economy was reflected in the staff. Candy Carter sold tickets from one side of her booth, candy and popcorn from the other. Scott collected the tickets at the entrance to the theater, did a brief stint as an usher, then climbed the narrow stairway to the projection booth. It was a real struggle on Friday nights, their only busy nights, when they played to a nearly full house, but generally there were less than two dozen customers, primarily teenage couples so preoccupied with each other he could have shown three hours of blank tape without their noticing anything. Scott would never have lasted three years in this job if it required any real initiative or brainpower; he operated the projector mechanically and possessed no understanding at all of the means by which celluloid images were transmitted to the screen. His boss occasionally made disapproving sounds about his shoulder-length blond hair, of which Scott was inordinately proud, but had never pressed the issue, perhaps because Scott was willing to accept such low wages.

Scott had long since stopped paying much attention to the movies, almost all of which he had seen several times before, preferring to spend the time lost in one daydream or another, usually involving the dispensation of large sums of cash or the resolution of dramatic political crises for which only Scott Barkin had the necessary personal qualities. Infrequently, there were sexual overtones, but carnal acts or nudity made him uncomfortable, on the screen or off it.

Which is probably why he noticed the girl in the torn dress during *Godzilla versus the Smog Monster*.

It was the third of three Godzilla movies that night, and Scott was anxious for it to end so that he could rewind the film, check to be certain the theater was empty, and lock up for the night. The smog monster had just taken to the air on its latest rampage when the camera shifted to a crowd shot, the usual aggregation of frightened figures running for whatever ineffective shelter they could find. At the forefront of the crowd, a slender Japanese woman fell to the ground, her blouse slipping from one shoulder. As she struggled to rise, someone stepped on the hem of her dress, which tore all the way to her waistline, briefly revealing a swath of white thigh before she was swallowed up by the crowd.

Scott only noticed it because even that small hint of sexuality seemed anachronistic in a Japanese monster movie of the 1970s.

A week or two later, while the original *King Kong* was passing across the screen, Scott was startled by the giant ape's rather revealing exploration of Fay Wray's clothing, at one point exposing a clearly naked breast for a split second. He vaguely recalled reading that some censored footage from the original print had been restored, so he just shook his head and chuckled.

It was the torrid love scene between Anne Francis and Leslie Nielsen in *Forbidden Planet* that finally led him to suspect that something was wrong. It was part of a double feature, opening with the classic *The Thing.* Margaret Sheridan had seemed somewhat lightly clad for a posting in Antarctica, and she displayed a rather fuller figure than Scott remembered, but otherwise there had been no note of incongruity in that film. But when Nielsen and Francis began clutching at one another in evident passion during the next show, Scott knew something was up.

"What the hell?" He rose from his chair and moved forward, peering out through the small window at the screen shimmering below. Nielsen had one hand closed quite obviously over a breast, while his free hand worked at the fastenings of her blouse. The ultimate revelation was only put off when Dr. Morbius, portrayed by Walter Pidgeon, put in an untimely appearance.

When the theater had emptied some time later, Scott stood staring at the coiled film. There had been no discernible reaction from the audience; could he have imagined the entire sequence?

"Hey, can I go now?"

Startled, Scott turned to see Candy standing nonchalantly in the projection-room doorway.

"Yeah, I suppose so. Everything all set downstairs?"

She nodded, chewing gum energetically. "Of course. I'll deposit the box office take on my way home. You okay? You look kind of funny?"

"Me? I'm fine. See you tomorrow." He was aware that he sounded distracted, but he couldn't help it. Absentmindedly, he followed her downstairs to the lobby.

"Okay, sure. See you." She watched him another second, then turned and left.

That's when he noticed the kid with the thick-rimmed glasses standing at one side of the lobby.

"Excuse me, mister." The kid stepped out of the shadows. Scott judged him to be barely into his teens. "Was that some special cut of *Forbidden Planet* or something?"

So he hadn't imagined it! But he didn't want to give anything away to this kid. Not until he had a chance to think. Scott kept his expression neutral. "What do you mean? It looked fine to me."

The boy seemed confused. "Some of that stuff wasn't in the original film. I thought maybe it was a restored version, like they did with *King Kong*, you know."

Scott shrugged. "I don't know, kid; I just show 'em. Sometimes we get the old ones spliced together wrong. Come on, let's go. I have to lock up."

Later that night, somewhere deep in his brain, Scott conceived the idea that this odd variant of the original film might be valuable, but try as he might, he could think of no way to take advantage of the situation. It would have to be sent back to the distributor in the morning; even if he had the facilities to copy it first, he had no idea how to make use of his discovery. The thought that he was missing a chance to make money, possibly quite a lot of money, was disturbing.

The very next weekend, Scott realized he had misjudged the situation.

It was a triple feature this time, starting with Gene Barry in *The War of the Worlds*. Scott paid little attention until the final moments, then moved his seat to a better vantage point. Next up was *Silent Running*, one of the few movies he still enjoyed watching, primarily because of the cleverly conceived robot characters. He had heard somewhere that they had actually hired amputees to play the parts, standing on their hands inside the confining costumes, and he never tired of trying to imagine how each shot had been constructed.

Within minutes, Scott realized that something was wrong. He knew without question that the crew member named Wolf was not a tall, slender redheaded female. At least, not until now. He was so stunned that he never even noticed later when, during the fight scene between Raquel Welch and Martine Beswicke in *One Million Years B.C.*, the former's furry bra was completely removed.

He waited impatiently for the last disheveled couple to fix their clothing and leave the auditorium, then descended to the lobby and helped Candy finish her cleaning up. She looked at him suspiciously—he had never offered any kind of assistance before—but made no comment.

"Walk me to the bank?" There had been two muggings in downtown Managansett that week, and Candy had expressed concern about her own safety.

"Sorry." He shook his head. "I've still got things to do before I leave."

She bit her lip. "I can wait, I guess. I'd feel better if I had some company while I'm carrying all that money."

Scott made an impatient noise. "It's not even a hundred dollars, Candy, for Christ's sake."

"The muggers don't know that!"

He shifted his weight from one foot to the other. "Look, just leave it for me. I'll make the deposit myself on my way home, all right?"

She looked dubious. "I don't know. I'm really supposed to do that myself."

"Then do it and stop whining at me!" he exploded. "I'm not paid to be your bodyguard or your nursemaid."

Candy's eyes widened and her mouth opened as though she were about to respond in kind. But then her features twisted angrily and she snatched up the deposit bag, whirled, and stormed out of the theater.

Scott carefully remounted the film on the projector and restarted it, convinced that his fortune was made. The credits played through and the story began.

Wolf was once again a young actor named Cliff Potts.

That evening, lying awake in bed, Scott Barkin reviewed the possibilities. There had been an opportunity for someone to switch copies while he was downstairs arguing with Candy, but that seemed highly improbable. He might be going crazy, have hallucinated the entire thing, but he dismissed that immediately because clearly that kid had seen the same thing he had in *Forbidden Planet*. The only other alternatives that occurred to him were that . . . somehow . . . the images from the film were being altered before they reached the screen, or that there was a way to make more than one person hallucinate the same way. He had no idea how this could e achieved, but perhaps some brilliant but reclusive inventor had developed such a device and was testing it secretly. Certainly Managansett, Rhode Island, was pretty remote, intellectually if not physically. The entire town seemed to lag a decade or more behind the rest of the world.

There still might be some way he could take advantage of the situation, but to do so, he would have to identify the source of the alterations. Tomorrow was comedy night, *Arsenic and Old Lace* and *A Funny Thing Happened on the Way to the Forum*. He was familiar with both movies and should be able to spot any variations. Somehow he would have to devise a method of tracing these changes back to their source. He passed the night restlessly trying to develop a strategy to deal with the situation.

Disappointingly, Sunday's screening passed without event, as did those throughout the week. Scott was ready to chalk everything up to fatigue and tension when he showed up for work on Saturday.

The Blob passed uneventfully enough, Steve McQueen saving the day in the final moments. The classic was followed by the darkly humorous sequel *Beware the Blob*, one of the few Scott had not seen before. His unfamiliarity caused him to miss some subtle divergences from the original, the highly revealing dress Carol Lynley wore during the party sequence, the dissolving of Cindy Williams's clothing during her death scene. The third feature, however, was another of his favorites.

Originally, Bradford had ordered *The Stuff*, another Blob-like film to complete the triple feature. The distributor had accidentally substituted *Close Encounters of the Third Kind*, which, while mismatched, was to Scott's thinking a far superior movie.

His enjoyment turned to excitement during the scene in which Richard Dreyfuss and Teri Garr had a hysterical argument in the bathroom. Frustrated, confused, even frightened, Dreyfuss/Roy struck out at his wife. Garr/Ronnie fell back against the bathroom wall in astonishment, then began to struggle as her distraught husband tore at her bathrobe and began making violent love to her. They were both naked when their children arrived to investigate the disturbance.

Scott rushed downstairs as the film was ending to ensure that he could surreptitiously watch the patrons on their way out. To his disappointment, everyone looked perfectly ordinary. There were several young couples who came regularly to neck in the back row, two young males who appeared to have arrived separately, a couple of elderly men, one distracted woman who constantly subvocalized to herself, and the kid with the glasses.

Scott crossed to intercept him, trying to be casual. "How'd you like the show?"

The kid peered up at him dubiously. "I don't know where you get these cuts, mister, but if my mom finds out what you're showing here, she'll never let me come again."

"Let's not tell her then, right?"

When the theater was empty, Candy locked the door from the inside. She hadn't forgiven him his churlishness. "Don't you have things to do?" She glared at him until he turned away, but he hadn't even noticed. His mind was racing at full speed.

Just to be certain, he rechecked the tape before leaving for the night. The film now displayed the original version.

Obviously, whatever device was being used was quite small, virtually undetectable. Even if it was some kind of hallucinatory gas, it would have to be contained in something. Perhaps he could at least identify who was bringing it into the theater. Scott began paying more attention to the movies he showed, but as he had expected, nothing happened during the next several days. He had concluded by now that whoever was responsible came on Saturday nights only, for the science-fiction program.

The following Saturday, a notebook and pen were at hand. Scott knew few customers by name, but most of them were familiar enough that he could mark down some significant characteristic by which to separate one from another. He made twenty-seven entries in all, either while taking tickets, or later, during a leisurely stroll through the theater before bringing down the house lights.

The Creature from the Black Lagoon passed uneventfully, but *Barbarella* was transformed.

Scott knew something was up right from the opening sequence when the nude Jane Fonda received her assignment. He couldn't remember how explicit the original had been, but this screening was downright lewd. Judging by the murmuring from the audience, the explicit sex on screen had even attracted the attention of the back-row patrons. And it didn't end there. Each encounter was altered in some fashion, always designed to provide longer and more revealing glimpses of Barbarella's body. The scene involving the now transparent pleasure machine was so erotic that it evoked a shocked outcry from someone in the audience.

The kid gave him a strange look at the end of the show, but rushed out of the lobby without speaking.

The next several weeks involved a painful process of elimination. Scott had decided to drop from his original list anyone who was absent during a subsequent incident. David Warner's rape of Mary Steenburgen in *Time After Time* eliminated seven people the very next weekend, but it took two more films to eliminate another five, and there were still eleven contenders. Confusing the issue was an influx of new viewers, primarily high school students lured by rumors of X-rated films. Scott's quarry must have noticed something amiss as well, because there were no alterations for almost a month, long enough for attendance to dip back to its usual level.

Scott was on the verge of giving up when the changes resumed. They had been growing increasingly daring all along, and the single-mindedly sexual nature of the alterations continued. But now the sex was frequently distorted, even violent. The mute girl, Nova, was subjected to some sort of painful electrical stimulation in *Planet of the Apes,* and the Morlocks tied Weena over an open fire for a prolonged sequence in *The Time Machine.*

For three straight weeks, Scott was unable to eliminate any of his candidates, the list of whom now consisted of two teenagers, the woman who talked to herself, an elderly man who seemed to fall asleep frequently, a man in his mid-twenties suffering from the worst case of acne Scott had ever seen, and an overweight middle-aged man whom Scott had chosen for no particular reason as the most likely culprit. The kid with the glasses stopped coming after Dian the Beautiful was brutally ravished in *At the Earth's Core.*

On the last Saturday in November, Scott got lucky.

For one thing, it was sleeting and promised to get worse. Candy had been glancing nervously outdoors ever since she arrived, even though she lived only six blocks away. Only seven people bought tickets, and two of them were among those whom Scott had already eliminated. There was also a middle-aged couple he'd never seen before. That left the acne case, the middle-aged man, and one teenage boy, the only one who always sat by himself.

The first feature was *Night of the Comet.* For a long time, Scott was afraid that there would be no change in the script, that this would be another fruitless night. But when the insane stockboys stripped and spanked the two sisters before tying them up, he knew his quarry was in the theater.

But there were still three possibilities.

Then the middle-aged man rose and walked up the aisle to the door, zipping his coat as he did so. Scott ran quickly downstairs and confirmed that the man had indeed left the theater. Two suspects remained, Acne Face and the quiet boy.

The second feature was *Wavelength,* a relatively low-key story about a young couple who stumble on a secret military base where three extraterrestrials are imprisoned. Scott watched intently but with growing unease. If nothing changed, did that mean the older man was his quarry? The brief nude scene early in the movie passed without alteration, and Scott settled back in his chair thoughtfully, trying to decide how best to approach the man.

The story unrolled before him, but Scott's mind was elsewhere as Robert Carradine and Cherie Currie made their way through the tunnels, eventually to be discovered and captured. He was so preoccupied, in fact, that he never did see how the girl's sweater was lost during the struggle with the guard, and only the brutality of the beating administered afterward was enough stimulus to startle him from his reverie.

Scott was downstairs waiting even before the closing credits began to scroll across the screen. Just possibly something in the demeanor of one of the two remaining suspects would tip him off. Acne Face walked by, eyes downcast, hands tucked into coat pockets, and never even looked in Scott's direction.

The quiet boy never came out at all.

Scott checked the theater thoroughly, but there was no sign of him. Something of his perplexity must have shown because Candy asked him what was wrong.

"One of the customers never came out," he explained. "That mousy little kid with the glasses who's in here all the time. Maybe I should check the rest room again."

"Don't bother." She sighed. "He took off right after the first picture ended. I heard him asking for a ride."

Reality seemed to freeze in place. "Are you sure? He left before the second feature started?"

She shrugged. "About then, yeah. The older guy who comes in here a lot is his neighbor, I guess. What difference does it make?"

Scott never answered her question, never even heard it, and a few seconds later, Candy turned away, shaking her head.

The following Saturday, Scott was waiting for Acne Face, having decided upon his strategy the night before.

"I know what you've been doing," he whispered as he accepted the ticket. Startled eyes met his own, then darted away.

"I don't . . ." The sound drifted off.

"Wait for me outside, half an hour after the show ends." Scott spoke more firmly. "I won't tell anyone if you do what I say."

There was no reply, but the look of guilt that passed over the acne-scarred features was as good as a confession.

There were no changes in that evening's double feature.

"I'm Scott." He offered his gloved hand in the darkness outside of the theater. The slouched figure standing in the shadow made no effort to respond. "What's your name?"

"Chuck. Chuck Scusset."

"Pleased to meet you, Chuck. Look, it's freezing out here. Why don't we go to some place quiet and talk about this, somewhere warm?"

And so it was that they ended up in Chuck Scusset's cluttered apartment less than six blocks from the theater.

Scott was no fanatic about neatness, but he was appalled by his surroundings. Chuck lived in what amounted to a bed-sitting room with an adjoining half bath on the third floor of one of Managansett's seedier apartment buildings. Other than the bed, there was a single folding chair and a card table, no other furnishings. Chuck's clothing was apparently stored in two cheap suitcases and a half dozen cardboard boxes he had retrieved from behind one of the local markets. Chuck had taken the chair, so Scott was forced to sit on the bed, the only relatively uncluttered area available.

It was evident that Chuck was a science-fiction fan. There were piles of genre paperbacks and digest-size magazines lining every wall, covering the card table, under the bed, filling the few shelves mounted on the walls. A model of the starship *Enterprise* stood in one corner of the room, surrounded by figurines of monsters, aliens, and space-suited humans. There was no other indication whatsoever of human habitation except for an occasional candy wrapper or empty potato chip bag.

"So how do you do it?" Scott asked.

"I didn't do anything," came the sullen reply.

"No shit? The movies just changed themselves and you let me come up here just because you're a nice guy."

No response.

Scott leaned forward, hands on knees. "Listen, Chuck, you're messing with copyrighted material here. You could get into a lot of trouble doing that."

"I don't hurt anything!"

Scott sat back, sighing with satisfaction. "Ah, but you do change things, don't you?"

For a few short seconds, it seemed as if Chuck were going to retreat into denial once more, but at last he nodded.

"All right, then, we can work out a deal, can't we?" Scott didn't wait for an answer. "Show me what you do it with."

Chuck looked away, apparently staring at a water stain on the far wall. "Can't."

Scott made an impatient noise. "Cut the crap, Chuck. You already admitted you're doing it, now show me the goddamned thing, whatever it is!"

The head snapped back in his direction and the lips grew firmer. "I can't! I do it with, you know, my head. Like, I imagine how I want the story to be, and it changes."

This wasn't at all what Scott expected, and he wasn't sure he liked it.

"You mean, there's no machine or anything like that? It's just something you can do and no one else?"

Chuck nodded.

Visions of a vanishing fortune raced through his head. But perhaps everything was not lost. He could arrange private showings, charge hundreds, maybe even thousands of dollars for the privilege of viewing an altered version of some movie or another. Maybe Chuck could substitute Cary Grant for Clark Gable in *Gone With the Wind* or something. But wouldn't the studios want a big cut if he did that or maybe even file an injunction or lawsuit against him?

"Listen, Chuck, there might be a lot of money in this for us."

"What do you mean?"

Scott gave a general summary of his ideas, not wanting to be too specific, partly because he didn't want Chuck to realize how nebulous his plans were, partly because he wanted to give the impression that arcane knowledge was necessary. It wouldn't do to allow Chuck to believe he could manage on his own.

"How much can you change things anyway? Could you maybe do a whole movie from nothing?"

Chuck shook his head and almost smiled. He'd begun to

relax a bit, Scott noticed, but the set of his shoulders and neck was still alert, intent. "No, I can only, you know, guide things as they go along. If I try to change too much, I lose control. It's like there's too much to keep track of."

Scott nodded. "Too bad, but I kind of thought that might be the case. That's why you only changed some of the movies, right?"

"I guess." With the sudden mood swings that Scott had already begun to recognize, Chuck was taciturn again.

"How come all the sex anyway? That's what gave you away, you know."

Chuck looked away, his hands twisting in his lap, unspeaking.

"Come on, we're going to be friends, you and me. We don't need to have any secrets. If we're going to get rich, I have to understand how this works, how you make it happen, how much you can do."

Without turning away from his contemplation of the wall, Chuck shook his head.

Exasperated, Scott slapped his knees with his palms. "Listen, Chuck, I'm trying to be nice about this. Remember, I know about you; I can tell people what you've been doing."

His companion didn't speak, but he began twisting in his seat and his head moved nervously. Scott thought he had things sized up pretty well, decided it was necessary to push his point now, before Chuck had time to think things through.

"How would you like it if I told people you were a sexual pervert, Chuck? Would you like that?"

Chuck's head swung around, eyes wide, mouth moving now, hands clenched together so firmly that the knuckles were white. "I wasn't hurting anybody! It was all just pretend!"

"Sure, just pretend sex. And pretty rough sex, too. Rape and beatings and pain, right, Chuck? That's the way you like it, isn't it?"

Head twisting from side to side, Scott's companion seemed to be searching for an escape route. Convinced that he had his victim securely hooked, he leaned back, lying full length on the bed.

"But that's okay, Chuck. I won't tell anyone that you're a sicko whose only value to anyone, including himself, is that he has this trick with his head that lets him change the ways motion pictures appear on the screen. As long as you play ball, your secret is safe."

"No! No one's gonna tell again, not ever."

At first, the words and the tone were so out of place, Scott didn't register the meaning. He raised his upper torso, balancing on his elbows, and saw that Chuck's posture had altered completely. He was leaning forward now, hands raised and clenched into fists, and now his eyes met Scott's squarely.

"I'll do you just like I did my old man." And suddenly, inappropriately, Chuck began to smile.

Scott felt the change first in his chest, a funny, itching sensation that fell just short of pain. For a second, he thought he might be having a heart attack, unconsciously glancing down at his own body. Slowly but perceptibly, his chest was swelling out, forming a recognizable, if somewhat overstated, shape. The buttons on his shirt popped and the material peeled back, revealing not his familiar, mildly hairy chest but, instead, a creamy, abundant female bosom.

When he felt the itching between his legs, Scott panicked and tried to rise from the bed, only to discover that somehow the covers had twisted around his wrists and ankles, holding him firmly in place. Chuck Scusset rose, smiling broadly now, eyes preternaturally bright. The itching sensation grew more intense, and Scott felt the muscles in his thighs and calves shifting, assuming different contours. There was an odd pull at the base of his back, as though his pelvis had assumed a different shape, and his buttocks felt broader.

"What the fuck are you doing?" He tried to put force into the words, but they sounded desperate even to him. And the voice wasn't quite right; it was higher pitched, softer than he had expected.

"You've got good hair," Chuck spoke quietly, standing beside the bed. "I won't even have to change that." Scott's bonds pulled him back down onto the bed, retracting so that his limbs were drawn taut.

Chuck was holding a knife in one hand now, bending slowly down to undo Scott's belt with the other. "It's not just movies I can change, you know. They're just easier."

Scott was frozen by shock as his jeans were lowered, revealing far less than he was accustomed to seeing there. The blade flickered in front of his eyes.

"But this is much more fun," Chuck breathed as the knife lowered, for the first time.

A HARD MAN IS
GOOD TO FIND

R. Patrick Gates

She was wet. Again.

Why the hell did I sit by the window?

The answer was obvious. Right outside the window a crew of bare-chested men were digging up the road. Several of them had decent bodies. One of them was drop-dead gorgeous.

She crossed her legs. The food came.

"This doctor at the hospital says I suffer from chronic fatigue. That's a very 'in' disease, you know. Shelly, the head nurse on my floor, says he's just trying to get in my pants, but I don't know." Her friend, Darlene, stopped talking long enough to pick through her chef's salad with a fork and remove all the onions.

"Jeff, that's the doctor, called it 'the yuppie disease.' One of the other nurses said it was contagious and I must have caught it from someone, but when I asked Jeff, he said that was baloney. Still, if it is contagious, I bet I got it from that weirdo Roger. I mean, Lisa, he is just *too* strange, even if he does drive a Ferrari and have a condo on Martha's Vineyard."

Darlene rattled on, but Lisa wasn't listening anymore. Everything her friend was saying she'd heard a hundred

251

times before from her. The gorgeous one was running a jackhammer, making his muscles ripple and dance.

"When was the last time you really, *really*, got laid? I mean laid till you cummed your brains out and collapsed?" Lisa asked Darlene, never taking her eyes from the jiggling muscle outside the restaurant window.

Darlene, interrupted in the middle of listing the merits of Martha's Vineyard, looked in shock at Lisa. She blushed a deep red, but a twitch of a smile played at the corners of her mouth. "Lee! The way you talk! You sound like one of the guys!" Darlene giggled.

It was true. Lisa knew it. She'd always sounded like one of the guys. It was part of the problem.

The jackhammer stopped. The gorgeous one had noticed her practically drooling over him as he worked, and now he paused and looked at her. Lisa couldn't help herself; she licked her lips. He smiled.

"I only got . . . had . . . you know, sex like that once, I guess," Darlene said softly, self-consciously. "It was on the night of my senior prom in a vibrating bed at the Dew Drop Inn. A bunch of us rented a whole slew of rooms for a party—" Darlene stopped, suddenly realizing that Lisa wasn't listening. She followed her friend's eyes to the window. A good-looking construction worker was standing, hips thrust out, hand on crotch, beckoning to Lisa. Darlene could read his lips as he mouthed, "You want this?"

Darlene gasped in shock, then gasped again when she saw that Lisa was nodding and smiling back. "Lee!" Darlene exclaimed, embarrassment blushing in her cheeks. "My God! You're incredible! You'd better cut it out or he's going to think you're serious. That's how women get raped you know."

Lisa looked at her friend sideways, then back at the construction worker who was gathering up his coat and lunch pail, his eyes still on her, beckoning. "I'm sorry, Dar," Lisa said. "I've got to go."

Darlene sat agape as Lisa left with the construction worker.

The weekend was a blur for Lisa. They guy's name was Rod and he was a weekend cokehead working his way up to a full-time habit. Lee didn't care. She'd tried the sexual enhancements of coke before, was even into it heavily for a while. If it wasn't for her deviated septum, which gave her voice its nasal twang and often prevented her from snorting and getting off, she could have easily been a coke addict, too. Now she was a lot of things, but a nymphomaniac cokehead would have been hitting the bottom of the barrel. If she'd gone that route, it would've only been a matter of time before she would have been reduced to prostitution to support both her habits.

As soon as they got to his apartment, Rod produced a large baggie of nose candy. She did a few lines and was on her way. When Rod used an artist's feathery brush to apply some of the South American jungle dust to her nipples and other sensitive areas, she was lost.

She had snatches of memory: Rod doing line after line of coke, then making wild, gymnastic love to her for hours on end; drinking Jack Daniel's from the bottle, Rod using the bottle on her, filling her, drinking from her; people coming and going (did she make it with several of Rod's friends—*Hey guys, check it out! This bitch is a nympho!*—at once?). The overall memory, though, was of a blurring, bubbling endless eruption of sexual pleasure that sent her soaring into the depths of orgasmic unconsciousness.

When she woke, late Saturday night, her body ached everywhere and her mouth felt as if the proverbial army had marched through it—twice! Rod was asleep next to her, the rim of his nostrils caked with the remains of his last hit.

Lisa looked at his naked body in the moonlight coming through the window and felt the burning desire begin again deep in her groin. The past forty-eight hours had been the best sex she'd ever had. She'd come as close to the perfect orgasm as she was likely to get; it had taken drugs, liquor, and group sex, but still she'd come up short; still, she was left unsatisfied.

In the moonlight, she played with him, and despaired. She was never going to get what she needed. She was never going to reach the perfect plane of orgasmic fulfillment. There was no man alive who could satisfy her. She was thirty-two years old and had been searching for the perfect orgasm since she was ten and had lost her cherry to a bicycle seat on a long ride, during which she had also discovered her addiction to orgasms.

Since then she'd suffered every bizarre sexual humiliation and degradation, from having to be taken to the hospital at the age of fifteen to have a chunk of pepperoni stick removed from her womb, to taking on the entire football team after the Thanksgiving game her senior year in high school. Two decades of sexual adventurism and the closest she'd ever come to the perfect cum was this pitiful weekend with Rod and company. If AIDS didn't get her, boredom surely would.

Still asleep, Rod was stirring under her touch. He moaned deeply in his throat and his breathing became shallow. Lisa stroked him and felt the fire in her loins begin to spread. Moaning, more a cry of pain than of lust, Lisa went down on him, awakening his sleeping lust with her tongue and lips.

Rod moaned and Lee heard an echo of her pain in it. She worked on him faster, swelling him to the point of release, then backing off. Rod slept on, but his desire was fully awake and standing tall.

With a whimper of despair at the futility of it all, Lisa mounted him in the moonlight, pulling him inside her, wanting to pull all of him, his entire body, inside her as if that were the only way she could ever be satisfied.

His breathing became choppy. He began to buck beneath her. She rode him, tiny orgasms starting before she even had him all the way inside her, and sighed at the frustration of it all.

Rod began wheezing loudly with exertion as he convulsed beneath her. Just when she thought he would wear out, he began to make strange gargling noises and his bucking took on new energy. His writhing awakened the start of what she knew was going to be a truly momentous orgasm.

"Yes! Yes!" she cried. *Please don't come too soon!* she prayed.

His hands closed on her arms and he began to shake her. The first wave of the orgasm washed over her, electrifying her hips, driving their grinding motion to a pistonlike frenzy. Rod let go of her arms and reached for her breasts. He clutched at them feebly as the second wave hit her, much stronger than the first. Her stomach shimmied like a belly dancer's.

"Don't stop!" Lisa cried as Rod's hands collapsed to his sides. *He's finished!* she lamented. He lunged up into her once, twice, then a third time that drove so deep into her that the fourth and fifth waves of the orgasm rolled over her simultaneously.

Rod was unmoving beneath her. Lisa rode him faster, trying to keep him from wilting. *Just a little longer!* she silently pleaded. She was never going to make it. He was going to get soft. She was going to lose it. Again!

The unexpected happened: Rod didn't get soft. In fact, he got *harder!* It felt like he was swelling inside her. Lisa shrieked with joy.

Orgasms six through one hundred were a chain reaction, constantly bombarding her within the space of twenty minutes. After that, they all ran together into one endless, super-duper orgasm that incredibly got better and better and felt like it could go on forever.

It was still dark when she woke, but of what night it was, she was unsure. She had the feeling that more than just a few hours had passed. She woke on the floor at the foot of the bed, her legs tangled beneath her, thighs glued together, a bump the size of a golfball on the back of her head.

I fell out of bed, she thought, and she giggled. Despite the pain in her head and the soreness in her body, she felt fantastic. "It's happened," she whispered to the darkened ceiling. "I've done it." The itch was satisfied, the burning was quenched. She didn't know for how long, and didn't care at the moment. This was the first time since that fateful bike ride long ago that she was fully and completely satiated and satisfied with sex.

And it was fine; it was oh so fine.

Massaging her legs out from under her, she got to her knees. From there she was on eye level with the bed. She looked, blinked, looked again, and gasped at what she saw in the moonlight. The sleeping Rod was *still erect!* In fact, he was *more* than erect. His already ample size had swelled thicker and seemed to stand taller. The memory of it doing so inside her made Lisa smile until a hysterical cackle of joy was streaming from her open mouth. Laughing herself breathless, she climbed on Roger for another ride and was instantly consumed by another endlessly perfect orgasm.

The next time she woke it was daylight and she was dying of thirst, lying upside down in bed, her face only inches from Rod's testicles. They were shriveled and blue, but the rest of the organ was still hard and raging, though it was now a deep purple color. It had something on it. Lisa blinked her eyes and tried to focus. The something began to move.

It was a cockroach. The pun eluded her as, just for a second, she saw the bug in perfect detail: its chestnut brown exoskeleton, its antennae waving in the air, the legs clinging to the purple flesh, the mouth nibbling at the head of Rod's rod.

Lisa screamed a loud, long horror-movie scream—the kind of scream she'd always despised hearing from B-movie damsels in distress—and ran from the room. She barely made it to the bathroom before puking up the bile in her guts. Ten minutes later, after dousing her head under a long and cold shower, she crept back to the bedroom and peered around the doorjamb.

The cockroach was gone, but Rod's nibbled manhood still stood ramrod straight. Its color was very bad, as was most of the rest of him. His skin had taken on a grayish-purple tint that deepened to black and blue around his neck, under his arms, at his ankles, and, as she'd already noticed, at his groin.

His face was the worst. The eyes were open and staring at the ceiling. The skin was blue-gray and the lips were white and parted slightly as if awaiting a kiss. Inside his mouth, and filling his nostrils, vomit had dried to a hard crust.

Lisa went into the kitchen and made coffee, trying to keep calm. She had to think this through or she was going to be in major trouble. But even more important than her involvement in Rod's death and whether or not she was guilty of any crime, she had to know if his deadly erection was a freak occurrence or a commonplace thing. After all, she'd finally discovered a method of achieving the perfect orgasm, and she had to know whether it was a fluke or not. She felt bad that Rod was dead but—she was a realist if she was anything—she *had* barely known him. And as far as consciences went, hers had died a long time ago on a Thanksgiving Day in the boys' locker room.

Lisa drank the coffee, then called Darlene at the hospital. She tried to keep her voice light. "Hi Dar, it's Lee. How are you?"

Darlene's voice was icy in return. "I'm very busy right now."

"Look, Dar, I'm sorry about our lunch the other day."

"The other day? You mean last week, don't you?"

"Uh, yeah," Lee said hesitantly. How long had she been screwing a dead man? "Yeah, I mean last week. I'm sorry about that. Really."

"Hmm," Darlene answered doubtfully. "That's why it took you a whole week to call."

"Aw, come on, Dar. I said I was sorry. What more can I do?"

Darlene was silent.

"Listen Darlene," Lisa ventured, "I need some medical information."

"Well then, you'd better speak to a doctor. There's one here right now, and I hear he has a big cock, too, so you can make a fool of yourself over him." The phone thumped in Lisa's ear.

"Darlene?" she called.

A muffled male voice not too far from the phone said, "I have a big what?"

Lee was about to hang up when the male voice came on the line. "Hello? This is Doctor Peter Ruttles, can I help you?"

"Um, hello," Lee answered awkwardly.

"Are, uh, you a friend of Nurse Lemay's?" the doctor asked, matching her awkwardness.

"Yeah, well, at least I used to be."

"Oh. Uh, was there anything I can do for you?"

Lee hesitated, then decided to plunge ahead no matter how awkward she felt. This was too important. "Yes, actually, you can answer some questions for me," she replied in her best feminine in-need-of-help voice.

"I'd be delighted," the doctor said. "Perhaps you'd care to ask them over dinner at my place, say tonight?" he added in a suave voice.

Lee ignored the invitation for the moment. "All I need to know is: Is it unusual for a man to die with an erection?" she asked boldly, getting the reaction she expected.

"What? Are you kidding?" The doctor sounded shocked, but excited, too. There was a nervous giggle behind his words.

"No, no. You see, I'm having an argument with this friend

who's always trying to put stuff over on me. I say she's pulling my leg and I want to show her up," she lied.

"Oh," the doctor said, trying to sound like he understood, or even believed her, but he was unconvincing. A hint of lechery crept into his voice when he spoke again. "I still think we could discuss it at my place. I can show you that live erections are much more fun than dead ones."

Don't bet on it, buster, Lee thought with a wry smile. "That might be nice," she said flirtatiously, "but I need this information right away. I'm meeting my friend for lunch."

"All right. If we can call it a date, I'll answer your question." Lisa agreed. "Your friend is right," the doctor explained. "It is very common for the blood to collect in the groin causing the penis to become engorged and erect in death."

Lisa smiled into the receiver. "Uh, how long would something like that necessarily last?" she asked.

"Oh, I guess until an undertaker removes the blood from the body or the thing rotted away, I guess," the doctor said, laughing awkwardly. "There's a statue in France of a fallen general, taken from a body cast of him days after he died, and his erection is very clear in the bronze. Now what time shall I pick you up for dinner?"

"Make it seven. And Dr. Ruttles, do me a favor? Please don't tell anyone that we have a date. I know from Darlene what gossips those nurses and doctors are there." The doctor readily agreed, and she gave him her address.

Lisa hung up and went back to the bedroom. From what Darlene said, Lee knew it had been at least a week since she had first shacked up with Rod. She wasn't absolutely sure when he had died, but she had a good idea it was Saturday night because from the look of him he was at least a couple of days overripe. She did some calculating and figured she'd been screwing a corpse for at least three days before it had begun to attract bugs. She gave a shiver of disgust at the thought of the roach, but not at what she'd done.

Lisa got dressed quickly and, taking an ounce of Rod's Bolivian marching powder and several of his syringes with her in her pocketbook, left the apartment quietly. No one saw her. All she had to worry about now was Rod's friends. She was counting on the fact that all they knew of her was her first name and what she looked like, and, because of the heavy cocaine use that had gone on, they probably wouldn't want to get involved.

When Doctor Peter Ruttles showed up at her door that evening, Lee greeted him in her hottest leather outfit and easily talked him into taking her to the local Holiday Inn where she had taken the liberty of reserving a room for them in his name. What she didn't tell him was that she had reserved the room for exactly three days.

At the end of the three days, during which time a "Do Not Disturb" sign hung on the door constantly, Lisa slipped out of the room and out a side exit of the hotel unnoticed. When the cleaning lady finally saw the "Do Not Disturb" sign taken from the door of the room the next day, she entered and found Dr. Ruttles dead. He was naked and bound to the bed with nylons. An empty syringe was sticking out of his arm, his decomposing member was still erect, and an eternal smile was etched on his face.

BEDROOM EYES

Michael Newton

They knew him at the Ecstasy Arcade. Which is to say, they recognized his face, receding hairline, business suit (invariably gray or black), the raincoat which he wore or carried with him every day, regardless of the weather. No one knew his name, but that was unimportant. They had seen the color of his money, and he never caused a scene.

Milo Grymdyke was a regular. He was predictable, arriving shortly after six o'clock each Friday night and purchasing his two five-dollar tokens, eyes averted from the cashier's face, proceeding quickly to the booths in back.

The booths were tucked away behind a threadbare curtain, out of sight from patrons in the shop. They were no more than simple plywood cubicles, unpainted, furnished with a single folding chair. One wall in each consisted of a heavy metal shutter, which concealed a plate glass window and another room beyond. Insertion of a token in the proper slot would raise the shutter to reveal a woman, seated on the far side of the glass. On cue, she would disrobe, performing for her one-man audience until their time ran out and the shutter fell.

Five dollars for five minutes. It was cheap at half the price. No contact or communication with the woman was allowed, but Grymdyke often found the windows marked by palmprints, smudged by lips and tongues. The customers were theoretically forbidden to expose themselves, but Milo found the claustrophobic atmosphere was often redolent of sweat and what he took to be the musky smell of sex.

He could not be precise about the latter smell, of course. At thirty-seven, he was still a virgin.

Grymdyke chose the third booth on a whim and closed the flimsy door behind him, checking out the metal chair before he sat. He scooted closer to the shutter, told himself that it was for convenience, so that he could reach the coin slot without rising.

Milo put a token in the slot; the shutter rose. He did not recognize the woman, although several of the regulars were now familiar to him. She was dark and slender, of indeterminate age and nationality, with blue-black hair grazing her shoulders. She wore a purple T-shirt, cut above her navel, with bikini panties in a matching shade.

Grymdyke studied her face for a moment, aware of fleeting time, the tingle in his groin. He lingered over flawless olive skin, almond eyes vaguely reminiscent of the Orient, the full lips moist and dark, without embellishment.

Seated on a chair like Milo's, she began without preamble, running long fingers over her breasts. Her nipples came erect beneath the fabric, and she nudged the hemline upward, teasing Grymdyke with a glimpse of soft, round flesh. Her eyes were closed, lips slightly parted, revealing the tip of her tongue between perfect teeth.

Her performance was less mechanical—more *sincere*—than many of the others, and Milo felt himself responding. There was sudden color in his cheeks, and he could feel the perspiration on his face, beneath his arms.

The woman stretched now, catlike, pulling the T-shirt off over her head. One hand returned to her smallish breasts while the other slid into her panties, making a fist in her crotch. Milo's eyes flicked back and forth between the hands, unable to choose.

She finally made the decision for him, rising and turning her back to the window, rolling the panties down across round, tan buttocks. Milo sat mesmerized as she skinned them down her thighs, below her knees, raising one leg after the other to step clear, affording him his first glimpse of pubic hair.

Both hands disappeared between her legs, invisible until the fingertips poked through in back and she leaned forward, thrusting her hips toward the window. A ripple passed along her spine—*just acting?*—and she turned slowly, easing back into the chair, raising one leg at a time and planting the soles of her feet on the glass. Placing herself on display.

Milo felt light-headed with the evacuation of blood to his groin. The triangle of pubic hair was neatly trimmed and glistening. Her fingers walked around it, growing bolder, finally probing for the heart, and Grymdyke *felt* her shudder this time, as she spread her lips.

A single bloodshot eye stared back at Milo.

Winked.

The shutter fell.

He jerked back in his chair, nearly losing his balance. For a moment, he was dumbfounded by what he had seen. *(Imagined?)* It was idiotic. Physically impossible. And yet . . .

He fumbled for the second token. Trembling, he clutched the chair with both hands as the shutter rose.

A different woman sat beyond the window, waiting. Grymdyke recognized her as a listless blonde whose platinum was showing dark around the roots. She was unbuttoning a see-through blouse when Milo bolted from the cubicle.

Impossible.

Insane.

He took a moment to compose himself before reentering

the shop. His legs felt wooden as he moved in the direction of the register, the cashier perched behind it on a stool. He cleared his throat to draw the younger man's attention from a bondage magazine.

His name was Hector, stitched across the left breast of a nylon jacket. Rodent eyes examined Milo for a moment, dull and listless.

"You need somethin'?"

"Yes." It came out as a whisper and he cleared his throat, commanding vocal cords to function. "There's a girl in number three."

"There better be. That's what we pay 'em for."

"I mean, she isn't there right now. . . ."

The cashier frowned. "Oh yeah? Well, go on back there, sport. I'll getcha somethin' nice."

"There *is* a girl," he said before the man could leave his seat. "It's just that . . . well . . . she's not the same."

"The same as what?"

"Before." He felt the words begin to tumble out and wondered if he sounded incoherent, or if it was only in his mind. "I put a token in, and she was dark. A tall brunette. The time ran out, and when I put another token in, there was a different girl. A blonde."

The cashier visibly relaxed, deciding he had not been served a loony, after all, but merely some poor jerk who hadn't gotten off before the clock ran down. The worrisome became routine.

"Must be her coffee break. It's the law. Go figure."

"Coffee break?"

"They switch, ya know?"

"I need to see her."

"Sure, no sweat. They only get ten minutes, 'less she's gone to lunch. That's half an hour."

"No. I need to see her privately."

The young man's manner changed. "That's what the booths are for."

"I need to see her privately . . . *outside.*"

"No dice. The ladies ain't allowed to mix with any of the customers."

He felt a sudden pang of desperation. "Surely you could let me have her name?"

"I'm not supposed to give 'em out, you unnerstan'? I mean, you look okay to me, but hey—" He spread his hands and smiled.

Milo palmed a fifty-dollar bill and placed it on the counter, near the register. "I understand the need to be discreet."

A moment passed in silence. Hector frowned and made the fifty disappear. "Okay, I figure you're a stand-up guy. She's tall, dark hair, you said? Nice tits, but maybe just a little on the small side?"

"Yes." The urgency had nearly robbed him of his voice.

"That's Laney Thatcher, but she don't come cheap."

"How much?"

A lazy shrug. "Search me. Free enterprise, you know? Don't sound too hungry when you call, she might negotiate."

"The number?"

Hector had retrieved his magazine by now, directing his attention to the centerfold. "She's in the book."

In fact, he found that there were sixty-seven Thatchers in the phone book, none of them named Laney. Loran Thatcher was the closest he could find, but two were listed simply by the first initial "L," without a hint of gender to assist him.

Hector might have lied, but Milo didn't want to think so, and he pondered other explanations as he lay in bed that night. The woman—*Laney*—could have purchased an unlisted number, or she might not have a telephone at all. The two "L. Thatchers" were his only hope, and it was too damned late to try them now.

The next day, his hand was shaking as he dialed.

The first "L. Thatcher" was a gruff old man whose voice reminded Grymdyke of a rasp drawn over rotting wood. His given name was Lawrence, and he lived alone, if it was any of the goddamned nosy caller's goddamned business.

Milo cradled the receiver, swallowed his embarrassment, and tried the second number. It was answered on the first ring by a woman's voice—expressionless.

"Hello?"

"I'm calling . . . that is, may I speak to Laney Thatcher?"

"Speaking."

Milo felt the room begin to spin around him. For a moment he could think of nothing else to say.

"Hello?"

"My name is Milo Grymdyke."

"Yes, I've been expecting you."

"I beg your pardon?"

Laughter. Tinkling like broken glass.

"I said, 'What can I do for you?' "

A trick. His own imagination taunting him again.

"You don't know me," he said. "I've seen you—"

—*naked*—

"Yes?" She sounded curious, amused.

A sudden pang of doubt constricted Milo's throat. "I wonder if . . . I mean, *are* you—"

"A dancer? Yes."

The telephone was welded to his palm with perspiration. Was it possible that she had read his thoughts?

"One night last week—"

Her voice became a husky tenor. "I remember you," she told him. "I've been hoping you might call."

"Did Hector speak to you?" The words were out before he knew what he was saying.

"Hector?"

"Nothing. I'm amazed that you remember me."

"You're much too modest."

Milo's heart was hammering inside his rib cage, aftershocks were reverberating in his groin. He spoke before he had a chance to change his mind.

"I'd like to see you."

"You've already seen me, Milo. *I've* seen *you.*"

—*the eye*—

His cheeks were flaming. "I just thought, if we could meet . . ."

"Of course."

His heart stopped, shuddered, found its beat again.

"I don't suppose tonight—"

"Why not? I get off work at nine."

His mind refused to function. "Nine o'clock?"

"Let's make it ten. I need some travel time, a chance to freshen up. You have my address?"

"I—"

She offered him directions to her house.

"Tonight, then. I'll be waiting."

She hung up before he had a chance to thank her, plead insanity, or use any of the other options that immediately came to mind. They had a date, of sorts, and Grymdyke knew that he would never have the nerve—the will—to cancel out.

He knew that he might never have this chance again.

The housing tract was new, so recently completed that a number of the homes stood vacant, windows dark, their yards small deserts waiting for new tenants and the landscape artists to arrive. As Milo parked in front of Laney Thatcher's house, he was aware of empty, darkened homes on either side.

There was no car in Laney's drive; the door to her garage was closed and padlocked. Milo wondered if she drove herself to work and then realized that he was stalling, wasting time. He locked the car, remembering to take the gift that he had purchased on the slow drive over.

Milo had considered flowers, changed his mind when he

could not decide which sort might be appropriate for the occasion. Blind date–cum-seduction was a tricky category. He had settled for a candy store that offered gift wrap for a dollar extra.

He rang the doorbell, listened to the tiny chimes inside. When there was no immediate response, his brain began to toy with him, suggesting Laney might have changed her mind, gone off somewhere instead of facing Milo now that safety glass no longer stood between them. He would not have blamed her, but he thought the disappointment and embarrassment might kill him.

Muffled footsteps, drawing closer. Milo gave a last tug at his tie and tucked the box of candy underneath his arm. If possible, he would have run—or melted where he stood— before she had a chance to look at him and laugh.

The dead-bolt latch snicked open. Milo grimaced in approximation of a smile as Laney Thatcher stood before him, framed in silhouette.

"Good evening, Milo."

"Guh . . . good evening."

"Please, come in."

She stood aside, and Grymdyke caught a whiff of some exotic fragrance as he stepped into the narrow foyer. Incense or perfume? He couldn't say.

"I'm glad you came."

He forced himself to look at her directly, conscious of the color flaming in his cheeks. She wore a plain black velvet dress which flattered her figure without being suggestive.

"I brought you this."

She took the package, sniffed it once, and smiled. "I love dark chocolate, thank you. Would you like to see the house?"

"Yes, please."

"I've really just moved in. You'll have to picture furniture."

He followed her through the parlor, dining room, and

kitchen, fascinated by the motion of her hips. The furnishings were sparse, as advertised. Where she had started decorating, Milo found surrealistic paintings on the walls, small graceful sculptures occupying shelves and counter space.

She offered him a drink while they were in the kitchen. Milo took a glass of wine and waited while she poured one for herself.

"To passion."

Milo touched his glass to hers and took a healthy swallow, startled by its potency and fire.

"You don't look like your name," she said.

"I've never thought about it," he replied, although, in fact, he had considered it on several occasions. "You don't, either."

"May I tell you something?" The fluorescent fixture overhead struck highlights in her hair and cast her face in shadow.

"Yes . . . I think so."

"Laney Thatcher is my stage name. I'm an actress . . . or, I will be, soon. I have auditions scheduled. The arcade—"

"I understand."

"I knew you would." She smiled. "My parents came to the United States from Greece in 1949. The civil war. My real name is Thanatos. Lamia Thanatos."

"Lamia." He turned the strange name over on his tongue. "I think it's more attractive than the other."

"Do you?"

"Yes."

"I'm glad." She drained her wine and Milo followed suit. "Shall we continue?"

"Please."

The house was small by modern standards. Milo wondered what there might be left to see.

"The bedroom."

She had finished decorating here. The bed was queen-size,

flanked by windows with their drapes drawn tight. A lamp and ornate telephone adorned one nightstand; an alarm clock and a decorator box of Kleenex graced the other. The chest of drawers and vanity were hand-rubbed wood, and Milo took them for antiques. The lights were soft, seductive.

"I enjoy the decorating."

"Yes, it shows."

She moved into the room, and it felt natural for him to follow her. She turned to face him, standing close enough to touch—if only he possessed the courage.

"This is what you wanted?"

Milo blinked and dropped his gaze, unable to respond coherently. She cupped a hand beneath his chin and raised his face until their eyes were locked.

"You must not be embarrassed. I am everything you wanted. You are everything I need."

She slowly turned her back and bowed her head, presenting Milo with her zipper tab. "Undo me? I can't seem to reach it."

Milo knew she could—how else had she got dressed?—but he was flattered by the gesture, burningly aroused. He ran the zipper down to Laney's waist and watched the two halves of her dress peel back, revealing silken flesh beneath. Against the plain black velvet, Laney's skin seemed pale. She wore no bra.

A shrug, and now the dress lay pooled around her ankles. Laney wore no panties, either, and from where he stood, her buttocks looked soft to the touch, covered with a layer of perfect down.

Another turn, and she was facing him. He had already scrutinized her body once, in intimate detail, but this was very different. He could touch her now, unless she stopped him at the final moment, and his fingertips were tingling with anticipation.

Laney moved in close to Milo, rising on her toes to kiss him. Dizzy, trembling, he allowed his palms to rest against the soft swell of her hips. She moved against him, heat communicated from her flesh, through Milo's clothing, and he stroked the curve of Laney's spine. He wanted desperately to feel her flesh against his own.

She eased the jacket off his shoulders, draped it on a chair, returning for his shirt and tie. He raised his arms to make removal of his T-shirt easier, and then her nipples brushed against his chest, sharp exclamation points of animal desire that made him gasp.

His belt delayed her briefly; as she grappled with it, Laney pinched her lower lip between her small, white teeth. He was amazed to see the beads of perspiration on her forehead, in the valley of her breasts.

She let him kick his shoes off, step out of his slacks and shorts. He kept his socks on as she led him to the bed and saw him seated on the mattress, pressing backward with a slim hand on his chest until he stretched out supine.

When Laney came to join him, Milo felt a sudden urge to run away, but he was helpless as the naked woman crouched above his face, thighs straddling his head. He could not see her face, but he was perfectly familiar with her smell, the fleshscape of her breasts and stomach looming over him. He had committed every pubic hair to memory.

Her laughter rippled in his ears like wind chimes, and she spread herself for Milo, showing him the eye. Its scrutiny was piercing, inescapable; he lay exposed in body, mind, and soul.

The woman understood his hunger; she had seen it with her secret eye. A shudder rippled through her body as the eye blinked once, rolled back—and disappeared. She settled over Milo's face, warm lips pressed tight against his own.

He feasted on her, ravenous, not caring that his nose and mouth were covered and he could not breathe. A skillful tongue flicked out to spar with Milo's, worming in between his teeth, another sweet surprise, and he was drowning, happily oblivious to galloping asphyxia.

She pulled away from Milo, sudden deprivation and the rush of oxygen to starving lungs producing spastic tremors in his rigid body. Crouching at his side, she gently drew his foreskin back and ran her tongue around the swollen glans, his shaft on fire.

Without another moment's hesitation, Milo opened to her, staring back at Laney with *his* secret eye, his small tongue flicking out to trace the sharp edge of her teeth. There was delight in Laney's laughter as she mounted him.

"I was afraid I'd never find you," Milo said.

"You have."

"I see."

She poised above him, open, trembling, ready.

"Kiss me."

Grymdyke raised his hips to meet her, and the velvet darkness swallowed him alive.

ATROCITIES

Lucy Taylor

*D*erek Mosby, you're a no-good son-of-a-bitch. A bad, bad boy. But it's over now. For good. Radell is out of your life.

The Piedmont jet banked on its approach into the Richmond Airport, giving Derek Mosby a view of checkered farmlands lightly dusted with snow between rows of winter-blasted trees and the frozen gray ribbon of I-95 heading into the city and beyond, toward Derek's suburban home. He knew he'd done the right thing, breaking it off with Radell, and that he should be pleased with himself, but the old, old tapes of his father's voice—*bad boy, Derek, cheating on your math test, bad boy to forget your mother's birthday, bad, bad, BAD*—the ancient, bitter scoldings drowned out the marshmallow-sweet voice of the stewardess telling passengers to buckle their seat belts.

It was late afternoon on Saturday. He'd called Jess from New York the day before to tell her he was cutting short his business trip and coming home. A slightly embellished version of the truth, to be sure, but one tailored to Jess's capacity for reality and his own sometimes limited courage.

The truth was he'd planned to stay another two nights with Radell, seeing the Apple (Radell had never been to

273

New York and he had planned to take her to the Oak Room at the Plaza for drinks, then on to Maxime's for dinner), but it was no good. Radell was marriage-minded. The more seriously she talked about their future together, the more he thought of his family. And when Radell asked in the middle of their coupling, "So when are you going to tell your wife we're in love?" he'd felt as if someone spilled ice water between his legs.

In love with Radell? In lust, sure, but how had passion made the treacherous transition to permanence this fast? How had occasional desktop sex with his redheaded dental hygienist led, seemingly inexorably as summer into fall, to talk of his divorce and their marriage? He'd wanted only to forget his problems—the kids, his age (forty-three in February), Jess's overfondness for brandy Alexanders—not overturn his life.

He was a parent, after all. Divorce might come when the kids were grown and on their own, but not before. His own father, for all his pious words and reprimands, had taken off when Derek was barely nine. Even now Derek still had moments of insecurity and loneliness, when he felt no older than when his father left, when that part of him that Brenner, the therapist in the office next to Derek's, called his inner child shrieked out for nurturing. It was during such a time of want that Derek had imagined—incorrectly—that peace and bliss and orgasms everlasting could be found between Radell's thighs. So what the hell—he had no idea how to parent himself, he could still do right by his own kids.

Did Jess suspect? Probably, if she wasn't too bombed. The kids? No, impossible. Blair was barely thirteen, preoccupied with clothes and pop stars and Madonna makeup. Fifteen-year-old Woody was a rising star on JFK High's baseball team and a downright prude in some ways—Derek had heard him once vigorously denounce a neighborhood convenience store for selling *Playboy*.

They were both good kids, more naive than they were willing to let on, kids who remembered not only Jess's and his birthday but Mother's and Father's Day as well. Old-fashioned kids, actually. They valued family.

And they deserve a helluva lot better than you, Derek Mosby.

He told the paternal voice in his head to go fuck itself and resisted the urge to slip his business card to a pretty stewardess as he exited the plane.

He drove home slowly, mindful of the icy edges of the road and the badly aligned front wheels of the Chrysler. No time for accidents now. He was almost home.

Blanketed with snow, the two-story brick house at the back of the cul-de-sac looked somehow smaller, like a faded dowager huddled frail and bony inside an ermine coat. He fumbled his way, feeling slightly miffed that no one came to greet him. As he stepped inside the hallway, though, the comforting aromas of dinner cooking entered his nostrils, did a fragrant twirling little dance along his nasal passages, and brought a rush of well-being that he hadn't felt since he and Jess first married.

Home, yes! Wasn't this what it was all about?

He started to call out, but a pang of something—guilt, fear?—silenced him as effectively as a hand across the mouth. Dread swamped him. For one fierce, irrational moment the thought came to him that maybe it wasn't too late yet to undo the actions of the past twenty-four hours, to tiptoe quietly out of the house, suitcase in hand, catch the next flight back to New York and hope to God Radell had taken him up on his offer to enjoy the City on her own in the paid-for hotel room, that she'd sympathize with his confession of terminal wimphood and welcome him back. So that he'd never, ever have to walk into this house again and smell dinner cooking and feel seduced by all the homey, *Father-Knows-Best*-ness of it all.

He took a deep breath. The moment—thank God—

passed. It had felt for a second like his heart was careening loose inside his chest; now it was in place, steady.

Just the little kid inside me, he thought, the little boy feeling scared 'cause he knows he's been bad, that he's cheated. But it's all right now, because I fixed it. I did the right thing.

"Daddy! You're home."

Blair galloped to meet him, her black hair swept back in a glossy horsetail, an apron knotted about her middle. In spite of her plump hips and conspicuous breasts, her gait seemed still little-girlish—a bouncing child.

"We missed you, Daddy. How was the dental convention?"

"Boring. Like all of them." He kissed her flushed cheek and was immediately aware of the heat from her, the smell of chocolate somewhere in her hair, the smudges of flour on her fingertips, transferred now to the jacket of his suit.

"You helping Mom with supper?"

"No, Daddy." She reached up, gave him a quick, sweet peck on the jaw. "I'm fixing it by myself."

"Where's Mom?"

Blair either didn't hear the question or chose to ignore it. He followed her dark, chocolate-scented hair into the kitchen, where his nose told him a roast was basting in the oven. "I asked where's your mother?"

"She said she was going over to Linda's to watch an exercise video."

"I see."

What the transaction really meant was this: Has Mom been drinking again, and, yes, she's getting tanked over at her girlfriend's and will be back when she arrives. But such words were never said explicitly. Disappointment seethed in his guts like termites. He'd left the scented hollows of Radell, her quick, inventive mouth—for this?

But, of course, he had, for Blair and for Woody. They needed a father. Moreover, he needed to *be* a father.

"Where's your brother?"

"Dressing for dinner. He helped me with the layer cake."

"Woody? Our Woody?" To this point in his life, Woody's crowning domestic achievement had been learning to operate the microwave so he could thaw out burritos at 7-Elevens. "Woody's into baking now? Amazing!"

Blair smiled serenely and stirred a pot of gravy on the back burner. Lima beans were bubbling in a pot on the front.

"Go wash up, Daddy. I'll be ready soon."

The phone in the living room sounded. Blair dashed past him, seized the receiver and listened less than a second before slamming it down.

"Who was that?"

"Just this boy at school. He's been bothering me for a date. A real nerd."

"Just the same, Blair, that was rude. Even nerds deserve some consideration." *I was a nerd myself in high school,* he started to say, but decided not all confessions, especially to a thirteen-year-old daughter who still thought Daddy was a hero, were good for the soul.

She pouted at him prettily, her mother's expression. He'd never seen much resemblance in Blair to either him or to Jess, but today her face seemed more womanly, its heart-shaped mouth set in an expression of wifely efficiency.

Then he realized that the illusion of similarity to Jess was heightened by what Blair wore beneath the apron—Jess's black woolen skirt with the elastic waist and a white knit top. Strands of Jess's malachite beads cascaded down the front; matching malachite clips were affixed to her ears. Even her lipstick was Jess's favorite shade, a rich plum much too dark for her age and skin.

"Did your mother tell you you could wear her things?"

"She doesn't care."

"It's not as becoming on you as your own clothes, you know."

She did a saucy pirouette, basting spoon in hand, a look both coy and defiant on her face. "I think I look nice. *Very* nice. I think I look better than I ever have."

He started to reply with a rebuke, something like he didn't appreciate having a daughter dressed like she was thirteen going on thirty, but decided this time to let it pass. It was all too rare that he heard Blair say something good about herself. More often, she bemoaned her oily hair or the twenty pounds she vowed to begin dieting away right after one last Almond Joy. To hear Blair defend her appearance was both encouraging (maybe she was at last outgrowing the pity-pot stage) and at the same time a little jarring. *How fast they change,* thought Derek, and he felt his age dragging him down.

The phone rang again. Blair was taking the roast out of the oven and lost time setting it down. She ran, but he beat her to it.

Radell's voice was a tight, bitter crackle.

"Listen, you little bitch, don't hang up on me again or—"

"Hello!"

There was a small gasp. "So you're home already, babe. Fast flight."

"I can't believe you called me at home. I thought you understood—"

"Oh, I understand fine. Your daughter and I had a nice little talk. She's pretty smart, you know. You sure she's yours? She tells me I'm not the first one. She says you've turned your wife into an alkie, that the whole family knows what a scumbag you are."

She broke off into braying laughter. Half cackle, half sob. A sound that made his heart go cold and thunderous. He slammed down the phone, bent quickly and yanked it out of the plug.

Blair watched from the doorway. She held a red mixing bowl full of chocolate icing tucked into one arm and she was stirring with a wooden spoon, slowly, with Zenlike ease. She might have been a stranger, so fixed, so coolly placid was her tiny smile. Mona Lisa with the mixing bowl, thought Derek, and realized, even as it dawned on him how little he really knew her, how much he loved her, too.

"Who was that, Daddy?"

He managed an embarrassed laugh. "You were right. A nerd. Let's have some peace. Don't answer the phone for a while."

"Your hands are shaking."

"I guess the trip wore me out worse than I thought."

He went to the sink and rummaged under it until he located one of the bottles in Jess's stash, a pint of Johnnie Walker behind the Windex and the Lemon Pledge.

Taking a glass down from the cabinet, he poured an inch, then doubled that for good measure. Christ, his hands shook like there were battery-powered vibrators in each finger.

"You can't drink that, Daddy."

"What?"

Blair's little-girl face set in a prim, cold stare. "Woody and I made a rule. No drinking in the house. I thought I got all the bottles, but I guess I missed that one."

"Well, sweetheart, don't forget you and Woody don't make the rules here. I'm damned near frozen from the cold. I need something to get my juices flowing."

He raised the glass.

"I told you you can't do that!"

Blair's hand swept out, plucked the glass away, and flung it at the back wall. Glass shattered and dark whiskey streamed along the patterned wallpaper.

"What the hell's got into you!"

"I *told* you, Daddy!"

"Goddammit, Blair, I won't have this!"

"No drinking!"

They glared at each other. Blair raised the mixing spoon as though prepared to deliver a blow. It was Derek who broke eye contact. He sat down heavily at the kitchen table, massaging a lightning-bolt-shaped pain in his temples. Blair put a consoling hand on the back of his neck and he felt again—unpleasantly—how very moist and warm her flesh was, how floral her perfume. Jess's perfume. That Estée Lauder scent he hated.

"I'm sorry I did that, Daddy. Only, you were being bad."

He started laughing. Who, indeed, was the parent here? With wives out boozing and ex-lovers on the phone? Good God, how had things gotten this out of control?

"Daddy, don't worry. We'll make things all right."

Astonishingly, she picked up the pint bottle and fetched him a new glass. She poured two golden jiggers. "This is an exception, Daddy. Because you're upset and because that crazy woman called. Just this once."

He gulped the drink gratefully, felt it loosen and warm him. A hot dark glow blazed in his belly, and his rage receded. Outside, snow was again pelting the window. Icicles fanged the sill, but here he sat cocooned in the smells of good food and warmth. To hell with Radell and her deranged mistress act. The truth was, in spite of Blair's temper tantrum, he felt safer, more relaxed here at home than in the steamy clinch of Radell's greedy embrace.

"You look so tired, Daddy."

"It was a long trip home."

"We waited for you."

Blair slid her small, soft hands with their unvarnished, badly bitten nails around his neck. He stood up and she nuzzled into him. She smelled of cinnamon and chocolate and Estée Lauder lilac, a luxuriant profusion of scents. Her closeness dizzied him. But when she began to undulate her hips in ever-narrower figure-eights, he jumped back as though she were on fire. Her bright lips fastened to his, her tongue warm and chocolaty. He was inundated with her various perfumes and sickened by the sudden, alarming realization that, incest taboo be damned, his lower portions hadn't heard of it and were firming up accordingly. Shame scoured him. He shoved her away and cracked an open palm with more force than he'd intended across her face.

She reeled back, nearly falling, then righted herself and glared at him with venomous contempt.

"Blair, wait, I—"

"I hate you," she whispered and ran out of the kitchen. As she fled past the table, her hand shot out long enough to collide with the roast and send it careening in a greasy arc, an oiled football, across the floor.

Derek rushed after her, trying as he did to find a way to put the blame on Jess, Radell, on anyone but himself, for his daughter's concupiscence. Maybe Blair really had talked to Radell and concluded that if Jess had failed at holding on to Daddy's sexual interest, the task now fell to her. A frightening possibility, but less mortifying than the fact that he'd actually gotten a hard-on, that while disgust was registering in his brain, the neurons in his groin were firing to a different drummer.

At the top of the stairs he stopped, caught his breath. The heat there was oppressive, stifling. The thermostat must be turned to ninety. Dust motes rotated slowly in the air, mimicking the patterns of the snowflakes outside the windows.

"Blair?" For once the house was absolutely quiet. Woody's stereo, normally ablast, was silent. No showers ran, no doors slammed. The effect was of expectant waiting, of inheld breath. He moved quietly, furtive as a prowler, until he came to Blair's door and tapped.

"Blair? Honey, I'm so sorry."

He knocked again, then waited a few seconds and tried the knob. To his surprise, it was unlocked. The door opened easily.

She was in bed, the covers tugged up over her, one arm thrown out as if to ward him off. The exposed hand was small and pink with smooth red-lacquered nails—Jess's hand.

His flesh went cold and crawly. He flung back the sheet, and Jess regarded him, her lips dark blue, her eyes rolled up into the whites. She was dressed in Blair's Farmer Johns and red pullover, and, bizarrely, someone had pierced her ears—a quick and brutal job, to judge from the way the lobes were gouged so that a pair of Blair's gold hoops could be driven through. From the angle of her broken neck, he figured she had hung herself. The kids must have found her, taken her down.

He touched his wife's dead face: eyelids, cheeks, chin. Her skin felt like warm putty, as though it might adhere to his fingertips and pull away like flesh taffy when he removed his hand.

"Don't touch her! You'll wake her up."

Blair stalked into the room. She kept her eyes fixed on the twirling snow outside the window, not looking at the contents of the bed.

"I told her she could take a nap till dinner, then do her homework. You can help her with her algebra."

"Christ Jesus, what—?"

"We have to raise her right, you know. Do the right thing. Parenting isn't easy."

The words were achingly familiar. He'd uttered them himself or some pious variation in the late-night conferences with Jess before the two of them stopped speaking in any meaningful way, before Radell and Johnnie Walker became the official consorts.

"Jesus, what's happened? Why didn't you tell me?"

"She probably didn't think you'd give a fuck," said Woody, stepping into the room beside his sister. He was wearing Derek's gabardine suit—much too big for him— and the paisley tie Blair had given Derek last Father's Day. In one hand, he held the wooden bat that had hit the winning home run against Martin Luther High the spring before.

Blair looked her brother fondly up and down and made a little tie-straightening gesture, which Woody ignored.

"Goddammit, Woody, what's happened?"

"We found her last night. She'd been on the phone with your girlfriend. I listened in on the extension for a while. Your bitch was telling Mom about the time you picked her up and carried her around the hotel room, fucking all the way—"

"Stop it."

"—and how you have this favorite thing she does to you with high heels—"

"Stop!"

"—and how you keep your stash of porno locked up in a briefcase in—"

"Nooo!"

He lurched up from Jess's body, screaming in his agony, and saw, an instant before he felt it, the worse and coming agony as Woody raised the bat and swung it. Crack! A brutal, lancing pain slashed up his arm, deadening it to the elbow. The next blow pulverized his kneecap, the third broke ribs. And still the muscled arms were coming up, again and again. The shadow of the bat loomed on the ceiling . . .

"It's good the children are asleep now," said Blair as she put dinner on the table.

"Blair, come out of it," said Woody. "It's Mom and Dad up there. They're dead. We killed them both. You gotta hold on to reality."

"You mustn't say such awful things, even kidding. No one's dead. The children are just tired." She spooned lima beans onto his plate. "Do you think we'll be good parents? I hope we will. Maybe we should have another child."

She moved to where her brother stood gazing out at the deepening snow and snuggled up against him, cooing sounds of comfort both maternal and seductive. "Woody?" she whispered finally. "We're all we have now. Please?"

Her brother gave a little sigh, took her in his arms and kissed her. The snow fell and they were all alone.

PEARLDOLL

John Shirley

It was one of those nights that releases trapped odors. The August heat steamed the reek of rotten fast-food grease and urine from the alley behind the Fatburger place on Santa Monica Boulevard. It made the smog seem to coagulate in the air, so a breeze that should have been a relief reeked of benzene and monoxides and ozone. The heat brought out the deepest layers of human sourness from the tramps slouching in the doorways. When you passed the discos, it summoned the hidden tincture of animal glands in the perfume of the fantastically coiffed ladies who stepped out of white limos, the underscent of lab-animal suffering and caustic chemicals in the cologne worn by their golden-chained escorts. It seemed to emphasize the cyanide and carcinogenic tars in cigarette smoke; it cooked the sewage under the streets . . .

And the semen left over in your pussy, or so Candy thought.

She'd douched after that creep Guido had come in her, but she couldn't quite get it all out, imagined she could smell it cooking and curdling in her . . .

It's too fucking hot.

She was walking down Santa Monica Boulevard, wishing

she hadn't worn pumps, wondering if maybe there were some flats in the trunk of her car she could put on.

Sometimes you can't remember a dream—until later on. When something calls it up. Prompts it from the back of your head somewhere. She was passing a boutique, tight stripped-back leather skirts and tops for women in the window. Standing in front of it were these two skinny blond hustlers. One was wearing a Levi's jacket with some sort of rock-band emblem on the back. And she heard that one talk about the Face Eater. "It's no shit, Face Eater got Butterbuns and Darla, got both of 'em, put 'em on a pentagram thing and tied 'em down and ate their fuckin' faces, man—"

"Bullshit," the other guy squeaked.

"No, for real, dude!"

For real? She'd always thought the Face Eater was something in a movie or . . . but now that she thought about it, she remembered seeing some headlines . . . Some sick "Night Stalker" type in Hollywood who . . . She didn't even want to think about it. She glanced at the hustler as she passed to see if the guy was, like, serious or what. He looked serious . . . And then she saw the window reflection, and it made her stomach jump like a scared cat. Because it was something she'd seen in a dream. A dream about Frank. The snarling, toothy, bloody mouth superimposed over a girl's face. Took her a full two seconds to realize it was a reflection of the rock-band logo—a wide-open shark's mouth— superimposed by reflection against the face of a mannequin in the store window. She'd seen that in a dream, hadn't she? A dream about Frank? Frank . . . She tried to remember . . . and couldn't quite.

Hurrying past the store, she glanced up at a different mannequin in another store window—and thought she saw another reflected face, this time superimposed over the mannequin's crotch . . .

Frank's face. She turned and looked for the source of the reflection. He wasn't there.

Big surprise. He couldn't be there. Frank was dead.

She took a long, ragged breath, and walked on. *Think about something else.*

She passed the black dude with the badly conked hair who was selling his phony sensimilla, which was just California pot dusted with PCP, and her feet hurt, and she still couldn't make up her mind what bar to go to . . . when she saw Frank. For real this time.

God damn it, Frank, you're *dead.*

She stopped in front of Bleeding Heart Records, under the big animated bleeding-heart logo, neon blood dripping on her head, and stared down the street at Frank Cormanstadt, and said, "Oh I'm *sure.* I mean is this too weird or what?" to herself. Bleeding Heart Records was open, it's open late, and Metallica was smacking the air from the record-store speakers. She guessed it was one of those Arthur Koestler synchronicity things her spacey brother Buster talked about because they're talking about the dead on the song—and here comes Frank.

Okay, so he's not dead. After all, she never saw his body, never heard it from anyone but people on the street. But it just felt so right she never questioned it. I mean, everyone was expecting Frank to die, from one thing or another, right? Drunks or drinking and driving or something. AIDS, maybe, from some whore.

But Frank was coming down the street wearing a kind of David Byrne oversize suit, forties-type thing, blocky with padding, his long curly black hair dancing over those cubistic shoulders, his black eyes glittering with neon, the hollows of his cheekbones pooling shadows. He smiled as he saw her, a smile like a squiggle from a can of white Day-Glo spray paint.

She was going to ignore him. Just cross the street. If he

wasn't dead, then he'd ditched her. He hadn't tried to contact her, he'd swept her under the rug, or under some girl's skirt . . .

Under some girl's skirt
Like a pile of dirt

If she got that band started with Sachet and Ellen she'd use those lyrics. If they let her sing.

Ignore him. Cross the street.

But she lingered, mad at herself for it, checking herself out in the glass of the record-store window. The little ponytail on top of her head like a water-fountain splash up there, kind of Valley Girlish, she thought now, but the neoprene shortpants and the skin-tight neoprene imitation snakeskin bikini top and the heels, they were killer, they ought to make Frank suffer.

As she'd suffered. How long had it been? (He was about twenty yards from her. There was still time to cross the street.) Six weeks? No, more like ten weeks. After three weeks of it, she'd heard he was dead. After five weeks—including two weeks getting drunk every day as a kind of endless wake for her dead Frank—meeting that mulatto dude in the Dead Monkey and getting it off with him, the whole thing another kind of drinking, really; and then the Skateboard Nazi, a skinhead jerk with a lot of tattoos. But his intensity had done something for her. Until he'd pushed his skateboard down on her face while he . . .

And then Lonny, three days with Lonny, surprised he didn't just split the next morning.

But he'd had to go back East to see his parents. Called once.

Last night with Greaser Guido hardly counted. But Lonny . . .

Come on, get real, that wasn't going to happen. Lonny was, like, a real prep type. And she was a bit relieved (Frank was about ten feet away—just time to dash across the street if she went now) that it hadn't happened with Lonny; it was too soon after Frank . . .

Frank and that bitch Pearldoll.

I mean, what kind of name is Pearldoll?

"Hi," Frank said, and it was too late to cross the street.

"Hi," she said. Saying it so it'd sting him, she hoped. *Hi*.

The sounds of the street, all those Saturday night cruisers, those lowriders in their chopped convertibles and Beverly Hills kids in their Mustang convertibles and those bored celebs in their limos, all of it a thousand miles away, somehow, when Frank stood there looking at her, talking softly . . .

Telling her he was sorry. A lot of weird shit had come down. He had been out of touch with everyone, even his agent. So you know it's serious.

"What kind of weird shit?" she asked.

"I was really sick," he said. "From . . . an OD. And Pearldoll—she died."

Her heart jumped. She was a little ashamed when she recognized the provenance of the sensation. "She died? You were doing up shit together and she OD'd?"

"No. No, I was alone, afterwards, when I OD'd."

"So you OD'd because she died?" She said it accusingly. Though she knew she should be nice about it, because his old girlfriend had died; I mean, oh wow, death was pretty heavy shit.

But she couldn't help it. That tone.

"No. I . . . No, she died and . . . Well, I don't know, maybe. But, you know, I wasn't even thinking about Pearl, I was going with you then, and, you know, I guess I, like, hadn't seen Pearldoll in like—"

"Come on, you were always thinking about her." Comparing *me* to her, Candy thought.

And thinking: I could always feel Pearldoll there, in the background, feeling like if she came around he'd leave me in a second. Well, he lived with her for three years, when he had that TV series on HBO, but when that fell apart and there was no more money, Pearldoll just *cruised on,* just left him, which should have told him what kind of cunt she was, but *no . . .*

"No," Frank was saying, "I wasn't thinking about her when I OD'd. I wasn't thinking about girls. I was thinking about acting. I guess Joey thought I was dead, I mean I guess I *was* dead, but they revived me, you know, got my heart started again, and I guess they didn't tell anyone . . ." He shrugged, with elegant dismissal. Life and death, a shrug.

He was so cool, the asshole.

"You mad at me?" he asked.

"What do you think? What's it been? Ten weeks? You haven't been in the hospital all this time."

"Yes I have. But not the . . . not that kind."

She stared at him. "Oh Jesus. They put you in the—? A fifty-seven-fifty?" The *mental* hospital.

He nodded. Milking it, though she didn't realize it at the time.

"Oh shit, honey," she said, taking his hands in hers.

Then she broke away. "You still could've called me from the ward."

"I was on all these meds . . . I could barely remember my name. And then when they let me use the phone I was, like, making crazy calls to the FBI and shit, didn't know what I was fucking doing, so they wouldn't let me use the phone after that . . . I'm lucky they let me out."

"Oh."

Feeling like the one in the wrong, now. How did he do it? Always leave her feeling like it was *her* that had screwed up.

"You wanna get a drink with me?" he asked.

Wham bam, thank you ma'am.

An old, old David Bowie tune playing on the sound system of Booty's. A mostly gay club, where Hollywood

Kidz hung out, a lot of fag-hags and a few guys hoping to cop some X or some blow or something.

Candy and Frank stood at the bar, Candy drinking a seabreeze, Frank with his eternal margarita. He was talking, and she was nodding, but only half listening at first. It was hard to make out with the disco banging away—now it was Jody Watley—and, anyway, her mind had taken a step back from him. Was looking him over. What was it that looked different? The suit? All bulky like that. Just heavier and . . . clumsy when he moved.

She thought she knew what it was. Meds. He was still on meds. Some antidepressant or maybe even stelazine.

Don't embarrass him by saying anything about it.

She was thinking pityingly about him, which invariably led to thinking tenderly about him, when he said, "It was really weird, how Pearldoll died."

God damn him. He was going to talk about her.

She remembered when she first realized how Pearldoll was always going to be there. She was at the Anticlub with Frank, their second date, they were, like, making out in the corner, walking everywhere holding on to each other, it was really close and sweet—and then Pearldoll walked up. And he changed. Just like that. Kind of froze up. Pulled away a little. "Hi, Frankie," Pearldoll said, like some torch singer in some old gangster movie. *Hiya, Frankieboy.* But real smug, too. Pearldoll was a cruelly pretty, painfully petite girl, half Japanese and half Swedish, her parents some kind of MDA-dealing hippies. Pearldoll smiling like the Mona Lisa at Candy. Condescendingly. Obviously an ex of Frank's. The look said, You might have him, but he's always mine. Just check him out if you don't believe me!

And it was true. Frank looked slack-mouthed after Pearldoll, gawked at her as she walked away.

"Okay, Frank," Candy had asked him, that night. "How long did you go with her?"

"Uh—kind of obvious, huh? About—couple years."

"Pretty serious."

"Yeah. Pretty serious."

"What happened?"

"I don't know. She's kind of schizy. I got freaked out one night when she said we should do a death pact."

"A *what?*"

"That we should commit suicide together to declare, I don't know, ultimate love or something."

"I think, guy, you're kind of better off without her. I mean, death pacts? Or *what?*"

"Yeah. I'm better off without her. For sure."

But every time he saw Pearldoll in the clubs, he had that gawky longing in his face. And she had that smug knowledge about her. And now she was dead and he was *still* thinking about her.

"Okay," Candy said, now. Tonight, in this hot, sweaty, loud club. They had to yell their conversation in each other's ear over the music. "So how did she die?"

"Sacrificed."

"What?"

"She was into Espiritu."

"What the fuck is that?"

"Espiritu Bebida. It's some Spanish cult from . . . Cuba or someplace. Like Santaria. Kind of an offshoot of it."

"I thought you said she was Japanese and . . . and Danish or something."

"Her roommate was Hispanic, got her into it. Pearldoll hated Japanese stuff, 'cause she hated her mom. She was into Latin stuff."

"Half Japanese, half whatever, Norwegian or something—"

"Swedish."

"Half Swedish—but into Spanish stuff. I never noticed her maracas."

He grinned. "She had some."

"So her roommate sacrificed her?"

"No, her roommate killed herself about two weeks before that. The police talk like Pearldoll was murdered by someone. They even hassled me about it. But she wasn't murdered. She did it to herself. Killed herself. Which is weird, how Japanese that is, like hara-kiri—kind of funny."

"Oh hilarious."

"She killed herself in an Espiritu suicide ritual."

"I told you she was fucked up. And it wasn't just jealousy." Candy looked around at the club, suddenly conscious that it was crowded and noisy and choked with cigarette smoke. A fat girl wearing too much makeup was trying to shove past her to get at the bar. Candy said, "This party sucks."

"It's not a party, just the usual crowd on—"

"That was from a song, 'This Party Sucks.' You *have* been put away."

"You wanna get out of here? Go to my place?"

"Your place?"

"Not mine. Where I'm staying."

"I better not." But hoping he'd talk her into it.

"Come on. I won't make moves on you. I just want to listen to records and talk. Let's fortify first." And he ordered two double Cuervo Golds. And then two more. She was wobbling on her heels when they finally got out, giggling and gasping, onto the sidewalk, and he guided them back to her car, seemed to know where it was without asking. Probably spotted it earlier.

Frank seemed hardly even drunk. He drove her up into the Hollywood Hills, one of those old bungalows built split-level into the hillside. The little porch kind of overgrown with shrubs and bird-of-paradise and morning glory, their blossoms closed and wrinkly for the night, like girls with their legs crossed, labia folded away . . .

Inside, air-conditioned shadows. Santa Fe–style furniture.

"Awesome view," Candy said. She stood in the dark living

room, at the picture window, looking over the tapestry of light, electric blue and sulphur yellow, that was Los Angeles. The night sky was dark violet, somehow, and an eternal stream of cars swept in rivers of headlight glow along the boulevards.

She stood in a deep rug, enjoying its feel on her toes, holding her pumps in one hand; one of Frank's cigarettes, a Sherman, dangled in the other.

Suddenly music, The Cult's "Sonic Temple," was playing from somewhere. He'd put on a CD. "I thought you didn't like this band," she said.

"I like 'em, now," he said, coming up behind her.

She could feel the heat from her cigarette on her knuckles; she could feel heat from Frank as he stepped up behind her. Put his arms around her waist. She could feel a rod of warmth at his crotch, pressing against the crack of her ass.

"Forget it," she said.

"It was you," he said. "I realized that when I was in the hospital. You were the one. The only one."

"Frank, don't—" But she wanted to hear more. To cover the doubts. His story about the hospital had come out too rehearsed. But playing it back in her head again, it sounded reasonable. Sort of. She turned around, knowing she shouldn't. "I still don't think—"

But then he was kissing her, hard, had his arms around her. It felt like he was around her and up under her. That was how it felt to her, with men, when it felt really good. Around you and coming up under you. Protecting and coming *into* you at the same time. He wasn't actually in her yet, but she could feel it pushing, straining at his pants, and there was an answering rush of oozing melt in her pussy . . .

"You . . . goddamned . . ." she tried to say. And then his tongue was in her mouth and it was like plugging into an electrical socket, the current was flowing. He felt different now, to her; he felt bigger and sometimes his tongue felt like it was—

Wait. He was carrying her in his arms.

She couldn't believe it. He wasn't that strong. She looked around and saw he was carrying her up a flight of stairs, which was even harder to do, and then he had toted her effortlessly into a bedroom. There were candles lit here. Blue and red candles. Nice. Romantic.

He put her gracefully on the bed, which was bare but for a sheet, and knelt beside her, kissing and groping. Only now, mixed in with the excitement, there was an anxiety, a feeling that someone was watching them . . .

Whose house was this? Not his. Some sicko voyeur, maybe, some flake he'd met in the nut house, watching them from a two-way mirror?

He was peeling her clothes off her, she was nude almost before she knew it, and he had taken off his coat and shoes but still had his pants on, how rude, but there was a certain excitement to that, too, a feeling that he was out of control with lust for her, wanted her that badly . . .

And then he was on top of her, wriggling into her. She was looking dreamily over his shoulder at the candlelight. Her eyes adjusting, the dark room coming gradually into focus. Little dolls, figures made of cornhusks and straw and rags, and a ceramic Mother of Mary but a Mary with the muzzle of a dog, and on a wall someone had painted a slogan or something, ornate in red letters. She could only make out a couple of words.

Hermano demonio . . . consagrar . . .

Spanish.

Panic surging, she looked around, seemed to see Pearldoll everywhere now. Saw her face in the folds of the curtain, in the curl of candlesmoke, in the shadows gathered on the ceiling.

Candy yelled hoarsely, tried to push Frank away. His cock in her no longer felt like a connection—it felt like an intrusion. "This is *her* place isn't it! Pearldoll's house! You pig! I don't want to be here—"

"Chill out. She left it to me."

God. Maybe he *did* kill her. Maybe he was a murderer. Maybe he was into this Espiritu stuff. Maybe he had sacrificed her.

She managed to pull her hips away from him, turning under him to crawl away. Saw the sheet for the first time clearly. There was a pentagram painted on it, in red, and some Spanish words. And a brown stain.

"I'm glad you turned over," came the voice from his mouth. "I want you from behind like a dog."

It was not his voice.

He was holding her down with arms that were just too strong; they were like metal bars; she felt like a rabbit in a cage that was too small for it, and then he was entering her from behind—god damn him, this was rape—and it hurt, and now he was shifting his cock, putting it up her ass—"Oh you bastard you *shit!*"

"What's the matter, sweet Candy?"

Not his voice?

She heard his clothes ripping. He had both his hands clamped down on her wrists, his knees on the bed, so how could he be ripping his clothes? There must be someone else in the room helping him. Maybe she wasn't dead. Candy hadn't heard anything about it on the news. Maybe Pearldoll wasn't dead, maybe she was here and they were going to sacrifice her on this pentagram—

And then she saw the woman's hands closing on her forearms. Those little white fingers with their oxblood nails. Pearldoll's. Digging into her forearms from behind. Then moving up to her breasts, digging into them with her nails, hurting, piercing, blood running over her nipples. A scream caught in Candy's throat.

They were taking her together. Pearldoll had hidden herself up here—must be lying close beside him.

Candy squirmed, trying to turn around to spit in the bitch's face. Frank held her down, and Candy only managed a glimpse over her shoulder. Saw only Frank's face, laughing without sound, something weirdly faggy in it. Maybe he was a repressed gay and that's why he was raping her up the ass and, God, they were going to kill her——

Panic went off, burned like a Fourth of July sparkler in her, and she thrashed and screamed at them, tried to see Pearldoll so she could kick her, could only see Pearldoll's arms, fingers clawing at her eyes. Tried to wriggle free, it was hurting more and more and more . . .

The red candle on the little blue Santa Fe–style end table beside the bed had been burning awhile, was pooled with quivery molten candle wax. Candy shot a hand out, grabbed the candle, flung its hot wax over her shoulder into the grinning bastard's eyes . . .

He shrieked with a sound like a cat under a car's tire, and his grip loosened for a moment, Pearldoll's, too. Candy wrenched loose, clawed free of them.

Scrambled around to face them, looking for something to throw.

Froze.

Frank's clothes lay in tatters beside the bed. There were two of them, facing Candy—two of them there, nude. The light made it seem . . . No. It wasn't the light.

There was only one. Made of two. Frank's head and shoulders and arms. And *her* arms, growing out of his torso, down under his arms. Pearldoll's arms and hands looking too small on Frank's body, making Candy think of Buster's Revelle model of a Tyrannosaurus.

He had no dick. He had no cock. He had a . . .

"No way," Candy said. "No fucking way."

It was Pearldoll's face. (Where was the door?) Pearldoll's face in his crotch, instead of his genitals. (Find something to throw.) Pearldoll's giggling, rabid-animal face.

Looking out from Frank's crotch, Pearldoll opened her mouth. Frank's cock came out of her mouth instead of a tongue. *She had his cock for her tongue.*

Frank opened his mouth, and then she saw that he had two tongues, one smaller and pinker than his own. Her voice came out of his mouth. Her voice mixed with his. "Want you. Always wanted you. Frank said you wouldn't share." Taunting. "Frank wouldn't kill you. Wouldn't hurt you. Bitch. Bitch. Brother Devil gave Frank to me and me to Frank and you, now. Bitch, bitch, bitch—"

Candy sprinted for the door. White fingers with oxblood nails closed on her wrist, jerked her off-balance so she fell facedown, skidding. The air knocked out of her.

Pearldoll's voice chanted in Spanish. A wave of weakness washed over Candy. A sweet, warm weakness. A weakness that soothed and murmured comforting lies. She was limp, like that time she'd taken three ludes, like a jellyfish, and someone was dragging her to the white sheet with the red pentagram . . .

It felt nice, being dragged that way. Like the rug was a big tongue licking her whole body, warm and wet. *Stoned. Stoned on something. Magic or drugs or both. Fight it.*

There was no fighting it. Not even when Frank straddled her and she saw Pearldoll's face descending toward hers, filling her vision, a pretty Japanese-Swedish face surrounded by pubic hair, legs to either side, coming down at her. Mouth opening. Quivering from inside that mouth, veinily tumesced, his cock, plunging toward Candy's mouth . . .

Suck, something commanded, and she did, and choked, and then Pearldoll pushed closer and began to chew off Candy's lips, and it all took a long time, and it was funny how little it hurt to be eaten alive . . .

"Love to eat Candy," said Pearldoll and Frank.

Before she was drawn in to a puddle of warm blood and liquid flesh, like red candle wax melting, she wondered what part of Frank's body her own face would look out of.

THE KIND MEN LIKE

Karl Edward Wagner

She was better than Betty Page," said Steinman. "We used to call her *Better Page!*"

He laughed mechanically at his own tired joke, then started to choke on his beer. Steinman coughed and spluttered, foam oozing down his white-goateed chin. Chelsea Gayle reached across the table and patted him ungently on his back.

"Thanks, miss. It's these cigarettes." Morrie Steinman dabbed at his face with a bar napkin, blinking his rheumy eyes. He gulped another mouthful of beer and continued: "Of course, that always made her mad. Kristi Lane didn't like to be compared to any other model—didn't matter if you told her she was ten times better. Kristi'd just pout her lips that way she'd do and tell you in a voice that'd freeze Scotch in your mouth that there was *no one* like her."

"And there wasn't," Chelsea agreed. "How long did you work with her?"

"Let's see." Steinman finished his beer and set down the empty glass with a deep sigh. Chelsea signaled to the barmaid, who was already pouring another. She guessed Steinman was a regular here. It was an autumn afternoon, and the tired SoHo bar was stagnant and deserted. Maybe soon new management would convert it into something trendy; maybe they'd just knock it down with the rest of the aging block.

"I was working freelance, mostly. Shooting photo sessions sometimes for the magazines, sometimes for the mail-order pin-up markets, sometimes for the private photo clubs where you could get away with a lot more. Of course, 'a lot more' back in the fifties meant 'a lot less' than you can see on TV these days.

"Thank you, miss." Steinman sipped his fresh beer, watching the barmaid walk away from their booth. "I remember doing a few pin-up spreads of Kristi for Harmony Publishing back about '52 or '53—stuff for girlie magazines like *Wink* and *Eyeful* and *Titter*. They'd seem tame and corny now, but back then . . . "

The paunchy photographer rolled his eyes and made a smacking sound with his lips. Chelsea thought of a love-stricken geriatric Lou Costello.

"After that I shot several of her first few cover spots—magazines like *Gaze* and *Satan* and *Modern Sunbathing*. That must have been the mid '50s. Of course, she was also doing a lot of work for the old bondage-and-fetish photo sets, same as Betty Page. I heard once that Kristi and Betty did a few sessions together, but if that's true no one I know's ever seen them."

"Did Kristi Lane do any work for Irving Klaw?"

"Not a lot that I can recall. I remember introducing them sometime about 1954, or was it 1953? I think they may have shot a few sessions—high heels and black lingerie, pin-up stuff. No bondage."

"Why not?"

"Word was that Kristi Lane was a little too wild for Klaw, who was really pretty straightlaced." Steinman wheezed at his joke. "People said that Kristi could get a little too rough on the submissive model when she had the dominant role. I know some of the girls wouldn't work with her unless they played the mistress."

"Where did she get all her work, then?"

"Mostly from the private photo clubs. And from the mail-order agencies who'd change their drop-box number every few months. You know, the ones with the ads in the back of the girlie mags for comics and photos—'the kind men like.' They could get away with murder, and poor Irving got busted and never showed so much as a bare tit in his photo sets."

While Steinman sucked down his fresh beer, Chelsea opened her attaché case and withdrew several manila envelopes. She handed them to Steinman. "What can you tell me about these?"

Each envelope contained half a dozen black-and-white four-by-fives. Steinman shuffled the photo sets. "That's Kristi Lane, all right."

The first set showed the model in various pin-up poses. The white bikini would have been too daring for its day, and Kristi Lane's statuesque figure seemed about to burst its straps. Her hair was done in her characteristic short blond pageboy, her face held her familiar pout (Bardot's was a careful copy), and her wide blue eyes were those of a fallen angel.

In the next set Kristi was shown dressed as a French maid. Her short costume exposed ruffled panties and lots of cleavage, as she bent over to go about her dusting.

"I shot this one," Steinman said, licking his lips. "About 1954. She said she was twenty. Anyway, they ran it in *Beauty Parade,* I think."

Kristi was tied to a chair in the next set. She was wearing high heels, black stockings and garter belt, black satin panties and bra. A black scarf was knotted around her mouth, and her eyes begged for mercy. She was similarly clad in the next set, but this time she was lying hog-tied upon a rug. In the next, she was tied spread-eagled across a bed.

"All shot the same afternoon," Steinman judged. "Do a few costume changes, give the girl a chance to stretch between poses, and you could come up with maybe a hundred or so good stills."

The next series had Kristi wearing thigh-high patent leather boots and a matching black corset. Her maid, attired in heels, hose, and the inevitable skimpy uniform, was having trouble lacing up Kristi's boots. Over the subsequent poses, the maid was gagged and bound facedown across a table by Kristi, who then applied a hairbrush to the girl's lace-clad bottom.

"Could have been done for Klaw," said Steinman, "but none of these were. The numbers at the bottom aren't his numbering system. There were a lot of guys doing these back then. Most, you never heard of. It wasn't my thing, you gotta understand, but a buck was a buck, then same as now."

Chelsea pulled out another folder. "What about these?"

Steinman flipped through a selection of stills, color and black-and-white, four-by-fives and eight-by-tens. In most of them, Kristi Lane was completely nude, and she was obviously a natural blonde.

"Private stock. You couldn't do that over the counter back then. Even the nudist magazines had to use an airbrush."

"Here's some more."

Kristi Lane was wearing jackboots, a Nazi armband, an SS hat, and nothing else. The other girl was suspended by her wrists above the floor and wore only a ball gag. Kristi wielded her whip with joyous zeal, the victim's contorted face hinted at the screams stifled by the rubber ball, and the blood that oozed from the welts across her twisting body looked all too real.

"No. I never did any of this sort of stuff." Steinman seemed affronted as he handed her back the folder.

"Who did?"

"Lot of guys. Lot of it amateur. Like I say, it wasn't sold openly. Hey, I'm surprised a girl like you'd even want to know about this kind of stuff, Miss . . . uh . . ." He'd forgotten her name since her phone call yesterday.

"Ms. Gayle. Chelsea Gayle."

"Miss Gayle. I thought all modern girls were feminists. Burning their bras and dressing up like men. I guess you're not one of them." His stare was suddenly professional, and somewhere in his beer-soaked brain he was once again focusing his 4×5 Speed Graphic camera.

Chelsea tasted her rum and flat cola and tried not to look flustered. After all, she was wearing her wide-shouldered power suit with a silk blouse primly gathered at the neck by a loose bow, and there was no nonsense about her taupe panty hose or low-heeled pumps. Beneath the *New Woman* exterior, she was confident that her body could as easily slither into a *Cosmopolitan* party dress. Her face took good close-ups, her blond hair was stylishly tousled, and she wore glasses more for fashion than necessity. Let the old fart stare.

"It's for an article on yesterday's pin-up queens," she said, repeating the lie she had told him over the phone. "Sort of a nostalgic look back as we enter the nineties: The women men dreamed of, and where are they now?"

"Well, I can't help you there on Kristi Lane." Steinman waved to the barmaid. "I don't know of anyone who can."

"When did you last work with her?"

"Hard to say. She was all over the place for those few years, then she moved out of my league. I'd guess the last time I shot her would have been about 1958. I know it was a cover for one of those *Playboy* imitations, but I forget the title. Didn't see much of her after that."

"When did you last see her?"

"Probably about 1960. Seem to recall that's about when she dropped out of sight. A guy told me once he'd run into her at a hippie party in the Village late in the sixties, but he was too strung out to know what he was seeing."

"Any ideas?"

"Nothing you haven't heard already. Some said she got religion and entered a convent somewhere. There was some talk that she got pregnant; maybe she married some Joe from Chillico and settled down. There was one story that she was climbing in bed with JFK, and the CIA snuffed her like they did Marilyn Monroe."

"But what do *you* think happened to her?"

Steinman chugged his beer. "I think maybe she got a little too wild."

"Too wild?"

"You know what I mean. Maybe got in too deep. Had to drop out of sight. Or somebody made sure she did."

Chelsea frowned and dug into her case. "This one is pretty wild."

It was a magazine, and on the front it said, *Her Satanic Majesty Requests,* and below that, *For Sale to Adults Only.* The nude woman on the cover was wearing a sort of harness about her hips with a red pointed tail in back and a monstrous red dildo in front. Her face was Kristi Lane's, blond pageboy and all.

Steinman flipped to the centerfold. A writhing victim was tied to a sacrificial altar. Kristi Lane was astride her spread-eagled body, vigorously screwing her with the dildo.

Steinman slapped the magazine shut, shoved it back to Chelsea. "Not my bag, baby. I never shot any porno."

Chelsea replaced the magazine. "Was that Kristi Lane?"

"Maybe. It sure looked like her."

"But the magazine has a 1988 copyright. Kristi Lane would have looked a lot older—she'd be in her fifties."

"You can't tell about that sort of smut. Maybe it was bootleg stuff shot years before. You don't worry about copyrights here."

"The publisher is given as Nightseed X-Press, but their

post office box now belongs to some New Age outfit. They weren't helpful."

"The old fly-by-night. Been gone for years."

"Who was shooting stuff like this back then? This looks fresh from the racks on 42nd Street."

"So it's a Kristi Lane lookalike. Hey, I saw Elvis singing at a bar just yesterday. Only, he was Jewish."

Steinman reached again for his empty glass, gave it a befuddled scowl. "Look. It's all Mob stuff now. The porno racket. Don't ask. Forget it. But—you *really* interested in the old stuff, the pin-up stuff? I got all my work filed away at my studio. No porno. Want to come up and see it?"

"Come up and see your etchings?"

"Hey, on the level. I could be your grandfather."

"Do you have any shots of Kristi Lane?"

"Hundreds of them. Say, have you ever posed professionally? Not pin-ups, I mean—but you have a wonderful face."

Chelsea smiled briskly and closed her case. "Tell you what, Morrie. Here's my business card. See what you've got on Kristi Lane, and then phone me at work. Could be I'll come by and take off my glasses for you."

She gathered up her things and the bar tab, and because he looked so much like a gone-to-seed gnome, she kissed him on top of his balding head.

"Hey, Miss Gayle!" he called after her. "I'll ask around. Look, doll, I'll be in touch!"

Chelsea played back the messages on her answering machine, found nothing of interest, and decided on a long, hot bath. Afterward, she slipped into a loose T-shirt and cotton boxer shorts, and she microwaved the first Lean Cuisine dinner she found in her freezer. A dish of ice cream seemed called for, and she curled up with her cat to consider her day.

The old geek at the used books and magazines dump off Times Square had given her Morrie Steinman's name after she had purchased an armload of Kristi Lane material from him. Apart from adding to her collection, she had really gained nothing from it at all—although it was a thrill to talk with someone who had actually photographed Kristi Lane back at the start of her career.

Chelsea gave her cat the last of the ice cream and hauled the heavy coffee-table book on Kristi Lane onto her lap. It had recently been published by Academy Editions, and she had lugged it back to New York from the shop in Holland Street, Kensington, certain that there was not likely to be a U.S. edition. Its title was *Kristi Lane: The Girl of Men's Dreams,* but Chelsea had already been dreaming of her for years.

She turned through the pages, studying photo after photo of Kristi Lane. Kristi Lane in stripper's costumes, Kristi Lane in high heels and seamed tights and pointed bras and lacy panties and bulky girdles and all the clumsy undergarments of the fifties. Kristi Lane decked out in full fetish gear—boots and corsets and leather gloves and latex dresses and braided whips. Kristi Lane tied to chairs, lashed to tables, spread-eagled over wooden frames, chained and gagged, encased in leather hoods and body sheaths. Kristi Lane tying other women into stringent bondage positions, gagging them with tape and scarves and improbable devices, spanking them with hairbrushes and leather straps.

Chelsea already had many of the photos in her own collection. However familiar, she kept paging through the book. Perhaps this time she might find a clue.

Of course, there was nothing new to be learned: Kristi Lane. Real name unknown. Birthplace and date of birth unknown. Said to be from Ohio. Said to be a teenager when she began her modeling career in New York. Much in demand as pin-up and bondage model during the 1950s. Dropped out of sight about 1962. End of text. Nothing left to do but look at the pictures.

Chelsea shoved the book aside and plopped her cat onto her vacated warmth on the couch. It was bedtime for the Chelsea girl.

Her dream was not unexpected. Nor surprising.

She was wearing one of those funny conical bras that made her breasts stick out like Dagmars on a fish-tail Cadillac—that was her first impression. After that came the discomfort of the boned white corset that pinched her waist, and the tight girdle that squeezed her hips and gartered her seamed hose. She tottered on six-inch-high heels, as her mistress scolded her for some imagined offense. Her mistress looked very stern in her black corselet and spike-heeled boots, and it was only the flip of a page before she was punishing her clumsy maid.

There was a wall-length mirror, so Kristi could watch herself being tied across a coffee table. Her ankles were tied to the table legs at one end, her wrists bound to the legs at the other end, forcing her to support her weight with her flexed legs and arms. Another rope secured her waist to the tabletop, and a leather gag stifled her pleas. Kristi wriggled in helpless pain in her cramped position, rolling her eyes and whimpering through the leather strap. Her thighs were spread wide by her bondage, and she flushed as she saw her mistress smiling at the dampening crotch of her girdle. Her cunt was growing hotter and wetter the harder she struggled . . .

Chelsea awoke with the pulse of her orgasm. After a moment she decided that, in the morning, she would try to search out the photo set and make a notation. She had made hundreds of such notations.

Her secretary told her: "Your grandfather phoned while you were at lunch."

"What?" Chelsea studied the memo. "Oh, that has to be Morrie."

"Said he has some new etchings to show you. Your grandfather is quite the kidder."

"He's a randy old goat. I'll see what he wants."

Chelsea returned the call from her office. Morrie's answering machine said that Mr. Steinman was at work in the darkroom just now and to please leave a message and number at the tone. Chelsea started to speak, and Steinman picked up the phone.

"Hey, doll! Got something for you."

"Like what?"

"Nightseed X-Press. The porno mag you showed me."

"Yes?"

"Most of them aren't really models. Just hookers doing a trick in front of a camera. I had a friend ask around. Discreetly. Found a girl who says she did some work for Nightseed about a year ago, gave me the address."

"Did she say anything about Kristi Lane?"

"The bimbo's maybe eighteen. She wouldn't know Kristi Lane from Harpo Marx. No phone number, but it's a loft not far from here. Want I should check it out?"

"I can do that."

"I don't think so. Not a job for a lady. Why don't you come by here sometime after five, and I'll make a full report. I got some photos you might like to see as well."

"All right. I'll come by after work."

Chelsea hung up and opened her shoulder bag. Yes, the can of Mace was right on top.

Steinman's studio was a second-floor walk-up above a closed-down artists' supply shop a few blocks from the bar where they'd met. The stencil on the frosted glass read *Morris Steinman Photography*, and Chelsea tried to imagine what sort of business he might attract.

The door was unlocked, and the secretary's desk had probably been vacant since Kennedy's inauguration. It was going on six, so Chelsea rapped on the glass and walked inside. The place was surprisingly neat, if a bit faded, and the wastebasket contained only a beer can. A row of filing cabinets had been recently dusted.

Chelsea let herself into the studio beyond the front office. She smelled coffee. There was a green davenport, a refrigerator, a hot plate, and an electric percolator, which was steaming slightly. There was a large empty room with a lot of backdrops and lighting stands and camera tripods. In the back there was a darkroom with a red light glowing above the DO NOT ENTER sign on the door. As she watched, the light winked out.

"Morrie?" Chelsea crossed to the darkroom. "It's Chelsea Gayle."

The door of the darkroom slowly opened. Morrie Steinman shuffled out into the studio. He was holding a still-damp print, but he wasn't looking at it or at Chelsea. His face was a pasty mask, his eyes staring and unfocused. Steinman stumbled past Chelsea, moving dreamily toward the couch. He was a puppet whose strings were breaking, one by one. By the time he collapsed onto the davenport, there were no more strings to break.

Chelsea pried the photograph from his stiff fingers. Blood was trickling from beneath the frayed sleeve of his shirt, staining the four-by-five print as she tore it free. The photo was smeared, but it was a good pose of Kristi Lane in a tight sweater with a bit of stocking-top laid bare by her hiked-up skirt. She was seated with her knees crossed on the green davenport.

"Morrie always did good work," Kristi Lane said, stepping out of the darkroom. "I thought I owed him one last pose."

She closed her switchblade and pouted—teenage bad girl from the 1950s B-movies. In face and figure, Kristi Lane hadn't changed by so much as a gray hair from the pin-up queen of 1954. Chelsea reflected that her pageboy hairstyle was once again high fashion.

"Why kill him?"

Kristi slowly walked toward her. "Not too many left from the old days who could recognize me. Now there's one less. You shouldn't have prodded him into looking for me."

"There's thousands of photographs. You're a cult figure."

"Honey, if you passed Marilyn Monroe jogging in Central Park, you'd know she was just another lookalike."

Chelsea reached for the can of Mace as Kristi stepped close to her. Kristi's hand closed like steel over her wrist before she could work the spray. The can flew from her grasp, as Kristi effortlessly flung her across the studio. She crashed heavily against the wall opposite and slid down against it to her knees.

Kristi reached down for her throat, and the switchblade clicked. "We can make this as rough as you want, honey."

Chelsea lunged to her feet and caught Kristi beneath her arms, lifting the other woman and hurling her through a backdrop. Kristi lost her switchblade as she crashed down amidst a tangle of splintering wood.

Struggling free, she swung a heavy light-stand at Chelsea's head. Chelsea caught the blow with her forearms and wrenched the bent metal stand away from her. Diving forward as Kristi stumbled back, she tackled the other woman—pinning her as the two smashed through the wreckage of another backdrop.

Kristi Lane suddenly stopped struggling. She stared in wonder at the woman crouched on top of her.

"Who are you?"

"I'm your daughter," Chelsea panted. "Now tell me *what* I am!"

Kristi Lane laughed and pushed Chelsea off her. "Like mother, like daughter. You're a succubus."

"A succubus!"

"Dictionary time? A demon in female form—a temptress who haunts men's dreams, who draws youth and strength from their lust. Surely by now you've begun to wonder about yourself."

"I'd found out from agency records that you were my mother. I thought that if I could find you, you might explain things—like why I'm unnaturally strong, and why I look like I'm still twenty, and why I keep having dreams about being you."

"I think it's time we had our mother-daughter chat," Kristi said, helping her to her feet. "Let's go home."

"Chelsea Gayle," Kristi murmured. "I gave you the name, *Chelsea.*"

"Why did you give me up?"

"No place for a baby in my life. The social agency had no problems with that, although they hardly could have guessed the full reasons. Most offspring never survive infancy. You've been feeding off my energy all these years—and you turned out very well."

Chelsea tugged off the remains of her blouse and slipped into a kimono. She couldn't decide whether her mother's gaze held tenderness or desire.

"Who was my father?"

"All men. The thousands who fucked me in their wet-dream fantasies, who jacked off over my pictures. Their seed is our strength. Sometimes the combined energy of their lust is strong enough to create a child. It happens only rarely. Perhaps someday you'll bear another of us."

"I work in advertising."

"Selling false dreams. Already you were becoming one of us."

Kristi took away Chelsea's kimono and unhooked her bra. Chelsea did not resist.

"You shouldn't hide your beauty," Kristi told her. "We

need to feed from their secret lusts. Both of us. Now it's time you were weaned. Get rid of those clothes, and I'll find you something better to wear."

Chelsea was naked when Kristi returned from another corner of the loft. Her mother had changed into spike-heeled boots and a studded leather bikini. Her arms were loaded with leather gear.

"I'll teach you," she said. "They need stronger stimulation now than they did when I began. I almost waited too long; I'd become nostalgia to them, no longer their sexual fantasy. My comeback will also be your coming out."

Kristi Lane led her over to a small stage area. Lights were coming on, and Chelsea sensed cameras and presences behind them in the encircling darkness, but she couldn't see beyond the lights.

"Now then, dear." Kristi set down her bondage paraphernalia and picked up a riding crop. "I am mistress here, and you must obey me in every way. Do you promise?"

"Yes, mistress. I promise."

"After all," her mother said softly, "this is what you've always known you wanted."

Then, sharply: "Now then! Let's get you into these!"

Meekly Chelsea put on the leather corselet and thigh-high boots, then submitted to having her arms laced tightly behind her back in a leather single-glove. By then it was pointless to struggle when Kristi strapped a phallus-shaped gag deep into her mouth, then brought out what at first glance had looked like a leather chastity belt. Choking on the gag, Chelsea moaned as the twin dildos penetrated her vagina and rectum, stretching her as they pushed inward to rub together against the thin wall that separated their bulbous heads.

Her mother leaned forward to kiss her face as she padlocked the belt securely into place. "You'll stay like me, Chelsea—forever young and beautiful."

Kristi helped her lie down on top of a long leather sheath.

As Chelsea writhed on her belly, Kristi began to lace together the two edges of the leather sleeve, tightly encasing her daughter within a leather tube from her ankles to her neck.

Kristi kissed her face again, just as she fitted the leather hood over Chelsea's head and laced it across the back of her neck. "Their lust is our strength. I'll help you."

Chelsea lay helpless, blinded and gagged, barely able to wriggle so much as her fingers. She felt her ankles being strapped together. Then, slowly, she was lifted into the air by her ankles until she was completely suspended above the stage.

Hanging upside down, tightly wrapped in her leather sheath, Chelsea could sense the gloating touch of the cameras. She writhed helplessly, beginning to experience the warmth that flowed into her from the hard rubber penises swollen inside her mouth and cunt and ass. She did not feel violated. Instead she felt the strength that she was drawing from an unseen prey.

Suspended and satisfied, Chelsea Gayle waited to be released from her cocoon, and wondered what she had become.

THE BRAILLE
ENCYCLOPAEDIA

Grant Morrison

*B*lind in the City of Light, Patricia walked carefully back through the Cimitière Père-Lachaise.

"Are you all right?" Mrs. Becque said again. "Now be careful here, the steps are a little slippery . . ."

Patricia nodded and placed her foot tentatively on the first step. Through the soles of her shoes she could feel the edge of a slick patch of moss.

"Are you all right?" Mrs. Becque said again.

"I'll be fine," Patricia said. "Really."

All around, she could feel the shapes of sepulchers and headstones. The echoes they returned, the space they displaced, the subtle patterns of cold air they radiated; all these things gave the funeral monuments of Père-Lachaise a weight and solidity that lay beyond sight. From the locked and chambered earth, a fragrance arose. The elaborate alchemy of decay released a damp perfume which combined with the scent of spoiled wreaths and hung like a mist around the stones. Rain drummed on the stretched skin of Patricia's umbrella.

"So what did you think?" said Mrs. Becque. "Of Wilde's monument, that is? Did you like it?"

"Lovely," Patricia said.

"Of course, the vandals have made a terrible mess, writing all over the statue, but it's still very impressive, don't you think?"

Mrs. Becque's voice receded into a rainy drone. Patricia could hardly mention how amused she'd been when she'd run her hands over Epstein's stone angel, only to discover that the balls of the statue had been chopped off by some zealous souvenir fiend. Mrs. Becque would most certainly disapprove of so ironic a defacement, but Patricia felt sure that Oscar Wilde would have found the whole thing thoroughly entertaining. Mrs. Becque, in fact, seemed to disapprove of almost everything and Patricia was growing desperately tired of the woman's constant presence.

"We must get in out of this awful rain," Mrs. Becque was saying. They crossed the street, found a café and sat down.

"What would you like, dear?" asked Mrs. Becque. "Coffee?"

"Yes," Patricia said. "Espresso. And a croissant. Thanks."

Mrs. Becque ordered, then eased herself up out of her seat and set off in search of a telephone. Patricia took her book from her bag and began to read with her fingertips. She found no comfort there. More and more often these days, books did nothing but increase her own sense of isolation and disaffection. They taunted and teased with their promise of a better world but in the end they had nothing to offer but empty words and closed covers. She had grown tired of experiencing life at second hand. She wanted something that she had never been able to put into words.

A waiter brought the coffee.

"Something else for you, sir?" he said.

Patricia started up from her book. Someone was sitting at her table, directly opposite. A man.

"I'm fine with this," the man said. His voice was rich and

resonant, classically trained. Every syllable seemed to melt in the air.

"I hope you don't mind," the man said. He was talking to Patricia now, using English. "I saw you sitting all alone."

"No. Actually, I'm with someone," Patricia said. She stumbled over the words, as she might stumble over the furniture in some unfamiliar room. "She's over there. Over there." She gestured vaguely.

"I don't think you're with anyone at all," the man said. "You seem to me to be alone. It's not right that a pretty girl should be alone in Paris."

"I'm not," Patricia said flatly. The man was beginning to disturb and irritate her.

"Believe me," the man said. "I know what you want. It's written all over your face. I *know* what you want."

"What are you talking about?" Patricia said. "You don't know me. You don't know anything about me."

"I can read you like a book," he said. "I'll be here at the same time tomorrow, if you wish to hear more about the Braille Encyclopaedia."

"I beg your pardon?" Patricia's face flushed. "I really don't . . ."

"Everything all right, dear?"

Patricia turned her head. The voice belonged to Mrs. Becque. Foreign coins chinked into a cheap purse.

"It's just this man . . ." Patricia began.

Mrs. Becque sat down. "What man?" she said. "The waiter?"

"No. That man. There." Patricia pointed across the table.

"There's no one there, Patricia," Mrs. Becque said, using the voice she reserved for babies and dogs. "Drink up your coffee. Michel said he'd pick us up here in twenty minutes."

Patricia lifted her cup in numbed fingers. Somewhere the espresso machine sputtered and choked. Rain fell on the silent dead of Père-Lachaise, on the streets and the houses of

Paris, covering the whole city like a veil, like a winding sheet . . .

Patricia raised her head. "What time is it?" she said.

In her room, in the tall and narrow hotel on the Boulevard St. Germain, Patricia sat listening to traffic. Outside, wheels sluiced through rain.

Rain sieving down through darkness. Rain spattering on the balcony. Rain dripping, slow and melancholy, from the wrought-iron railing.

She sat on the edge of the bed, in the dark. Always in the dark. No need for light. The money she saved on electricity bills! She sat in the dark of the afternoon, ate another slab of chocolate and tried to read. It was hopeless; her fingers skated across the braille dots, making no sense of their complex arrangements. Unable to concentrate, she set her book down and paced to the window again. Soon it would be evening. Outside, in the dark and the rain, Paris would put on its suit of lights. Students would gather to argue over black coffee, lovers would fall into one another's arms. Out there, in the breathless dark and the flashing neon, people would live and be alive; and here, in this room, Patricia would sit and Patricia would read.

She sat down heavily and, unutterably miserable, slotted a cassette into her Walkman. Then she lay back on the bed, staring wide-eyed into her private darkness.

Debussy's "La Mer" began to play—the first wash of strings and woodwind conjured a vast and empty shore. White sand, desolate under a big sky. White waves smashed on the rocks. Patricia was writing something on the sand. Lines drawn on a great blank page of sand. She could not read what she was writing but she knew it was important.

Patricia licked dry lips, tasting chocolate.

What did he look like? The man in the café. The man with the voice. What would he look like if she could see him?

She unzipped her skirt and eased her hand down between

her legs. The bed began to creak faintly, synchronizing itself with Patricia's harsh, chopped breathing . . .

She was stretched out on watered silk in a scented room of flowers and old wine and he was there with his voice and his breath on her body his breath circulating in the grottoes of her ear and in her mouth and his skin and the mesh of muscles as he went into her

. . . Debussy's surf broke against the walls of her skull. White wave noise drowning out the traffic and the rain, turning the darkness into incendiary light.

The music had come to an end. The room was too hot. An airless box. Patricia was suffocating in the dark. She rose, unsteadily, and faced the mirror's cold eye. She knew how she must look: a fat, plain girl, playing with herself on a hotel bed.

"Stop it or you'll go blind," she said quietly. She felt suddenly sick and stupid. She would never meet anyone, never do or be anything. It all came down to this stifling room. No matter where she went, she found herself in this room. Reading. Always reading. Nothing would ever happen.

The dark closed in.

"I knew you'd be here," the man said. "I knew it."

"I don't see how you could just know," said Patricia and felt stupid. She was saying all the wrong things.

"Oh, I know," he said. "I'm trained to recognize certain things in people. Certain possibilities. Certain . . . inclinations." His hand alighted on hers and she jumped. "I can tell we're going to be friends, Patricia."

"I don't even know your name," she said. She was becoming frightened now. She felt somehow that she was being *circled*. His voice was drawing a line around her. Sweat gathered between her breasts.

"My name?" He smiled. She could hear him smile. "Just call me L'Index."

"Sorry?" Patricia felt sure she must have misheard him. She tried not to be afraid. Being afraid was what had made her lonely.

"L'Index," the man repeated. "Like a book. L'Index."

"I can't call you that," Patricia said.

"You can. You must." He reached out and took her hand. It was like a soft trap, fastening around her wrist. "Dear Patricia. You must. You will. I will show you such things . . ." The fear was almost unbearable. She wanted to run. She wanted to go back. Back to that room, that book, like the coward she was. The man was holding open a door. Beyond lay darkness, it was true, but then again, Patricia was no stranger to the dark.

"L'Index," she said.

When Mrs. Becque returned to the café to collect Patricia, Patricia had gone. One of the waiters had seen her leave with someone but found it impossible to describe the man. No one could describe the man. He had come and he had gone: a gray man in the rain. Invisible. The police were alerted. Half-heartedly they scoured the city, then gave up. Patricia's parents mounted their own futile search. The newspapers printed photographs of a rather plump, blind girl, smiling at a camera she could not see. Her eyes were pale blue, their color diluted to invisibility. Eyes full of rain, like puddles in a face. Very soon the papers and the public lost interest. Patricia's room lay untenanted. A stopped clock. The girl was never found and the police file stayed open, like a door leading nowhere.

The Chateau might have seemed like a prison were it not for the fact that it appeared to perpetually renew its own architecture. No door ever led twice to the same room, no corridor could ever be followed to the same conclusion, no stair could be made to repeat its steps.

Additionally, the variety of experiences offered by life in the Chateau was of such diversity that life outside could only be timid and pale by comparison. Here, there was no sin which could not be indulged to exhaustion. Here, the search for fresh sensation had long ago led to the practice of continually more refined atrocities. Here, finally, there were no laws, no boundaries, no limits, no judgment.

And the motto above the door read simply "Hell is more beautiful than Heaven."

Tonight was to be a special night. In the red room, in the room of the Sign of Seven, whose walls beat like a heart, Patricia lay in a tumble of silk cushions. She found a vein in her thigh and slowly inserted the needle. After the first rush, her head seemed to unlock and divide like a puzzle box. Her nervous system suffered a series of delicious shocks and smoke spilled into her brain. She licked red lips and began to shake. The tiny bells pinned to her skin reacted to her shudders. Her body became a tambourine. She drew a long breath. The room was hot and sweat ran on her oiled skin, trickling from the tongues of the lewd tattoos which now adorned her belly.

Above the pulse of the room, Patricia could hear the boy spitting, still spitting. L'Index had allowed her to touch the boy—to run her nails through his soft hair, to pluck feathers from the clipped and ragged wings he wore on his back and to finger the scars of his castration.

"What's he doing?" she said dreamily. "Why is he spitting?"

L'Index had come back into the room. He closed the door and waited for the boy to finish.

"He's been spitting into this glass," L'Index said. "Here."

Patricia took from him a beautiful crystal wineglass.

L'Index knelt down beside her. Heat radiated off his body and he smelled faintly of blood and spiced sweat.

"The boy is an angel," L'Index said. "We summoned him here from Heaven and then we crippled and debauched him."

Patricia giggled.

"Our own little soiled angel," L'Index continued. "Come here, angel."

The boy shuffled across the room, slow as a sleepwalker. His wings rustled like dry paper.

"What shall I do with this?" Patricia asked, weighing the glass in her hand.

"I want you to drink it," L'Index said. "Drink."

Patricia dipped her tongue into the warm froth of saliva.

"He has AIDS, of course," L'Index said casually. "The poor creature has been the plaything of god knows how many filthy old whores and catamites. As you might expect, his spit is a reservoir of disease." He paused, smiling his almost-audible smile. "Nevertheless, I do insist that you drink it."

Patricia heard the boy whimpering as he was forced onto his hands and knees. She swirled the liquid round in the glass.

"Drink it *slowly.*"

She heard the chink and creak of a leather harness. A match was struck. Was there no limit to what he would ask of her?

"All right," she said, nosing the glass like a connoisseur. It smelled of nothing. "I told you. I'll do anything."

And she drank, slowly, savoring the bland, flat taste of the boy's saliva. The whole glass, to the dregs. As she drank, she could hear the boy gasp—sodomized. Patricia licked the rim of her glass.

"You were lying," she said. "AIDS. I knew you were lying."

The boy cried out, with the voice of a bird. L'Index had done something new to him. Patricia waited for L'Index to undo the harness and sit down beside her.

"I knew I was right about you, when I saw you all those months ago," L'Index said. He tugged on the ring that was threaded through her nipple, pulling her toward him. Automatically, she opened her mouth and allowed him to place an unclean treat on her tongue.

"I knew you were worthy of admission."

"Admission?" said Patricia. "Admission into what?" The sound of her own voice seemed to recede and return. She was beginning to feel strange.

"Do you remember when I mentioned to you the Braille Encyclopaedia?" L'Index asked.

"Yes." Fragments of music flared in Patricia's head. Choral detonations. She felt that she was falling through some terrible space. "The Braille Encyclopaedia. Yes. What is it?"

"Not a thing," L'Index said. "A society. Here. On your knees. Touch me."

He took her hand.

"But you've never let me . . ." she began, growing excited. White noise blasted through her, like a stereo pan, from ear to ear.

"I'm letting you now," he said. "You've shown a rare appetite for all the sweet and rotting fruits of corruption. Sometimes, I'm almost frightened by your dedication. Now, I think it's time you were allowed to taste the most exquisite delicacy." He set her hand to his bare chest. Her fingers brushed his skin and she started.

"What is it?" Patricia lightly traced her fingertips across tiny raised scars. Alarm returned as she realized that his entire body, from neck to feet, was similarly disfigured. She ran along a row of dots, suddenly unable to catch a breath.

"It's braille," she said. "Oh, God, it's braille . . . I feel so

323

strange . . ." He filled her mouth and stopped her speech. Like a nursing child, she sucked and swallowed and allowed her hands to crawl across his skin.

"You drank angel spit," L'Index said. His voice was full of echoes and ambiguous reverberations. "You drank the rarest of narcotics. Now it's time to read me, Patricia. Read me!"

She read.

Entry 103   THE DEFORMATION OF BABY SOULS
Entry 45   THE HORN OF DECAY
Entry 217   THE MIRACLE OF THE SEVERED FACE
Entry 14   THE ATROCIOUS BRIDE
Entry 191   THE REGIMENTAL SIN
Entry 204   BLEEDING WINDO . . .

Patricia snatched back her hand and pulled away, terrified. L'Index came into her face, spattering her useless eyes.

"What are you?" she whispered. She blinked and sperm tears ran down her cheeks. Somewhere, the fallen angel whimpered in the darkness.

"There are several hundred of us," L'Index explained. "And together we form the most comprehensive collection of impure knowledge that has ever been assembled. Monstrous books, long thought destroyed, have survived as marks on our flesh. Through us, an unholy tradition is preserved."

"And what about me," Patricia said.

"One of our number died recently," L'Index said. "It happens, of course, in the due process of time. Usually, we initiate a relative, often a child. My grandfather, for instance, was the Index before me. In this case, however, that was not possible. Part of my job is to find a suitable successor . . ."

Gripped by an extraordinary fear, Patricia dropped to the floor.

"Don't be afraid, Patricia," L'Index said. "Not you."

As she lay there, he pissed on her hair. She lifted her face into the hot stream, grateful for an act of degradation she could still understand. It helped her to know he still cared.

"Will you abandon your last claim to self? Will you embrace the final release, Patricia? That is what I'm asking of you. Will you step over the threshold into a new world?"

"You sound like an evangelist," she said. His urine steamed in her hair. Patricia breathed deeply, inhaling a mineral fragrance. Slowly her heart rate came to match the pulsing of the room. She thought of what she had been and of what he had helped her become.

She held her breath for a moment. Counted to ten.

"Yes," she said hoarsely. "Yes."

They came singly, they came in twos and in groups: the Braille Encyclopaedia. Some were driven in black limousines with mirrored windows and no registration plates. Others walked, haltingly. Men, women, hollow-eyed children. They came from all directions, traveling on roads known only to a few mad or debased souls. They came and the doors of the Château opened to receive them. There was an almost electrical excitement in the air. The current ran through enchanted flesh, conjuring static in the darkness. Blue sparks played on fingertips as the Braille Encyclopaedia made its way into the Chateau. They were, each of them, blind, even the youngest. Silent and blind, blue ghosts, they entered the darkness. And the doors closed behind them.

Patricia did not hear them enter, nor did she hear L'Index welcome his guests. She sat in her chamber, listening to the fall of surf on an interior beach. On the bedside cabinets were vibrators, clamps, unguents, suction devices, whips: all the ludicrous paraphernalia of arousal. She was familiar with each and every item and she had endured or perpetrated every possible permutation of indecency that the body could endure.

Or so she had thought.

She touched her own smooth skin. She had removed the bells and the rings and toweled the oil away. Her skin was blank, like a parchment upon which L'Index wished to write unspeakable things. The music of Debussy crashed through her confusion.

We are all of us, she thought, written upon by time. Our skin is pitted and eroded by the passage of years. No one escapes. Why not then defy time by becoming part of something eternal? Why not give up all claims to individual identity and become little more than a page in a book which renews itself endlessly? It was, as L'Index had said, the final surrender.

Patricia removed her headphones and made her way downstairs.

L'Index was waiting for her and he introduced her to the members of the Braille Encyclopaedia. Blind hands stroked her naked body and, finding it unmarred, lost interest. She trembled as, one by one, they approached and examined her with a shocking frankness. Shameless fingers probed and penetrated her: the dry-twig scrapings of old men and women, the thin furtive strokes of wicked children. By the end of their examination, Patricia teetered on the brink of delirium. Her darkness filled with inarticulate flashes and fireworks displays of grotesque color and grossly ambiguous forms.

"They don't speak," she said. It seemed terribly important.

"No," said L'Index simply.

She felt them crowd around her in a circle, felt the

pressure and the heat of unclothed flesh. No sound. They made no sound.

"Are you ready?" L'Index asked, touching Patricia's shoulder gently. She nodded and let him lead her into a tiny room at the back of the Chateau. Soundproofed walls. A single unshaded bulb, radiating a light she could not see. L'Index kissed her neck and instructed her not to move under any circumstances. She wanted to say something, but she was too afraid to speak. The words jammed at the back of her throat.

And then the door opened. Someone she did not know came into the room. Patricia suddenly wanted to run. The light was switched off and candles were lit, filling the room with a sickly sweet narcotic scent.

Patricia heard then a thin metallic ring. A sharp-edged sound. The brief conversation of scalpels and needles and blue-edged razors.

"L'Index?" she said nervously. "L'Index, are you there? I'm afraid . . ."

No one answered. Patricia rocked on the balls of her feet. The air was too hot, the candlesmoke too bitter. She gulped lungfuls of oily, shifting smoke.

Someone came toward her, breathing harshly, sometimes mewing.

"L'Index?" she whispered again, so quietly that it was no more than the ghost of a name. In her head, the noise and the colors mounted toward an intensity she felt she could not possibly bear.

The first cut caused her to spontaneously orgasm. Her brain lit up like a pinball machine. She swayed and she cried out but she did not fall as hooks and needles were teased beneath her skin.

Moaning, coming again and again, Patricia was delicately scarred and cicatriced. Alone on a private beach, she realized what word it was that she had scrawled in the sand.

And in that moment of understanding, the surf surged in and obliterated every trace of what she had written. Her identity was finally erased in the white glare of a pain so perfect and so pure that it could only be ecstasy. Fat, awkward Patricia was at last, at last, written out of existence by articulate needles.

She came to her senses and found that she was still standing. Thin spills of blood streamed down her body, pooling on the floor. She touched her stomach. The raw wounds stung but she could not help but run her fingertip along the lines of braille. She read one sentence and could hardly believe that such abomination could possibly exist let alone be described. Her whole body was a record of atrocities so rare and so refined that the mind revolted from the truth of them. How could things like this be permitted to exist in the world? She felt dizzy and could read no more.

"I'm still alive. I'm still alive," was all she could say. At last, she fell but L'Index was there to catch her.

"Welcome to the Encyclopaedia," he said, salting her wounds so that they burned exquisitely. "Now you are Entry 207—The Meat Chamber."

She nodded, recognizing herself, and he led her out of the room and down an unfamiliar corridor. She could feel herself losing consciousness. There was something she had to ask him. That was all she could remember.

"The Chateau," she said, slurring her words. "Who owns the Chateau?"

"Can't you guess?" L'Index said.

He brought her into the ballroom, where they were all waiting for her. Hundreds of people were waiting for her. She smiled weakly and said, "What now? Can I please sit down?"

"These gatherings happen only rarely," L'Index said. "The entire Encyclopaedia is not often assembled together in one place and so our lives take on true meaning only at these moments. I can assure you that what is about to follow will transcend all your previous experiences of physical gratification. For you, this will be the ultimate, most beautiful defilement. I promise."

He sat her down in a heavy wooden chair.

"I envy you so much," he said. "I'm only the Index, you see. The mysteries and abominations of the flesh are denied to me."

He pulled a strap across her arms, tugged it tight and buckled it.

"What are you doing?" she said. "Is this the Punishment Chair? It's not, is it?" She began to panic now as he clamped her ankles to the legs of the chair. The Encyclopaedia was arranging itself into a circle again. Footsteps sounded down the corridor.

"This is the Chair of Final Submission," L'Index said. "Goodbye, my love."

And he clamped her head back.

"Oh no," she said. "Wait. Don't . . ."

A clumsy bolt and bit arrangement was thrust into her mouth, chipping a tooth and reducing her words to infantile sobs and gobblings.

The footsteps advanced and the Encyclopaedia parted to make a passage. Shiny steel chinked slyly in a leather bag. L'Index leaned over and whispered in her ear.

"Remember, you may always consult me . . ."

She bucked and slammed in the chair but it was fixed to the floor by heavy bolts.

"Oh my sweet," L'Index said. "Don't lose heart now. Remember what you were: alone, lonely and discontented. You will never be lonely again." His breath stank of peppermint and sperm. "Now you can pass into a new world where nothing is forbidden but virtue."

A bag snapped open. A needle was withdrawn. It rang faintly, eight inches long.

"Give yourself up now to the world of the Braille Encyclopaedia! Knowledge shared only by these few, never communicated. Knowledge gained by sense of touch alone."

And she finally understood then, just before the needles punctured her eardrums. Her bladder and her bowels let go and the odors of her own chemical wastes were the last things she smelled before they destroyed that sense also. Finally her tongue was amputated and given to the angel to play with.

"Now go," L'Index said, unheard. There was sadness in his voice. His tragedy was to be forever excluded from the Empire of the Senseless. "Join the Encyclopaedia."

Released from the chair, The Meat Chamber stumbled into the arms of her fellow entries in the Braille Encyclopaedia. Bodies fell together. Blind hands stroked sensitized skin. They embraced her and licked her wounds and made her welcome.

She screamed for a very long time but only one person there heard her. Finally she stopped, exhausted.

And then she began to read.

And read.

And read.

AUTHOR BIOGRAPHIES

Paul Dale Anderson

Anderson's short stories have appeared in *The Horror Show*, *New Blood*, *Masques III* and others. The Illinois writer's recent novels include *Claw Hammer* and *Superstitions*.

Gary Brandner

California horror writer Brandner has twenty-seven novels in print, including the popular *Howling* series. His latest work is *Doomstalker*.

Kurt Busiek's

Busiek's writing is familiar to comic book readers of *Wonder Woman*, *Liberty Project*, *Open Space* and others. The Connecticut writer's short fiction has appeared in the *Newer York* anthology.

John L. Byrne

Byrne's prolific comic book career includes *X-Men*, *Spider-Man*, *Batman* and *Superman*. His first novel, *The Fear Book*, appeared in 1988, while *Hotter Blood* marks his first appearance as a writer of short prose fiction. He lives in Connecticut.

Lisa W. Cantrell

North Carolina's Cantrell won the Bram Stoker award for her first horror novel, *The Manse*. Her recent work includes *The Ridge* and *Torments*.

Nancy A. Collins

Collins is the author of *Tempter* and the *Sunglasses After Dark* vampire series. She lives in Louisiana.

Don D'Ammassa

Rhode Island's D'Ammassa is the author of *Blood Beast* and is a reviewer for *Science Fiction Chronicle* and *Mystery Scene*.

Stephen Gallagher

Gallagher's work includes the acclaimed *Valley of Lights* and *Rain*. Upcoming projects include *The Boat House* and *The Unforgiven*. The English writer's first short prose fiction appears in *Hotter Blood*.

Michael Garrett

Garrett is an Alabama writing instructor whose published work includes *Keeper* and numerous short stories for publications like *Twilight Zone*. His upcoming books include *Hangman*, co-authored with Jeff Gelb.

Mick Garris

Garris's prolific screenplay writing credits include *batteries not included* and *Fly 2*. The California writer's short fiction credits include *Hot Blood*, *Silver Scream*, and *Midnight Graffiti*. He recently directed Anthony Perkins in *Psycho 4*.

Ray Garton

California's Garton has penned over half a dozen novels, including his latest, *Trade Secrets*, and *Live Girls*, which was nominated for a Bram Stoker award.

R. Patrick Gates

Gates is the author of *Fear* and *Grimm Memorials*, which he calls a modern-day version of "Hansel and Gretel." He lives in Massachusetts.

Jeff Gelb

Gelb has authored short fiction for *Scare Care*, the novel *Specters*, and co-edited the first *Hot Blood* anthology. Upcoming projects for the Los Angeles resident include the editorship of rock and roll horror anthology *Shock Rock*.

Stephen Gresham

Alabama's prolific Gresham has authored 11 horror novels since 1982, including his latest, *Bloodwing*. *Hotter Blood* marks his initial foray into short fiction.

James Kisner

Kisner has penned more than eight novels, including *Poison Pen* and *Dead-End Job*. His short fiction has appeared in *Masques III*, *Phantoms*, *Stalkers* and *Scare Care*. He lives in Indiana.

Richard Laymon

Los Angeles resident Laymon is the author of over a dozen horror novels, including *Flesh*, *Resurrection Dreams* and the recent *Funland*.

Graham Masterton

Masterton's popular horror fiction has seen print worldwide. The England resident's most recent works are *Walkers*, *Empress* and *Night Places*.

Rex Miller

The prolific Miller has authored two non-fiction books and nine novels in less than five years, including the acclaimed Jack Eichord sextet. The Missouri resident's first short fiction was published in *Hot Blood*.

Grant Morrison

Scotland's Morrison is a well-respected comic book writer of such titles as *Animal Man, Doom Patrol* and the Batman graphic novel "Arkham Asylum." *Hotter Blood* marks his first published short prose horror fiction.

Michael Newton

Newton's work includes more than 82 books, including over 30 installments of Mack Bolan. His recent work includes the *VICAP* series. Newton lives in Indiana.

Elsa Rutherford

Rutherford is the author of *The Water and the Blood* and *Hoodoo*, and conducts writing seminars in her home state of Alabama.

John Shirley

California's Shirley is the author of *In Darkness Waiting, Cellars* and *Dracula in Love*, and the acclaimed short story collection *Heatseekers*.

Kiel Stuart

Stuart's short fiction has appeared in *Tales of the Witch World I, Magic in Ithkar 3, Pulpsmith* and *The Horror Show*. She lives in New York.

Lucy Taylor

Florida resident Taylor's short fiction has appeared in *Women of Darkness, Women of the West, Thin Ice, Cavalier* and others.

Karl Edward Wagner

North Carolina's Wagner has written or edited over 35 horror and science fiction books, including *At First Just Ghostly* and *The Fourth Seal.*

Chet Williamson

Williamson is the author of four novels and numerous pieces of short fiction, which have appeared in such diverse magazines as *The New Yorker, Playboy* and *Twilight Zone.* He is a Pennsylvania resident.

J. N. Williamson

Williamson has written over 30 novels and 90 short stories, and is the editor of the popular *Masques* anthology series. He lives in Indiana.

Pocket Books presents
its collection of
EROTIC
HORROR

HOT BLOOD	............66424-7/$5.99
HOTTER BLOOD	.........70148-5/$5.99
HOTTEST BLOOD	........75367-3/$5.50

THE HOT BLOOD SERIES:

DEADLY AFTER DARK	.........87087-4/$5.50
SEEDS OF FEAR	...............89846-3/$5.50
STRANGER BY NIGHT	........53754-7/$5.99

EDITED BY JEFF GELB AND
MICHAEL GARRETT

Simon & Schuster Mail Order
200 Old Tappan Rd., Old Tappan, N.J. 07675
Please send me the audio I have checked above. I am enclosing $_____(please add $3.95 to cover
postage and handling plus your applicable local sales tax). Send check or money order ---- no cash or C.O.D.'s
please. Allow up to six weeks for delivery. You may use VISA/MASTERCARD: card number, expiration date and
customer signature must be included.

Name _____

Address _____

City _____ State/Zip _____

VISA/MASTERCARD Card # _____ Exp.Date _____

Signature _____

POCKET
BOOKS

1029-03

Innocent People Caught
In the Grip of
TERROR!

These thrilling novels--where deranged minds create sinister
schemes, placing victims in mortal danger and striking horror
in their hearts--will keep you in white-knuckled suspense!

- ☐ CABAL by Clive Barker 74288-4/$5.99
- ☐ GHOST STORY by Peter Straub 68563-5/$6.99
- ☐ FLESH AND BLOOD by D.A. Fowler 76045-9/$4.99
- ☐ THE VOICE IN THE BASEMENT by T. Chris Martindale 76012-2/$4.99
- ☐ SCARECROW by Richie Tankersley Cusick 69020-5/$4.99
- ☐ PHOBIAS: Stories of Your Deepest Fears Edited by
  Wendy Webb, Martin Greenberg and Edward Kramer 79237-7/$5.50
- ☐ UNDER THE FANG
  Edited by Robert R. McCammon 69573-8/$6.50
- ☐ SHOCK ROCK Edited by Jeff Gelb 70150-9/$4.99
- ☐ SHOCK ROCK II Edited by Jeff Gelb 87088-2/$5.50
- ☐ PANIC by Chris Curry 74947-1/$4.99
- ☐ VIPER QUARRY by Dean Feldmeyer 76982-0/$4.99
- ☐ SUCCUMB by Ron Dee 87110-2/$5.50
- ☐ SAVANT by Rex Miller 74848-3/$5.99
- ☐ JIMJAMS by Michael Green 88148-5/$5.50
- ☐ NEAR DEATH by Nancy Kilpatrick 88090-X/$5.50
- ☐ MORE PHOBIAS Edited by Wendy Webb 89547-8/$5.99
- ☐ SWEET WILLIAM by Jessica Palmer 88017-9/$5.50

All Available from Pocket Books

POCKET
BOOKS